PRAISE FOR

No Longer Alone

"Soft stunning and lyrically captivating, *No Longer Alone*: *Based on a True Story* grabs onto the reader as quickly as a prairie thunderstorm. Avery and Prentis's journey to love and renewed faith in the days leading up to World War I resonates as much today as it did one hundred years ago. A wonderfully engaging reading complemented by Inman's vivid depiction of Oklahoma history and richly layered Christian characters."

—L. B. Johnson, Award Winning author of *Small Town Roads*

"In *No Longer Alone*, Melinda Inman imagines what her great grandparents' early marriage and courtship were like a hundred years ago when men courted women and worked to earn their heart. Set between the Oklahoma Land Rush and the beginnings of World War I, her novel explores how people lived as pioneers who wrestled with the land, the weather and their own history. I cared deeply about Prentis, Avery, their families and even their animals because they were so well drawn.

No Longer Alone is a fast, lyrical read that explores how people on the eve of the Great War worked out their salvation, with as much thought, prayer and angst as we do today. Even though happiness is nearly impossible to write, Inman draws a beautiful portrait of a couple who fall in love and start a happy marriage, that was as refreshing to dive into as mountain lake."

—Katie Andraski, Author of *The River Caught Sunlight*

"It was a pleasure to read this book from start to finish. Readers who come from a background of the homestead era and prairie farming traditions will recognize this story as an authentic portrayal of the dreams and struggles of a young couple as they forge a life together. The author's descriptions of everyday life on a farm in the early 20th century are rich in detail. It is as if we were there, witnessing daily occurrences. The conversations in the story come across as genuine and underscore the importance of constant communication in any relationship. One section that was particularly delightful involved the young couple discovering things about each other they didn't know before they married. So true to life!

The incorporation of historical events lends additional authenticity to the story. It demonstrates how people's personal lives are affected by both positive and dire circumstances at home as well as on the other side of the world.

The faith element of the story is especially strong. There are many couples who enter into marriage hoping to meld their families' different religious beliefs into a healthy whole. This is not an easy process, as all of us are influenced by our early experiences. Many families keep the peace on religion by not getting involved in any faith tradition. The author has used Avery and Prentis as models of not giving up on God and seeking a way to live together in faith for the benefit of their future family.

No Longer Alone is an outstanding example of family memories incorporated into an intriguing novel."

—Carol Johnson Parker, Educator

"Have you ever read a fictional book where you were drawn into the lives of the characters, and then a few chapters in find yourself contemplating your own responses to life because of how the characters are processing theirs? This book did that. I was drawn into the pain and struggles of Prentis and Avery, each unique, but drawing them toward the Lord as He worked in their lives. The more they contemplated their family responsibilities and issues of faith, the more I loved them for their authentic responses - no platitudes or "Christian-eze". Avery and

Prentis truly grappled with what it meant to be followers of Christ in a family, community, marriage, and church—the everydayness, ups, and downs.

This book stretched me and caused me to laugh, cry, and learn right along with the characters by challenging my heart to seek after what GOD wants for me, my marriage, and the use of my gifts as a Christian woman. Prentis and Avery BECAME real people to me as I turned each page. Well written – characters, history, life events, faith struggles. Biblical truths were realistically applied to all relationships and situations. I want to know what happens next—and so will you when you get to the last page! Yes, there is a sequel coming . . . how will the war brewing in Europe affect their little farm in Oklahoma?

—**Kristin Lewis Robinson,** Life Coach, Author

Melinda elegantly writes a historical love story all while reminding us that God's plans are undeniably perfect. In hardship, loss, and joy, His divine provision is a thread that binds us all, regardless of generation or race. A wonderful example of a relationship done well, *No Longer Alone* is the type of story you want readers to take note of. What more will the characters teach us in the sequel? It will be difficult to wait and find out."

—**Karina Herring**, Artist, Entrepreneur

"This is the story of Avery and Prentis and the challenges they encounter on the path of life. These characters are so vividly portrayed that it seems as if you actually know them as you laugh with them and cry with them while following their many and varied activities. The storyline keeps you trying to guess what will happen next as the tale continues. A key element in the story is the relationship between Prentis and God. The story combines personal successes and failures with a religious theme threaded throughout the book. I was touched by the depth of character portrayal of both Avery and Prentis. This book is definitely a 5-star book. Thank you, Melinda Inman, for sharing your storytelling talent with your readers. I do hope there is a sequel coming!"

—**Barb Amstutz**, Avid Reader

No Longer Alone
by Melinda Viergever Inman

© Copyright 2017 Melinda Viergever Inman

ISBN 978-1-63393-423-8

Published by

ShowKnowGrow
PUBLISHING

Ypsilanti, Michigan

BASED ON A TRUE STORY

NO LONGER ALONE

MELINDA VIERGEVER INMAN

ShowKnowGrow
PUBLISHING

DEDICATION

Because of their inspiration, research, encouragement,
storytelling, fact-checking, historical input, and love,
this story is dedicated to my parents, my aunts, and my uncles:

Jacqueline and L.D. Garrett
Elaine and Dan Viergever
Dottie and Roger Koeppen
P.J. and Linda Pinkerton

This story wouldn't have been possible without you.
All of you contributed to my knowledge of the characters of
this novel,
the geography and customs of northern Oklahoma,
and the historical times in which Avery and Prentis lived,
moved, and breathed.
I am grateful for you and for all you contributed to make this
story come alive.
And to all the progeny, each and every one.
Enjoy this story of our family.

ONE

THE HARD-RED CLODS OF Oklahoma dirt cascading onto the baby's pine coffin devastated Avery. She would never forget the sound. Nor would she soon forget the blue lips of her pale little brother, the swarms of sympathetic faces, the guilt she felt over her attempts to squeeze in Bible school homework, and the wails of her momma. But the thud of the dirt was the worst.

Avery couldn't recall the last time she'd felt happy. But today promised to be different. Today might turn out to be glorious.

Tugging at her cheeks stiffly, as if ill acquainted with this unfamiliar expression, her lips stretched into a smile. This was a long-gone sensation. Spreading wide her arms, she reached for the prairie sky, staring up into the deep blue vault. Beside her, Daddy softly chuckled.

It was a blessing to be out under the bright sunlight rather than sitting in the darkened house with Momma. And now that she'd cracked wide, Avery couldn't seem to stop smiling.

The past weeks since baby Russell's death had been difficult and Momma inconsolable. Since the railroad ran nearby, all but Floyd had come by train to Kingman, Kansas, home of Grandma and Grandpa Slaughter, hoping family would help put them back together. The boys' shouts of laughter sounded from behind the barn. They were in the garden with Grandpa, needing this escape, too. Momma remained safely in Grandma's care.

The familiar niggling of guilt sprang up now that Avery was going out, but Daddy had insisted she accompany him to buy horses. He was always considerate like that. She had needed a break. Avery sucked in a deep breath, relaxed her shoulders, and swung her arms freely as they headed into town.

Since they'd be riding home bareback, she wore her ride-astride apparel. She usually only wore the split-skirt at home, but the ensemble was comfortable and modest with its full divided skirt and matching jacket. Surely it wouldn't be too scandalizing for such a brief trip.

But, of course, there was a crowd at the Pinkerton Livery Stable, and she received some hard stares from the local women who waited in their buggies. She always seemed to be shocking the citizenry. Today she didn't care. She turned her attention toward the task at hand.

Barely able to see over the livery's corral fence, she stepped onto the bottom rail, feasting her eyes on the horseflesh. She loved horses as much as Daddy.

"Nice mare over there." She pointed at the far corner.

Her daddy nodded. "What about the bay gelding . . . there?"

"You know I prefer mares." She laughed softly. "So does Momma."

"You both think they're easier for women to handle, don't you?" He smiled at her.

"We do. But you need the gelding."

Barely visible over the horse's back, Avery detected movement inside the darkened livery. In the far corner, a tall man cleaned stalls with focused intensity.

"Daddy, who's that in the barn?"

Her father peered into the livery. "That's Prentis Pinkerton."

"Prentis! The last time I saw him was at his father's funeral . . . how many years ago?"

"Hmm. March 1906. Been seven-and-a-half years now."

"Seven! I can scarcely believe I haven't seen him since then."

"He's been working hard. Thomas's death changed his life."

Avery nodded, considering the implications. Thomas Pinkerton had died young, age forty-five, leaving a widow and four children, the youngest only one year old. Prentis had been barely fifteen. During the funeral, from a few rows back, Avery had stared at his fresh haircut. Sitting in a new suit, his head had remained bowed throughout the service. When he and the other pallbearers hoisted the coffin onto their shoulders, his face had been contorted with such naked despair that it had broken her heart. It still hurt to recall it. Dazed, he had pressed his head against the casket, hopelessness permeating his countenance and posture. That box had contained his dearest friend.

Thomas Pinkerton's early death had propelled her childhood friend into adulthood, taking him from school—a thoughtful, intelligent young man—and transforming him into a farmer, livery-stable owner, and provider, all while still a spindly boy. Prentis had been supporting the entire family since that day, splitting his time between their land south of town, their Oklahoma farm, and their livery. This made Avery sad. While she had been preoccupied with her own concerns, her friend had lived a different life.

Yet another instance of death rearranging life, Avery thought. *What would we do without Christ?*

"Avery, let's check out the gelding and the mare," her father said, drawing her attention.

After waving to Fred Pinkerton, Daddy entered the corral and inspected the horses—teeth, hooves, and temperament. He rode each about the enclosure; both responded well. Avery opened the corral gate so he could ride up the road, putting one horse after the other through its paces. Narrowing her eyes, she examined each animal in turn. Now was the time to be hard to please, persnickety even, but she could see nothing wrong with either horse. When her father finished he smiled and nodded, his assessment the same—both had passed inspection.

Fred spoke now with some other customers who needed horseshoeing done, so Avery and her father stepped into the barn, heading toward Prentis. He appeared nearly finished with the task of shoveling all the filthy straw and manure out of the back stall.

"Prentis," Avery's father hailed. "Good to see you, son."

Prentis straightened and turned, hesitating a moment when he caught sight of her. Then his face creased into the familiar, shy smile she remembered fondly. Quickly, he stripped off his leather gloves and thrust out his hand.

"Good to see you, too, Mr. Slaughter. It's been a while."

They shook hands warmly and then her daddy turned toward her, resting his hand on her back. "Prentis, you remember . . ."

"Of course I do," he said softly, tipping his Stetson. "Avery, nice to see you again."

The manly octave of his baritone surprised her. Seven years ago, he'd been in a higher register. Looking up into his face, she discovered that he stood quite a bit taller than she. He was now over six feet, not at all the image in her memory. Piercing eyes, cornflower blue—this she recollected, but the modest friendliness and manly strength behind his eyes, coupled with his strong broad shoulders, created an appealing package. Used to bearing responsibility, he was now a handsome, mature, and capable man.

"Prentis." She smiled up at him. "It's been a long time."

"My father's funeral, I think."

"That's what we thought, too. How are you?"

"Ready to focus all my efforts on our Oklahoma farm. Moving down there after Fred gets on his feet. Now that he's out of school, he's taking over here, and my uncles are helping out with the livery. How you been, Avery?"

"I've been all wrapped up in my schooling. I graduated from the Normal School for Teachers in Alva. Now I'm teaching in the schoolhouse on our section and completing a Bible degree by correspondence, so I've been doing quite a bit of studying."

"You always liked that."

"Yes, I did. I still do."

"Well, Prentis," her daddy jumped in, "we'd like that bay gelding and the mare over there."

"For Avery?" Prentis glanced down at her.

"Nope. She's keeping her old horse—can't part with it. This is for her momma's use while Avery's teaching."

"They're good riding horses, healthy—quite a few years left in both. Come on into the office, and I'll make you a receipt."

The two men stepped into the small livery stable office, and Avery strolled back toward the corral, preoccupied. She hadn't expected her heart to flip-flop under Prentis's gaze. This was disconcerting. Self-conscious, having spent his adolescent years working alone in the fields, he had kept his head slightly inclined, as if he couldn't quite look at her head-on. His smile bashful, he had peered up at her from under his brows. Knowing that solitary habits had been thrust upon him by tragedy, Avery found his shyness endearing.

Seeing him after all these years affected her heart strangely. This was unexpected—she needed time to compose herself. Having decided at her baby brother's burial that she would never marry, she couldn't allow her heart to dictate. A momentary vision of Russell's miniscule coffin flashed across her mind. This gave her pause. Losing babies as her momma had done would be impossible to bear. No, she would focus on her career. A twenty-three-year-old professional woman must be in command of her affections. She must be composed.

There was also the fact that Prentis had never attended church. What did that mean? When they were children, it hadn't mattered. But now, he was a man. Had this circumstance changed? Should she even consider him, if he expressed interest? Fortunately, her father and Prentis remained in the office quite a while, affording her plenty of time to readjust her thinking.

Careful, Avery, eyes and heart set on heaven.

When the men returned, all was calm within. Placidly, she watched as they put new bridles on the horses. Daddy slid up bareback onto the gelding. Performing according to old habit, Prentis stepped toward Avery without a word and stooped so she could plant her left boot in his bare hands. It felt natural and right that he would do so. Palms open, his fingers were interlaced and readied. Without hesitation, as if by reflex, she stepped, he boosted, and up she went.

As she settled herself, the mare shied, and Prentis grasped the halter. Avery bent forward to stroke the mare's neck, speaking soft, reassuring words. The mare calmed, and Prentis released the horse. Avery sat back and smiled down at him.

"You were always good with horses." Prentis returned her smile. Then, his expression sympathetic, he turned his attention to include her father. "Should've mentioned earlier how sad we were when we heard of your baby's passing. Didn't hear until after the funeral. If we'd known, we would've been there."

"Thank you, Prentis," her father responded. "Wound's still fresh. Christ and prayer are holding us up."

Prentis nodded and then turned his gaze toward Avery, the shy smile reappearing. "Good-bye, Avery. It's especially good to see you again."

"I'm glad to see you, too." She hoped she appeared tranquil and serene.

But as Avery and her father rode across the dusty stable yard and onto the road, she couldn't resist a glance back. Still standing in the yard, Prentis watched her departure. Swiftly, he lifted his hat and waved. She smiled demurely and then turned back toward the road. The joy in her heart gave away her true feelings entirely. *Silly me.*

* * * *

Prentis stood staring after Avery until she was out of sight. From the first moment he'd seen her face, his heart had been thudding. *Mucking out manure!* Not a very romantic pastime for a reunion with the girl he'd pined after for so long—Avery, always calm and genteel, poised and serene, but now transformed into a beautiful woman, the proper schoolteacher. Thankfully, her eyes had been friendly as she'd watched him strip off his heavy work gloves, filthy from his earthy work. He was certain he'd reeked of the stuff. Good thing she'd been raised on a farm.

She'd been wearing one of those skirts his mother and sisters discussed in appalled tones. Avery had always rocked the boat, but now she did it in such an elegant manner. He grinned.

Her mass of shiny hair had been piled high, her voice soft and low. Those entrancing black eyes had pierced him through, as if pinning him down, demanding that he profess his hidden love. Her Cherokee eyes had always seemed to look right inside him. He hoped he hadn't gawked. She was a stunning woman.

How had he waited seven years for her? It had about killed him. He was glad she had no idea yet. It would be impossible to sleep tonight.

* * * *

Avery's entire family relaxed on Grandma and Grandpa Slaughter's front porch after supper. All watched as a horse cantered up the lane. From her seat, Avery recognized Prentis Pinkerton. As they'd ridden home from the livery a few days earlier, her daddy had informed her that Prentis would come to see how the horses were doing, since the Pinkerton's good reputation as fair horse traders and businessmen was of paramount importance.

Since she'd been forewarned, Avery hadn't expected his appearance to provoke any emotional fervor. She'd been wrong—she practically fluttered with anticipation.

Prentis reined in, even more handsome in the saddle. "How're those horses doing for you?"

"Horses are fine, Prentis." Her father leaned back in his porch chair. "Can hardly get Avery off her mother's new mare. We finally convinced her to come in for meals."

They all laughed, Avery the loudest. It was true.

"P.J.," Grandpa Slaughter called to Prentis, "get down off that horse and have some of this iced tea. Just chiseled into a new block of bought ice. It's good and cold."

"Thank you." He swung out of the saddle. "I'll take that tea. I can stay a bit before I have to head home. Need to be back by dark."

Prentis looped the reins over the hitching rail, and his horse began to graze. He acknowledged all the porch-sitters with a shy but friendly nod, coupled with a slight tip of his hat. As if sensing Avery had been watching him, his eyes briefly caught on hers. Then he shook John's hand and Jerry's before joining her brothers on the porch steps.

"How you boys been?" he asked.

"Great," Jerry replied. "Workin' hard. Done with school. You?"

"Good. Keepin' busy." Grandma Slaughter emerged from the house with the promised glass of tea and handed it to Prentis. "Thank you, Ma'am."

Grandma nodded and sat back down.

As they all talked, Avery enjoyed listening to the melody and cadence of Prentis's new voice. Opinions thoughtful and informed, he expressed himself well.

They discussed the mild weather and Grandpa's recent trip to the fiftieth anniversary Civil War encampment. Conversation then turned to plans for the upcoming Settlers Day celebrations held in northern Oklahoma within a few weeks—the twentieth anniversary of the Land Run for the Cherokee Outlet. Fall planting was then considered, including the merits of hard red winter wheat—Grandpa still called it Turkey Red Wheat. Tractors came next—most of them used both tractors and horse-drawn plows for farming.

"So, P.J.," Grandpa said with a twinkle in his eye, "Avery's been trying to convince her daddy to buy an automobile, now that he has a tractor. She's bound and determined to have one. What are your thoughts on the subject, boy?"

Before responding, Prentis turned to scrutinize her expression. His eyes fixed intently on hers. Perched on her porch chair, she leaned forward, eager for him to side with her, hoping he would. Her long black braid swung toward him, and his eyes softened as they stared into hers. She detected a decision in his eyes.

Prentis turned back toward Grandpa Slaughter. "You're asking a livery stable owner for his opinion on automobiles?"

"Sure am." Grandpa's eyes had a mischievous gleam. "Figured you'd take my side and stand against these newfangled contraptions."

"Must confess that I'm attached to the horse and buggy. Not merely for economic reasons, but also for the leisure and time to contemplate that traveling by horse provides. Gives you time to think. And, in the buggy, it gives you time to talk." Prentis's eyes flicked toward hers. "However, I think progress will overrule my position."

Avery rewarded this statement with a wide smile.

"Carefully spoken." Grandpa chuckled. "You certainly don't want to rile Avery. Once she gets going, there'll be no peace."

Everyone laughed heartily.

"Grandpa," Avery interjected, "I'm not that bad."

They all laughed because she was.

"That's why I chose my words with care," Prentis said.

Everyone laughed again. This time, Avery joined in. They were right.

"Avery," her daddy said, "sun's near setting. Take Prentis down to the corral, so he can inspect those horses before he leaves.

Then he'll be certain he's made us an honest deal—that being his purpose in coming. We want him to know that all's well."

Avery puzzled over her father's suggestion. They'd already assured Prentis that the horses were fine. But, seeming to be a wonderfully fortuitous coincidence, it synchronized completely with her traitorous heart's desire. Regardless of rational consideration, apparently her heart wasn't set on spinsterhood. Married women bore babies, one after another, often losing them. Yet, knowing this, still her heart had cast off her hasty funereal resolution.

Without speaking, the two rose and walked toward the barn. Flush with happiness, she took several slow deep breaths, hoping to calm herself.

From low on the horizon, the setting sun glowed golden. Insects and motes of dust and pollen floated or propelled themselves through the warm haze above the corral. Across the backyard, the barn cast a long dark shadow, and the cicadas whirred their nightly late-summer symphony. Prentis and Avery stepped up to the corral and stood contemplating the horses.

"See, Prentis." To her ear, her voice sounded a bit shaky. "They're fine—good horses."

After regarding the horses for a moment, he turned to face her, leaning against the corral and casually hooking his arm on the top rail. One side of his face was in shadow, the other in the glow of the setting sun, the angle of the sunlight making his blue eyes lucent.

"Avery, I was wondering if I could call on you at home."

Her heart warmed as she stared into his hopeful eyes. "I'd have to speak to my father."

"I already have." He chuckled softly. "I'm guessing that's why he sent us back here."

"He already said you could call on me?"

"He did." Prentis smiled.

"Is that what took you so long in the office at the livery stable?"

"It was. But that wasn't the first time he and I have discussed this."

"It wasn't?"

"We've talked about it for quite a while. I'm just now at the place where the support of my mother and Millie is taken care of. Money's laid by, and Fred's taking the home responsibilities. I'm developing our Oklahoma land as my own homestead. Buying it from the estate so it's mine, free and clear. That's why I'd like to call. The time is finally right."

"You've been planning this?"

"For a long time."

"I didn't realize, Prentis." Avery wondered how she had been entirely unaware of something so important. "I've been preoccupied with my own life."

"That's exactly how I wanted it. What if circumstances had prevented this for even longer? What if I'd kept you waiting and it never came to pass because some economic disaster prevented it? Didn't want you to know I was interested in you. Wanted you to have a happy girlhood, finish your schooling, and do whatever you wanted, just in case I was prevented. Didn't seem fair to let you know how I felt, if I couldn't do anything about it."

The selflessness of this gesture overwhelmed her. Anything could have happened, including another man asking to court her, but Prentis hadn't spoken until he was able to provide for her and was therefore free to put his emotions into action. This was entirely noble and masculine.

"How long have you felt this way?"

"For as long as I can remember." His eyes looked into hers sincerely, gently, the manly strength of patient waiting in their depths.

"I would be honored to have you call on me, Prentis," she said softly.

"Thank you. Would you like to attend the Settlers Day dance with me? The Wakita dance is in the Miller's barn near our homestead. It's the first day I can get free, since I'm still going back and forth between the two farms."

"I'd love to go."

"Good." He smiled broadly at her. "Thank you. I'll come get you on the afternoon of the sixteenth. Now that we've seen that these horses are fine, I'd better head home."

"Yes, we can report to the interested crowd on the porch that the horses are indeed fine."

They laughed together. Making pleasant conversation now,

instead of walking silently, they strolled side-by-side back toward the house. When they came around to the porch, the parents and grandparents still sat comfortably. All studied them with knowing smiles.

"Daddy, it would appear the horses are fine, and that fact has been duly noted by Prentis."

"Well good, daughter."

The older generations all chuckled. Confused, the boys looked up at them from the porch steps. Clearly, they didn't understand why this was funny.

Prentis swung up onto his horse, settled into the saddle, and lifted his hat to all before smiling down at her, his eyes twinkling.

"See you soon, Avery."

"I look forward to it."

Avery stood staring after him as he rode down the lane. At the end he looked back, exactly as she had done at the livery stable. She waved, and he lifted his hat, a parting tribute.

Then he took off fast on his horse, racing the setting sun.

TWO

WITH HOWARD SLEEPING BETWEEN her arms, Avery rode her childhood mare home from the first day of school. It had been a long day for a five-year-old. Against Avery's chest, his head lolled back and forth to Frisky's clopping pace, her filly name no longer apt. Howard's saliva dribbled onto Avery's right sleeve, darkening the fabric. She bent to kiss his hot little head and spied a trickle of moisture trailing from under his little-boy sideburn.

Gene and Abe had raced home the minute Avery dismissed school, taking off with unusual haste while she tidied the schoolroom, arranging everything for the following day. Little Howard had been her assistant. She would ask others to stay tomorrow to help, and when she arrived at home, she would speak to Gene and Abe about their rapid departure.

Since Howard slept and didn't keep her occupied with his usual chatter, she evaluated the day. There had been the typical first-day adjustments—assessing new students and placing them into grade levels while keeping the others occupied with their studies. This had gone fairly well.

Early on she had gotten the older boys involved as leaders. They would set a good example for the younger. Lavishing praise on every good attempt, wise choice, and kind action, she had motivated all the children to work cheerfully and cooperatively. Of course, the adolescent boys hadn't arrived yet. They were still helping with planting, their schooling dictated by each family's farming needs. One particular student would be a handful. She pondered on him for a moment then turned back to the day.

A wasp nest in the girls' outhouse had resulted in shrill screaming and one sting, the school outhouses having been abandoned over the vacation months. One of the newly appointed boy leaders had knocked it down, chucked it into his lunch pail, capped it, and carried it off while Avery tended to the sting. Other than the wasp incident, it had been a good day.

The children had played *Ante Over* at recess, a game she couldn't resist. To establish discipline, she usually maintained decorum during the first month, but she had seen no potential or looming disciplinary problems so had participated. Racing around the school building with the children had disheveled her carefully arranged hair, so she had simply pulled out the pins to wear her thick braid down her back for the remainder of the day.

After her careful review, she allowed her mind to wander where it had longed to go all day—to Prentis and his confession. He had waited for her, all the while allowing her to move through her life freely. Since the trip to Kingman, this had frequently been on her mind. Pausing to thank God for the gift of a good man's selfless heart, she smiled.

Frisky now plodded up the lane and around the house. As they rounded the corner, Avery gaped, completely taken aback. There, sitting by the barn, was a shiny new Model T. Arms crossed, her daddy leaned against it, grinning at her.

"Well, Avery, what do you think?"

She was speechless. The boys all roared with laughter at her reaction, Gene and Abe laughing so hard they fell on the ground. This was surely why they had run home. It was obvious they'd known about the surprise. Howard awakened, as stunned as she when he sat forward, gripping the saddle horn to stare at the automobile.

Finally, she found her powers of speech. "You changed your mind."

"Yes, indeed."

Avery passed Howard to their father and swung down. In awe, she approached the coveted "contraption," as her grandfather called it. It was beautiful—a 1913 Ford Model T Touring Car, shiny black. She ran her hand along its frame—smooth and metallic, the feel of progress. It sported a glass windshield, so they wouldn't need to wear goggles. The roof would prevent the need for hats and protective gear. It had a leather front seat and a wide and spacious backseat. They could all squeeze in.

She grinned at her father. "Let's drive it."

"I thought you'd feel that way. I've already taken your momma and the boys for a ride. You and Howard jump in. I need to educate you on the proper use of this automobile."

Avery sat in the front, beside her daddy. Howard crawled into the back. When he stood up on the floorboards, his head was far below the high roof. Daddy cautioned him to keep his head and arms inside the automobile. Right beside Avery, Floyd stood outside the Model T, watching the entire start process again.

"The responsibility for safety belongs to the driver," her father said.

She nodded seriously.

"Floyd's going to show you how to complete the passenger's responsibilities."

She smiled at Floyd, who hadn't quit grinning since she'd arrived home. He'd probably grinned all day, since the moment the Model T had arrived.

"Now watch, Avery," Daddy said. He schooled her on the intricacies of starting the new automobile, then paused and looked at her seriously. "Got all that?"

"I do. Control lever up, throttle almost all the way up, hand brake set, mixture-control knob facing forward. Now what?"

"Step out, and Floyd will show you the passenger's job."

Floyd opened her door, walked her to the front of the automobile, and demonstrated how to pull out the choke ring. She grabbed it and tugged. Out it came. She held it firmly.

"Now," Floyd said, "you've got to be careful. Ask Daddy if he's got the control lever all the way to the top. That retards the spark so it doesn't start up until we're ready."

She stared at Floyd. They'd seen their father do this. "Ask him?"

"Yep. It's a safety precaution—we're supposed to ask. If it's not set, the starting crank can rotate back and break your arm."

Through the glass windshield, she peered at her father. "Daddy, do you have the control lever all the way to the top?"

"Yes, I do, Avery." He nodded. She looked back at Floyd.

He showed her how to hold the choke ring while turning the starting crank twice. Avery made the two turns and stopped at the top.

"Now," Floyd said, "let the choke ring go and turn the starting crank two more times. Tell Daddy when you're done."

Avery complied. "Ready, Daddy," she called.

He beckoned to her through the glass. "Step around here, so you can see what's next. This is the power switch. I'm moving it to the right—to the battery setting. Now watch Floyd."

Floyd pulled up the starting crank one more time and the engine fired. *Chucka-chucka-chucka-chucka, sproing, chucka-chucka-chucka-chucka.* The Model T's motor ran smoothly. They all grinned at one another. Her father motioned for her to get in.

"Now, see here," he spoke loudly over the engine noise. "I'm moving the power switch from battery to magneto. That keeps the battery from draining. Now I turn the mixture control a bit counterclockwise, easing off with the fuel. I put my foot on the brake. Look here, Avery."

He demonstrated which handbrakes to release and detailed the final adjustment with the spark and the gas before slowly lifting his brake-foot. With a slight jerk, they moved forward.

"And we're off," he said. "The rest is like driving the tractor."

Making a wide circle, they rolled smoothly through the barnyard before heading up the lane and onto the road, travelling south. Avery laughed out loud the entire way. As they drove along the dirt path of a road, her father made her review the start process, so he was certain she could do it without damaging herself or others. They weren't to let anyone help them other than a family member. That way he'd be certain that whoever touched it knew what to do.

Both starting and driving an automobile were serious business.

"How do we go faster?" she said.

"Pull down on the throttle control to give it more gas. Like this."

Their speed increased. The windows had been lowered, and the wispy hair that had escaped Avery's braid whipped about her face. She turned to look at Howard, who was standing and staring out the window as the scenery sped by—it was like being on the train.

"How fast are we going?" she asked her father.

"Look here—twenty-five miles per hour." He pointed at the speedometer.

"Let's go faster."

He smiled widely at her and pulled down the throttle, giving it more gasoline. They surged forward. The needle on the speedometer pointed between the thirty and the forty.

"Give it more gas, Daddy."

"I think that's enough, Avery. We don't need to be reckless."

"What's the top speed?"

"Forty-five miles an hour."

"Amazing!"

"But don't you go trying it." He shot her a serious glance.

"I won't," she said. "I promise."

She didn't want to make him nervous, but she knew it would be difficult to resist. Her father glanced over again, giving her a stern look.

"I'll hold you to that," he said.

Nodding, she leaned back in the seat, recognizing how hard it would be to keep that promise. She sighed. Any speed in this automobile would be a treat, she reminded herself.

"What about hills?" she asked.

"When you go uphill, put it in low by retarding the spark. Move the spark control lever up. I'll drive you around to demonstrate. If it ever dies on a hill, you may have to take it backwards."

Thinking he was joking, she looked hard at him. But he merely shrugged and nodded.

They eventually reached the corner and headed up the dirt road east toward Wakita. Blowing by the fields, they left a cloud of dust in their wake. Avery couldn't believe they were moving so rapidly. The trip usually took them more than an hour by wagon, if the horses trotted. This was why they shopped in Gibbon—

it was closer. When she saw Wakita looming before them, she studied the timepiece pinned to her shirt bodice. It had taken only fifteen minutes to make the eight-mile trip.

Amazing! This would change everything!

As they entered town, her father pushed up on the throttle and shifted into a lower gear, driving slowly. Along the street, numerous buggies were parked, and many horses were tethered to the hitching rails. People stood about chatting and loading their wagons. Everyone stopped their work and stood still on the wooden sidewalks, gaping as they chugged by.

The Slaughters smiled and waved. Avery felt like a dignitary. Some waved back, but most merely stared. After circling through Wakita, they headed toward home, stopping on the west edge of town to switch drivers. Daddy wanted to watch her drive, so he could help her. Almost killing the engine, she took off with a jump.

"Let the brake out slowly, and more gradual on the gas next time."

She nodded, focused on recalling all she had learned. This was different than a tractor in a field. They might meet people coming from the opposite direction. The main road was rutted and barely the width of two wagons. Each must move slightly off the road to pass. That would be difficult. In fact, up ahead she saw someone headed toward them. She decreased the gas so as not to spook the neighbor's horse, steering the Model T to the right side of the narrow thoroughfare.

As they drew nearer, she was horrified to see that the rider looked like Prentis. After not seeing him for over seven years, he seemed to appear everywhere. What if she killed him with the automobile? She cut the gas and slowed to twenty.

As they chugged by Prentis, he wore a wide grin. Her daddy and Howard waved. She could only meet Prentis's eyes for a moment, lest she forget herself and lose control on the rough road. But in that moment, she saw the look of pride he gave her. Her heart swelled with satisfaction.

She couldn't return his smile; she had to concentrate on her driving. They flashed by him, and then he was gone, growing smaller in the side rearview mirror. Bouncing her eyes back to the mirror several times, she watched him fade away. He'd surely have something to say about this when he took her to the dance next week.

* * * *

After a relaxing weekend with much time spent driving the Model T, Avery had a surprise visit from the man who had hired her, the superintendent of schools, who stopped by after Sunday night's suppertime. Harold Cink informed Avery that his adolescent son Billy would attend school the next day. This was the problem student who had occupied her mind. Billy Cink was fifteen and had caused trouble with every previous teacher. Because of this, his parents had attempted schooling him themselves for the past several years. They now wanted him to have the formal education necessary to get him through eighth grade. He was only in fifth grade, so it would be a challenge.

Billy Cink had a habit of taunting teachers and then running out the door when they attempted to chastise or discipline him. The boy was fast. Teachers in hot pursuit were easily outdistanced with Billy laughing all the way. Needless to say, this deteriorated classroom discipline. Now that the winter wheat had been planted, Avery was to tame this young man, since he was the ringleader of the adult-sized boys who would filter back into school.

"Miss Slaughter, you have my full support," Harold Cink said. "If that boy comes home early, skips class, or even leaves the schoolyard, I'll give him a whopping he'll never forget."

"Well, Mr. Cink, between the two of us, let's hope we can avoid that."

"If he needs a lickin', I'll be givin' it to him."

"Thank you for your support. We'll get the boy through his schooling."

Mr. Cink thanked her and then stepped out to admire the automobile.

Avery ascended to her room to pray about the problem. *What to do?* As the sister of six brothers, she was certain she could handle the situation. She formulated her plan. There would be no playing with the children at recess tomorrow.

The next morning, she rose and dressed in serious attire—a starched white blouse with a black ribbon tied at the neck, a black skirt, and her hair in a carefully pinned knot. Desiring to be at the schoolhouse settled and ready before the students arrived, she left early on Frisky after eating a good breakfast and praying with her mother. Since she knew the older boys were coming, she arranged their desks. And then, she sat down to pray as she waited. There would be no daydreaming about Prentis today.

Eventually, the students arrived, stabling their horses in the small barn or staking them to graze. One by one, they entered silently, each depositing their lunch pails in the cupboard. She greeted each one kindly, but all appeared apprehensive and subdued, hardly speaking. They probably reckoned this would be the last day of school—they'd lose their teacher after the coming dreaded confrontation. She didn't think that would be the case, so she carried on as if no such concern weighed on her mind.

Finally, the adolescent boys appeared, several in a group, all clustered around the culprit—Billy Cink. They were tall and broad shouldered, towering over her. Avery shot up a prayer as she studied their stubborn faces. A pimply-faced, fifth-grade pubescent boy was always a handful, no matter where a person encountered him—a chip on his shoulder at completing lessons with the younger children, opinionated and loud in his attempts to appear wise, behaving as though school were a punishment rather than a privilege, resentful that he had to leave the world of men to be dictated to by a schoolteacher, particularly a woman teacher.

Her day would be a challenge.

Welcoming each of the new male students formally, Avery removed the sting by addressing them as if they were men, using their surnames, *Mr. This* and *Mr. That*. Assessing their places in their studies and starting them in their lessons, she moved among them assuring them that because of their advanced years they would move more quickly than the younger students and would soon surpass them. Because they were men now, they would pack more learning into a shorter time. Her own brothers had done the same.

Most of them responded with relieved expressions and cooperative looks, her respectful tone and encouraging words having won them over. Moving from desk to desk, Avery discussed with each one their individual placement.

During all of this, Billy Cink sat slumped in his desk, scowling and obstinate.

"Mr. Cink." Avery stepped over to complete his assessment. "Can you please tell me which reader you're using?"

Silence met her request. She waited a moment.

"Perhaps you didn't hear me, Mr. Cink. Which reader do you use at home?"

She stood, calmly regarding him as he looked out the window with an insolent expression. Not budging, she awaited his response.

"Mr. Cink."

"I don't have to answer no girl teacher, and I ain't doin' what you say."

Deliberately, solely to irk her, he had used poor grammar. Billy rose to his feet, edging his way toward the door, probably expecting the switch and the chase that usually ensued when he spoke thus to a teacher. Looking him right in the face, Avery stood her ground.

"I'm a man," he declared. "I don't have to put up with sittin' here in your dumb school. You're just a stupid girl."

Then out the door he ran.

Calmly, Avery walked back to the front. The only sound in the classroom was the *tap, tap, tap* of her boots up the center aisle. As if paralyzed, the students sat stunned and appalled. She picked up the fourth reader and set the work for the oldest students, writing it on the board and taking any questions before they began their assignments. Next, she gave direction to students in the lower grades; then she sat with the youngest students to listen to their lessons.

Glancing at Howard, she noticed he sat still as a statue, his face white and eyes large. He probably wondered what would happen next. Nothing would happen. If Billy Cink wanted to run off the property, miss school, and take that whopping, it was entirely up to him. She placed the responsibility for his behavior squarely on his own shoulders. Out the window, she glimpsed him. Confused, he stood on the school property line, looking back at the building, expecting her hot pursuit. He was going to be disappointed.

All morning, the students worked diligently, keeping their

noses in their books, occasionally sneaking furtive glances out the window at Billy. He still stood. Then storm clouds blew over, lightning cracked, and rain fell. Billy retreated to a shade tree, attempting to shield himself from the downpour. Avery stuck her head out the door and invited him inside, but he turned his back, stubbornly crossing his arms over his chest—he wouldn't come.

Lunchtime arrived.

"Students, we'll be taking our lunch in here because of the rain. Would one of you young men circulate with the water bucket so everyone can have a drink?"

One of the boys who had come in with Billy volunteered, completing his task efficiently. Another offered to pass out the lunch pails. The children relaxed as they ate their lunches, and the older boys circulated among them, models of decorum. Maybe all would be well. Apparently too embarrassed to come in and face the room, Billy remained outside for the rest of the day. A sodden scholar, he took off on his horse the moment school was dismissed.

Avery cleaned the board. Abe, Gene, and Howard stayed with her, straightening the desks and taking the erasers outside to knock out the chalk dust. Their posture was protective. She could tell they were proud of her for facing down such a big boy. They all rode home together, Howard with her again. Abe and Gene shared their momma's new horse.

At the house, the boys left to help with the chores, and Avery stepped inside, the beginnings of a headache throbbing at her temples. On the outside, she had appeared calm. But inside, she had been tense, hoping her assessment of the situation and human nature would work when accompanied by prayer. It had been a relief to see how the day had gone, but she still had to face tomorrow. Would he come back? Would the conflict repeat itself?

"Momma, I'm going up to lie down," she said as she passed through the kitchen.

Her mother looked up from the bread dough. "Headache? Did it go well?"

Avery nodded to both and trudged up the stairs. Arriving in her room, she cracked the windows and pulled down the blinds that faced the setting sun. After taking down her hair, she removed her serious attire, put her wrapper on over her undergarments, and lay down on the bed, forearm thrown across her eyes. Hearing the gentle rustle of her mother slipping into the room, Avery peeked from under her arm. Momma carried a cold wet compress, a glass of water, and two aspirin. Anxiety creased her forehead. She always worried about Avery's headaches, but having so recently lost Russell, she seemed especially apprehensive.

"Here you go, darlin'," she said, passing Avery the comfort measures. "And here's another thing for you." Momma handed her an envelope, addressed in a strong, scrawling hand to Miss Avery Slaughter. "Came in the mail today."

Puzzling over who had written, Avery downed the aspirin and inspected the envelope, turning it to examine any identifying markings. There weren't any, other than the ink stamp over the postage that read: *Wakita, Oklahoma*. Before opening it, she rested with the compress across her eyes, the envelope lying upon her chest.

Momma sat on the bed, pressing her hand against Avery's forehead. As usual, her mother's hand was warm. An exhalation of relief followed—no fever, apparently. Momma stroked Avery's hair and gently massaged her temples, humming her way through several hymns. Feeling her shoulders, neck, and forehead relax into Momma's soothing touch, Avery sighed, but her curiosity wouldn't leave her alone. Who had written?

Lifting the compress, she examined the envelope again then reached for a hairpin to slice open the top. She pulled out a handwritten note in a masculine hand.

September 8, 1913

Dearest Avery,

Imagine my surprise when you passed me so rapidly in a new Model T! I'm sure you were quite pleased with your father's purchase. Automobile notwithstanding, I hope you don't mind me doing my courting in a buggy—slower transportation and thus more time for looking at your lovely face, talking to you, listening to your voice, and hearing your opinions. I look forward to seeing you on Tuesday afternoon—I have a difficult time focusing on my work as I consider it. My heart is filled with joy and anticipation at the mere thought of seeing you.

Affectionately,
Prentis

This was the handwriting of a man who had abandoned his education to take care of his family, no longer patient with producing the perfect Edwardian script that Avery taught her students and labored to produce in her everyday handwriting. This was the writing of a man with work to do, a man in a hurry. But, assessment of his penmanship aside, schoolteacher that she was, his words touched her heart.

He had called her "Dearest Avery." What did he mean? How dear was she?

He'd signed his name "affectionately." How affectionately? He wanted to hear her voice and listen to her opinions. Focusing on his work was difficult. Obviously, he'd spent some time daydreaming over the coming night of dancing, as had she. He said her face was "lovely."

Reflecting on each word, she read the note again, running her fingertips across the ink. *Silly sentiment*, she told herself, but he himself had written it there.

Momma had stepped out, Avery realized, leaving her alone to ponder Prentis's words. She smiled as she mused over his bashful expression when they had shaken hands at the livery stable, his eyes when he had asked if he could call, and his smile as she had passed him in the Model T. She felt the same about him.

Transportation by buggy would be just fine—longer driving

time, more time to talk. There was obviously a flaw in the new automobile. It moved too fast. Avery's headache had dissipated; this was a relief. Right then, Momma called her down to eat supper.

* * * *

The next day at school, Billy Cink entered quietly, sat down, and got to work. Avery never had another day of trouble from him. With her encouragement, he quickly surpassed his friends. The healthy, academic competition between the older boys spurred the younger ones to try harder and made the school more intellectually challenging, all round.

She thanked God for the idea He'd given her and for the fact that it had worked.

THREE

TUESDAY, SEPTEMBER 16, 1913, WAS SETTLERS Day in Oklahoma, a school holiday. Avery loved the yearly celebration. Today was the twentieth anniversary of the 1893 Land Run for the Cherokee Outlet, the final settlement of Indian Territory. Once everyone had staked his or her claims, the land had become known as Oklahoma Territory. Statehood had only come recently though, a mere six years in the past on November 16, 1907.

The Land Run celebration was a big event in each community, including a local parade and picnic. Everyone in the surrounding countryside headed to Gibbon for the local occasion.

Avery enjoyed rehearsing the history. To prepare her students for the holiday, she had instilled in them the facts of Oklahoma's settlement. She took pride in their heritage. The Land Run had been life-changing for almost all the families in the region. She still remembered the day. Like a number of others, her family had made the race as Cherokee Indians[1] *and* as American citizens. Their path to get there had been circuitous.

Before their tribe had been driven out of the Great Smoky Mountains, the Cherokee had been well-educated, respectful citizens, and good farmers. They had their own written language, a newspaper, a translation of the Bible, and a representative form of government. Many had converted to Christianity, including Avery's family, the Moravian, Presbyterian, Baptist, and Methodist missionaries having been effective. Since they attended the same churches, some had intermarried with other believers of European ancestry.

But President Andrew Jackson had viewed all Indians as "savages," including those of mixed heritage. He wanted to drive the Cherokee out of the Southeast, along with the Seminole, Choctaw, Creek, and Chickasaw—the *Five Civilized Tribes*. Avery's great-grandfather had seen what was coming. To save their family, he had packed up the entire clan and had slipped away from tribal lands along with hundreds of other Cherokee families, heading separate directions to avoid detection.

Passing through the Appalachian and Allegheny Mountains, her ancestral family had journeyed safely to the northwest corner of Virginia. With their common faith, they had blended into Virginia church life, eventually marrying locals who were members of their church. They had integrated and survived.

Her Grandpa Slaughter had been born safely in Virginia, thus, avoiding the Trail of Tears, the government's brutal removal of the Cherokee to Indian Territory in the winter of 1838-1839. Raised there, he had grown to manhood and had married Grandma, a woman whose European lineage went back beyond the Revolutionary War. While a young husband and father, Grandpa had fought for the North in the Civil War, leaving for battle right after Avery's daddy was born.

After the conflict, Grandpa Slaughter had brought his young family west to be near the Cherokee who had been resettled, hoping to reestablish connections. They had settled near the border of Indian Territory, in Kingman, Kansas, and he and Grandma had raised their family. Here Momma and Daddy had met and married, both with similar histories.

When the government stripped the final sliver of this western soil away from the Cherokee in 1893, Daddy had thought it right to try for the free land, since it had been promised to their people for "as long as grass shall grow and rivers run." And so, he and Momma had raced for the land and had obtained their homestead of 160 acres, a quarter section.

And now, twenty years later, all who had made the Land

Run rode in the parade, Avery's family in their Model T this year, rather than on horseback, half of them anyway. Since the younger half had been born after the race, they piled out to watch the older half parade by. The watching crowd consisted mostly of newcomers and of youngsters their age.

As they passed by the crowd, her brothers John, Abe, Gene, and Howard cheered with the others. Avery grinned at them and waved. Over the Model T's engine and the yelling voices, she could only faintly hear the bullhorn voice booming from the bandstand announcing each Land Run participant: "Abraham and Minnie Slaughter; Floyd, Avery, and Jerry Slaughter."

After the parade, a potluck picnic spread out on the grassy pie-shaped hunk of land across the tracks from the town's first building site. From the bandstand, patriotic music played, pausing whenever a train clickety-clacked past their festivities. The town and surrounding area had several hundred people now, all gathered to celebrate their joint heritage. Many were of Cherokee extraction, many of European emigrant stock. Most were an all-American mix. All were Oklahomans. It was a celebration of people united to eke out a living from the plains.

When the picnic concluded, the family headed for the Model T so Avery could dress for the dance. Floyd would drive now. Avery laughed as they attempted to squeeze Hattie into the already full back seat. She would be spending the day at their house, unless she and Floyd also decided to attend the dance. Floyd kept glancing over his shoulder, his straight black hair flopping into his eyes as he grinned at Hattie. Their wedding was in less than two weeks.

Avery had done everything she could to prepare for tonight's dance, including bathing. The entire ritual had been performed the night before: heating the water, sitting in the washtub, scrubbing with Momma's homemade soap, and then trickling the warm water over her head. She had rinsed twice to remove the soft lye soap from her hair, wanting it to gleam and shine.

Once they arrived home, she merely refreshed with a quick wash of her face and upper body. After patting dry, she applied powder and the perfume she kept for special occasions. Then Avery stood in her cambric-and-lace knickers and chemise surveying each outfit Hattie pulled from her wardrobe. If she wanted to dance comfortably, she couldn't wear the currently fashionable, slim silhouette—no hobble skirt for her. But she didn't want to appear dated.

They chose the fuller red skirt with matching fitted jacket—it had a double-breasted, woven-herringbone bodice of narrow red-and-black stripes, fitted three-quarter-length sleeves, and a snug black waistband. Her thin black boots were comfortable for dancing and complemented her outfit. Her ankles would show, so she would wear her matching calfskin gloves.

Decision made, Hattie laced Avery into her corset, worn only for formal events. She relaxed as Hattie pulled the laces tight. Then she dressed with care, glad she was slender so the corset wasn't torturous as it was for some girls.

Using jeweled combs to add sparkle, they piled her hair up like a Gibson Girl, inserting extra hairpins since she'd be dancing. Hattie secured Avery's hat with a hatpin for the buggy ride while Avery tied the large bow under her chin. This was a dressy function, so the hat was appropriate. Revealing the combs and beautifully arranged hair, she would leave her hat in Prentis's buggy when they arrived.

As they labored over the final details, they heard a buggy pull in. Hattie peeked through the curtain. It was he. Turning from the window, she grinned at Avery, and Avery couldn't resist grinning back. Time for the final touches. Applying the tiniest pat of red rouge to her lips, Avery stared at her transformed reflection in the mirror. She was ready, at least outwardly. Inwardly, she quaked. Standing behind her, Hattie met her eyes in the mirror.

"Avery, you look perfect—exactly like a fashion plate."

"Do I? I don't feel fashionable. I'm a bundle of nerves."

"You'll be fine. You're always so poised."

"Is everything really all right?"

"Oh yes, very much so. He'll think you're beautiful."

"I hope so."

Their eyes met in the mirror, all their hopes and dreams remaining unsaid. There was no need to speak of it. Hattie's expression told Avery that her hopes were known and understood.

"Let's get this show on the road!" Avery rose.

When Hattie opened the bedroom door, Avery heard the deep

rumble of Prentis's masculine voice speaking with Floyd in the living room. The rest of the family appeared to be outside under the shade trees, chortling as the little boys performed antics.

As Avery descended the stairs, Hattie trailed behind her. Both men looked up. Their conversation ceased. Prentis had on a three-piece suit with a gray-striped waistcoat and a stiff-collared shirt. He sported a fresh haircut, trimmed close on the sides and long on the top, the typical manly cut of the day. With his thick brown hair combed neatly over the left side of his forehead, he was handsome, and his eyes were fastened on her.

"Avery, you're lovely," he said softly.

"Thank you, Prentis. I hope my hat stays on for the ride."

"We'll go slowly. There's plenty of time."

"Sissy," Floyd said, "you look swell. Did you help, dearest?" He smiled at Hattie. She nodded, hooked her arm through his, and turned to admire Avery.

"Well," Avery said, her cheeks warmed by all the compliments, "let me get the cake, and then, we'd better go, since the buggy is a slower form of transportation." Wanting Prentis to know she was pleased to drive slowly, she smiled up into his eyes.

Stepping into the kitchen, she picked up the cake, already prepared and ready in a woven picnic basket. Excitement made her jittery. She almost didn't trust herself. Drawing a deep breath, she attempted to calm down. Steady now, she returned to the front room. Prentis gave her his shy smile when she entered.

"Let's go then," he said quietly.

Going ahead, he opened the door for her. Avery stepped out onto the porch.

When they emerged, her family called from the shade trees, praising her appearance. Trying to keep her nerves calm, she smiled and waved her goodbyes as the two of them strolled toward Prentis's buggy—a two-seater drawn by a glossy brown, well-groomed horse. The top was up for shade. Avery handed him the picnic basket, which he set carefully on the floorboard. Then, taking her hand, he steadied her as she stepped in.

Adjusting her skirt, Avery settled back against the comfortable upholstered seat, drawing another deep breath as Prentis circled around the front before climbing in. Smiling at her, he grabbed the reins. Then he spoke the horse's name, "Ulysses," and off they went, wheeling up the lane before heading south, the horse assuming a slow gait.

"Can't even begin to tell you how happy I am to spend this day with you," he said.

"I feel exactly the same, Prentis. Thank you for the letter."

"After seeing you in the Model T, I thought you might not want to travel by buggy."

"I'm sorry I didn't smile or wave. I was concentrating so intently that I couldn't."

"You did look awfully serious."

"It was more difficult than I had expected. When I saw it was you, I was mortified. I was afraid I'd hit and kill you."

He chuckled. "I would have gotten out of your way."

"Good." She joined him in laughter.

"Did you enjoy your celebration in Gibbon? We had a big one in Wakita."

"I did enjoy it! We drove the Model T in the parade."

"Do you still recall much of the Land Run?"

"I remember from a child's perspective, since I was only three. I'm certain some of my recollections are all mixed up with what my parents and Floyd have told me. Clear as day, I remember the loud booming of the cannons at noon. All the horses jumped. I did, too!"

He laughed. "I can picture you in that wagon in your sunbonnet. You looked so sweet then with curls poking out the ends of your little braids."

"I did have on my sunbonnet; it matched Momma's. I'm surprised you remember."

He fixed his eyes on hers. "You occupy a significant portion of my memories."

"Why, thank you!" Smiling at him, her heart reacted warmly to his statement.

"What else do you recall?"

"Having lived nearby for so long, Daddy already knew what land he wanted. He was on his fastest horse, hoping he could reach it, but when all the horses reared up at the sound of the cannon, another horse came down on its hoof. That's why Daddy only got two miles in before he staked his claim, far shy of what he wanted. Still, even though the horse went lame, Momma could hardly keep up in the wagon. She was supposed to take the flag marking the land after Daddy pulled it, so he could pound in their stake and defend the property."

"My dad told me about that. He was racing with Miss Blanchard, trying to help her get to good land, since my folks had backed her. He saw your father's horse stumble and your mother's struggle with the horses, but had to keep riding. What was it like in that wagon?"

"Bouncy! I'll never forget that!"

He laughed. "I'll bet!"

"One time we careened onto two wheels. Momma was praying out loud as she drove, shouting her prayers at God, really. Other riders flashed by, riding hard and yelling at their horses. They kicked up dirt as they passed. I was in the back, rattling around, peeking out between Floyd and Momma as she tried to follow Daddy. Since she needed two hands to control the horses, Floyd held the shotgun, ready to defend us, if need be. He was only six, but he seemed so grown-up sitting there with that gun."

"Imagine he took his duty pretty seriously. That would be Floyd through and through."

"Yes. It wasn't a laughing matter."

"Where was Jerry?"

"I was too little to hold him safely, so Momma pinned him between her boots. He screamed all the way."

Prentis nodded. "Glad you made it safely. Many got injured."

"Near us, someone got shot. Momma shouted at me to lie down when that happened. I didn't see anything after that, or when they defended their claim once it was made."

"Dad told me there was violence in the camps, too."

"Yes, there was. We camped for several days beforehand. I slept in the wagon with Floyd and Jerry while Momma and Daddy took turns patrolling outside. Their weapons were always loaded. Daddy kept instructing us children not to touch the firearms. Every night we heard a ruckus of some sort. New arrivals to the camp were breaking the law and sneaking across the border before the appointed time, leaving someone hidden there to claim their land. But at the time, I didn't really understand what was happening. I only knew we were leaving home, and everything was changing. Gunshot was a common sound."

"Were you frightened?"

"In the wagon during the run I was, especially when we almost tipped over and then after Momma told me to lie down. But in the camp, for some reason I felt safe. Momma and Daddy were both there. What could happen?"

He glanced at her and smiled. "Felt that way as a child, too. Nothing could possibly go wrong when my parents were around. It's different now that we're older, isn't it?"

"Yes, I've seen my parents go through hard times completely outside their control, losing so many babies for instance. They can't keep everyone in our family safe. I'm sure it all changed for you when your father died. What you've done for your family is very noble. Giving up your schooling and supporting them all was a sacrifice, but you did the right thing."

Prentis looked away, keeping his head turned. Avery realized she'd embarrassed him.

"I'm sorry for drawing attention to what you've done," she said quietly.

"Didn't do it for attention." He turned toward her, his patient eyes making her keenly aware of the strength and depth to this man she had known so well as a boy.

"I know you didn't."

"Like you said, it was right. I was almost a man. Didn't want to rely on the charity of our extended family when I was capable of working and providing. Would have been degrading for my mother. Dad would have wanted me to take care of things."

Once more, Prentis fixed his eyes on the road, and they rode silently for a long stretch. Mentally, Avery berated herself for causing him discomfort. It seemed she was always getting herself into trouble with her mouth; she hadn't meant to offend him. Unsure of how to remedy the situation, she studied the surrounding landscape, determined to keep her mouth shut until he'd recovered from her blunder. Maybe that would ease his shyness. Many minutes ticked by.

"How was the start of school?" His voice was kind; he sounded interested.

She gave him a brief synopsis of the first week and then the arrival of the pubescent boys, including how she'd dealt with the problem. When she explained how she'd handled Billy Cink,

Prentis laughed out loud and told her she was a wise woman. She hadn't felt very wise a few minutes ago. Ending her account, she detailed the improved behavior of the older boys. He was glad. She asked how the last two weeks had gone for him.

"Been plowing my fields, breaking new ground, and getting ready for the planting—using the horses."

"You don't have your wheat in yet?"

"No. I'm old fashioned. Don't plant until the fall equinox."

"Do you pasture your cattle on it in the winter?"

"I do. Just put them out a little later—at home anyway. Haven't built my herd down here yet. I'm surprised your dad doesn't plant at the equinox—most of the old farmers do, especially the Cherokee. Both your granddads in Kingman always planted late."

"I talked Daddy into being scientific."

"Don't know that scientific is best for farming, but I may be wrong. I'm willing to give you that. My father swore by planting at the equinox—it's probably our Scots-Irish heritage, sticking stubbornly with tradition. We tend to do that."

He smiled at her, eyes warm and friendly, the joke on himself. She smiled back, feeling relieved that her earlier blunder hadn't done any harm. Everything was comfortable again.

"Do you get better yields?" she asked.

"I have good yields, but it's not something you can run an experiment on. You can keep track of it, year after year. But you can't plant it early then turn back the clock and plant it late, replaying the same year and the same conditions."

"That would be the truly scientific way to go about it. I see what you mean."

"It's all in God's hands anyway. A farmer understands that better than most. I certainly understand that with the way my life has gone."

"Everything's in God's hands." Avery sat quietly for a moment, distressed that she had to upset the cart again after everything had been restored to comfortable friendliness. However, she had to ask. She took a deep breath then plunged in. "Prentis, I've never asked you about this, but it seems like a good time—"

"Why don't I go to church?"

"Yes, if you don't mind my asking. You believe in God, and you trust Him."

"And He's helped me through the most difficult circumstances in my life."

"Do you mind telling me?"

Turning toward her, Prentis studied her eyes. In the clear-blue depths of his eyes a flash of sorrow displayed itself; then he turned and stared off at the horizon. Several minutes ticked by before he looked back. Keeping his eyes on hers, he swallowed hard then started in.

"My father was raised Roman Catholic, and my mother Protestant. When they fell in love and wanted to marry, neither of them wanted to change their religious views. Keep the previously mentioned stubbornness in mind." He paused; she nodded. "Catholics can't marry non-Catholics—the church considers it a sin. And Protestant pastors aren't particularly fond of their people marrying Catholics—they probably think it's a sin, too. The priest didn't want my father to turn Protestant, and the pastor didn't want my mother to turn Catholic. Don't know if things have changed, but that's how it was then. My father's priest and my mother's pastor said they'd have to take a vow that they would never attend church if they married each other."

"That's ridiculous!" Avery couldn't help herself. "I'm sorry. I don't mean to be offensive, but isn't that counterproductive?"

"That's how I feel about it."

"So what happened?" she said.

"Neither of those clergy would marry them, so they married at the courthouse. That's why we didn't attend church growing up. But our mother always told us what she believed, and our father told us what he believed. Mother read to us out of the Bible. Dad taught us the rosary; occasionally, he'd mention one of the saints. In Kingman, we studied the Bible at school, and I decided to read my Bible every day, trusting that God would help me to comprehend it."

"Was it difficult?" she asked.

"Understanding the Bible or growing up that way?"

"Both."

"Yes, both were difficult. There was strife between the two families. When I was still a baby, while Mother was in town, Dad had the priest come out to baptize me. He was afraid I'd go to hell. Mother came back early, and there was the priest. She was angry with Dad—felt he'd betrayed her. But my grandparents on my father's side said he'd done the right thing. That caused division in the family, between my Pinkerton grandparents and my mother and the Dir grandparents—a war of religion, like in Europe from the Reformation until the late 1600s. After that, ever once in a while, my mother would take us to visit her Protestant church against my father's wishes to spite him. There would be a fight when we got home. It was a mess. Church became a battlefield, and we kids were caught in the middle."

"That would be a mess. With all that, how did you know what to believe?"

"Well, I prayed about what I read in my Bible. I spent a lot of time by myself after Dad died. Everyone else was at school, and I was out there plowing, planting, and harvesting, then riding my horse to the livery and working there. I was alone most of the time—really isolated and lonesome. Missed my dad terribly."

Avery made a soft sympathetic sound; Prentis paused to look at her.

"I'm sorry I interrupted," she said. "It's so sad that you had to experience that."

"God took care of me. It was difficult, but being alone caused me to recognize that God was near and that He cared for me. Felt as if He was watching me somehow, as if I was being observed, and He was helping me. Then I began to understand some things in my Bible that had puzzled me for a long time, and I didn't feel alone anymore."

"What did you understand?"

"Sort of saw the big picture. I comprehended that God had made the world and had a plan to redeem us from before He made mankind. At just the right time, He sent Christ to die for our sins on the cross, and then He raised Him from the dead, proving that Christ was who He had said He was—God in human flesh. When He helps us realize that we're sinners and can't do anything to make ourselves good or clean, He touches our hearts, and we place our faith in Him. Then He changes our hearts and begins to make us like Himself. For me, that takes a lot of work." He smiled at her. "As I was working, I had plenty of time to pray and to think about what I read in the Bible. That's what I came to believe."

"That's what I believe, too. There are churches that teach that—every single one that I've ever attended. Why don't you go to a church like that?"

"Avery, try to understand this from my perspective. Please know I'm trying really hard not to offend you. I know this is important to you, but I'm afraid of churches. There's always fights over doctrine and, in my family at least, conflict that splits the entire family, causing parents and grandparents to yell at one another while both sides claim to be Christians."

"I understand. Do you think you'll ever overcome your fear?"

"I hope so." He pinned her with his eyes. "I know it's important. But I see so many church people who don't act like the Bible says believers should. I don't trust the church."

"Goats."

"I'm sorry?"

"Goats—you know, the parable of the sheep and the goats."

"Oh!" He laughed softly. "You confused me. You mean people in the church you think are sheep—true Christians. But they're actually goats—people who've never lived changed lives?"

"That's correct. There are goats in with the sheep and tares in with the wheat. It's my opinion that they're usually the ones causing all the problems. I studied those passages in my Bible correspondence course this summer. I'm sorry you've been hurt, Prentis."

He studied her face. "Are you still my friend, then?" he said softly.

"Of course, I'm your friend! You were afraid I wouldn't be?"

"My heart was pounding when you asked about church. Feared I'd lose your good regard—I look somewhat like a heathen. Figured you'd tell me to swing this buggy around and take you home. But I had to tell you the truth, even if I lost you and had to endure that hardship again."

Turning toward him on the buggy seat so she could look directly into his eyes, she laid her gloved hand gently on his. "Prentis, you're not a 'heathen.' You're one of the most worthy men I know. You've had hard times, but you've responded in a way that honors God and your family. It wasn't possible that I would have asked you to turn the buggy around. In every interaction with you, I see evidence of your faith."

"Thank you, Avery," he said softly. "Pray for me about this."

"I certainly will."

Removing her hand from his, she slid back, leaning against the backrest as she smoothed her skirt. That had been an intense conversation. Not knowing if he wanted to continue in this vein of discourse, she looked off toward the horizon, sitting calmly, letting him choose the next topic. To keep from swaying against him, she braced herself, her gloved fingers gripping the seat's front edge. He glanced down at her nearest hand then looked up into her eyes.

"May I hold your hand?" he asked quietly.

Would this be granting a liberty? Avery looked intently at Prentis. Evenly, he met her appraising look, his eyes kind and humble, relief showing that his confession about his beliefs hadn't destroyed their newly budding relationship. She considered all those years he'd been alone and waiting, not saying how he felt about her.

She reached for his hand. "Yes, you may. I actually held yours first."

Prentis blew his breath out in a puff. As he enfolded her hand in his, he crinkled his eyes at her. Silently, they continued for a moment, staring at one another as they rode along.

"Thank you for being so understanding," he said.

"And thank you for being so patient."

"You're a prize worth obtaining. I hope I can win your heart."

FOUR

THE MILLER'S BARN HAD been built with both dancing and livestock in mind. The bottom of the tall structure was a typical barn—dirt floors, stalls, and hay, the farm animals taking advantage of those amenities, but the upstairs had been designed for community functions. To enter the social hall, Avery and Prentis ascended a covered staircase outside the barn and passed into a large room with a high ceiling. The airy space was all of natural wood—wooden floors, walls, and rafters. It was crowded with people of all ages. Avery recognized many familiar faces.

Along the side of the room were tables laden with refreshments. Avery added her cake and placed the picnic basket underneath. Several men she knew headed toward her: Joseph Pitzer—Hattie's older brother, Leroy Rapp, and Clarence Tippin. She'd known these Wakita boys her entire life. Their parents all knew one another, so they'd been acquainted since they were children and had attended events and dances around Manchester and Gibbon. She couldn't even remember when they'd first met, as she couldn't recall when she'd met Prentis.

"Pink!" Joseph Pitzer clapped one hand on Prentis's shoulder, pumping his hand with the other.

"Pitzer," Prentis replied evenly.

"You've brought the prettiest girl, I see. How are you, Avery?"

"I'm doing well, Joseph. How are you?"

"Perfectly happy in every way. But I'll be even happier when you put my name on that dance card of yours. I'll take the first dance and the second, unless Pink has beat me to it."

Prentis hadn't brought up the subject of her dance card. Protocol demanded that she accept the first request for a dance, so she took out her card and penciled in Joseph Pitzer.

Prentis bent and whispered in her ear, "I'm sorry I didn't think to ask. I was all caught up in our discussion in the buggy. Can I have the rest?"

Eyebrows raised, she looked up at him. "All of them?" she whispered back.

"If you'd rather dance with your friends, I don't mind. It's your decision."

His blue eyes were earnest as he said this—he was leaving it up to her. What should she do? Avery had to think about this. She should have consulted Momma or Hattie.

Avery hesitated for only a moment, then she wrote Prentis's name on the third line. As she did, Clarence and Leroy leaned in to indicate where she should write their names. While penciling them in, she noticed other male friends heading their direction. Needing time to think, she slid her card onto her wrist by its woven cord, tucked the pencil into her pocket, and turned to cut her cake. Fortunately, the music struck up as she finished.

Joseph Pitzer stepped over and led her out for the first dance of the cycle—the *Modern Waltz*. As they spun around the floor, he chattered non-stop. He had always been talkative. She gave him short answers, her mind distracted by what Prentis was doing. As he watched her dance with Joseph, he stood eating a piece of her cake. Every time she spun around, he smiled at her. He hadn't asked another girl to dance.

Since Joseph had claimed the second, Avery stayed with him. During the short break before the instruments played, he regaled her with humorous stories. She tried to be attentive, but kept thinking about Prentis, who stood pleasantly regarding her.

The *Quickstep* commenced. When she and Joseph came pacing around with their staccato, synchronized footwork, Prentis had disappeared. Trying to be inconspicuous, she scanned the room, but didn't catch sight of him. Where had he gone? Still, she managed to keep up with Joseph.

About halfway through the dance, Prentis quick-stepped by with Mary Beth Miller, hostess of the party. She smiled up at him, chatting as if they were old friends. He seemed interested as he listened, and he danced incredibly well. Obviously, he had danced before, possibly with Mary Beth. The pang of jealousy Avery felt surprised her with its intensity.

The dance ended. Joseph thanked Avery profusely and departed to find his next partner. Prentis materialized at her elbow; he was on her card for the third.

"You dance well." Avery struggled to keep her tone even.

"Two sisters."

"Sadie and Millie taught you to dance like that?"

"Yep, Sadie in particular. They said they needed the practice—even Millie. She intends to be a superb dancer when she's old enough. They wanted to make sure I wasn't a social misfit. Didn't want me to have two left feet, they said."

"Well, they succeeded. They taught you well."

"Thank you. I'll tell them."

"Do you dance often?"

"I've been working so hard, I've only been to one or two dances down here in all these years."

The music commenced. With a touch of bashfulness, he smiled gently and took her into his arms. "Here we go." As he looked down at her, his blue eyes shone.

Dancing the *Viennese Waltz*, they swooped round, all circling the dance floor. Prentis performed the requisite deep knee-bends and long steps splendidly, and he led well. Avery relaxed and let him push her backward around the floor, yielded to his lead. As he partnered her, he spoke quietly—words for her ears alone.

"I'm happy to be able to dance with you."

She smiled her agreement. It was downright blissful being held in his arms.

"You're a graceful dancer, Avery, light on your feet and easy to lead."

"Why, thank you, Prentis."

Eyes fixed on hers, he moved her in perfect time with the music. The flow of the rhythm washed over them as he piloted her, swirling with the others in synchronization.

"I ate about half your cake, I think."

Avery raised her eyebrows at this comment.

"Best cake I've ever had!" he said. "Awfully tired of my own cooking."

She laughed.

Too quickly, Prentis's dance ended. Clarence came for the *Slow Foxtrot*, followed by Leroy for the second rendition of the *Modern Waltz*—no controversial *Tango* here, this being Oklahoma. Gloomily, Avery watched Prentis glide by with two different Wakita girls, one dance after the other. She attempted to wear a pleasant expression as he sailed by with these glowing, talkative partners, but jealousy gnawed at her insides.

The musicians now paused for a short break before resuming the cycle of classical ballroom dances. They laid aside their instruments, stood, stretched, and walked toward the refreshments.

Prentis materialized at Avery's side. Hand on her elbow, he gently steered her toward the door. "Let's go outside," he said quietly.

With the others, they chatted as they descended the wooden staircase and stepped out into the farmyard. Several of the young men commented on a baseball game Prentis had recently pitched. He made an offhand, self-deprecating comment—a joke at his own expense. They all laughed. Then he guided Avery up the lane, away from listening ears.

A cool evening breeze blew softly about them. Brilliant stars blanketed the heavens, like a canopy of sparkling light. The three-quarter moon had recently risen on its journey across the nighttime sky, God's artistry providing a covering of magnificent beauty for their first outing.

"So," he said softly, "can you pencil me in for another dance?"

Cast in the silvery light of the moon, his eyes were dark, overshadowed by his brow. She was embarrassed. He had asked for all the dances, and she was miserable that she hadn't given them to him. After granting Prentis permission to call on her and thinking about him every single day for the past two weeks, it had felt strange to dance with Joseph and Clarence and Leroy. She didn't want to play this game.

"I can pencil you in for *all* the rest—if you still want them, that is."

"That's why I came." He dipped his head and smiled shyly up at her. "Sorry I didn't ask you before we arrived. Should have remembered your dance card as soon as we got into the buggy. But you were so beautiful! There you were, sitting right beside me, knocking my ability to think right out of me. I forgot my etiquette."

"And I forgot mine. I came to this dance with you."

"There's nothing wrong with dancing with your friends."

"Who were the girls?" she asked nonchalantly.

"Casual acquaintances. It isn't right for a man to leave unaccompanied women without a dance partner, if he's standing nearby. Or so my sisters tell me."

"They're right. You were a proper gentleman."

"Yes. But I'd prefer to dance all the rest with you. You're the one I came to dance with."

She smiled at him, and he smiled back. Then he tucked her hand into the crook of his arm and strolled back inside, dancing with her alone for the rest of the evening.

The ride home in the dark was companionable, filled with discussion of the particulars of the night. As they trotted along the country road guided by moonlight and the buggy's headlights, Prentis held her hand. He asked when he could see her next. She invited him to Floyd and Hattie's wedding in two weeks—she'd already checked with Hattie.

Until then, he'd be absorbed with planting wheat—a tedious task involving much stopping and starting as the seed was sown. He still used horses, he said, preferring them to a tractor. While sowing, he would stand on the running board, enabling him to see into the drill-boxes as he drove his horses at the right pace for distributing seed. Whenever the hoses got plugged with seed as it filtered down to the disks, he would stop and clear them. He enjoyed watching the disks fold the soil over the well-sown seed.

He chuckled. "I apologize. Didn't mean to deliver a discourse on planting wheat. It's sort of occupying my mind since I'll start next week."

"I'm interested in what you'll be doing. I don't mind." She smiled at him, recognizing how conscientious he was with all his work. These were the essentials of success in farming and in business. He would be a good provider.

Prentis's eyes gleamed at her in the moonlight—she saw a flash of his teeth. At home, he hitched the horse to the rail, assisted her out of the buggy, and escorted her to the door.

"I had a wonderful time, Avery. Look forward to seeing you in two weeks."

"I feel the same. Thank you for the beautiful evening."

He lifted her gloved hand to his lips and kissed it, smiling up at her as he did. Then he ran off into the darkness, calling a soft farewell as his buggy rolled down the lane. Avery stepped into the house smiling and humming.

* * * *

By the following Monday, another letter arrived for Miss Avery Slaughter.

September 22, 1913

My dearest Avery,

What a joy and privilege it was to take you to the Settlers Day Dance! I've coasted through the rest of this week on a cloud of happy remembrances. The most beautiful woman at the party agreed to come to the dance with me! How fortunate I am! I enjoyed talking with you, looking at your lovely face, listening to your voice—the most precious sound in the entire world, and holding you in my arms on the dance floor. Thank you for understanding the struggles of my faith. You are a compassionate and wise woman. And thank you for allowing me to attempt to win your

*heart. I'll endeavor to do so with all that
I am—with all the best that is within me.*

Very affectionately,

Prentis

Avery pressed his letter to her chest, his words tugging at her heart. For a shy man, he was articulate on paper and in speech, an intelligent, gentle man. Their beliefs were the same, and his life testified to his faith. She was comfortable with him. Given all that, the church issue seemed minor. She would pray for him, as he had asked, but God would have to take care of it.

Maybe married life would be a blessing. Maybe she could yield. At the dance, her jealousy had been illuminating. She had stronger feelings than she'd realized.

Still, the thought of dear baby Russell fresh in the grave was too much. Could she endure that, even if Prentis stood by her side? She needed more time.

Dead babies left a lasting mark.

FIVE

NOW THAT FLOYD AND Hattie's wedding approached, every evening the family moved more of Floyd's possessions into his new house. During the day, rather than helping Daddy, Floyd seeded his own fields, planting late like Prentis. As Floyd vacated, Jerry and John spread out, the three having shared a bedroom. Avery would be the oldest at home now. It would be strange not to have Floyd at home any longer. She would miss him.

While they were organizing the new house, Hattie shared a secret. Momma had told Hattie to prepare herself to host some of the family get-togethers now that she would be Floyd's wife. Because Avery was "frail," Momma had confided, Hattie was never to expect her to play hostess after she got married, assuming Prentis proposed and she accepted.

When Hattie told her this, Avery was taken aback. Apparently, her headaches worried Momma more than Avery had been aware. She didn't know what to say.

Glad to host the family events, Hattie laughed at Avery's dismay, telling her not to be offended. These sorts of things were always said when people were in transition. It was difficult for Momma to see her oldest son move out; she was worried about her daughter. She'd recently lost a baby, and her family was scattering. They should merely humor her.

In spite of Hattie's reassurances, this irritated Avery. It brought to mind the opinion of many of the women she knew. They didn't understand her career and educational aspirations and so accused Momma of coddling her—"pampering," some said. But, all along, Momma had thought she was sickly and weak. That was why Momma did so much at home. Avery needed to consider how to respond, if at all—Momma had been through so much.

* * * *

On the last Saturday in September, Prentis pulled up the lane to transport Avery to the wedding. He was debonair in his three-piece suit. Avery wore a white lace-covered blouse and one of the newly stylish hobble skirts, purchased for the occasion. There would be no dancing, so she wasn't concerned about ease of movement. She completed her ensemble by piling her hair high and wearing white gloves, a wide white hat, and boots shined to perfection. Today she desired to appear particularly fashionable.

As everyone loaded, Avery felt melancholy when they divided into different vehicles. She glanced up to see Momma looking at her, bravely pressing her lips together. Avery gave her a gentle smile. She would miss Floyd, too. After the post-wedding picnic, he would take Hattie to their new home east of Manchester. Therefore, Howard didn't ride in Floyd's buggy as usual, but with Avery and Prentis. Everyone else stepped into the Model T.

The first indication of a problem with Avery's new skirt occurred when Prentis had to lift her into the buggy. She couldn't take a wide enough step. Overflowing with happiness at seeing one another, they merely laughed. Avery dismissed it from her mind, distracted by their conversation. As they drove smiling up the lane, Howard snuggled in between them.

"How are you doing, little man?" Prentis asked him.

"Just fine, Prentis," Howard stated in his little man voice. "How are you?"

"Working hard. Just got all my wheat planted."

"We did ours much earlier," Howard stated in a proprietary way, as if proud of his decision to plant early.

"Is that right? How much yield do you think you'll get?"

"Reckon about twelve bushels per acre."

"That so?" Prentis smiled at Avery over Howard's head.

"Yep. That's what I reckon."

"I hope to get more."

"Well, maybe you will, and maybe you won't." That was a Grandpa Slaughter-ism.

Both Avery and Prentis laughed. Howard looked up at them as if he had no idea what was so funny. The rest of the ride, he pestered Prentis with questions about his buggy, his horse, and his property, attempting to make grown-up conversation. He ended by questioning Prentis's intentions toward Avery, making her nervous about where his interrogation was heading.

"What are you doing spending all this time with my sister?" Howard said.

"What do you think?"

"I think you're trying to steal her away from us."

"Don't intend to do any stealing."

Howard looked at her; she assured him there would be no theft. He thought a moment. "Well, Hattie's stealing away Floyd."

"Maybe Hattie's family thinks Floyd's doing the stealing," Prentis said.

This rendered Howard speechless; he apparently hadn't thought of it from this angle. Silently, they rode the rest of the way, Howard lost in contemplation of this conundrum, Avery grinning at Prentis, and Prentis hardly ever taking his eyes off her.

She felt particularly pretty on this autumn afternoon, and the affection in his gaze seemed to signal his agreement. The whir of the carriages wheels and the clippety-clop of the horse's feet on the packed-dirt road were the only sounds for the rest of the trip.

As Prentis hitched the horse, Howard clambered down and turned to regard him with suspicion—possible sister-stealer that he was—before joining Momma and Daddy. Holding Momma's hand, Howard headed into church, giving Prentis one final disapproving stare before marching in. Prentis chuckled then turned to extract Avery from the buggy.

"If I take your hand," she said quietly, "when I step down I'll have to hold up my skirt, showing my entire lower leg below the knee."

"We wouldn't want that."

"Prentis," she whispered, "this isn't funny."

He quickly removed his grin, but his eyes twinkled mischievously.

"I didn't think this through," she said. "Silly skirt! What do you suggest?"

"I'll simply lift you down."

"But everyone's looking. They'll know it's because of the skirt."

"Avery, if you look closely, you'll see you're not the only woman in this type of skirt, and several women came in wagons. Probably more than one woman had to be lifted down today."

She sighed. "I thought I would look so fashionable. I should have gone back in to change when you had to pick me up bodily. Why wasn't I thinking?"

"We were out of time, if I recall."

"Oh, everyone's going in . . . wait a minute for the crowd to thin."

Waiting for the signal, he stood patiently. Then, grinning at her, he put his hands around her waist and lifted her down, setting her lightly on her feet.

Struggling to maintain her dignity, Avery attempted to keep a straight face. It was one thing to be helped out of a wagon—that was the norm, but it was another thing altogether when your skirt fit so tightly at the ankles that you couldn't step out of a buggy. She wondered what had possessed her to buy this newly stylish, but entirely worthless piece of clothing. This was the ironic twist that made all the difference. She burst out laughing, causing the crowd in the churchyard to turn to stare at her, some disapprovingly.

"You've upset the goats," Prentis whispered.

That caused her to laugh even harder, drawing more disapproval of her indecorous behavior outside a church building.

"Jesus never laughed, you know," he said quietly.

Gleefully, she grinned at him, taking his offered arm. They straggled in with the last of the congregation then made the protracted march to sit with her family in the front. Long-legged Prentis took miniscule steps to match her constrained gait. Catching a glimpse of Joseph Pitzer regarding her slow progress with a grin and one raised eyebrow, Avery gave him a demure smile. At last they made it! She slid into the pew first, followed by Prentis.

Each wearing an expression of disbelief, her brothers gaped at her, clearly amused by how difficult it was for her to walk. As she met their eyes, she got the giggles. Turning away, she noticed Hattie's brother still had that eyebrow raised. Smothering her laughter, the slight shaking of her shoulders was the only indication. She often had to do this when teaching small amusing children. She didn't want to cause a ruckus.

Behind them, she heard a woman whisper, "It's that man. He hasn't darkened the doorway of a church his entire life, I don't think."

Suddenly, this wasn't funny. Someone was speaking ill of Prentis, as if he'd been the one responsible for her behavior, simply because he didn't attend church. People could be so cruel and judgmental. As she considered turning to see who had spoken, her shoulders made the slightest motion in that direction. Slowly, Prentis laid his hand directly on hers, covering her entire hand. He never took his eyes off the ceremony. Hattie's father had just handed Hattie off to Floyd.

Avery looked down at his hand, which was simply lying on top of hers, gently restraining her. This gesture let her know he was not offended. She relaxed and took a deep breath. As she did, Prentis lifted his hand and folded his hands together with a slight smile. Out of the corner of her eye, she caught the movement and leaned ever so lightly against his shoulder. He leaned back.

The rest of the ceremony passed without incident, though she remained distracted by her assumptions about who had made the comment and why. As Floyd and Hattie marched out, Momma dabbed her eyes and turned to smile at all her progeny and Prentis, seated in a row right behind her. They all smiled back. Avery decided not to mention the thoughtless remark. If Prentis could react so magnanimously, so could she.

"Momma," Avery leaned forward to whisper. "I'm having Prentis take me home to change this skirt. I can barely walk, and I couldn't get out of the buggy."

"I wondered if that would be a problem."

"We'll go fast so we don't miss anything."

"Very well." Momma nodded then addressed the entire row. "Let's all go out together—come with Daddy and me." With her eyes, she singled out Avery and Prentis. "Then you both head for the buggy as soon as we get outside."

They all stood. Out they went, walking as fast as they could, though not as quickly as they would have liked to, but for Avery's mincing steps. Prentis lifted her into the buggy, joined her, and then made good time up the country road. As they raced homeward, she held onto her hat and turned toward him.

"How did you do that?"

"Do what, Avery?"

"Keep from glaring at whoever said that."

"It doesn't matter what she said, whoever she was. God sees my heart. That woman's opinion doesn't matter to me. I've heard it all before."

"I hate that people would judge you like that."

"Goats, remember. You said it. Who knows the state of a person's heart?"

Contemplating this, she stared at the landscape flying by. The horse was galloping.

"Just remember," he said, glancing at her, "if I succeed in my quest and we become man and wife, people will talk about you because of me. They're talking about you now, merely because I'm courting you. Do you want that?"

"People already talk about me. They criticize the fact that I study and have different goals than most young women. And then there are some who notice our black hair and eyes. They puzzle over our distinctive blended appearance, wondering what in the world we *are*, until they figure out we're Cherokee, in part or in whole. Then they expect the tomahawks to come out."

He snorted. "That's ludicrous! Human beings are often absurd." He glanced at her; she nodded, resigned to the fact.

"You can see it dawning on their faces," she said. "Next the whispering starts or the evasive movement to the other side of the room or the street. Then someone hisses, 'dirty savages'."

"I remember comments like that when we were young—knocked another boy down once for saying it. But this is different. This would be criticism of your choice as a Christian. No one criticizes you for that now."

"I think some do. Men often tell me it's ridiculous that I'm getting a Bible degree—I'm a woman, after all. They don't understand it. They assume I'm a suffragette and laugh about it."

"Well, are you?"

"Yes, I am. I believe women should be able to vote."

"I agree. Other than the ignorant comments about your heritage, those criticisms come because you're a strong and intelligent woman. You're a teacher; you're pursuing an advanced degree; you want to vote. But if by some miraculous kindness of God I'm able to secure your hand and make you mine, you'll be criticized for things people believe about *me*. They'll question your choice and your spiritual discernment. Will that matter to you?"

"If God's estimation is the most important thing, then I shouldn't care one iota."

"So, is it?"

Taking a deep breath, she considered her motivations. "Unfortunately, I sometimes worry too much about what people think, such as when I was overly concerned about how to exit the buggy, or when I bought this ridiculous skirt, merely because it was fashionable. I probably need to grow. I need to put God's view of me first."

"If you want me to continue to court you, it will only get worse. Should we continue? Consider what it will mean."

There was her house. Prentis turned off the road, and they raced up the lane, dust flying as they came to a rapid halt.

"Wait here," she said. "Turn your head. I'm going to lift this silly skirt so I can hurry."

Pausing, she stared pointedly at him. He complied, turning away and shielding his view. Hiking her skirt up, she moved fast, climbing down and running into the house.

In her room, Avery changed into a fuller skirt, glad to have a moment to ponder his words. She felt ashamed of herself as she realized what a people-pleaser she was, especially within the church. How many of her good deeds were truly done because she loved the Lord?

After Russell's funeral Daddy had asked them to meditate on living lives that pleased God, setting their hearts and minds on Him. Did she serve Christ to be seen or because she adored Him? If done because she loved Christ then why did the opinion of others, even her own mother, bother her so much? She needed to meditate on this. Prentis challenged her, causing her to evaluate her relationship with the Lord, making it more pure and truthful.

The realization of this made her incredibly happy.

Hurrying, she scurried outside. Prentis had maintained his posture, his hand still blocking his view. When she slammed the front door, he turned, studying her face as she strode rapidly toward him. He looked as if he expected heartbreaking news. Before he could get out to help her, she reached across. Grasping her hand, he drew her in and then wheeled the buggy around. The horse galloped when he lightly flicked the reins, heading them back at top speed.

"In answer to your question, I absolutely want you to continue to pursue me."

"You do?" His voice broke. Turning, he searched her eyes.

In his eyes she perceived the pain he'd felt all his life as church people had judged him, first because of his parents and then because of his own decision not to join a church body.

"I was afraid I'd lost the opportunity to win you." He kept his eyes locked on hers a moment longer before turning them toward the galloping horse.

"No." She rested her hand on his arm. "When I went inside, I realized how much I need you in my life. You're helping me to consider my motives and my hypocrisy, enabling me to evaluate whether my love for the Lord is true and faithful. Do I truly care more about what God thinks of me than what anyone else thinks? The desire of my heart is to please Him. You're helping me to assess whether that's how I'm really living. Thank you."

He flicked his eyes away from the racing gelding, fastening them on her. "You benefit my life, too, Avery. You bring happiness and friendship again, easing my loneliness. Thank you for allowing me to pursue you."

She leaned against his shoulder, and he reached for her hand. They didn't speak for the rest of the trip. The distance was covered rapidly, and soon they pulled into the lane at Hattie's parents' house. Many people were still walking up from their buggies and wagons.

As Prentis secured the horse, Avery waited.

When he arrived at her side, he stood looking up at her, regarding her with loving eyes, all the hope restored to his gaze. Taking his hand and giving it a squeeze, she stepped down. Then he tucked her hand into the crook of his arm. Bound together by mutual affection, they strolled up to join the party, each perfectly content with the other.

* * * *

By Wednesday, Avery had received another letter. The next opportunity for her to see Prentis was the annual Open House at her school. It was a month away.

September 29, 1913

My very dear Avery,

I can't begin to tell you how relieved and glad I am that I may continue my quest for your heart and your hand. For a woman pursuing a Bible degree, I know I'm a most unorthodox suitor—a man who doesn't attend church. I value your friendship and good opinion more than that of any other person on God's green earth. You were an incredibly fun childhood playmate. The time we spent together as children built some of my life's best memories. I missed you during those years when I shouldered my father's responsibilities and worked and prepared to attempt to win you. The joy of getting to know you as a grown woman has been worth the wait. You're a blessing and an encouragement.

Having gotten used to seeing you every two weeks, it will cause me acute agony to be deprived of your company for an entire month. I'll miss you. I long for the end of October. Buying cattle, building a feeding area, and doing all the tasks involved with starting my herd will be no compensation for the loss of your company. How will I get through the month?

With all of my affection—

Prentis

His mention of their childhood brought back delightful recollections of riding horses, sprawling in the shade conversing as Prentis fished, and chuckling together—his blue eyes bright and clear—over some stunt their younger brothers had pulled.

She recalled watching the boys play baseball. Prentis had been a good pitcher even then. The ball had smacked hard into Fred's toughened bare hands whenever Prentis let loose with a fastball—*pop!* None of her brothers had been capable of hitting it, not even Floyd.

After sunset, all of them had played hide-and-seek while their parents talked on the porch. She remembered hiding in the darkness with Prentis, their fingers interlaced. His hands had always felt warm and solid. Into her memory flashed a long-ago evening.

"Wait, Avery," he had whispered, pulling her closer so he could speak right into her ear, his breath hot on her cheek. "Floyd's right around the corner."

Keeping a grip on Prentis's hand, she had edged behind him, sliding deeper into the shadows. Holding her breath, she had bowed her head, pressing it against his back as Floyd's soft tread passed them by. There was a pause and then Floyd's footfalls had moved onward. Cautiously, Prentis had pulled her forward by their linked hands, and the two of them had raced for base, laughing when they slammed jointly into the back door with Floyd's heavy footsteps sounding behind them.

"What a girl!" Prentis had said. "Not only are you smart, but you run as fast as a boy!"

Avery had taken this as the highest praise. The reminiscence made her smile—they had been about twelve. What fond memories she had of him!

A month was a long time. She was going to miss him acutely. How would *she* get through the month? She thought about writing him back. Since he had initiated this correspondence, it would be appropriate, however, she didn't know if she could write as openly as he did. Before she could pen her words for posterity's sake, she needed to be courted more thoroughly.

Prentis's words wooed her heart, pulling her toward him.

SIX

ON FRIDAY NIGHT, AVERY asked her parents if she could take the Model T to Anthony, Kansas, on the following day. She had received her first paycheck, and she needed a new coat. With her mother she had perused all the ladies' magazines and the Sears catalogue to determine the latest fashions. It was early October, and now was the time to purchase—the new styles were in the stores. Since she wanted to buy a quality garment that would last for many years, she needed to feel the fabric and try on the coat. Anthony was the place to go.

Daddy sent John along, giving him money for purchases for the farm and entrusting him with some of the adult responsibilities of running the place, now that he was sixteen. Since he knew how to start the Model T, he would also fulfill the passenger's tasks in the start-up process.

Before the purchase of the automobile, Avery would have gone by train, because it would have taken about three hours on a trotting horse. Anthony was more than twenty miles north. In the Model T, the trip would only take about forty minutes, if she didn't drive too fast. She had promised her father. However, as they traveled away from the farmhouse, she saw the needle edge up past forty several times. Whenever she noticed, she pushed the throttle up the tiniest bit, keeping her hand lightly upon it to facilitate quicker adjustments.

Flying over a slight hill, she and John waved at Mr. Smith, who lived directly north. Sternly, he stared at them, disgruntled.

"What was that all about?" John asked.

"Maybe he doesn't like to see a woman drive, or perhaps he doesn't like the automobile."

"Or maybe you're going too fast." John leaned to look at the speedometer.

Avery startled when she observed that they were almost up to forty-five.

"Or maybe that," she said, pushing the throttle upward. She removed her hand so she wasn't tempted to edge it downward.

The ride was bumpy on this farm road—two hard ruts made by the wagon wheels, grass growing in the middle, large potholes that she either dodged or hit, causing them to bounce into the air. Following this red-dirt road, they soon arrived at the state line and navigated the jog, turning right and then left as the Oklahoma road connected with the one in Kansas. This thoroughfare then joined a main highway north toward Anthony.

This more-frequently traveled Kansas thoroughfare was graded by Harper County. There were fewer bumps and less grass, but it was like a washboard. As the Model T clattered over the tiny ridges in the road, their teeth rattled. Avery had to go even slower.

"Sis," John said, "I'm in no hurry. What's the rush?"

"The new fashions will be gobbled up. It's imperative that we arrive early."

"You girls and your silly fashions. That hobble skirt wasn't much of a success, was it?"

"No!" She laughed with him. "You're absolutely right about that."

Between the washboard road and the potholes, the trip took them forty-five minutes, but they arrived as the shops opened on Main Street. After dropping John at the implement store, she headed back east toward the downtown.

Avery sought a new type of garment—a merging of the cape and the cloak into the long oriental coat currently fashionable. Older women still wore capes, but younger women like her preferred the coat. The oriental coat was like a cocoon, swathing a woman in warmth from neck to ankle, practical and stylish all the way down to her boot tops, and thus sensible for an Oklahoma schoolteacher. She wanted one with a fur collar and an oversized muff to match.

Buggies and a few automobiles lined the broad dirt-packed Main Street. As Avery parked the Model T and hurried into the ladies' apparel store, she realized that she especially sought to impress others in the area of fashion. She would have to consider Prentis's thoughts on this, maybe even consulting him. Was it right for a young woman to be so swayed by fashion that she was ready to spend an entire month's wages on a coat? Her father had taught her to buy quality items, because they lasted longer, affording the best use of her money. But was she being vain? Perusing the store's offerings, she pondered this.

Avery stopped in her tracks. There before her very eyes hung the exact coat she sought! Long, black, and sleek, it was the height of fashion—oriental in cut, all wool, and satin-lined with a double-breasted fur shawl collar. As if that wasn't enough, there was a matching fur muff and a satin-lined, fur-and-black-velvet hat. *Oh my!* The thrill of finding precisely what she wanted gripped her. She checked the label—exactly her size.

The store was crowded. Quickly, she scooped it up. Instantly, a store clerk appeared at her elbow to assist her. Stepping into the dressing room, Avery practically fluttered with anticipation. It fit! She looked incredibly modern and stylish! Moreover, the price was exactly what she could pay, including the hat and muff.

For the eight-month term at her small schoolhouse, Avery received a $500 annual salary. Thanks to President Woodrow Wilson and the passage and ratification of the Sixteenth Amendment, federal income tax was now automatically deducted. Everyone was taxed at the same rate, no longer apportioned by the population of each individual state. She paid the exorbitant rate of 1 percent right off the top. It was robbery. But even Jesus had paid taxes, so she shouldn't complain.

Of her $61.88 paycheck for the first month, her tithe subtracted, she had $55.69 to spend. Daddy had said she could use the entire amount for the purchase, instead of giving him half as she usually did. Her purchase would cost $49.50. She had plenty with a few dollars left.

Should she pay it? She studied the coat again. It was quality. It was beautiful. If she walked out without it, she would regret it later.

When she picked up her brother, the coat and the muff were wrapped in brown paper and tied with string. The hat was in a hatbox, and the two bundles sat on the backseat. John placed his few items on the floorboard, and they headed home. As she described the coat, she bubbled over with excitement.

"I've never been so flustered about a coat," he said.

"Johnny, I know it's probably vain of me, but it's so pretty, and I want to look nice."

"For Prentis?" he teased.

"Well yes, for Prentis. But, silly boy, don't you know we women want to look nice so the other women think we look nice."

"If that's the case, you're the silly ones."

"I admit we are. But recently, I remember you strutting around in your new boots, making sure all your friends saw them. So we girls aren't the only ones."

"Guess I did." He laughed at her description.

"I've also seen you slicking your hair down with pomade so it lies down nice and flat. Then, with your nicely combed hair, I've watched you laughing and blushing as you try to get the attention of the girls at church."

"All right, I admit it. We're both silly."

"We definitely are."

When they arrived at home, Avery modeled her coat. Her parents were both pleased, thinking she'd done a mighty fine job choosing this particular coat. John had done well, too. But her father wanted to have a private conversation. They stepped into the front room.

"Mr. Smith rode down earlier to tell me that I needed to 'settle Avery down.' Do you have any idea why he'd say that?"

"I think I was going faster than I should have been when we drove by his house."

"That's what he said. How fast were you going?"

"I was going over forty, but under forty-five. Truly."

"I believe you. You gave me your word that you wouldn't

go as fast as forty-five. But let's talk about that. Was that a safe speed for that dirt track of a road?"

"Well, John and I were bouncing and jostling about, so I'm guessing it wasn't."

"You're guessing right. Did you go that fast on the road north to Anthony?"

"No, we didn't. We made bad time up that road."

"Watch your speed, Avery. Don't want you to have an accident. I also don't want anyone to have to tell me to 'settle down' my daughter, who happens to be the local schoolteacher."

"Your point is taken, Daddy. Thank you."

* * * *

Providentially, the following day turned unseasonably cold for Oklahoma. Blustery weather blasted in from the north, and the sky grew gray—a reminder that winter would soon be upon them. Avery was delighted to wear her new coat to church. As she came out the door to climb into the Model T, her mother gasped.

"Why, Avery," she said, "you look like a Martial and Armand fashion plate."

"Oh, Momma, do you think so?"

"I do, indeed."

But after a full morning of teaching Sunday School and hearing a challenging sermon, Avery noticed many envious looks as she left church. And now, she felt a pang of conscience. Should she have purchased the expensive coat? Was it too plush for their rural lifestyle? Was it all right for her to have such a fashionable item?

Later in the evening, after spending Sunday afternoon reading her Bible and praying about it, she asked her parents.

They looked at one another, and then Daddy spoke. "Avery, you work hard for your salary. We had hoped you would make such a purchase. Soon you may be a married woman, and that coat may have to last you for the next decade. I've always taught you that it's better stewardship to buy quality than to spend money on something that may wear out quickly."

"But at church some girls appeared to be envious."

"Were you suitably humble? Were you wearing the coat or was the coat wearing you?"

Silently, Avery considered his words before answering. "I think the coat was wearing me. My chin might have been a bit high this morning and my bearing somewhat regal."

"Well, you seem duly chastened. Confess your error to the Lord. Jesus's blood covers even fashion-oriented pride. Next time you're out in that coat, remember it's made of mere cloth, it's temporal, and it will perish one day."

"Prentis and I have been talking about that."

"Fashion or the temporal state of this earth?"

"Neither. We've been talking about being aware of whether God's approval is more important to us than man's."

"Now that's a serious topic worth contemplation. What did you decide?"

"I think I seek the approval of others far too much."

"Did Prentis concur?"

"Oh, he never said either way. He was simply concerned about me. Since he doesn't go to church, he wanted me to realize people will talk about my decision to allow him to court me. That being the case, he wanted me to be certain."

"What started this discussion?"

"We overheard someone say something about him."

Momma and Daddy glanced at one another, and Momma pursed her lips. Daddy turned back toward Avery with tired and patient eyes—his deacon expression.

"Prentis is a fine, hardworking Christian man. I wouldn't have given him permission to court you if he weren't."

"I know that, Daddy. I told him that I absolutely want him to continue."

"You're just the woman to soothe and heal his heart after all he's been through."

"Do you think so?"

"I know so. You have a delicate conscience, patience, and a gentle spirit. Look at you, worrying about whether or not the other girls were offended by your coat. Tells me a lot about your heart right there."

Avery sighed. "I still value the good opinion of others too highly, though."

"There are times we all do, daughter. We're human."

* * * *

When Avery arrived home from school on Wednesday, Momma handed her a letter. Prentis's handwriting was scrawled with more emotion than usual. The address practically covered the entire front of the envelope. She went up to her room to open it.

October 6, 1913

Precious Avery,

Yesterday I spent a miserable day sitting in this lonely house meditating on you, unable to focus on anything I read in my Bible and unable to rest. I know the Sabbath was made for man, so we can rest our bodies; but it wasn't restful.

I'm down here permanently now, and the cold weather brought something to mind. It occurred to me that I'm wasting the dry roads while I have them. Soon the roads will be bad and travel will be impossible on some weekends, and then I won't be able to see you, even if we've planned on it. The thought of that caused me quite a bit of despair. And so, since winter is rapidly approaching, I'd like to change my tactics.

What I really want is to look at your face, hear your voice, talk with you, and spend time in your presence. Here I sat, whiling away the hours on Sunday; and there you sat in your house, doing the same.

I want to spend normal hours of normal days with you. I hope I'm not being too forward, but I want to ride up and see you every Sunday afternoon that I can until the weather prevents it.

Is that asking too much? Would I be stealing away your Sabbath rest?

If you prefer we only see each other for special occasions, I'm willing to please you in this. With everything in me, I want to please you. Can you write me and tell me if I may come? I'm finding I can't keep my mind from working its way round to you, no matter what task I'm completing. Sunday was especially difficult. I miss you.

With all my heart—

Prentis

As Avery thought of him alone down on his farm and how often he'd been lonesome since his father had died, a spasm of sympathetic pain squeezed her chest. His request lined up exactly with her wishes. She now desired to know his opinion about practically everything. She wanted to spend time with him in normal everyday activities. The dance and the wedding had prompted some serious discussions, but quiet days at home had their value, too. She went downstairs to speak to her parents. They were in favor, as were all the boys, except Howard.

"He'll just steal you away faster if he comes." Looking like a wizened old man, his little five-year-old face wrinkled with worry. His lower lip quivered. Momma hugged him close, and Avery took hold of his hand.

"Howard," she said, "Prentis can never steal me from you."

"Hattie stole Floyd." Apparently, Howard hadn't been swayed by Prentis's logic.

"Floyd is still your brother."

"But I never see him," his small voice quivered, "and he used to sleep right across the hall and sit right across the table."

"That's true. Howard, do you think you'll stay a little boy all your life?"

"No," he said seriously. "I'll grow up."

"Yes, you will. Do you think we should all live with Momma and Daddy for the rest of our days, even after we grow up?"

"*I* want to live with Momma and Daddy all my life."

"That's how all children with loving parents feel. You'll understand when you're older."

Howard sighed. "That's what everyone always says."

"Have you considered that when Floyd married Hattie, she became your sister?"

He looked up at Momma for verification; Momma nodded.

"And, if Prentis were to want to marry me—though I don't know if he will yet, Howard; nothing's been said or decided—it would make him your brother."

"He doesn't look anything like us."

"Nevertheless, he'd be your brother."

"But Hattie looks like us."

"It's because she's Cherokee, too. But look at all of us, Howard. See how we vary in appearance? Some have a slightly fairer complexion, hair, or eye color than the others."

Howard turned to look at each family member in the room. Each met his eyes, smiling at him as he learned this familial lesson. Then he returned his eyes to Avery's, nodding seriously.

"We differ because the Cherokee often married people from outside the tribe," Avery said. "You can see it in our features. Why, Chief John Ross was only one-eighth Cherokee when he led the tribe during the *Trail of Tears*. With even one drop of Cherokee blood, we're still considered to be Cherokee. Our ancestors sometimes chose to marry someone they loved who wasn't Cherokee, often because they shared their Christian faith."

"But none of us have blue eyes like Prentis."

Avery laughed softly. "That's true. But the color of our eyes, hair, or skin isn't the important thing. It's the quality of a person's character that's his or her measure. Prentis would be a good brother; he's a very good brother to his own brother and sisters."

Recognizing that he'd been bested, Howard stalked off. It was obvious that he didn't like that his older siblings were all growing up and heading different directions. Listening to reason was something he didn't care to do.

Avery went upstairs to consider how to reply to Prentis. He had asked a specific question and needed a specific answer. Therefore, she had to write, no matter how shy she felt about it. She took out her pen and ink to draft a note—she could say all she needed to say briefly.

Dear Prentis,

Thank you for your thoughtful letter. Your words always touch my heart. Please come to visit every Sunday you are able. Howard's a bit upset with your request. He's afraid you're going to steal me away, but I very much want to see you. I miss you, too.

Sincerely,

Avery

SEVEN

ALL WEEK AVERY MEDITATED on her need for public approval. The conversation with Prentis had prompted more self-reflection on her personal growth and humility than she'd experienced in a while. The good opinion of others often did matter to her more than pleasing God.

Huddled under a pile of quilts, she lay in her room curled up with her Bible, keeping the lamp lit when she should have been sleeping. As she evaluated her motives, she prayed. Prentis's maturity challenged her, provoking her to consider her life and whether God's opinion was truly the one that mattered.

Midweek, Daddy came in to speak with her privately. Someone—he wouldn't say who—had complained about her new coat. It could have been anybody. She'd worn the coat everywhere since the weather had turned cold. This someone had told Daddy that he needed to "rein in Avery's extravagant spending." It was scandalous that she had spent an entire month's salary on a coat. The local schoolteacher's salary was a matter of public record. Anyone could have gone to Anthony and seen that coat in the store, therefore knowing its price.

Once more, someone thought her father needed to calm her down, rein her in, or keep her in check, even though she was an adult woman. Maybe she *should* become a more radical suffragette. She could march around with placards, picketing outside the homes and offices of lawmakers—all friends of her daddy, and make real trouble.

"I told this person that you were an adult woman," her father said, "an independent laborer. I'd taught you to buy quality goods, and I felt your purchase was a good one."

"What did he or she say?"

"That I needed 'to have better control' over my daughter."

"Daddy!" Avery felt humiliated.

"People are always going to say and do things we don't agree with, even hurtful things. There will always be unkind words. As someone you care for asked you recently, whose opinion is more important—God's or man's?"

"God's." Avery sighed.

"Baby girl, all these challenges cause you to grow as a Christian—you know trials always do. You've seen that worked out in our lives. It's true in your life as well. If we don't keep God's opinion first and rely on Christ, human frailty will drag us down and harm us. You know what happened to me. My drinking nearly destroyed our family. I must, and so must we all, set our hearts on Christ. God must be first in our lives."

Avery nodded; she knew this was so. These admonitions helped her to evaluate her motives. In every action, though her intentions were good, she detected a tinge of a wrong motive— resisting the rules just a bit, not considering others, desiring praise, or placing the approbation of others higher than God's approval. Usually, she hid these flaws and sins behind her own back, unaware that she even had these aims. She needed to grow—God would have to do some work within her. His bringing it to her attention was a beginning, calling her to repentance.

When she went to church the next Sunday, she wore the coat; the coat did not wear her. She knew she looked stylish, but remembered it would someday be worn and no longer fashionable, as her old coat was now. Her purchase had offended someone, so no highly held chin or fashionable posing occurred. The coat was simply worn. She wanted to be kind to her neighbors. Not everyone had an independent salary to spend on such a nice item, and she knew it.

Though she'd spent much time with the Lord in self-evaluation and reflection, it was difficult to concentrate on the church service, for Prentis would be arriving today. She didn't know when. He'd probably wait until after they'd finished their dinner. Floyd and Hattie were coming home with them this week. Of course, Prentis wouldn't know that.

Until today, no one had seen the newlyweds since the wedding. They'd disappeared for the past two weeks and hadn't even been in church for the past two Sundays. Floyd and Hattie both reddened when all the little brothers loudly inquired about this, right in the crammed entryway of the church as people left the service. Avery didn't ask. Then Howard squeezed into Floyd and Hattie's buggy. Avery could imagine the types of questions he was posing.

During the drive home in the Model T, Avery realized she couldn't recall the sermon topic. If Prentis's visits were to become regular occurrences, she'd have to master herself and pay attention regardless of her anticipation.

* * * *

Momma had set a big smoked ham into the oven, along with piles of greased potatoes. The right amount of wood in the cookstove kept everything cooking slowly. The night before, they'd made pies—peach, pumpkin, and apple. A pot of chopped carrots simmered in the Dutch oven on the back of the cookstove, right over the hottest part of the oven. When they arrived home, all would be perfect. They would smell the food before they even walked into the house.

As they pulled up the lane, Avery was surprised to see Prentis had already arrived. Sitting on his horse in the barnyard, he was bundled in a coat, scarf wound up to his eyes, awaiting them. With her eyes fixed on his—heart joy-filled, she beamed at him as her father pulled the Model T into the barn.

"I went into Wakita this week, Avery," Daddy said. "Ran into Prentis at the dry goods store and invited him for Sunday dinner, since he was coming anyway."

"Thank you! I know he's tired of his own cooking. Why didn't you tell me?"

"Thought a surprise might brighten your week."

"It certainly does!" She leaned over to kiss Daddy's cheek.

When she turned away from her father, Prentis stood waiting to assist her out of the automobile. As she slid across to take the hand he offered, she smiled up at him. With a shy smile for her, he tucked her hand into the wool-covered crook of his arm.

Gene offered to stable his horse; Prentis thanked him. They all walked toward the house, and Prentis greeted the rest of her family. Howard didn't look too happy to see him. Profusely, he thanked her parents for the invitation. When they arrived at the house, he stepped aside with Avery as everyone else filed in.

"I'm so glad to see you," he said. "You look particularly beautiful. Is this coat new?"

"Yes, it is. I bought it last weekend in Anthony."

"My goodness, Avery, what a good choice! Stylish, warm, well made—a wise purchase. You look like those pictures my mother and sisters are always poring over."

"Thank you, Prentis. Did Daddy tell you to say that?"

Prentis's eyebrows shot up. "Why no! Is there something I don't know?"

"I'll tell you about it later. For now, let's simply say that the last two weeks have been a learning experience. It's been good for me. I'm happy that you approve."

"So you weren't put off by the fact that I invited myself?"

"Not at all. I missed you. I *want* to spend normal hours of normal days with you."

As she quoted his letter, he smiled at her. But they could smell dinner. The fragrance practically pulled Prentis in through the door, and he pulled Avery in after him.

"You have no idea how dismal my cooking is," he whispered to her. "This is almost like being in heaven," he said to Momma. "Thank you, Mrs. Slaughter, for having me. I may starve down there in that stake house."

"We'll see if we can keep you alive from week to week." She chuckled softly.

"What did Avery make?" Momma indicated the pies. "Pie is my favorite," he told Avery.

"I thought you liked cake."

"I do. But pie is even better. I can't wait for dessert!"

Momma shooed him out of the kitchen. The three women

needed space to work efficiently. As they scurried about, Momma grinned from ear to ear—the entire family was present, even possible future members. Avery knew the sore place in her mother's heart was still healing, and family time salved the wound left from losing baby Russell.

When they had the food on the table, everyone around it, and grace had been said, her parents sat smiling at one another down the table's length. Having their entire family around the table was a blessing—like medicine for their souls.

Amid much laughter, the food was passed, eaten, and praised; Prentis was especially complimentary. He ate like a man who hadn't had a good meal in a great while.

After the main course, the women each carried in a pie. Prentis had one slice of each. Avery didn't know how he could eat so much and where he was putting it—he was a tall and slender man. He praised each pie and told her several times that she was an excellent cook before ducking his head to shovel in more. By the end of dessert, the pies had all been consumed by the tableful of hungry boys and men. Hattie, Momma, and Avery smiled at one another and rose to tidy up the kitchen.

Used to cleaning up after himself, Prentis carried in dirty dishes until Momma shooed him away, sending him out with the other men. She didn't like their system disrupted. Avery and Momma had it down to a science; Hattie was almost superfluous. But now, Momma did something unexpected. She sent Avery out to spend time with Prentis, saying she didn't need her help today, now that Hattie was there. At first, Avery was confused and frustrated, but then she remembered that Momma thought she was "frail." Now that Hattie could fill her shoes, she wondered if she would ever be allowed to help again.

Avery stepped out of the kitchen and into the world of men.

Gene and Howard already slept on the floor, curled up near the cast-iron stove. Sprawled on their bellies facing one another with the checkerboard in between, Abe and John played a game. Jerry wrote at one of the side tables. Sound asleep, Floyd slouched in Momma's armchair with his feet on the hassock. Snoring loudly, Daddy sprawled across the couch. Head cocked, Prentis stood reading the titles in their bookcase with one book in his hand.

"I've been sent out to spend time with you," Avery said.

Smiling, he slid the book back in. "That's fine by me. Do you want to go for a walk?"

"Will you be able to walk? As much food as you crammed into yourself, I wouldn't think that would be possible."

He chuckled. "I fortified myself for the coming week. However, I *am* able to walk. Though it's tempting, I don't want to waste my limited time sleeping on the floor. Have to leave in time to take care of my animals."

"How long do you have?"

"A couple more hours."

"Let's take a walk then." Avery headed into the hall.

As Prentis helped her into the new coat, he praised its purchase once more, admiring the smart hat and matching muff. In light of all the controversy this coat had caused, it gave her great satisfaction simply listening to his comments. He held the front door open. Out they went, stepping off the porch and strolling up the lane before either of them spoke.

"So, you've had a difficult time about your coat," Prentis said.

"It was an expensive purchase. I spent nearly my entire first month's salary."

"I believe it's better to buy quality items."

"That's what Daddy taught me. But I wished I could have consulted you, too. Your opinions are becoming increasingly important to me." She felt shy about admitting this.

"And yours to me. That's as it should be, I think."

"You're right." She walked a few paces, attempting to refocus. "After I bought the coat, I acted vain about it. I strutted around, and I offended a few people. Someone spoke to Daddy. I'm more absorbed in seeking the approval of others than I had realized."

"I think we all are."

"Thank you for bringing it to my attention so I could evaluate my motives."

"Have to evaluate mine all the time. Nice thing about farming is I have all day to do it. A farmer always lives a well-examined life. We have plenty of time with our own thoughts."

"My thoughts are tied up with lessons and children. I haven't done enough self-reflection. That's one reason I appreciate you, Prentis. You're aiding my growth as a Christian."

"Missing you causes me to rely more on the Lord. You're benefiting me, too."

Each turned to smile at the other.

With his teeth, Prentis grasped the tip of his nearest mitten and yanked it off. He tucked the mitten into his pocket and slid his hand into Avery's fur muff. His hand was warm against hers, flesh against flesh—it felt right and familiar, a nice way to hold hands on a cold day. She leaned against him as they walked a short distance, each huddled down into their coats, braced against the wind.

She asked about his farm. He'd enlarged his barnyard and had built a sheltered feeding area before acquiring a dozen steers and a bull: Rex, king of the cows. A large quantity of Dr. Roberts' remedies, necessary for treating the ailments of livestock, had been ordered. Hoping to purchase a stallion up in Kingman, he was constructing more pens for his animals. In wet years his creek flooded, so he was considering a way to redirect that water, if possible. The winter wheat was up, and soon he'd turn the cattle into it for feeding.

These details familiarized her with his days. She enjoyed learning about his daily concerns. Usually, her daddy only discussed the farm's day-to-day details with the boys. Prentis's open discussion made her feel as if she were part of his life. Now he peered up at the sun, a faint glow in the clouds indicating its position on this overcast day.

"Need to turn back."

As they turned, sadness at his coming departure washed over her. It was only a week, but she appreciated his companionship and his perspective. She was growing attached, and she wished she could see him every day.

He looked down at her, studying her face. "It's difficult to think about going."

"It is," she acknowledged.

"Tell me what you'll do after I leave."

"Well, I need to lie down and read my Bible."

"What are you studying?"

"Colossians. Daddy read from it the day we buried Russell, and then you and I had our conversations. So, I've been studying it—reflecting on who Christ is and what He's done for me. I'm attempting to set my affections on Him. Daddy reminded me of that again this week."

"Starting this week, I'll study it, too. Then we can discuss it next weekend."

She smiled at him. "The mere thought of doing that with you makes me happy."

"It will make me miss you less, I think, knowing we're contemplating the same things. It's awful lonesome down on that farm. With no one to talk to, I'm alone in my head, meditating on what I've been reading, thinking of you, or talking with God. The silence is loud."

Enjoying his turn of phrase, she met his eyes. "I could tell by your letter. The way you expressed yourself actually made me feel pain. You sounded so lonely."

"My loneliness prompted me to be too forward, inviting myself up here."

"I missed you, too. I'm glad you came."

"Good. Maybe I'm making progress in winning your heart."

Pausing, he stopped and stared into her eyes for a moment. Removing his hand from her muff, he cupped her chin in his warm palm, caressing her cheek with his thumb.

"So soft," he whispered.

Heart full, she gazed up into his eyes. Gently, he smiled down at her; then he re-tucked his hand into her muff, and they continued on.

"Capturing a memory," he said. "That will get me through the next week."

She laughed softly, happy with the way he wooed her.

EIGHT

THE FOLLOWING SUNDAY, PRENTIS arrived after the Slaughters had returned from church. He'd attempted to get there earlier, but it simply couldn't be done. The livestock had needed extra attention this morning. Trying to make up time, he'd pushed Ulysses hard.

At his knock, Avery flung wide the door, beaming at him. The warmth of her welcome provoked a moment of bashfulness. Ducking his head, he returned her smile, wishing he didn't have such an introverted streak. Being near her still roused his social awkwardness, especially on first greeting. Her proximity overpowered him. Smiling all the while, she admitted him. Abe offered to stable his horse and headed outside.

On the other side of the entryway wall, a conversation heated up in the living room. Masculine voices argued about a farming issue involving heifers. Stepping that direction, Prentis was surprised to find Joe Pitzer ensconced on the sofa arguing with Mr. Slaughter and Jerry. They debated the wisdom of raising one's heifers to maturity versus selling them, saving the feed, and buying new fourteen-to-fifteen-month-old heifers to breed. The issue was currently being considered by the US Department of Agriculture.

Prentis had strong opinions about keeping his own heifers, but he hadn't come all the way up here to spend the day disputing the matter. Pitzer had opposing views, and Prentis didn't want to get into a disagreement or have his time with Avery disrupted.

The three men looked up and noted Prentis and Avery in the doorway.

"Pink," Joe Pitzer greeted him loudly, acting the role of lord and master of the house.

"Pitzer," Prentis replied. "Mr. Slaughter, Jerry, good to see you."

"How are you, Pink?" Pitzer said as Jerry and Mr. Slaughter merely nodded, wearing amused expressions.

"Can't complain. You?"

"Still reeling from the last time our teams played and you struck me out."

"Couldn't be helped," Prentis said. "If I remember correctly, you caught my pop fly to leftfield for our third out. So we're even."

"Joseph came home from church with us," Avery explained quietly. "Why don't you join them while I help Momma?"

"All right," Prentis said. Avery smiled at him then headed for the kitchen, retying her apron. Wondering how this invitation to Sunday dinner had been issued to Joe Pitzer, Prentis realized that his expectations for the day needed to be adjusted.

Seating himself on the opposite end of the slick horsehair sofa, he listened to the argument. Though they urged him to join in, he agreed with Mr. Slaughter and Jerry and felt no need. He assured them that they had it covered adequately without his two-cents' worth. When Minnie Slaughter called them to eat, relief escaped him in a quick exhalation.

Avery seated him beside her, which reassured Prentis, but Pitzer took the chair right across the table. Each time Prentis became engrossed in private conversation with Avery, Pitzer chimed in from across the way, teasing Avery or bantering with her about some family or local matter of which Prentis had no knowledge.

It dawned on him that Joe Pitzer vied for Avery's attention, and perhaps also her affection. He recalled Pitzer's haste to get on her dance card and then considered how Pitzer had eyed Avery as they'd come down the aisle before Floyd and Hattie's wedding. Silently, Prentis watched their conversation, assessing the situation.

"Joseph Edward Pitzer," Avery exclaimed, "you know I had nothing to do with that!"

"Not what I heard, Avery Veretta Slaughter—since we're being formal. I think you were the one who took out Mr. Smith's tree that sits so near the road. A vehicle hit it."

"Johnny was with me. I did no such thing."

"She's right, Pitzer," chimed in young John. "I was there."

"Not the story I heard." Pitzer leaned across, arching one brow.

"There's not one iota of truth to it, Joseph Pitzer," Avery stated, "not one. If you repeat those lies, you'll be sullying my reputation."

"I think you can handle that yourself, what with your fancy new coat and your flying over hills in that automobile."

She burst out laughing. "Apparently, my reputation is known far and wide."

"Indeed!" His black eyes flashed as he grinned at her.

Prentis had to admit that Pitzer was a looker, an open and gregarious man—his exact opposite in every way. That was plain. They were both Cherokee, with their black hair and eyes and their shared heritage. Might Avery prefer a striking, congenial, black-haired husband with a similar history? Joe Pitzer appeared to be his competition.

After the meal, Avery and Mrs. Slaughter served dessert to a tableful of grateful men. Prentis ate two pieces of cake, quietly observing the continuing banter between the two. The Pitzers lived nearby and attended the same church; their friendship was convenient in every way.

After they'd all stuffed themselves, Pitzer shoved back his chair and announced his departure. He had promised to help Floyd move in Hattie's piano. They would have their hands full. Jerry, John, and Abe offered to help, and out they all went with Gene tagging along, swearing not to get in the way.

Avery sighed then turned to help her mother.

As Prentis observed all this—wondering about the meaning of that sigh, his eyes met Howard's. The boy still looked disgruntled that the family Sundays were being disrupted. Prentis decided to attempt to make some headway.

"Howard, what say we play some checkers? Hear you're a good player."

"I'll beat you. I beat everybody."

Prentis chuckled. "Let's see what you can do, little man."

As they set up the checkerboard, Howard complained. "Avery doesn't have time to play with me anymore."

"Why's that?"

"She has papers to grade, and Joe Pitzer drops by all the time. Today after church, he invited himself home with us. It's bad enough that . . ." Howard stopped short and stared at Prentis.

"Bad enough that . . . ?"

"Never mind."

Apparently, Howard was old enough to realize it would be rude to inform him that he resented his intrusion. However, unwittingly, Howard had provided some helpful information. Joe Pitzer had been visiting, and he had invited himself today. That was something to ponder. The first checkers match began. After the dishes were done, Avery joined them.

Prentis manipulated the games so Howard never suspected he had not earned his victories—the little man swelled more with each one, and Prentis demanded satisfaction each time, keeping the competition going. Every time Howard beat him, Avery laughed softly. Brow furrowed, Howard stared at her, once insisting she tell him why his victories were so amusing. Quickly, with a serious expression, she offered her sincere congratulations.

After numerous matches, Prentis pushed back from the board, admitting defeat.

"Come back next week," Howard said, "and I'll beat you again."

"I'll do that."

Prentis turned toward Avery. Her eyes told him she had understood his tactic with Howard. By silent agreement, they both rose and walked toward the entryway. After bundling up, they strolled silently all the way up the lane. She was unusually quiet. Prentis waited for her to open the conversation, but she seemed preoccupied.

"I'm sorry our visit was interrupted," she said at last.

Waiting to see if she had more to say, he glanced at her, but she kept her eyes fixed on the horizon, quietly contemplating some inner thought. Hands burrowed deeply into his coat pockets, Prentis walked wordlessly beside her. *All right, heavenly Father, now what do I do?* Choosing the high road seemed the right thing. Pitzer's interference need not change his tactics.

"Tell me what you learned in Colossians," Prentis said. "Been longing to know."

Pulling out of her reverie, Avery glanced at him, appearing relieved to turn her thoughts in this new direction. "I was in awe of Christ. He's so powerfully presented in the first chapter. It caused my heart to praise Him, not only for who He is, but also for what He's done for us."

"I felt the same. I read the chapter over and over again."

"I did as well. As I reflected on the text, I wondered what you were learning."

"It seemed to me that Paul was telling us we have all we need in Christ."

She smiled and turned toward him. "That's the same conclusion I reached."

"It was comforting to know our thoughts were occupied in similar ways."

She sighed, and her smile dissipated. "Why, oh why, did Joseph Pitzer come visit today?"

"You didn't want him here?"

Quickly, she shot him a look of consternation. "No!"

"But you seemed to enjoy his teasing."

"We've carried on like that since we were small children. He and Floyd are best friends—now brothers-in-law, so he's always been around. But he's not the kind of man I'm interested in, though he seems to have gotten it into his head that I desire his company."

"Any idea why?"

"None whatsoever. I don't know why he would believe I want him here. He's come over several times and now after church, all without my invitation."

"Avery, I don't think you understand the effect you have on men. With all those brothers, you're completely at ease around us, which is very attractive. You're so vivacious and beautiful that any man would be crazy not to want to spend time with you."

"Well, thank you, Prentis." She turned, looking him full in the face. "I don't see myself that way at all. Do you think I'm encouraging him?"

"There's a comfortable easiness between the two of you."

"He's like family—he's Hattie's big brother."

"There's only one kind of family he wants to be to you, and it's not as your brother."

"Is *that* what he's after?" She appeared astonished.

"Yep."

"Are you certain?"

"Absolutely."

"How do you know he's not simply being friendly?"

"I'm a man. It's obvious. If you doubt me, ask your father."

"But I'm not interested in him. He drinks and runs around! You *know* what alcohol did to our family after my parents lost all those babies and the first house burned down. Daddy lost a near-certain opportunity to be the first governor of Oklahoma because of strong drink. It about destroyed our family. It's hurt too many people I love. I want nothing to do with it. I don't want Joseph's attentions, but I can't be rude to my sister-in-law's brother. What should I do?"

"Evaluate your heart. You seem to enjoy his company."

"But I enjoy yours far more." She turned her adamant expression his direction.

"You spent much more time talking with him than with me."

"I wanted to talk with you, but he kept interrupting."

"Avery, when I asked to call on you, I knew you had male friends clambering after you—I play baseball with most of them. They talk about you. A man would have to be blind or addled not to be aware of your charms. But, regardless of my hopes, I want you to choose the man you feel will make you happy. Of course, I want you to choose me, but the decision is yours. If you choose him, it will break my heart, but God will take care of me. He always does. I want you to be happy, and I want the woman I'm pursuing to want me, too."

Avery had stopped walking. They stood on the dirt road, staring at one another in the late-afternoon sunlight, their time together drawing quickly to a close.

"Prentis, I want *you* to pursue me. Until you came to my grandparents' house asking if you could call on me, I was beginning to think I would never marry. Not only is it risky, but also none of these men are the kind of husband I want. Until then, I hadn't realized I'd been holding my breath, waiting to see what you would do, wondering if you would ever come after me."

Relief filled his chest. *Thank God!*

He stepped closer and nestled her face between his hands, staring into her eyes to discern her profession in their depths. Her black eyes had always fascinated him; they were like magnets, drawing him in. For a long while, he stood gazing into her eyes. They shone up at him, vulnerable and open.

"If you're absolutely certain," he said, "I would be honored. I *want* to win your heart."

"I'm certain. I've known you long enough to be positive about that."

"That being the case, you'll know what to do about Joe Pitzer."

Taking her hand, he turned back toward the house. He needed to get Ulysses saddled so he could pound down the road, hastening home before darkness fell. The days were too short.

It felt as if something had been settled between them. Reticence had been broken down. He felt no hesitancy—the uncertainty he often felt as a shy man had been vanquished. He would trust Pitzer's near proximity into God's and Avery's capable hands.

* * * *

Mid-week a letter arrived for Avery. After school, she ran up to her room to open it.

October 20, 1913

My precious Avery,

I feel as though there's a new understanding between us. Our discussion on Sunday has encouraged me. My pursuit of your heart consumes my thoughts.

Interrupted though we were, I enjoyed having the opportunity to sit with you, to walk beside you, to watch you gather your thoughts as you considered your responses, to hear your gentle voice, to gaze at your beautiful face, and to study your eyes—so lovely!

Your Cherokee eyes—like onyx! I focus on them, attempting to see into their depths; your soul peers out at mine. My soul adores what it sees. I look forward to seeing the success you're making of your school. I'm so proud of you! Then, I'll see you again in less than two days—laying by memories for when I won't be able to travel up as often. I'll miss you so terribly then. For now, my mind and my heart are fixed on seeing you at your school's exhibition in a few short days.

With all my heart,

Prentis

Avery read the letter again, pondering on the poetic portion in the middle. When he had held her face in his hands, he had tilted his head the smallest bit, studying her eyes.

She had been desperate for him to understand that she wanted his pursuit. His calm strength and patient gentleness attracted her. Her heart had been racing as she had looked back at him, regarding his blue eyes, so clear in the western sunlight—such dissimilarities of appearance between the two of them, but such similarities of heart. Apparently, he had been as affected by the moment as she had been. He wrote so beautifully about it.

How could she make it plain to Joseph Pitzer that she didn't want him? With her friendly manner, she had unintentionally given him encouragement. But he was not for her.

Prentis was the man she wanted. She couldn't wait to see him again.

NINE

FRIDAY AFTER SCHOOL, THE house buzzed with excitement. Avery was wound up and hadn't eaten all day. This evening her students would display their intellectual skills at the Open House and Exhibition. All morning had been spent reviewing the recitations and the spelling words. In the afternoon, they had cleaned the building from top to bottom—wiping down the windows with vinegar, so they would gleam by the lamplight, polishing the desks, and hanging up each student's schoolwork to be viewed. Everyone's excitement and nerves had bubbled over.

After the Exhibition, boxed suppers made by the girls would be auctioned off to raise money for the school. The boys would compete to buy the girls' boxes; then each girl would eat with the purchaser of her box. This provided a type of elementary courtship ritual for the students, all under the supervisory eye of their parents and community.

As Avery put the finishing touches on a boxed supper to eat with Prentis, she considered how pleasant it would be to share a meal. Most of the day, she had listened to the oldest girls talk about their hopes for the evening. Avery expected their boxes would bring the highest bids. Young men would compete, eager to dine with them. It was a chance for these girls, who were practically women, to show off their culinary skills and their scholarly expertise.

Her boxed meal readied, Avery patted Howard as she hurried past him to dress. Her three youngest brothers stood in a row preening in the mirror above the sideboard; Howard perched on Momma's hassock. Pomading their hair, they combed it repeatedly so the cowlicks and obstinate parts didn't stand up. It was the most cooperative location for slicking hair while sharing one can of pomade. The boys had on their nice shirts and suits.

Once upstairs, Avery dressed quickly. Wearing her serious attire, she stared into the mirror, pinning her hair more tightly than the Gibson-Girl look, but still in the general shape. The public would be viewing her school and hearing her scholars perform; her professional appearance and demeanor mattered. But Prentis would be coming too, so instead of the somber black ribbon, Avery wore a purple one tied under her high collar.

And now, they all loaded into the Model T and drove to the school, twenty-one-year-old Jerry taking a turn at the wheel. It was late afternoon as buggies, wagons, and the occasional automobile traveled toward the one-room schoolhouse at the corner of their section. Attempting to relax, Avery settled back into the seat and surveyed the fall scene.

The sun shed a golden light on the unvarying green of sprouted winter wheat, a veritable carpet of fertile growth, uniform, with grazing cattle dotted throughout taking their fill of the nutritious plant life. This aspect of fields in the fall calmed her. Though it was late October, the weather had cooperated. Indian summer had arrived. With a light cloak or jacket, everyone who spilled out of the schoolhouse afterward would be comfortable eating outside.

As they pulled in, Avery examined the buggies. Prentis hadn't arrived yet—he had a long twelve-mile drive late in the day. She scurried in and organized her scholars, packing them three to a seat, so there was room in the back for the assembled crowd.

The schoolroom filled rapidly with family, friends, and neighbors, everyone excited to see the young people strut their accomplishments. Though they were well prepared, each student's face appeared anxious. Staring straight ahead, their lips moved as they silently repeated their recitations. Each would face the crowd at one time or another, stand up straight, and speak out the information they had packed into their heads. It was truly terrifying.

Patting and soothing, Avery passed among them.

At the stroke of five, she turned to face the assembled audience. Scanning the crowd as she commenced her introduction, she noticed Floyd and Hattie arriving late appearing slightly disheveled. Then, at the very back, she spotted Prentis wearing his shy smile.

Pausing for a tiny beat, like an inhalation, she reacted to the impact of his presence. As she continued her small speech of welcome, she smiled at him with her eyes. Trying not to look exclusively at him, she explained the order of the evening, shifting her gaze from one spectator to another—bypassing Joseph Pitzer. Then she introduced the first class. Fixing her eyes one last time on Prentis, she sat to observe the efforts of her youngest scholars.

Howard rose with his classmates to recite a piece about George Washington. When they finished, the crowd burst into applause prompting wide smiles from the students. The next older students rose *en masse* to perform a group recitation, likewise followed by applause. Avery felt pleased with the efforts of both groups.

Silent and pale, the older students waited their turns, each lost in solitary agony, repeating their recitations to themselves— Billy Cink perspired heavily. After the younger students finished, one after another the older students rose. From the middle grades up to her most mature students, each spouted their individual recitations, all performing well.

Gene and then Abe spoke their pieces perfectly, even though Avery glimpsed Johnny sitting in the audience making faces at them. Feet planted wide and chests out, the younger boys spoke directly to their big brother, like little prosecutors before a hostile jury.

Gene completed *The Character of Jesus Christ* by Bishop Porteus, a difficult piece for a boy of ten. He delivered it to John with solemn conviction. Abe spoke *The Importance of Well-Spent Youth*, directed personally to John, a warning contained therein. Being a thirteen-year-old boy, Abe seemed to enjoy admonishing his older brother publicly.

Only a few of the other students forgot a portion, pausing, eyes momentarily blank. They quickly regained composure when they heard Avery's whispered cue, each continuing on and finishing bravely and with grace. Billy Cink bested them all with *The Celestial City* from McGuffey's *Eclectic Fourth Reader*, quoting Revelation 19-21. When the crowd burst into cheers and gave him a standing ovation, Avery smiled as broadly as he.

The students all rose together and sang the national hymn *America* in four-part harmony. This was rewarded with another deafening round of applause.

Then Avery handed the *Eclectic Progressive Spelling Book* to the superintendent. Mr. Cink posed spelling words to the students, beginning with the youngest, who stood side by side as competitors, two lone scholars facing the room. The first to miss a word sat down and then another student rose to take on the victor and continue the competition.

Each student advanced as far as their individual skills carried them, all performing admirably as one after another spelled down their competitors. At the very last, Avery's oldest students—Dorothy Aves and Blanche Penny—stood poised, well-dressed, and immaculately coiffed. It took a full thirty minutes before one finally out-spelled the other. Arms around one another, they collapsed into their shared desk, relieved it was over.

Exclaiming over how well they had done, Mr. Cink praised Avery, delivering congratulations and sincere thanks for her efforts. Embarrassed by his tribute, she remained in her seat facing the front, but he insisted she stand to face the gathered assembly.

As she rose, ringing applause filled the little room. The crowd—those who weren't already standing against the walls and in the back—jumped to their feet to cheer. After looking at Momma and Daddy, who were smiling at her, she fastened her eyes on Prentis, who appeared as if he were bursting with pride. The joy of the moment about overwhelmed her; the evening had gone exceedingly well.

Now her father stood to auction off the box suppers. The procedure was explained: After the auction was complete, all bidders would rise, file to the front, make their donation, and collect their meal to eat with the female student who had prepared it.

Working his way through the girls' boxes, Daddy finally arrived at the adolescent girls. Their boxes went for high prices. After a protracted battle, Jerry purchased Dorothy Aves's box for twenty dollars. Everyone looked shocked. Avery raised her eyebrows at Daddy, who stood appraising Jerry before continuing. Stoically, Jerry stared back at him.

Then Daddy surprised Avery. He brought forward *her* box to auction! She had expected to eat the meal with Prentis and had tied it with her favorite red ribbon for him to keep.

A good-natured bidding war developed between Prentis, Leroy Rapp, and Joseph Pitzer. Self-conscious as she heard the offers rising, Avery sat with warm cheeks and pounding heart, hoping for Prentis to triumph. Urging the men not to let the others outbid them, Daddy egged them on to ever-higher bids. There was a great quantity of jesting. Enjoying this friendly competition, the gathered crowd laughed loudly.

Eventually, Leroy dropped out, and only Prentis and Joseph Pitzer remained. Finally, Prentis was victorious. For a cool thirty dollars, he had won the privilege of eating her boxed meal and having her company for supper. The crowd cheered—the money benefited the school. Avery felt embarrassed but pleased.

"That's some serious money raised—a grand total of $325.50," her father said. "Well done! After I say grace, each of you purchasers knows what to do. Now, let's bow for a word of prayer." He paused while everyone settled down. "Thank You, Lord, for these children and the hard work they've put into becoming competent scholars. We're delighted with what they've accomplished, and we praise You for them and for their hardworking teacher. Bless our time together and this food to the good of our bodies, in the name of our Lord Jesus Christ. Amen."

"Amen," all agreed. Then everyone stood, and chaos ensued.

Eager men and boys packed the middle aisle, each paying their donation, grabbing their box, and searching for the girl who had prepared the meal. After finding her, both headed outside, conversing shyly. After the crowd had thinned, Prentis made his way to the front, paid his money, and picked up Avery's box. Now he stood smiling down at her.

"Prentis, I hardly know what to say." Her cheeks felt flush. "You didn't need to lay down that much cash tonight. You're eating with me for free on Sunday."

"And leave you to Pitzer, missing the opportunity to sit and talk with you?" He laughed. "That's not possible. I'm glad I can help your school. This exhibition was superb! You've accomplished so much, Avery. I want everyone to know how proud I am of you."

She smiled up at him. "Well, thank you—for all the named reasons."

"Do you want to eat inside or out?"

From the nearest window, Avery peered into the schoolyard, catching a glimpse of Joseph Pitzer eating with her family. She didn't want him to invade her time with Prentis.

"Let's eat in here by the raised window on the other side of the room. We'll catch a breeze, over there. I'm a bit overheated. I've been anxious about the students and the event."

"Fine with me," he said, squeezing in beside her. The narrow seat was barely wide enough for the two of them. Prentis's shoulder felt warm and solid. "What have you got in here?"

He untied the red ribbon, tucked it into his pocket, and lifted the lid. There was the requisite cold fried chicken, a small cherry pie, a tin of potato salad, a quart-jar of pickled beets, a small covered dish containing hard-boiled eggs, two quart-size jars of tea, and a loaf of bread. She'd also included silverware, two plates, two napkins, and a spoon for serving the potato salad.

"This alone was worth the trip." He grinned at her. "When added to the privilege of watching your students and sitting with you for a few moments, I've struck it rich tonight."

She smiled back at him.

"Did you make every bit of this with your own two hands?"

"Yes, I did."

"If this is as good as your desserts, I'll eat more than I should."

She laughed. "Let's see what you can do."

Heaping his plate, she loaded on ample servings before passing it to him. Then she fixed her own plate, taking half the amount.

Turning to look at her he said softly, "Thank you for preparing this meal *and* for serving it with your own two hands."

"You're most welcome."

As they gazed at one another, his eyes were soft and appreciative. It made her happy, not merely his presence but that he valued her work, both in preparing a simple meal and in teaching a roomful of children. She leaned into his shoulder, and he leaned back. Then they laughed out loud together, pleased to be in one another's presence.

Both ate with gusto. Relief that the exhibition was over now gave Avery appetite. Prentis ate like he always did when he encountered her cooking—like a starving man who had found sustenance. He complimented her excessively. He was probably comparing her cooking with his own, but still, it made her happy to hear his praise.

After the meal, he needed to head home, and she had to speak to parents and patrons of the school. She sent the box and the remaining food home with him and stacked the dirty plates and silverware to give to Momma. Together, they left the schoolhouse, first stepping over to her parents so he could greet them. The boys had now scattered, so Prentis looked for her brothers, walking over to congratulate or to greet each one.

From where she stood with her parents, Avery watched their interactions. When Prentis squatted to talk to him, Howard fought off a smile. Then Prentis pointed at her, and Howard nodded seriously. Prentis stood, they shook hands, and he returned to her side. She strolled over to his buggy with him to say goodbye.

"What did you say to Howard?" she asked.

"That's between us, man to man."

"Oh, a secret."

Prentis nodded. He took her hand in his and gave it a tender squeeze, caressing the back with his thumb before lighting the headlights and checking the horse's harness. After climbing into his buggy, he sat for a moment looking into her eyes.

"See you on Sunday," he said.

She nodded.

Then he spoke Ulysses's name, fixed his eyes on hers one more time, and rode off into the night.

Glad she'd see him in two days, she stood watching his buggy's headlights rolling away south down the darkening road.

His gentle affection warmed her heart. Too soon, he was out of sight.

Turning back to her responsibilities, she circulated among her scholars and their parents, congratulating each student, informing their parents of each one's exceptional work, and accepting their thanks. It was a joyous and completely successful evening. She was thankful.

All evening, her little brothers had been running interference for her with Joseph Pitzer by keeping him occupied. That had been the prearranged plan, and they had succeeded, but now he was the last person remaining. Since the schoolhouse had to be straightened and cleaned before they could leave, they all worked together.

Then Jerry lit the headlights and performed the passenger duties for the trip home, and Daddy drove the Model T. Joseph lived in the same direction, so he followed in his buggy. Avery declined his invitation to ride with him.

"Twenty dollars! What was that all about, Jerry?" Daddy asked as they pulled out.

"You know *exactly* what that was about, Daddy."

"That's what I figured."

They all laughed. John, Abe, and Gene teased Jerry about Dorothy all the way home. Howard sat silently. Avery peered at him, barely able to discern his little face in the darkness. Leaning against Momma, he had promptly fallen asleep. When they arrived home, he roused, insisting he could walk in "like a man" and holding himself stiffly upright as he climbed the porch steps. No chores needed to be done; they had cared for the livestock before they left. And now, everyone hurried inside to get to bed. The sun rose early.

Startled, Avery realized Joseph Pitzer had pulled in behind them and now walked toward the porch, barely discernible in the darkness.

"Avery," he called, "I need to apologize."

He reached the porch and mounted the steps, stepping near her before speaking.

"I'm sorry I couldn't beat out Pink," he said. "I don't have that kind of money."

"What do you mean?"

"Figured you'd be sore, since we're sweet on one another. Give me a kiss, so I'll know you're not mad at me."

In the darkness he leaned in to kiss her. She took a step back.

"Don't you dare kiss me, Joseph Pitzer!"

"You girls always tease."

Reeking of alcohol, his breath blew hot on her face as he attempted to pull her close. Placing both hands on Joseph's chest, Avery shoved hard. Completely surprised by her evasive action, he staggered backward out of balance. The back of his legs struck the porch railing, flipping him right over the rail and into the shrubs. She heard breaking branches, the thud of his landing, and his groan in the dark. Resolutely, she marched to the porch's edge.

"I am *not* sweet on you, Joseph Pitzer, nor have I *ever* been. Do not *ever* do that again! It should be readily apparent that my affections are with another man. That was scandalous!"

From the darkness, he moaned, but was otherwise speechless for once in his life.

She turned and marched into the dark house, decisively slamming the door. He could extract himself from the hedge, attend to any injuries, and get home on his own. Surprised, she found her father waiting right inside the door, chuckling.

"Daughter, you handled that well."

"You left me to deal with him alone?"

"I was here keeping an eye on things. You had everything well in hand."

"That was completely unexpected."

"Figured you had no idea of the poor misguided boy's intentions."

"I didn't until Prentis enlightened me."

"I also hoped the two of you had discussed the situation."

"We did." She gave him a hug. "Thanks for watching out for me, Daddy. Now I must go to bed. That was an exhausting conclusion to a bone-wearying day."

As she trudged up the stairs, she heard Joseph Pitzer's buggy pull away.

Avery lit her lamp, undressed, and slipped into her bedclothes. When she turned back her covers, she caught sight of a small, white envelope lying right in the middle of her bed.

In a familiar scrawling hand, her name was written on the front.

How had it arrived here? She sat on the bed and opened the envelope. Prentis's writing was sloppier than usual and in pencil, but what a relief to see it just now!

Beautiful and wise Avery,

As I write I'm watching your remarkable exhibition—your students are a reflection of your skill and wisdom in guiding their studies and shaping their lives. What fortunate scholars they are! How blessed I am to be pursuing such a woman, who produces such capable and disciplined scholars! I will shortly plunk down as much money as is necessary to secure your company for supper—I'll do whatever it takes. It benefits your school; I'll be able to sit near you, breathing the same air you're breathing; I'll gain your delicious food for supper, which is always satisfying; and I want all the assembled masses to know how precious you are to me. See you Sunday.

With pride and affection—

Prentis

Avery blew out the lamp and lay in the darkness holding the note over her heart, musing on how he had written it there in the back of the room, cramped and standing for the entire Open House, probably using a wall, window ledge, or seatback to pencil his words.

This was how she wanted to be pursued, not in the manner that had occurred outside. What an encouragement it was to read Prentis's gracious words at this moment! Apparently, Daddy had informed him that he would auction her boxed supper, so he could arrive prepared and she would be guaranteed to eat with him, rather than Joseph Pitzer. Prentis had arrived with plenty of cash. Both he and Daddy had looked out for her.

ON SUNDAY PRENTIS RODE in right after Avery's family had pulled into the barnyard. Joseph Pitzer had not invited himself home this week. In fact, he hadn't been in church today. Avery knew he would have to show his face eventually, but she hoped when he did, he had a better understanding of where he stood with her—she had made it quite clear.

It was a relief to see Prentis's modest smile as he led his horse over to the Model T. Beaming at him, she grasped his hand and slid out of the automobile. Though tempted to throw her arms about him, she remembered propriety and restrained herself, settling for grinning at him with all her might. Puzzled, he studied her face.

"I'm so glad to see you!" she said, by way of explanation.

"And I'm glad to see you. What's happened?"

"I'll tell you about it later."

After Abe took hold of Ulysses and headed for the barn, Avery had to remind herself to be composed. Overjoyed to see Prentis—such dissimilarities between the two men—she wanted to skip across the barnyard, gleefully dragging him behind her. Instead, she leaned on his arm, strolling sedately, a model of decorum. Perfectly happy, she smiled up at him.

"Thank you so much for the note," she said.

"You're very welcome."

"Its arrival was perfectly timed. It was exactly what I needed at that moment."

With a perplexed expression, he studied her face as they walked in.

The family enjoyed the savory pinto beans and potatoes that had simmered with the ham hock since daybreak. Momma whipped up some cornbread to accompany the beans, and they consumed warm apple cobbler for dessert. As usual Prentis ate all he could hold. Momma shooed them both out of the kitchen after the meal, and they headed out on their walk.

Prentis's face went ashen as he listened to Avery's account of Joseph Pitzer's attempt to kiss her. But when Joseph ended up in the bushes, he chuckled.

"Knew you'd figure out what to do about Pitzer," he said. "Never imagined you pitching him off the porch, though."

"He fell; I did not pitch."

"Nevertheless, you got your point across."

"You should have seen his face as he toppled over the edge. There was just enough moonlight that I caught a glimpse of his startled expression as he went over." She restrained a giggle. "I shouldn't laugh—it wasn't funny. He lay there moaning while I practically wagged my finger at him. I told him what I thought of his presumptuous behavior."

Prentis laughed; then his face grew serious. "Still, I'm glad your father was right inside, since Pitzer had been drinking. Could have gone another way."

"But it didn't."

"Wish I'd been here. He wouldn't have tried it at all. Like to make it clear that he can't treat you that way."

"I'm certain I took care of it," she said.

"But he needs to know he shouldn't try to take advantage of you."

"I'm sure he got that message."

"Avery, I'm used to being the provider and protector. I'm attempting to move myself into that role in your life. I want to *do* something."

"Does something need to be done?"

"Don't know. Have to wait and see."

"What do you mean?"

"I think he owes you an apology, and I hope it's forthcoming."

"Joseph Pitzer has never apologized to anyone in his entire life," she said, laughing. "That would be a first. I wouldn't hold your breath on that one, Prentis."

Before departing, Prentis drew her into his arms, as if overcome with the desire to shield her from harm—their first hug since they were children. He pressed his face into her hair.

"Though you handled yourself admirably, I'm sorry I wasn't here."

"God and Daddy were watching out for me."

"Wish I'd been the one who pitched him off the porch."

She chuckled quietly. "That would have been highly entertaining."

As his horse walked out of the barnyard, he kept turning back to look at her, as though he couldn't bear to ride away, leaving her exposed and vulnerable. With each glance, she waved back at him reassuringly. She valued his protectiveness.

* * * *

Mid-week Prentis rode into town, needing to make some purchases at the general store. After hitching Ulysses to the rail, he stepped onto the boardwalk, and there was Pitzer staggering out with a heavy load. The two men looked at one another evenly.

"Can I speak to you down at my wagon?" Pitzer said.

"Certainly."

After heaving the fifty-pound bag of feed into his wagon, Pitzer shoved his hands into his blue-jean pockets and turned to face Prentis.

"There's been a misunderstanding," he began. "I assumed Avery wanted me. We've been friends all our lives and have always teased one another. Thought she'd saved those first two dances for me at the Miller's. Then at Hattie and Floyd's wedding, she gave me a look that was different than I'd seen before. Thought she was flirting. I misunderstood. Meant no offense."

"Might have been wise to ask her before you tried to steal a kiss."

"Wasn't trying to put the make on her or anything. But you're right. I'd been drinking before the exhibition and then afterward in the buggy—always impairs my judgment."

"Alcohol tends to do that. An apology might be in order."

"Planned on it. Have to figure out how to approach her though, given that our last encounter ended with her scolding me while I was flat on my back in the shrubs. Don't want her to knock me down again."

Prentis chuckled. "You'll sort it out, Pitzer. Appreciate your speaking to me."

"Don't need you throwin' no high-and-inside fastballs at my head next time we face each other across the plate."

"No fear of that."

The two men shook hands and parted ways, both smiling.

* * * *

During the following Sunday's walk, Prentis informed Avery that he had run into Pitzer at the general store in Wakita. As he spoke, she listened, feeling increasingly sober and distraught. When Prentis finished detailing the conversation, he was smiling, but Avery felt as if her consternation might overwhelm her entirely.

"I'm going to have to reflect on that," she said slowly. "He thought I was flirting with him? I don't recall any interaction with him at the wedding."

"When you had on that narrow skirt, he smiled at you as we came up the aisle."

"Oh no." Avery felt sick—she recalled smiling particularly at Joseph. She came to a standstill. Prentis stopped walking and faced her.

"What is it?" he asked.

"He was grinning at me and had that one eyebrow of his cocked—I know that look. I aimed a grin back at him." She paused. "Oh my goodness."

Appalled by her behavior, Avery turned around and retraced her steps. A few paces up the road she stopped, keeping her back to Prentis. She hadn't considered the impact one coy smile could have—it had been provocative. While on the arm of one man, she had indeed flirted with another. On the porch, Joseph had said they were "sweet on *one another*." He cared for her, and she'd never noticed. She had knocked him off the porch and lectured him for something she had unintentionally invited with a flirtatious smile.

"Avery?" Prentis now stood right behind her.

She couldn't turn to face him. "I've just realized something about myself."

"Care to talk about it?"

"I'm so embarrassed."

Behind her, he stood waiting. She owed it to him to be entirely honest. Wrapping her arms about herself, she gnawed on her thumb as she braced herself. When he heard what she had to say, he would probably leave, bringing their courtship to an end.

"As we walked in, I smiled at him in a way that he obviously considered to be inviting. It's clear to me now that my smile was flirtatious. I was with you—I care for you; I wanted to be there with *you*, not him. Yet I smiled at him like that." She turned around to face Prentis, unable to look him in the eye. "I'm so sorry."

Gently, he grasped her chin between his thumb and forefinger, lifting her face. The blue eyes that looked back at her were filled with love. Tilting his head slightly, he studied her eyes, an action that was becoming increasingly familiar.

"Avery, you're vivacious—full of life. Your personality sparkles and shines. That's one of the reasons I love you. Can't even remember when I started to love you, but I love you with all my heart. Sometimes your effervescence spills over—you shine like those electric lights they've installed in town; I can see them from my farm several miles away. You radiate joy when you're happy. He assumed it was personal. It's hard for us men not to do that when you smile at us. Your smile seems to be especially for that one individual you've locked eyes with. Of course he would be attracted to you. Seems every single man I know is. You're open and warm. That's attractive to men. Please don't beat yourself up."

Breathless, she had listened to this small speech. He had declared his love and understood her so completely that it astonished her. She hadn't known any of this about herself. Now he stood watching her, awaiting her response, and she needed to answer him.

"So many things . . . First, you know me better than I know myself."

"I've had years to think about you."

"I'm beginning to comprehend that. You seem to be completely aware of my flaws, yet you love me anyway. I want to return that affection, but I'm not yet ready to make that proclamation."

"Didn't say it to provoke you to respond in kind. Just wanted you to know. It's my goal to win your love—I'm just getting started. I don't expect you to return my love yet."

"Thank you for not rushing me. That's what I thought when I came into the house after shoving Joseph off the porch. There on my bed was your note. I was grateful that you were wooing me so differently than he had in mind. I like the way you're courting me."

"Good." He smiled widely. "That's always helpful for a man to know when he's in pursuit of a woman."

"Are you certain you want such a flawed woman—one who isn't even aware she's flirting with another man, even when she's in your presence?"

"You weren't flirting. You were just being yourself. I know you're not interested in him."

"That's a relief. You're the one for whom I've been waiting."

"And you're the one I've been working, waiting, hoping, and longing for. So, let's see what I can do—I'm doing my best to win your heart."

"You're going about it the right way. I wouldn't change one particle of your tactics."

He grinned. "Then I'll keep it up."

Glad for each other's company, they walked back hand-in-hand, each leaning against the other.

ELEVEN

AVERY LOOKED FORWARD TO Prentis's visits with great anticipation. He came every Sunday in November, including a visit on Thanksgiving Day—five more harmonious afternoons spent together. His pursuit of her heart grew more ardent. Each week he came as early as he could and stayed as late as possible. During every visit he ate like a starving man, complimenting her and her mother on their cooking, overflowing with praise for every dish they prepared, and gratefully taking home whatever they sent with him.

The weekly letters continued. Prentis built on his alliance with Howard, including him in the delivery of other items during the week—notes and small gifts at unexpected times. Howard proved a good ally. Prentis's tactic was highly effective. Avery could see no reservation toward Prentis remaining in Howard's attitude. In fact, they had become close friends.

Each week Prentis surprised her with some thoughtful act, demonstrating that he'd been thinking of her and was aware of her person, desires, and preferences—a newspaper clipping of special interest, an item she'd mentioned, such as a new thimble from town, or a remembrance of something she'd said weeks ago.

Anchored by his earlier declaration of love, they revealed more of their hearts and grew in affection and attachment, sitting closely to one another, shoulder to shoulder as they whispered together in the front room. The depth of his attachment was like an unexpected gift or a kind word during a time of discouragement, drawing her toward him. She hadn't realized how much she needed him or how thirsty she had been for his affirmation—he was like water in the desert.

With her family, they played games—cards, dominoes, checkers, and charades. When the roads were good, they went for buggy rides. Discussing it each week, they moved slowly through Colossians together, comparing the truths they saw there with similar passages. Contemplating the Bible together made them feel connected to one another. Their simultaneous studies made Prentis feel less lonely, he said—not only was the Lord near, but Avery was near in heart as well.

But bad weather couldn't hold off forever. In early December, an ice storm hit. At week's end, Avery received his letter. Several of Prentis's cattle were sick and a horse had been injured. When the ice melted, the roads were soggy and impassable.

As week followed week, snow fell regularly, making a sloppy, semi-frozen red porridge of the Oklahoma roads. They passed the first weeks of December separated by weather and its consequences—Prentis had often reminded Avery that this would happen, hence the storing up of memories and as many visits as possible.

December 17, 1913

Beloved Avery,

The days I've dreaded are upon us. I can't get to you because of the bad roads. I don't want to complain, but I miss you so badly! I grew accustomed to seeing you each week. I long to fix my eyes on your face, to listen to your gentle voice, to gaze into your eyes—it's agonizing being here alone! I keep the red ribbon from your boxed supper in my Bible as a bookmark—it makes you feel near. It still smells like your hair.

I want to share with you all I'm learning in my Bible study. I see Christ exalted—Creator of all things, image of the Father, God in human flesh. I yearn to talk about Him with you; I want to know your opinions.

And, I want to talk with you about my everyday concerns—I'm still nursing my cattle with Dr. Roberts' remedies, and the horse is mending. I've been working inside the barn, preparing all the tools for the coming season of harvesting and planting.

How I wish your father's farm was nearer to my own! But God is sovereign. He must have a purpose—it makes me long for you more acutely. I am entirely yours—I love you completely. I hope I'm making progress in drawing your heart to mine. I've yearned for you for as long as I can remember. I'll close for now—I can hardly bear this absence from you.

Your devoted,

Prentis

Oh, he was making progress. Avery had the consolation of being surrounded by family and students—hers was not the solitary task of farming, but she missed him sorely. She put down the letter and prayed for him, asking God to relieve his loneliness, to make Himself near and dear and close to Prentis, alone in his daily work and in that farmhouse each night.

They would both have to hold on and rely on Christ.

It wasn't until December 21, that Prentis could visit again, the weather having warmed, drying the roads. The family had pulled into the barn, disembarked from the Model T, and headed toward the house when Prentis came clattering into the farmyard. He leapt off his horse and swallowed Avery up in his arms, lifting her onto the tips of her boots before releasing her. Then, seeming to realize what he'd done, he dipped his head—she'd seen this bashful expression before.

"My heart got the better of me," he said quietly.

Her entire family chuckled sympathetically then walked on into the house, except Howard, who stood grinning at Prentis before following the rest inside.

"I'm sorry for being so forward," Prentis said.

She smiled. "I'm not offended. Thank you for the exuberant hug."

Grasping her hands, he looked into her eyes. "It's a blessing simply to see your face. I'll be ruing the sun its course today. But God is in control of the seasons, months, and days. Have to be content. Hope we'll be granted a few Sundays before the next storm rolls in. I'm a lonely and impassioned man."

Lifting her hands out of her muff, he pressed his lips to her palms, first one and then the other, his eyes fixed on hers. His lips were warm on her skin—it made her heart race. Taking her hand in one of his and gripping the reins with the other, he led both her and the horse into the barn. Once inside, he pulled her into his arms again.

"I need to hold you," he said. "I've missed you so terribly."

Wrapping her arms about his waist, she returned his embrace, resting her cheek against his coat. It felt good to be in his arms, as if she'd been created to be exactly here, right against his heart. Pressing his face into her hair, he inhaled deeply then let out a satisfied sigh.

Releasing her, he fixed his eyes on hers for a moment then led Ulysses into one of the stalls for grooming. While he worked, he sought her input on the actions he was taking at his farm, looking into her eyes as he awaited her remark or nod before continuing. No time could be wasted—the sun was up only briefly; this was the shortest day of the year. Moving from one topic to the next, he spoke quickly, getting her opinion on all his decisions. Each choice affected the future prospects of his farm.

Once his horse was cared for, he grasped her hand again, and they walked toward the house—it was fried chicken for dinner today; they could smell it as they neared. He talked to her all the way across the barnyard and into the back entry, wrapping up his farming consultation as they entered the crowded kitchen. That he valued her advice pleased Avery greatly.

Dinner was delicious; Prentis ate piles of food. At the table, they discussed the weather, how beneficial the moisture was for the growing winter wheat, Prentis's cattle, and his upcoming livestock purchase. In the spring, he explained, he intended to sell the fattened steers so he could buy heifers. He would also purchase the stallion in Kingman. He was concerned with keeping his herds pure.

"I've been reading Dr. Roberts' recommendations for keeping mares and heifers from slinking their foals and calves. He says . . ."

Abruptly, Prentis halted in mid-sentence and blanched, his eyes fastened on her father's. Jerry, John, Abe, and Gene had all stopped chewing. They gaped at Prentis with their forks poised in mid-air. Only Howard kept working away at his food, oblivious. All the older boys now looked at their father. Rendered speechless, Prentis continued to stare at Daddy. Then all of them slowly turned to regard Momma and Avery.

When Prentis met her eyes, he dropped his head and focused on his plate, shoveling food into his mouth, cheeks mottling pink, obviously mortified that he'd headed the conversation toward livestock breeding. There were women present. It was inappropriate.

Her father chuckled softly and steered the table talk another direction—toward the end of Avery's school term. Could she tell them how the scholars were faring? Who would be going to the high school in town next year?

With his head down, Prentis kept eating. Avery could see that he was attempting to recover from his social blunder. Keeping her eyes off him so he could pull himself together, Avery discussed school. "I think Abe should pursue high school in town next year. He's doing so well." Abe smiled widely, swelling with pride. "I hope Billy Cink will go, too. He's become such a promising scholar. Of course, Dorothy should go."

At the mention of Dorothy's name, John started teasing Jerry. Out of the corner of her eye, Avery detected that Prentis was no longer buried in his food. Maybe he'd recover.

Momma sailed round the table, giving each one a heaping scoop of peach cobbler made from the preserves. They praised the delicious dessert, moving the conversation one more step away from procreation.

Everyone rose from the table. Out of habit, Prentis started his usual clearing of dishes. Head down, he remained silent. Smiling sympathetically, Momma scooted them out of the kitchen.

"Let's go for a walk, Prentis," Avery said.

The sun shone brightly, and the ground was dry. She wanted to get him outside, not only because of the weather, but to clear the air. As they stepped off the porch, she clutched his offered arm. Mutely, they walked across the barnyard and up the lane.

The problem with an embarrassing social blunder is that you can't talk about it, because in doing so, you're blundering again. Avery knew this from painful personal experience. Yet it hung in the air between them, showing in Prentis's posture and demeanor.

"What did you learn from our study this week?" she asked softly, heading an entirely different direction than farming.

"In light of my sinfulness, it's a good thing God planned to redeem me before He'd completed a single act of creation."

"That's Ephesians Chapter One, isn't it? I looked at that cross reference, too."

"Yes. I'm grateful that He would forgive my sins and adopt me as His own son."

"It's humbling, isn't it?"

"Utterly humbling," he said, head still down. "It's a mystery why He would choose me."

"I feel exactly the same. We're all merely human, sinners all. We commit human mistakes that we don't intend, and yet, there they are, standing between God and us. But God forgives us, even making us His own children. It's an undeserved blessing."

"It says there that our sins are forgiven 'according to the riches of His grace.' All week I've thanked Him for His grace and His forgiveness. Thank Him particularly today."

"As do I," she said. "I err so frequently—parading around in my new coat, driving the automobile too fast, worrying about what other people think of me, placing that concern before God's perspective, not considering how my friendliness might be adversely affecting some man, and on and on, day after day."

There. It had been discussed in an oblique way. He had been reminded of God's grace and her own equally frail human nature.

Prentis had fixed his eyes on her face when she listed her failings—she had glimpsed him out of the corner of her eye, but had kept her eyes straight ahead. Attempting to convey her sympathy, she now leaned against his shoulder, holding his arm tightly. He took her hand. Head uplifted now, he asked questions about how she'd spent the past weeks and chuckled as she shared a humorous story. Listening attentively, he asked follow-up questions.

They walked a long distance, but the day was short. Too soon they had to turn around. When they arrived at the house, the sun set low on the horizon. They went directly to the barn. As he saddled Ulysses, they discussed Christmas. His animals kept him from traveling to Kingman. She invited him to ride up on Christmas Day, as soon as he was able.

Ulysses had been saddled, but Prentis stood in the quiet stillness of the barn, appearing uncertain. Turning away from the horse, he opened his arms, and she stepped into his embrace. Engulfing her, he rested his chin on top of her head.

"I'm genuinely sorry for what happened earlier. I would never want to offend you in any way. I wasn't thinking and . . ."

"Prentis, it's nothing. I'm a teacher, a scientific woman. I'm not offended one iota."

"Truly?"

"Truly."

Breathing a sigh of relief, he lifted her face with his mittened hand. When she met his eyes, they bore into hers. "Thank you for your understanding heart—you're so precious to me. I'll see you on Christmas day."

"I'm glad. You're precious to me, too." She smiled up at him.

Prentis gazed at her a moment longer then released her and swung into the saddle. As horse and man stepped out of the barn, she walked alongside. He pulled his wool scarf up over the lower half of his face, peering at her over the top, his eyes intense upon hers, hesitating a moment, as if he couldn't bear to ride away. Leaning down from his horse, he cupped her face in his wool-covered mitten again, gazing at her over his wrapping.

"I love you," he said, voice muffled by the thick wool.

"And you, Prentis, are the most important man in my life."

"I'll have to be content with that. For now."

TWELVE

CHRISTMAS MORNING PRENTIS ROSE before dawn to tend his livestock then headed toward the Slaughter's. Ulysses trotted easily on the frozen roads. Prentis hoped to see Avery for several weeks in a row—no ominous weather threatened. But it was in God's hands.

This forced absence bound Prentis's heart ever more securely to Avery. Having longed for her since his earliest recollections, he had thought it would be impossible to become even more attached. But it was possible. Being away from her was wrenching agony. He hoped he could marry her before the next winter. Separation from her was simply too painful.

The barriers were coming down. His declarations of love, their growing affection, and their increasing transparency were solid evidence. He longed for intimacy; he longed for her. He wanted to talk with her about anything and everything; he desired to be free with his affection. The caged beast of his passion must be kept in check—he had to keep a grip on himself.

He'd been begging God for help.

Being alone on the farm was unbearable. Only Christ got him through it. It reminded him of those years after his father's death, when he had suffered the fresh loneliness of a fatherless boy. His growing awareness of God's eye upon him had sustained him through that painful loss. God had drawn him near, attaching him permanently when he had finally comprehended the loving sacrifice Christ had made and had committed his life wholeheartedly, once and for all time, into His hands. Nothing could ever change that.

This winter absence from Avery felt like that past time of lonely grieving. But now, human love pulled him toward a different kind of safe harbor. He longed to attach himself to her in every possible way. She didn't know it, but he was also studying marriage and its comparison to Christ and the church. Christ was the Head; the church was His body. Prentis wanted to make Avery his very own—his body, as Christ had made the church His own. He yearned for her.

The ride to her house and back always provided time to strategize. When would he ask her? How would he do it? The time had to be right. There was a season for everything. He'd already asked her father. Now he awaited Avery. When she loved him in return, he would ask.

The early-spring calving wouldn't be a good time to present his proposal—he'd be up in Kingman helping Fred, out at all hours, spending irregular days and nights assisting cows giving birth, caring for calves, governed by sleeplessness. He'd travel up on the train and would ride the young stallion home after the last calf was born.

Horse breeding would come after that, dependent on each mare's season, whimsical and unpredictable. He'd be patiently working with the stallion, establishing the breeding norms for his horse business, and familiarizing the animals with one another—waiting on each mare, governed by the attraction of kind for kind ordained by God on the sixth day.

Being a farmer taught a man that God was sovereign over His universe and the creatures He had made—a man reacted and worked within God's framework, overcoming the wreck that sin and death had made of God's creation, bringing order to chaos and animal madness. It was given into man's hands to till the earth and to rule over the creatures, so Prentis brought order within his farm's realm and his livestock's governance.

The garden had to go into the ground next. He would

seek Avery's advice and implement her decisions. When they planted it, the wheat wouldn't be ready for harvest yet and school would still be in session, the calm before the storm of reaping, threshing, and plowing. Right there would be a gap in the frenzied, springtime activity.

This might be the time to ask her.

It would give her time to prepare her possessions and household goods to join him in his house, *if* she accepted him. Would she be ready by then? Would she love him?

He couldn't tell from this vantage. Time would make it clear.

He hoped to marry her near summer's end, but he awaited her response to his wooing. Desperate though he was, he wouldn't rush her. He needed a good harvest, so they could marry.

Lord God, Father, please give me enough yield to marry this year.

After the harvest, he would launch his beef enterprise, breeding the new heifers with his well-chosen bull. This would establish his financial plan. Sometime between then and the fall equinox with its sowing of the winter wheat, perhaps they could marry. Maybe then—finally, at last—would be the best time to wed, *if* she accepted him, *if* she was ready, *if* he got his wheat in.

Oh please, Lord, let her be ready!

How he adored her! He loved her so dearly—small, dark, and lovely as a girl; mysterious, wise, and playful in their youth; intriguing, alluring, and precious in their adulthood. He dreamt of her at night and thought of her during the day, penning the tame version of his emotions onto paper, scrawled for her in his letters.

There was her house! Soon he'd see her face. His chest filled with anticipation.

* * * *

The wild turkey was stuffed with the traditional Slaughter-family dressing. It now baked in the cookstove, all the buckshot having been meticulously plucked out. The pies had been baked yesterday. Everything else was peeled and ready to cook. They awaited Prentis to open gifts. Hoping for a glimpse of him, Avery lifted the white curtains to peer through the glass, straining her eyes. *Wait!* His horse was coming fast up the lane!

"There he is," she announced.

This was the signal for John and Abe to tend his horse. Out they went. In he came, bundled in his great coat. He beamed when he saw her, his face lit with joy. Her heart filled with happiness at the sight of him and the pleasure of his nearness.

"Merry Christmas, Avery!"

"Merry Christmas to you, too, Prentis!" Hugging him an affectionate Christmas greeting, she pressed her face against the coolness of the thick wool, breathing in his outdoor fragrance. "God bless you on this joyous morning."

"And you as well."

Shaking hands warmly, he exchanged Christmas blessings with her family, who had all gathered to greet him. Avery took his coat. Her parents settled everyone around the tree, Prentis nearest the stove for warmth. John and Abe returned, and the gift opening commenced.

Handmade items were the order of the day, with a few books, tools, and other purchased gifts. For Avery's daddy, Prentis had brought *Dr. David Roberts' Practical Home Veterinarian,* an esteemed sourcebook. He was appreciative. For her momma, he'd procured a lace collar; she said it would go nicely on the new dress she was making. He'd bought a big set of Lincoln Logs for the younger boys and neckties for the older.

Wide smiles beamed on all the boys' faces. Gene and Howard dumped out the wooden pieces in the corner and got to work building log cabins. The older boys, who were beginning to take girls on outings or to court them in earnest, seemed quite pleased with their ties. Prentis had been watching and listening, as usual. These gifts were thoughtful.

Her family members gave him an assortment of practical items they'd heard him mention, a few tools and items for home and farm. The older boys presented him with exactly what he'd purchased for them. They all laughed together, comparing their neckties.

With Prentis's eyes fastened upon her, all the noise and activity faded as Avery opened his gifts: a thick volume of poetry—*Complete Poetical Works and Letters of John Keats*—edited by Horace Elisha Scudder, a bound-leather journal for recording her thoughts, and a lace shawl.

"Oh, Prentis! It's too much."

"No, it's just right—beautiful and thought-provoking gifts for a beautiful and thoughtful woman. I don't read Keats, but I know you do. Still, his poem *Bright Star* expresses how I feel about you. I hope you'll read it. It's as true today as when Keats wrote it."

Nodding that she would, she looked at him solemnly, overwhelmed by his generous and considerate nature. Each of these gifts touched her heart deeply—he knew her well.

Wrapping the shawl about her shoulders, she spread the scalloped edge to admire the delicate lacework. It was such an exquisite piece of work! Pleased, she smiled up at him. He had been watching her all the while.

Now he opened her packages—*A Puritan Catechism (With Proofs)* by Charles H. Spurgeon and two pair of thick handknit woolen socks, made by her own hand.

"Thank you!" Thumbing through the book, he examine the question-and-answer format with texts listed. "This catechism is exactly what I need for our studies. You've mentioned it several times, how helpful it is to you."

"Whenever I explained something from Spurgeon's catechism, you always had a hungry look, as if it would be useful to you."

"It will be. I'm grateful! And the socks—I'm strangely particular about my socks. Drove my siblings to distraction. You probably don't remember."

"Oh yes, I do! That's why I made them." She laughed.

Grasping her hand, he pulled her close, speaking softly, "Thank you for these personal items. That you made them yourself makes them even more precious."

"You're most welcome," she whispered back.

* * * *

As were all their days together, Prentis felt this one was too short. As always, the food was delicious and the time spent with Avery's family was fun. Floyd and Hattie's arrival in time for dinner made everything all the more lively. Rather than taking a walk on this sacred day, they stayed with her family. It was good to be together—Prentis loved her family. Around the pot-bellied stove in the parlor, they played games; laughter filled the house.

At one point, they all gathered around the piano, and Mrs. Slaughter pounded out the tunes while they sang Christmas hymns. Prentis stayed near Avery all day, watching her eyes as she hung on his words, paying heed to her opinions, enjoying her jokes and arguments, laughing at her stories, listening to her breathe. Too soon the sun dropped toward the horizon, and he had to leave. Avery bundled into her coat to go with him to the barn.

"Hope to see you in a few days." He smoothed the thick blanket on Ulysses's back. "Weather seems to be holding."

"We can hope and pray."

"It was a wonderful day. Enjoyed the argument you had with John about suffrage. You made your points well. He was playing the devil's advocate to rile you."

"He always does that. He likes to watch me get heated about a subject."

"It worked." He chuckled. "You were heated. Howard was a little nervous."

She laughed. "I noticed his eyes were wide. It's frustrating to have all the responsibilities of adulthood without the right to vote in an election, simply because I'm a woman."

"Can't imagine. We men take what we have for granted. Maybe by the next election, women will have the vote."

"I hope so, but enough about politics. It was a pleasure to spend an entire day with you. I always feel peaceful and contented when you're near."

"Feel the same." Hugging another farewell, he pulled her into his arms and placed a soft kiss into her piled-up hair that brushed temptingly against his lips. "Even though I need moisture for my wheat, I dread snow. Keeps me away from you. I'm thinking contrary to my usual opinions at this time of year."

Caressing Avery's cheek, he lingered over her expression as she gazed up at him. Did he detect adoration? Maybe he was succeeding in his wooing. It was always difficult to leave her.

* * * *

Surprisingly, they got three Sundays in a row before weeks of snow and ice followed, engulfing the second half of January in whiteness, blue light in the overcast dawn every morning.

Prentis was housebound for the rest of the month, entrapped by the weather.

Snow in Oklahoma made everything beautiful, white, and pristine. But it only stayed a day or so before dissolving in the sunlight, leaving mud and then partially frozen mud, followed by solidly frozen mud as the weather turned cold again. This was when Prentis could visit Avery, on frozen mud. But even then, if the crust wasn't deep, his horse cracked the surface and sank down to the soft, clay-like *terra firma* underneath, a not-so-firm foundation.

The partially frozen mud flung everywhere when a person rode through it, even if the horse merely walked, as Avery's horse did for the short trip to the schoolhouse. Prentis had noticed the telltale flecks of red mud thrown up by her horse's hooves onto her clothes, including the new coat. But his longer trip of twelve miles through the mud wasn't merely messy.

At a nicely paced trot on dry ground, the trip home took him an hour and a half. After going there and then back on a dry road, he would arrive home with a sore back and abdominal muscles. Keeping his seat in a way that protected the horse's back from injury left man more tired than beast for the effort. The following day he was always stiff and aching. However, through mud the trip was horrific, doubling the time and wearing out rider *and* horse, maybe injuring it by journey's end, twisting its legs and damaging the ligaments, not to mention its feet. Sometimes mud sucked a horseshoe right off, damaging the hoof if the horse stepped on the nails. Then the horse had to be re-shod, maybe doctored.

Prentis had a hard enough time keeping his horses' feet dry in the winter, attempting to prevent the injuries so common in horses and to forestall mud fever. Long trips through mud were foolish. They couldn't be undertaken.

* * * *

January 26, 1914

Beloved Avery,

Once more the mud and snow keep me from you. How will I bear it! It cannot be borne. God help me to set my affections on things above! I know He doesn't give me more than I can endure, but at this moment it surely feels like it. I pray for His grace.

The cattle and the horses have damaged feet; I'm spending all my time in the mud, bent over hooves, cleaning them, doctoring them, covered in mud—then attempting to keep mud out of every crack and crevice of this house as I come in each time. I'm not succeeding. Red Oklahoma mud is everywhere. Difficult weather is harder to bear when a man's heart is heavy with the agony of waiting.

Avery, I need you so badly. How I miss you! I can't write another word.

Love,

Prentis

THIRTEEN

EVERY DAY AVERY MEDITATED on the poem Prentis had said expressed his feelings: *Bright Star*. Penned by Keats nearly 100 years earlier, it expressed his love for a woman he could never have, for tuberculosis had destroyed his health and ended his life prematurely. As Avery read, Prentis's ragged emotions dawned on her. She comprehended his longing more fully.

Bright star, would I were stedfast as thou art—
Not in lone splendour hung aloft the night
And watching, with eternal lids apart,
Like nature's patient, sleepless Eremite,
The moving waters at their priestlike task
Of pure ablution round earth's human shores,
Or gazing on the new soft-fallen mask
Of snow upon the mountains and the moors—
No—yet still stedfast, still unchangeable,
Pillowed upon my fair love's ripening breast,

To feel for ever its soft fall and swell,
Awake for ever in a sweet unrest,
Still, still to hear her tender-taken breath,
And so live ever—or else swoon in death.[2]

While she appeared steadfast and bright, Prentis felt alone and solitary with only his affection for her as company down on his farm. Sleep evaded him as he waited for her while gazing at the "soft-fallen mask" of new snow that kept them separated. He longed to be pillowed upon her breast, to feel her chest rise and fall, to hear her breathe—that sound itself granting life. He felt it might kill him to wait for her. Under his patient demeanor, he suffered.

Avery was ready. This separation and loneliness hurt him too much. Why subject him to a long courtship when he had won her heart? She wanted to be his—his wooing had succeeded. Taking the risk of loving a man, come what may—even dead babies, she had plunged in.

* * * *

On February 1, Prentis came at last pounding hard over ground frozen like steel, horse's hooves clattering as if on stone. He leapt from his horse and engulfed Avery in his arms. Returning his amorous greeting, she clutched him to herself. He responded, swallowing her up, lifting her off her feet—suspended, affectionate, needing, and wanting him, too.

Her parents hustled the boys into the house.

Finally releasing her, Prentis dropped to his knees, down onto the frozen earth. Twining his arms about her waist, he gazed into her face.

"Avery, I need you—it's not good for a man to be alone; God said so Himself. I'm not complete without you. I need you to keep me together, to ease my loneliness, to make me a better man, to help me through this life. Will you marry me? In my desperation, have I asked too soon? Do you want me? Will you have me?"

She stared into his eyes—earnest, hopeful, filled with longing. "Yes, Prentis, I will. I would be honored to be your wife."

Instantly, his face spread wide with a smile. Leaping to his feet, he grabbed her up again, uplifted in his embrace. A query in his expression, he looked into her eyes.

"May I kiss you?"

Cupping his face, she answered by pulling him closer. Ardent blue eyes drawing so near, his lips pressed soft and warm, his kiss tender. Protracting their loving clasp, she wound her arms about his neck—their first kiss, so precious.

Pulling back, he stared into her eyes. Her heart was full of love as she met his gaze. Reacting to what he saw there, he pressed his lips to hers again, lingering.

"Avery," he whispered, "how I love you!"

"I adore you as well. You're the love of my life."

At this proclamation, there was another kiss, this one more passionate. She returned his ardor; it was like coming home, as if she were exactly where she was supposed to be.

He pressed his forehead to hers. "I need a good harvest. If I get it, can we marry before the fall? I *have* to secure you before next winter—between harvest and fall planting, sometime in August or early September. I need to make you mine."

"Yes. I'll marry you then."

"Thank you! Thank you so much!" He threw his head back and laughed. "Let's go tell your family. This is the best news of my life, the most wonderful thing to happen to me other than God's redemption. Can't even begin to tell you how happy I am."

She smiled widely at him. "I feel the same. I love you."

Grinning back, he scooped her up and carried her bodily across the barnyard. Before entering, he set her down and kissed her again.

They stepped in. Everyone stood in the kitchen.

Simultaneously, all turned toward them as if synchronized; all wore guilty expressions. Jerry held Howard, who was grinning. Obviously, they'd been watching from the kitchen windows.

"Congratulations!" they all said together.

"You watched?" Avery said, shocked.

"Couldn't help it," Jerry said. "Had to see how it was done."

"I think you could figure that out on your own," she said, bursting into laughter.

"I'm sure I could. That was pretty dramatic, though. Don't

know what it is about you girls that makes us boys lose our heads—but we sure do."

Now the entire family laughed. It was true.

* * * *

Avery's welcoming embrace had told Prentis all he needed to know. He had won her.

Out had popped his proposal, as if by reflex, thus turning them down a new path earlier than he had originally planned. They spent the rest of the day with her family, detailing the year's course and considering what was essential for setting up housekeeping. The boys all had opinions, as did Mr. and Mrs. Slaughter.

Howard sat on his knee throughout grinning at him, clearly glad to gain a brother. They expected him to stay with them on occasion, Prentis told him, once they were married.

As everyone strategized, Avery smiled at Prentis across the table. The joy sparkling in her eyes prompted such gladness of heart that he almost couldn't contain it. *Thank you, Father!* When he left, there was another kiss. Now he had to make it to their wedding day.

As he rode home, Prentis mulled over their next obstacle. In a few weeks, he'd go to Kingman to help with the calving. He would discuss with his mother the details of the property and the wedding. He'd already written about his pursuit of Avery, and she was supportive. Still, he realized the religious wars might surface again.

His father's family considered him a Catholic, though he'd only stepped inside a Catholic church for family funerals and weddings. That furtive infant baptism made him Catholic in their eyes, maybe a lapsed Catholic, but definitely not a Protestant. They would want Avery to convert to Catholicism and would press for a Catholic service. This would upset his mother, who would want a Protestant service. That in turn would anger the Catholic Pinkertons.

But Avery held the important opinion. Besides God, she was the only person Prentis cared about pleasing. Her family's country church was just fine with him. He would not let that get lost in the fray. This part of the process caused him anxiety, bringing all his fears of church to the fore. He would strive to honor God—doing what was right, what didn't trouble his conscience, and what pleased his bride. Before he journeyed to Kingman, he and Avery needed to talk. But first, he would write, giving her time to consider her preferences.

February 2, 1914

My beloved Avery,

What joy fills my heart! You'll be mine by the end of the summer! I'll live through the winter! Now I have to hold on until our wedding day. Beautiful, precious woman, you're a prize worth obtaining and so difficult to wait for. I'm filled with longing.

We were so caught up in our plans that we didn't discuss what we had studied during our weeks apart; yet I see there a remedy for my impatience. "For in Him dwelleth all the fullness of the Godhead bodily. And ye are complete in Him..."[13] I have all I need in Christ to sustain me as I wait for you. I will rest in Him. He will help me. I'll beg Him for His help every moment, Avery. I'll trust in Him.

And, I'll attempt to stop complaining. See what hope your love gives me! Consider my last letter—I wrote mainly about mud and my loneliness. I was at the end of myself. But your love encourages me and *draws me to Christ. I hope to see you next weekend. By God's grace it will be so. If not, He will sustain me.*

When I come, we must talk about all you hope and dream for our wedding day. Soon I'll travel up to Kingman, and I need to know before I speak to my family. Fulfilling your desires and yours alone is my intention.

Loving you with all my heart,

Prentis

* * * *

All week, Avery had mused on Prentis's proposal—his proclamation, the tenderness and desperation in his eyes. Often, she had daydreamed when she should have been listening to a recitation. "Miss Slaughter?" a student would say, calling her mind back to her duties. She attempted to save her meditations on Prentis for her time alone. But she often failed.

Reflecting on how her love encouraged him, she considered what he had written about the Colossians passage they were studying. This would be true of their married life: her love would strengthen him, and his would strengthen her. Sharing what they learned would uplift them both—his letter had heartened her. Contemplating his coming trip to Kingman, she decided that uplifting his heart was the important thing. She pondered how best to do this.

* * * *

When Prentis came the following week, Avery had plotted her course. After Sunday dinner, the weather being warm—a brief taste of the coming spring, they set out on the country road. With her arm tucked up against his side, she leaned into him.

"I've thought about your words since your letter came," she said.

"Yes?" He glanced at her.

"Your reliance on Christ encouraged me."

"Have to rely on Him all the time. When I cry out to Him, He helps me."

"He even enables us to wait."

"Yes." He smiled down at her. "No matter how difficult it is."

"Like you said in your letter, we're complete in Him. That means no one can impose extra religious requirements on us. None of that need affect us."

"Explain that." His brow knit as he turned toward her. "With your seminary training, I hoped you'd understand the end of that chapter. That's what you're referring to, isn't it, the end of Colossians 2? Couldn't make heads nor tails of it."

"It relates to Jewish and cultic practices of that era. In short, on the cross and through His resurrection, Christ accomplished all that was necessary. Therefore, no other rituals or ascetic practices are required."

He nodded. "In Him we have all we need. Nothing more needs to be added."

"Yes. That being the case, I want to apply that principle to our wedding."

Prentis glanced at her, his expression doubtful. "Not sure what that has to do with it."

"Please, hear me out. When you go to Kingman your family will insist that certain religious requirements are necessary for our wedding ceremony. You're going to be pulled in two directions—Catholic Pinkertons and Protestant Dirs, each claiming we'll be godlier if we do it their way." She glanced at him. With a grim expression, he nodded. She continued, "We need not submit to their demands—we're already in Christ, and He's done everything necessary. But, neither should we alienate your family by having a wedding at my church. God gave no instruction about *how* a wedding must take place. So we need not marry in any church if the religious wars will erupt or if it will offend your family. We simply need to be married legally. I'll marry you anywhere. All I want is you."

This declaration arrested their walk.

Facing her now, he studied her eyes. "Thank you. I understand your application. But I don't want you to sacrifice everything."

"And I don't want you to be torn in two."

"I want you to have exactly what you want for your wedding day."

"You want me to be selfish?" she said.

"No, but a woman dreams about her wedding day. I have two sisters. I know this."

"When I marry you, I'll be fulfilling my dream: You love me, and you'll be mine."

"You've never thought of the particulars—the ceremony, the dress?"

"Of course, I have."

"Those things are important," he insisted.

"Yes, but they're minor considerations. In marrying you, I'm to love you selflessly. That includes the wedding day itself."

"I'm to love you selflessly as well. Because of that, I want us to marry in your church. Seems as though a wedding ceremony between two Christian people should occur in a church. My parents wanted that, but couldn't have it, given the circumstances."

"Ideally, that would be the case. But it isn't necessary."

"I don't know, Avery—"

"To make you happy, I'll wear a beautiful white dress."

He smiled at her. "That would make me happy. But I still want us to stand in front of your pastor to be married, exactly as you've always wanted."

"But I release you from that, Prentis. Keep that in mind while you're up in Kingman. You're more important to me than the location of our wedding. I want what's best for you."

"Now we're back where we started." He laughed softly. "I want what's best for you as well. If both of us keep this attitude, we'll have a remarkable marriage."

"We will."

FOURTEEN

WHEN PRENTIS LEFT THE Hutchinson & Southern Railroad car in Kansas, he hadn't expected to find so many things altered. He'd been down in Oklahoma full-time since October, and it was now only the end of February. All had been constant before then, when he traveled back and forth between the two farms and the livery. But now, everything had changed.

The farm was right between Kingman and Cleveland, so he'd written that he'd get off there. No reason to backtrack. Fred was there to meet him with a horse. As they rode toward home, Fred kept up a steady stream of conversation peppered with obscenities, a new habit for Fred.

When he'd lived at home, Prentis had tried to check this in his little brother. But Fred was nineteen now—the age at which young men don't listen. And so, after Prentis's first remonstration, which went unheeded, he saved his breath. Though he was only twenty-three, he'd taken a parental role in Fred's life. But now Fred was running the home farm and the livery, getting help from Uncle John, Uncle Grant, and various Pinkerton cousins as needed. There was no need to listen to an older brother. He probably wouldn't have listened to a father either.

The first family news out of Fred's mouth had been

shocking—something Prentis had never considered possible. He felt naïve for not realizing this might occur. Their mother was being courted. Mother was forty-three years old—a mature woman, but not an old woman. She'd been only thirty-five when their father had died, and she owned a business and land in two states. This shouldn't have been a surprise.

What shocked Prentis was the age of the man. George Bellew was only thirty-one.

Prentis tried not to be suspicious—he hadn't even met the man, but to his mind sprang the apprehensive notion that this man might be after his mother's land and money. Immediately after this came the jolting realization that all his plans with Avery might have just been destroyed. He had expected several years to establish his farm and launch his horse-and-cattle business. Then, with cash in hand, he would purchase the land from Mother, free and clear.

Instead, he might need to buy now. He'd recently sunk a pile of money into steers as well as improvements. He planned to purchase the stallion with the last of his cash. Though cash would come in when he eventually sold those steers, he didn't want to touch his savings. A farmer always needed to keep a reserve. Then there was the wheat—it couldn't be depended on yet.

Buying the land now might gobble up all his reserves and his profits. Quickly, he did the calculations. The going rate for unimproved Oklahoma land was $17.50 per acre. That meant he needed $2,800 for his quarter section, more if his mother charged him for the improvements. Perhaps $5,000 if that was the case. He didn't have it.

The dream of having Avery before next winter faded before his very eyes. He might not even have a farm by then, depending on what his mother and this man decided. Fred was still talking, but Prentis couldn't focus on his words.

Lord, help me! What do I do? Hold me up and give me wisdom.

Now Fred's voice grew impassioned, capturing his attention. "Dang it! Don't know how she can do this to us—expecting us to buy her out so she can marry this man and move to Attica. Just pickin' up and leavin' everything here."

"Attica?"

"George's farm and business are there. He's a pharmacist."

"So he has money? He's not after Mother for her assets?"

"No." Fred snorted, glancing at Prentis. "That's what I thought, too. He's only eight years older than *you*—don't even want to think about that. But he appears to be solid."

"That's a relief."

"Do you have the cash in hand? Are you ready to buy that Oklahoma farm?"

Slowly, Prentis answered, "No. That's what I've been considering."

"I think Mother needs to sell one farm or the other right now. She's been vague, says she has to talk to you. Uncle John or Uncle Grant will buy her out of the livery if we don't. And there goes our business interest and all our hard work. I don't have cash for the farm here."

"Neither do I for the farm down there. Other than that, is George Bellew a good man?"

"The devil if I know! Seems to be solid financially. But he's just appeared on the scene since last summer."

"Last summer! I was here. How did I miss this?"

"It was nothing at first, a friendship." Fred glanced over. "You were busy—back and forth between the two places, both of us working at the livery. But you weren't in Kansas half the time. I didn't even notice it at first, and I was here. Seems he wrote frequently."

"I think Mother's welfare should be our first consideration at this point, while we're scrambling to put our lives in order. When can I meet him?"

"He's up every weekend."

"That's a trip!" Prentis was impressed by the man's tenacity.

"Comes by rail."

"How did they meet?"

"Met in Anthony, of all places. She was down there doing some shopping. And he was downtown, over from Attica on that particular day. Considerin' whether he would expand his business by opening a shop in Anthony."

"So, they randomly met in downtown Anthony, and . . ."

"And, apparently, he liked what he saw. Gosh dern it, Prentis, I'm nineteen. Can't talk about Mother like this! Makes me sick at my stomach. Let's talk about that stallion."

Prentis listened as Fred described the stallion—the one he was no longer certain about purchasing. He knew all about the stallion. It had recently turned three, and he wanted that horse to build his business. If he bought the horse, he could eventually gain capital by selling his own horses. The purchase would provide steady income to supplement his farming. But cash on hand was the important thing right now. Should he buy the horse?

They trotted into the farmyard. There was his dog! Sam came streaking across the yard, jumping up on Prentis as he dismounted, smothering him with dog affection. He squatted to scratch behind Sam's ears. The dog was overcome with joy; his entire body wagged.

"Sam! Good dog. Hadn't realized how much I missed you."

Fred took Prentis's horse so he could run in to greet Mother and Millie. Sam trotted alongside him as far as the back door, wagging all the way. The familiar fragrance of home assailed Prentis's senses as he stepped inside. *What a relief!* It was good to be back.

Sadie had married a couple of years ago, leaving only Fred and Millie at home now, and Fred had one foot out the door, not at home much of an evening or weekend. Considering that, Prentis thought he understood Mother's desire to remarry. Though Millie was only nine, Mother's home was emptying and her youth fleeting.

"Prentis!" Mother and Millie exclaimed when he dashed in.

Both hurried to embrace him. He smiled down at them, one arm around each. Probably another catalyst for Mother's decision, he hadn't been home since October—his longest absence. She had leaned hard on him the past eight years.

"It's good to see you both! Millie—why, look at my pretty little sister! You've grown about a foot, I think."

"No I haven't, and you know it!" She laughed with him.

"So, tell me how you've both been."

Mother and Millie spilled the news from the past five months. Millie told him about school, despicable boys, new clothes, and her horse. Then Fred entered, and they sat down to supper, the bubbling female discourse continuing. Glowing, Mother chatted about George, sprinkling his name throughout the home details. Across the table, Fred raised his eyebrows at Prentis then ate silently, ignoring the conversation. Whatever the make of the man, Mother obviously loved him. Her expression softened whenever she said his name. Prentis hadn't ever expected to see his mother look like this. It was disconcerting.

"We have business to discuss, Prentis," Mother said after the dishes had been done. "But let's talk tomorrow morning. You're tired—no sense getting into it yet. But any day now, you'll be out with those cows, so we can't put it off after the morning."

"All right, Mother. Fred gave me a general idea of what we need to discuss. We'll tackle it at breakfast. I'll turn in now."

Prentis climbed the stairs to his room and surveyed his boyhood items. He'd probably need to haul everything out of here when he left—a new consideration. He might need to take a wagon home with the stallion tied to the back, *if* he bought the stallion.

Suddenly, reading his Bible and writing to Avery felt like urgent necessities. Opening the well-worn book, he thumbed to Colossians 3 and read the first four verses. This was the portion Avery's family had meditated on after the baby died.

These commands to seek the things above and set one's affection on them were the basis for all godly behavior—this was how right actions resulted. This was a good reminder. He sat for a while, contemplating how to apply that to the current situation; then he wrote to Avery.

February 23, 1914

Dearest Sweetheart,

How I miss you! I saw you yesterday, but it feels like a long time ago now that we're separated by distance and circumstances.

I received shocking news when I arrived—Mother's going to remarry. I haven't met the man yet, George Bellew is his name. Fred says she needs to sell one farm or the other. Fred's nowhere near ready to buy this farm. The responsibility will fall on me, but I don't have the cash yet. This may change our plans.

I'll write more later. I'm talking with Mother in the morning. I just had to unburden myself before I went to bed. I'm trying to set my heart on things above and trust Christ.

Missing you desperately—

Prentis

* * * *

When Prentis stepped downstairs in the chilly morning, his mother was already waiting with two cups of coffee steaming on the table. The aroma had pulled him out of bed. After greeting her, he settled across the table and downed a fortifying quantity of the brew—strong, black, and hot. Then he tilted back in his chair, his eyes on hers, the signal that he was ready to listen.

"Let's jump right in," she said, "since Fred already gave you the essentials."

"Sounds good to me."

"I want to sell one of the farms before I marry George. He's expanding his business and needs the cash. I want to give it to him."

"Did he ask you to sell?"

"No!" Eyes on his, she laughed. "He doesn't know what I'm planning."

"Then—?"

"I want to surprise him. Noticed his hesitation about his business expansion, so I did a little investigation and discovered the need."

"So, it wasn't his idea?"

"No. He's not that type of man, Prentis." Pausing, she pursed her lips, regarding him with a perturbed expression.

He shrugged. "I haven't met him yet. I wouldn't know."

"That's true," she conceded.

"I'm trying to look out for you."

Reaching across the table, she patted his hand and smiled. "Thank you. Must be a surprise to come home and find all this."

Concealing his dismay, Prentis buried his face in his cup, finished his coffee, and rose to refill from the coffeepot on the hot stove. The warmth was nice, and Mother's eyes weren't boring into him, so he lingered there.

The sting of rejection was surprising. He pushed it aside, trying to be objective. Gently, he was being bumped from the position of importance in his mother's heart. A husband's concerns came before a son's, marriage being the primary relationship. She had every right to make these financial decisions without consulting him. Still it hurt.

"When do you need to sell?" he asked.

"Before summer. We'll marry when Millie's school year is over."

"Makes sense."

Racing through Prentis's mind were all the particulars of his finances, the value of the land, and how much his mother might want for the improvements.

She turned to face him. "Do you need time to think about it?"

"Not really. Of course, I'll buy. Need a home for Avery and me." Keeping his eyes on his coffee, he stepped back over and plopped into his chair. "But before we hammer out the details, I'd at least like to meet the man. Might help me wrap my mind around it."

"I understand. You need to be certain he is what he says he is."

Nodding, he raised his eyes to meet hers.

"Prentis, you've done a mighty fine job caring for our family since your father died."

Tenderly regarding him, she wore a familiar motherly expression of pride, one she always showed when he had done something well. That look softened the pain a bit. Reaching across, she patted his hand again then rose to start working on breakfast.

Prentis finished his coffee, grabbed his coat, and stepped out to check on the cows. He was glad he'd have plenty of time alone during calving to work this out in his head and his heart.

* * * *

That weekend, when Mother and George Bellew returned from Sunday services at the Methodist Church in Kingman, Prentis planned to assess the situation firsthand. He'd been out all night with the cows and had missed George's arrival.

Last night, he and Fred had been forced to pull a calf. Cow and calf were fine now, but it had been touch-and-go, stressful, and messy. None of the cows were currently calving, but at least five calves had been born each day. It had been hectic all week. Much Antisepto and Umbilicure had been applied. Fred was inside sleeping right now.

When the carriage wheeled into the farmyard, Prentis was still in the barn with Sam beside him paying no heed to its arrival. The dog had stuck closely to Prentis each time he'd emerged from the house. Sam was his dog, and it was obvious he'd missed his master. Peering through the slightly opened barn door, Prentis watched the man help Mother out of the carriage and into the house. Millie walked alongside, talking non-stop; they were smiling at one another, amused over something she'd said. Every weekend, they went to church together, Fred had said.

All seemed friendly and proper. Prentis considered this first impression: Millie liked George Bellew, and he had treated Mother with care and consideration. It was beneficial that Mother and Millie could go to church with the man.

Prentis headed for the house. At the back-porch sink, he scrubbed his entire upper body with lye soap, keeping the farmyard out of the house. Feeling the stubble on his chin, he realized he needed a shave. It could wait. Clean at last, he pulled a towel and fresh shirt from the shelf Mother kept stocked. He dried, dressed, left his boots on the porch, and stepped inside.

An assured bass voice sounded from the dining room conversing with Millie, who was chattering away about the events of her week. The man asked Millie questions that demonstrated his awareness of the circumstances. Obviously, they had previously discussed these subjects. Mother bustled about in the kitchen, scurrying to get the meal onto the table.

"Prentis." Mother held out a bowl of baked potatoes. "Can you carry these in?"

Prentis nodded, received the bowl, and walked into the dining room. His habitual shyness made him hesitant. Eyes on the potatoes, he set them beside the roast beef. The man had risen. Once Prentis was free of the potatoes, his mother's suitor thrust out his hand.

"George Bellew."

"P.J. Pinkerton."

Meeting his eyes, Prentis shook the offered hand and evaluated the man—well-dressed, hair slicked down with pomade, open smile, crinkly-friendly eyes, mature for his thirty-one years, a handsome man. George's handshake was firm and confident; he wore a friendly expression.

Mother entered and set the last of the food on the table. Turning to slip her arm through George's, she smiled at him before turning toward Prentis with an eager smile.

"You've met now," she said. "I'm so glad. George, this is my son Prentis, who's taken such good care of us since Thomas died."

"Your mother's very proud of you, P.J. I've heard a lot about you."

Prentis hadn't ever really looked at his mother. She was his mother; that was all. But now, clutching another man's arm—a man who was not his father, he had to consider that she was also a woman. He felt the pang of disloyalty. As he observed Mother's smile and how she leaned against George, the protective offended emotions he felt regarding his father's rights almost took his breath away. Another man was courting the woman his father had loved.

But his father had been gone for eight years—dead and buried in the cemetery. It had been horrific to lose him, not merely his person, but his provision, sustenance, and fatherly input in their lives. And Mother, also dearly loved by Prentis, had lost the care of a husband.

Smiling and happy, she stood before him now, looking as if something vital had been missing, exactly as it had been missing for him. He had lacked a father, but she had lacked a husband. Today she looked more alive than she had since his father died.

When Mother had married Father she'd only been seventeen, and he'd been twenty-six. There'd been so much arguing during his youth—the wars of religion tearing the house apart—that he had never thought about his parents' relationship. At some point, they had loved passionately. They probably had still loved one another when his father died.

How could a fifteen-year-old boy discern such a thing? He only recalled the arguing, inflexibility, and stubbornness. Scots-Irish folk were passionate in their loving and in their fighting. Nevertheless, his parents had been committed to one another and had made a good life together. Millie had been only a year old when his father had died, so Prentis knew there was physical affection in their marriage.

But his mother's expression right now told him that she was *in* love. She felt for George what he felt for Avery. Why hadn't he ever seen his mother look at his father like this? Had he not been paying attention? He'd probably never know the answer to that question. He didn't know if he wanted to know. But he knew what it was like to be in love.

Therefore, his conscience urged him: *Be forbearing.* God was giving him the grace to respond as he should. He would forgive his mother for her absorption with George and her plans. She wasn't considering the financial crisis into which she might be throwing him. She probably assumed he had the money already banked.

Prentis would secure the money for the farm. He would not burden her with the difficulty this would cause him. He would merely do it. This was the best way he could love her and care for her. He had to have the farm, or he couldn't marry Avery. A mortgage seemed to be the only solution. For that, a thriving cattle-and-horse business would be good collateral. He'd buy the stallion. If he worked hard, he could pay off a mortgage in a few years.

All of these decisions were made and considered in a flash, and now he realized that George and his mother stood looking at him, awaiting his response.

"I'm sorry," Prentis said. "I was distracted a moment. Had to readjust my thinking."

George chuckled. "I'm sure that's true. Here's some man you've never met, coming in to waltz away with your mother."

"Yes, something like that."

George pulled out Mother's chair, helping her to seat herself, and then he sat next to her. He hadn't assumed he would have the chair at the end opposite Mother, the place Prentis always sat. This was considerate.

As Prentis reached for the potatoes, Mother and Millie bowed their heads, and George began to say grace. Growing up, mealtime prayers had never been said in their home—it had always caused a war: Should the Catholic prayer or the Protestant prayer be repeated? They'd never been able to compromise. This was a good change: God was being thanked for the food. Prentis bowed his head and joined them. George seemed to bring out the best in his mother.

A pleasant meal followed. George was personable and informed. They all conversed easily. Mother had kept him abreast of the particulars of Prentis's life. He asked about Avery. Prentis told George their plans and warmed to his favorite topic; he found that George was already acquainted with much about her.

Then George informed Prentis of all his current business and farming concerns and his future plans for expansion. His objectives were to provide for Mother and to see that Millie received a good education. He didn't have any concerns other than those. Mother was past childbearing. George loved her and aimed to take care of her. Her family would be his.

Prentis felt relieved. The care of his mother and Millie was soon to be lifted from his shoulders. He'd taken on that responsibility so young that it was merely a fact of life to him, but soon he would be accountable for only himself and Avery. Maybe his mother's marriage wasn't a tragedy after all. He could focus on Avery.

Before he lay down to take a nap after dinner, he wrote a quick letter.

March 1, 1914

Dearest Avery,

I only have a moment to write. I've been up all night with the cows and need to catch some sleep. I've met George—a nice man, mature, good for my mother. He'll take good care of her and Millie. Seeing them together helped me adjust my thinking.

Mother wants me to purchase the Oklahoma farm soon, before she marries George. I have about two-thirds of the cash needed. I'll be seeking a mortgage for the balance—I can make it go. I'll visit the banks in Kingman, Anthony, and Wakita to find the best terms, and then I'll talk it over with you before I sign anything.

We haven't discussed our wedding yet. No sign of any war of religion; but I'll soon see Grandpa Dir and all the aunts and uncles on both sides—everyone gathered at Sadie's next weekend. Dirs will upset Pinkertons, who will upset Dirs. Pray that I trust the Lord with all of it.

I hope to be home in two weeks—twenty-five calves born, about fifty to go. None lost yet. We'll do the branding before I leave, adding injury to insult. It always seems wrong to pull that on a calf so soon after the struggle of being born, but it has to be done.

Loving you with all my heart,

Prentis

When the Dirs and the Pinkertons gathered to discuss the upcoming wedding, this battle of the religious wars was even worse than Prentis had feared. He felt torn in two. The following week he licked his wounds, contemplating the war of words. As he awaited the births of the final calves, much time was spent in solitude.

Neither side was pleased with him. He had remained noncommittal until he could discuss everything with Avery. He couldn't see a reasonable solution that wouldn't offend someone. Avery's happiness was paramount, and he wanted peace. However, there would be no peace if they married in any church at all. She had released him from the expectation of a church wedding, but still, he longed for her to have one.

It grieved him that this was the condition of his family. He knew Avery's family wasn't perfect, but he admired their unity, love, and acceptance of one another. They were all believers, followers of Christ. That was the important fact.

His chest tightened as, once more, he envisioned all the impossible, unworkable solutions.

Prentis was still afraid of churches.

FIFTEEN

PROGRESS WAS SLOW. ADJUSTING his position on the spring bench, Prentis maneuvered, attempting to get comfortable. So far the trip home had taken two-and-a-half days in the farm wagon, camping along the way. His seat was sore. But the weather had been perfect—sunshine, balmy breezes, and dry roads. Alert with ears forward, Sam sat on the seat beside him, surveying the road with keen eyes.

The stallion was hitched behind the wagon, now part of his collateral for the mortgage he would obtain. It was a beautiful horse—spirited, broad chested, and perfectly formed. In a couple years, the foals from this stallion and his mares would sell for a profit. When he arrived home, he'd launch that business by familiarizing the animals with one another.

George and Fred had helped him load his possessions into the wagon. He now had all his furniture, tools, and personal items, including his dog. The wagon, the two horses drawing it, and all of these possessions were now his. No money had changed hands. Mother wouldn't even take it when he had offered.

"Stop being ridiculous, Prentis," she had said. "You've run this farm for eight years."

The Oklahoma farm was his home now. Once Avery had moved in, it would feel like home. Until then, it lacked the essential ingredient—his new wife. For now, he felt displaced and disquieted by this upheaval, as if he were a homeless child, even though he was a grown man of twenty-three. The fact that he had Sam was a comfort. At least he'd have a companion.

When Millie's school was out, a quiet wedding would occur at Mother's minister's home in Kingman. They would load everything into George's wagons, and Fred would live in the nearly empty home where Prentis and all his siblings had been born and raised. They had never discussed Prentis's purchase of the Oklahoma land in front of George—he had no idea. It would be Mother's wedding surprise. The fact that Prentis would have to take a mortgage to make the purchase was his secret. Mother had no idea—one secret on top of another.

Keenly aware of the stallion, the mares kept nickering back to him, causing the horse to toss his head and whinny in return, becoming acquainted before they even arrived at the farm. This would ease the breeding. The mares would soon be in season. These additional mares from the home stock would give him more foals to sell in two years, assisting with his cash-flow problem.

The banks in Kingman and Anthony had given him good terms, mortgages at 1.1 percent interest—he had impeccable credit. Of course, everything depended on a good harvest this year. It seemed he had to take this financial plunge, but he needed to consult Avery.

If he took the mortgage and the harvest failed, they wouldn't be able to marry this year. Not paying at least the interest on the note would put the entire farm in jeopardy. All it would take was hail, tornado, fire, or some other calamity—all outside his control.

If that occurred, he would be behind and therefore unable to pay the note. He would then have to renegotiate, but at a higher rate with the unpaid interest folded into the loan, adding even more debt. He didn't like taking the risk, but it was all in God's hands, either way.

Anxiety permeated his considerations. The need for a mortgage put a cloud over everything. He would have to trust the Lord more thoroughly; He would care for them. *Set your mind on things above*. Following his own advice, he reviewed an encouraging passage from Hebrews.

"Seeing then that we have a great High Priest . . . "

The two mares pulling the wagon stopped, staring back at him with twitching ears, trying to discern his command. No persons were present, so his words had to be directed at them.

"Talking to myself, girls," he said. "Giddup."

Simultaneously, both mares turned their heads, eyes, and ears forward. Obedient, they focused on the road and plodded ahead. Prentis chuckled and shook his head. *Where was I?*

Finishing his recitation silently lest he confuse the horses again, he was glad he recalled the entire passage. This was the encouraging fact: Jesus knew how he felt. He had been tempted as a man, though He had never sinned, being God in human flesh. Because Jesus empathized and Prentis belonged to Him, he could approach Him and beg for mercy. Jesus would help him.

Pouring out his fears and uncertainties, Prentis prayed for mercy and grace. He needed the Lord's sustaining help. Articulating his concerns took a while. Pulling his attention from his prayer, he realized the sun settled low on the horizon. He urged the horses to pick up their pace. The mares were weary; the load was heavy. Thankfully, the Slaughter's house was near.

He'd written Avery, asking if he could break his trip there. They would discuss the religious wars. These last days in the wagon had given him time to pray and to hash through the war of words, demands, and expectations. He had found no solution. Pleasing Avery above all other people on earth was his desire, but he knew Avery would have a different opinion.

There was the house. Someone in white moved toward him—*Avery!* Obviously, she had been watching the road. She grew larger before his eyes, wearing a broad, white hat, her hair braided over her shoulder, falling across her white blouse and blue sweater.

Grinning, he plucked off his hat and waved it.

She returned his wave. He urged the horses forward, arresting their progress when they reached his goal—the beautiful woman coming toward him so joyously. He jumped down and swept her up into his arms. How he'd missed her!

"Avery!"

"I've longed to see your face," she whispered into his ear.

Inhaling the fragrance of her hair—soapy clean with a scent of floral and fresh air, he nuzzled against her neck, holding her about the waist. Her toes barely brushed the dirt road.

"You're like breathing in springtime," he said. "Simply seeing you makes me feel hopeful and relieved." Leaning in under her hat brim, he kissed her enthusiastically.

She kissed him back and then gazed at him with her sparkling black eyes. "I've missed you. Please, tell me all about it. I see you've brought Sam."

Prentis set Avery on her feet, and she scratched under Sam's chin. The dog seemed to recall her from their youth; they took up right where they'd left off. His tail wagged vigorously as she spoke to him. Sam had always liked her.

"Couldn't leave my dog, now that home isn't home."

She gave him a sympathetic look.

Prentis took her hand and stepped toward the stallion, grasping its halter. "Let me make the introductions. I need to show you this horse."

Until he had the horse completely in hand, Avery lagged behind. But when he turned toward her, excited to show her the horse, she stepped up to stroke the stallion's muzzle.

"This is Apollo," he said.

"The sun god?" She laughed. "You named the horse after a Greek god?"

"Actually, I was thinking of Louis XIV, the Sun King. I've read that artists portrayed him as Apollo. He was the absolute monarch of his domain, exactly as this horse will be. Meditating on the wars of religion gave me the idea. Couldn't very well name him Louis XIV."

"No, you couldn't." She couldn't seem to quit laughing.

"This is serious." He chuckled with her. "He'd get no respect in Oklahoma named Louis XIV. Half our profits are in Apollo. His traits will show in every foal our farm produces."

"*Our* farm—that's a happy thought!"

"It will be yours and mine by the time the first foals are born."

They stared at one another as the thought sank in. Then they both grinned.

"These," Prentis said, continuing the introductions as they

stepped around the wagon, "are Daisy and Mabel—friends of long acquaintance."

Avery stroked Daisy's forelock; then she patted Mabel's silky chestnut cheek.

"They're good mares," she said.

"Steady and mature. They'll be good for Apollo. This is his first season." Quickly, Prentis moved the conversation away from horse breeding. "And these things . . ." He swept wide his arm indicating the loaded wagon. "These are all my earthly possessions."

The heaped pile was roped down and covered with canvas tarps. None of the furniture or boxes could be seen, merely the impressive mound.

"It had to be strange to empty your childhood home."

"Felt somewhat orphaned again. Even though my mother's still living, her affections are engaged elsewhere."

Grasping both his hands, Avery looked up at him. "I'm sorry for that loss. Nothing stays the same. Everything changes while we're here on this earth."

"That's true."

"But now you've engaged my affections, and you'll soon be loading my things into your wagon. Then I'll be the dislocated one."

He smiled. "Hope you won't mind leaving your childhood home. I'll be so glad to have you in that house with me. I hope you'll be happy there."

"I will be," she said with certainty.

"You'll have been there to put in the garden and then later for the harvest. Hope it will feel like home to you by then."

"It will. You'll be there. Home will be wherever you are."

Those words prompted him to kiss her again. He lingered over this second kiss. Pulling back, he gazed into her eyes—how he loved this woman!

"Think of this wagonload as the beginning of the establishment of our home," she said.

"That's an uplifting thought."

Grabbing Daisy's halter, he clicked his tongue. All three horses moved forward, rolling the wagon toward their destination. Fingers intertwined, Avery and Prentis walked beside the mares.

"So," she said, "tell me about the wars of religion."

He sighed. "Exactly as I thought it would be."

"We were prepared for that."

"True."

"What do you want to do?" she asked.

"Whatever you want."

"Regardless of whom we offend?"

"Absolutely!" He grinned. He knew she'd know he was teasing.

She laughed. "But what do you think Christ would have us to do?"

"Now that's the difficult part. What *would* He have us do?"

"Let's study together before we even discuss it. We need to examine what the Bible says about not offending others."

"Good idea. Gives us time to pray and think first. We may have to give up what we want for the sake of peace."

She nodded. "Usually, that's the case."

"True, Avery—you're wise." By their linked hands, he pulled her against himself, shoulder to shoulder. "So, anything exciting happen to you since your last letter?"

"Well, a couple of things occurred. Joseph Pitzer rode over to apologize."

Surprised, he looked at her. "About time. How did that go?"

"He was cordial. I said I was sorry for giving the wrong impression. He hoped we could still be friends, and I said we could. He didn't tease for once in his life."

"Sounds like you handled that admirably."

"Thank you." She smiled at him. "He seemed appropriately chastened."

Prentis laughed. "And with good cause."

"The other event wasn't so cheerful."

"Oh?" He fixed his eyes on her face. Her voice held the familiar mix of consternation and embarrassment; she'd done something grievous.

"There's a storm brewing in the Sunday School department because I'm engaged to a man who doesn't attend church."

"Warned you this would happen."

"Yes, you did. But I acted rashly. I gummed up the works, as my brothers say."

"Avery—"

"Yes, you guessed it. I said something I shouldn't have. You know me well enough to suspect that. Mrs. Alfonse Riley is head of the Sunday School. I'm certain she made that comment at Floyd and Hattie's wedding. When she asked why you didn't attend church, I said, 'Primarily because of people like you.' That probably wasn't a very wise answer."

Suppressing a grin, he chuckled softly. "You're probably right."

Mrs. Alfonse Riley was a prim and finicky woman. Prentis found it humorous that she was so attached to her husband's flowery first name. The man himself went by Alf and was a kind and unpretentious man. Her insistence on the use of the entire formal matrimonial title amused most of the population of north-central Oklahoma.

"They're reviewing the matter," Avery said. "Daddy is one of the deacons, and I know he'll vouch for you."

"You don't need to defend me. God is the one I'm concerned about."

"I know. I was impetuous, and I'm going to have to apologize."

"You're a humble and gracious woman."

"I don't think Mrs. Alfonse Riley would agree."

"Another thing to pray about," he said.

"Yes, let's add it to the list. Joseph Pitzer and my scandalizing of the Sunday School department aside, what about the mortgage? Is it the only option?"

"My mother doesn't want cash for the improvements. She says I worked for so long to support her that she can't charge me for that."

"That's a relief! Your mother was well aware of your contribution those eight years."

"Yes, it appears she was, and I'm grateful. I have more than two-thirds of the total in savings. So I'm almost there, but a mortgage seems to be the only recourse."

"Then let's pray about that, too," she said.

"All right, we'll pray."

"God will give us the answer."

Prentis nodded. He felt peaceful merely being in her presence.

* * * *

A period of early spring rain followed Prentis's return from Kingman, keeping the roads a muddy disaster for horse and man and parting them for two more weeks. But then, the rain eased, the sun shone, and the roads dried. During the separation, they had planned by mail when Avery and her mother would come, *if* the roads were good. They were. At last! The garden needed to go into the ground, especially the cool-season vegetables.

Avery drove south from Wakita—past the prairie cemetery, monuments in stone to the dearly departed—and then turned west, traveling three sections, watching for a house on the road's south side. If they crossed the wooden bridge, they'd gone too far. Excited for a first glimpse, she scanned the distant farmland. In the Model T, the trip that took Prentis an hour and a half on a trotting horse was completed in about thirty minutes with ease and no discomfort.

As they went through the final intersection, the road sloped uphill. There was the house! It faced east with a good view of the road. Avery liked it. That meant all the fields they had just passed on the left belonged to Prentis. The mares had been grazing. The wheat fields spread out behind them, separated by a barbed-wire fence—exceptional horses and plush wheat. Here came Sam, dashing out from behind the house, the first member of the welcoming committee.

A square frame house on a stone foundation crowned the hill. To build the foundation, Thomas Pinkerton had hauled stones up from the creek bottom, intending for each son to have a farm, either this one or the one in Kansas. Prentis's father had built for his sons in either place, so he'd taken care with the details. Well-planned farms were his legacy. Prentis had told Avery of laboring alongside his father with Fred, even as small boys, carrying stones, digging ditches, and laying fence. The stone foundation gave the small claim house an air of permanence.

Behind the house stood dense cottonwood, willow, and red cedar lining the creek that snaked along the base of the bluff. About fifty yards behind the house the bluff dropped off sharply, according to Prentis. Avery turned into the drive. It circled past the house and toward the barn, built on the winding creek's diagonal—off at an angle from the surveyors' arrow-straight road, instead of strictly horizontal or perpendicular to it.

Settling his Stetson in place, Prentis stepped out the front door. Clearly, he'd been watching for them. He strode down the hill smiling and obviously as excited as she. Planting this garden and viewing the house were both important steps toward their wedding day.

Gene and Howard jumped out and ran to him, both exclaiming excitedly about the ride, Prentis's horses, and his wheat. He tousled Howard's hair and shook Gene's hand. Then he clapped a hand on the shoulder of each, and they walked back toward the automobile. Sam trotted beside the boys, wagging and friendly. The dog had always had an affinity for boys, having had such a kind master. Avery smiled at the sight.

Prentis welcomed Momma and embraced Avery. "I'm glad to show you your future home."

"I'm glad I can see it!" She smiled up at him.

Lacing his fingers through hers, he led them up the path toward the house. The front was symmetrical—the door right in the middle, one window on each side. A small, wooden porch stood in front, a shady place to sit in the evening.

They climbed the front steps, Prentis opened the door, and they filed into the front room. A potbellied stove stood in the middle of the far wall. Two comfortable chairs, each with a hassock, were arrayed to the left on the south wall. They neatly framed a window in the center. A table between the two chairs held an oil lamp, Prentis's Bible—with Avery's red ribbon hanging out one end as a bookmark—and several other books.

A bookcase stood in the corner. Avery paused to investigate. It was packed with a wide variety of literature, from classics—*David Copperfield* among them—to Dr. Roberts' veterinary guidebook. Livy's *The Early History of Rome* sat on the end of one shelf, *The Iliad* on another. Consulted frequently, Dr. Roberts' dog-eared guide was pulled out farther than the others. Abutting this bookcase, under the east-facing front window, sat Prentis's desk.

Avery could imagine him here each lonely night, reading and studying. Soon, they would sit in this room and read together. She smiled at him as she thought of it. The way his eyes gleamed, he seemed to have been thinking the same.

A doorway left of the pot-bellied stove led into the bedroom. The room held neatly arranged bedroom furniture, probably from his home in Kansas, including a crisply made bed. There were two windows, one on the west and one on the south. Sunlight would stream in there in the wintertime. Avery felt shy about stepping into the bedroom, so she didn't.

Everything was tidy; he was fastidious. Having been lifelong friends, she had known that, but this well-kept home occupied by a young bachelor was proof. Prentis let her make her own observations, standing quietly as she studied each detail.

At the opposite end of the front room, under the north window stood a small drop-leaf table with two chairs, both pushed in precisely. They would sit there and eat.

The other doorway, right of the potbellied stove, led into the kitchen. Stepping across the threshold, Avery scanned the room. To the left was a shiny cookstove; by the back door stood a small icebox. The north wall consisted of a bank of cupboards with the sink set right in the middle. It had a convenient hand pump.

The top cupboards extended all the way to the ceiling from the height of Avery's chest. These were about a foot deep. The lower cupboards, reaching the level of her hips, were about two-feet deep, leaving a two-foot-wide work ledge in the gap between the upper and the lower—the perfect height. The top of the bottom cupboards formed a ledge of highly polished wood on which to work and mix food. It was convenient, easier than working from a tabletop. Momma didn't have this. All her kitchen work was done on the table.

Above the sink a window overlooked a small patch of grass and trees, the bluff seeming to fall away not far from this corner of the house. The view would be pleasant. To grab an escape from the confines, Avery could look out the window and gaze at the trees.

She would be in the kitchen more than she'd been accustomed, but she didn't mind. She'd be cooking for Prentis—one man she adored. *Happy thought!* She glanced up and saw that he was studying her face, anxious about her opinion.

"This is perfect, Prentis," she said.

He smiled, looking relieved.

"I'm pleased. It's so convenient and has so much storage space. I'll be able to look out the window as I work."

"Thought you might like that. When Dad put the sink there, I remember he said the same thing about Mother. I was just a little boy, but I handed him the tools."

"The cupboards look newly painted."

He nodded. "They are. Put them in this winter."

"You built all of these cupboards during the wintertime?"

"Yes, I was thinking of you."

"You built these for me?"

"I did. They're sized to your height, so it will be convenient."

The thoughtfulness of this gesture overwhelmed her. The idea of him planning and measuring specifically for her height was almost more than she could fathom.

"I appreciate this, Prentis. Thank you," she said softly, hoping she conveyed her pleasure adequately. "They're perfect. The work ledge is ingenious. Everything is so handy. It will be easy to be in this kitchen."

"That's exactly what I hoped as I built them."

"It's lovely," Momma contributed her opinion. "You've done this so well."

He smiled at her then took Avery's hand. "Step out here and see the back porch. Then I'll show you the barnyard before we plant the garden."

He opened the back door. Five steps led down into the enclosed porch. A hand-poured cement floor was at ground level. There was another sink with a hand pump and an area where boots and tools were all neatly organized.

As Avery stepped down the stairs to the concrete floor, on her left she saw more steps that went down under the house, the root cellar conveniently accessed without having to go out into the weather. This would be handy for retrieving canned goods and root vegetables, and for taking cover when tornadoes threatened.

That trip out of the house, across the yard, and down into the cellar was the worst part of the typical tornado routine in spring through fall, especially if there was hail. She and Prentis would only have to run out their kitchen door and down the stairs to arrive safely underground—no dodging of hail and torrential rain driven by gale-force winds.

"Oh!" she said softly. "I like this, Prentis."

"Convenient, isn't it? When Dad built here, he improved on the Kansas house."

"I can't even begin to express how happy I am! This house is perfect, as if it were made to order. I feel perfectly content merely thinking about living here with you."

"Good." Satisfaction spread across his face. "Happy you're pleased. Let's take a look at the barnyard and the animals."

He opened the back-porch door, and they filed up a path that duplicated the angle of the land. Following the serpentine bed of the unseen creek below the bluff, thick trees and brush edged this northwest corner. On this wedge of ground the garden spot had been tilled only a short stroll out the back door. They walked past the swath of fertile, prepared red earth.

Approaching the barnyard, the path joined the drive. Prentis pointed at various details and Avery examined each as they strolled toward the barn, arriving first at the variety of pens. There stood Apollo in the nearest pen, his head up, alertly regarding them. Howard and Gene were already perched on the fence admiring him. They had raced away after peeking into the house. At their age, if you'd seen one house, you'd seen them all. Sam sat beside them. They all turned now and grinned at Prentis, Sam wagging.

"Prettiest quarter horse I've ever seen," Gene said with appropriate awe. "I think he remembers us from when you stopped at our house."

Howard nodded enthusiastically.

"He's swell, isn't he?" Prentis said. "Hope the foals get all his best traits. He's quick and agile—good for working and riding."

"How many of the mares will you breed?" Gene flicked his eyes in Avery and Momma's direction, blushing as he awaited Prentis's response.

"All of them."

Sagely, Howard and Gene nodded, as if their vast amount of farming experience compelled them to agree with his business decision. Avery smiled at their attempt to appear manlike.

The group continued through the well-organized barn. Beyond stood Rex's pen. He was a registered Hereford—white of face, chest, and belly; broad and manly of stance; sturdy and solid; an intelligent head; short curved horns; clear eyes; a calm expression; straight across the back; heavily covered with flesh—in short, all a bull should be.

Gene whistled long and low when he saw Rex. "Now that's a bull!"

"Half the herd," Prentis said.

In silent admiration of the magnificent creature, all stood gazing at him. Then, reverently, they turned, walking away from Rex as one leaves church, in silent contemplation. Avery had never seen such an impressive bull. Prentis was known for being a good judge of livestock, and now she knew why. Next to Rex was a wide, fenced area where the steers were penned, all large and ready to sell.

"The steers are nice and fat," Howard said.

"They are. Brought them up to the barn so Avery could see them today. Fed them on prairie grass, alfalfa hay, oats, and as much corn as I could afford. I needed to fatten them up fast. Selling them at the cattle sale on Tuesday."

Avery smiled inwardly at the preparations he'd made for her. Everyone stared at the proverbial fattened calves, pondering their fate. Their certain doom unknown, the steers stood placidly chewing their cud. For some odd reason, Avery found their unwitting serenity amusing. She stifled a giggle.

Beyond the pen that held the steers, separated from the prairie-grass pasture with barbwire fencing, the green wheat woke from its dormancy, prepared to grow tall. All was well. Avery's heart filled right up to the top. This would be her home, and Prentis had accomplished it all while laboring to gain her. Eyes soft and appreciative, she turned to search for him; he was already gazing at her, adoration in his eyes.

SIXTEEN

AFTER CHURCH THE NEXT day, the sunshine lingering, Prentis pulled into the barnyard. When Avery saw that Apollo was hitched to the buggy, she looked down, smoothing her skirt front to hide her apprehension. Straightening, she detected not a trace of concern on his face. Prentis relaxed under the shade of the buggy top, reclining against the seat. Hat tipped back and sleeves rolled up, he appeared to be in perfect control of the stallion.

"Avery, he has to do something other than stud the mares," he told her when he coasted to a stop. "His reign isn't that much of an absolute monarchy."

Apparently, her anxiety showed.

Leaning toward her, he offered his hand, keeping hold of the reins and through them the horse. He didn't leave the buggy to help her. Clearly, he wasn't as lackadaisical as he appeared. Trusting his expertise, she latched onto his hand, and he pulled her in.

"I apologize for my bare arms," he said. "I know it's impolite, but keeping this horse in check on the trip up here overheated me. Hope you'll forgive me."

"Of course."

Apollo's withers quivered; he whinnied and tossed his head, anxious to get moving. Once Avery was settled, Prentis sounded the signal, and they took off like a shot.

"He's got to burn off some energy; the mares aren't in season yet."

Moving fast, Apollo galloped up the road. The surrounding fields flashed by. Periodically, the buggy bounced them into the air. The roads were rutted with dried mud left in whatever shape it had taken when last wet. Attempting to keep Apollo in check, Prentis's hands were both engaged, the muscles in his forearms bulging as he strained with the reins.

Avery held onto the armrest, gripping it with all her might.

Smiling widely, Prentis bounced his gaze back and forth from her eyes to the horse, obviously enjoying watching Apollo run, accompanied by the exhilaration of moving fast.

"Too bad we didn't have him when we had to switch that skirt of yours."

He aimed his playful eyes her direction, and she smiled a tiny smile.

"It's all right, Avery. He's been trained to pull the buggy. He's not a racehorse, merely a high quality farm-and-buggy horse, but still a cow pony, as the old farmers say. He's responsive. I could stop him short if I wanted. Did you notice how well he responded to my signal?"

Another glance. She nodded.

"He's energetic. He can smell the mares. Even though they're not in season yet, they will be any day. Sorry for discussing horse breeding. It's occupying my mind. You're going to be marrying a rancher." He gave her a longer look.

"I don't mind. I want to understand."

"Good. Let's let him go. He'll tire soon. He ran all he wanted on the way up here."

"I like to go fast, in the automobile at least. If you trust the horse, I'll trust you." She scooted closer to Prentis, released the armrest, and gripped the seat with both hands. "I won't touch your arm so your hands aren't impeded."

He shot her a quick smile before fixing his eyes on Apollo's racing hindquarters. "Can you converse while moving at top speed?"

"I'm able. Are you?"

"Absolutely. I love a running horse—best way to travel, much better than a Model T."

He flashed her a grin. That was debatable, but she didn't want to tackle that subject today.

"All right," she said, "I'll tell you what I've been considering since you returned from Kingman and we decided to pray."

"Sounds wonderful."

"First, I don't want you to get the mortgage. I want to give you my savings so you don't have to borrow the money. I have $1,000 banked right now, and I want you to have it."

Eyebrows raised, he gave her the longest look he could with Apollo tearing up the road. Twice, he stared into her eyes, checking the horse in between.

Finally, he spoke, "I can't take your money."

"Why not?"

"I want to do the providing."

"But why can't I help you? I'm going to be your wife. What's mine will be yours."

"And what's mine will be yours as well. But it doesn't seem right. I want to take care of you. Taking your money would make me feel as though you were taking care of me." He kept his eyes fixed on hers for a long while, then looked back at the horse.

"But, Prentis, it will be *our* farm."

"Yes," he agreed, "but I need to stand on my own two feet, work hard, and pay the bills."

"You've been doing that since you were fifteen."

"Guess I've grown accustomed to it."

"Let's suppose you get the mortgage and some disaster occurs. Will you allow me to give you my savings then?"

Apollo seemed to have gotten his frustrations worked out— he slowed.

As Apollo eased up, Prentis looked hard at Avery. "Can you let me consider that? Need to pick apart my motives and think about what would be pleasing to God, right for me as a future husband, and encouraging to you."

"Yes, of course. I won't bring the subject up again. It's up to you."

"Thank you. I love you, Avery." He passed the reins into one hand and reached over to caress her cheek. "It's generous of you to offer, but I'd like you to spend that money on yourself. You deserve it."

"And you deserve to have a wife who wants to help you. I love you, too."

Prentis leaned in for a peck of a kiss. "You're a wonderful woman."

"I'm certain not everyone agrees." She sighed. "My next news involves Mrs. Alfonse Riley and the Sunday School department."

"Tell me what happened."

"I've been relieved of my duties."

"Avery, I'm—"

"Don't even say it, Prentis! This isn't your fault. I shouldn't have retorted as I did. Even though I apologized, I know my tongue was the cause of her decision, Daddy's good words about you notwithstanding."

"But it wouldn't have even come up if—"

"No, Prentis. I take the blame for this. She asked whether I thought you *might be* a believer, as if I would *ever* become engaged to a non-Christian man." The mere idea still left Avery fuming. "Her assumption riled me. I took up an offense too quickly. I thought she was condemning you and judging me. If I had explained calmly, all would be well. I was wrong."

"Still, I'm sorry to have put you in this situation. I can't attend church. This is why."

"You can't throw out the entire institution because of one sinner, or in this case two. The church is comprised of sinners, Prentis. It always has been."

"Regardless, this makes me sick. I don't want you to lose something so precious to you."

"I'll be fine. I have you. Most of my spiritual growth this year has been provoked by your faith and the resulting realization of my many flaws."

He leaned in to kiss her forehead. "You cause me to grow, too, Avery. But I wish there was something I could do. Other than attending church, that is."

"You can simply be yourself. That's enough for me."

His brow knit together; she knew he considered himself culpable. But she held herself responsible. She had overreacted, instead of praying for God's grace to respond as she should. The humbling was good for her.

"I need to grow," she said. "I should have assumed the best about her and replied graciously. God is good to work in my life."

They rode silently. Prentis seemed to be digesting all she had said.

At last, he spoke. "Thank you for taking the pressure off me, but I'm grieved this happened. I'm grateful for your love. I can't wait to marry you."

"What do you think we should do about the wedding?"

"Everyone's feelings are injured so easily—you and Mrs. Riley included. We need to be careful of the feelings of my family."

"Yes, we certainly do. We don't want to offend them or cause them to stumble."

"Paul gave a good example in Acts 21." He glanced at her.

She nodded. "Yes, he put the interests of the Jewish Christians in Jerusalem ahead of his own. Unfortunately, most of us aren't as willing as Paul to yield to the preferences of others."

"Especially in my family," Prentis said.

"I want us to let go of disputable matters and hold onto the essentials: Christ died for our sins, was buried, and rose on the third day for our justification. Salvation is in Him and no other. Those are the life-changing truths, not where or how we choose to marry. Like Paul, we need to let go of our preferences about disputable matters for the sake of unity and peace. We can't be rigid about what we want, merely because they are."

Prentis nodded.

Feeling sheepish, she glanced at him. "I'm sorry. I sounded like the Sunday School teacher I am—or used to be, didn't I?"

He chuckled. "You did. You'll be a Sunday School teacher again. They value your Bible learning and humility, exactly as I do. You help me understand. So, what do we hold onto and what do we sacrifice?"

"That's the issue. How do we show deference? I don't want to offend your family, and I want whatever you want."

"What *I* want? If the courthouse in Medford were open today, I'd drive this buggy down there, not tell a soul of my squabbling relatives, marry you, and take you home." He grinned.

"That sounds wonderful." She grinned back.

"That said, I want to do what's best for you. I want to do what's right. I don't want to be selfish, and I want us to please God by doing our best not to offend others."

"That being the case, here's my suggestion." She paused to collect her thoughts. "Let's travel up to Kingman sometime after the harvest and visit everyone, maybe having a meal or a party together, if they desire. Then, so no one's offended, let's go to the courthouse together and be married by the judge, only you and me. Afterward, we can board the train and come home."

He fixed his earnest eyes on hers. "Are you certain that's what you want?"

"I'm certain. I've thought about it and prayed about it, and I want peace."

"Will you wear a white dress?"

"Yes, I will."

"Who should we bring as witnesses?"

"How about each of us bringing one sibling who is of age?"

He nodded. "Good idea."

"Do you mind if we sing a song?"

"The two of us?" He looked at her, eyebrows raised.

"Yes, the two of us, the witnesses, and anyone else who wants to sing along."

"Which song?"

"Let's sing *For the Beauty of the Earth*."

"I like that one." He flashed her a wide smile. "I'd probably do anything you suggested, you know."

She returned his smile. "Is there anything in particular you want?"

"A double-ring ceremony. I want to wear the symbol of my commitment to you for all the world to see."

Touched by his decision, Avery sat regarding him for a moment. "Why, Prentis, thank you. I'll buy your wedding band. See, it's all decided."

"Still feel like you gave up too much."

"No, I didn't. I get to have you."

Pulling slightly off the roadway, Prentis spoke a few calming words to Apollo and then enfolded her in his arms. His eyes smoldered like blue flames, holding in their depths an intensity she hadn't before witnessed. Passionately he caressed her mouth with urgent lips, taking her breath away. He kissed her quite thoroughly.

"I love you so much." His voice was rough with emotion when they came up for air. "When you said that, I felt like I'd finally found my way home."

"You have," she whispered.

Tossing his head and stamping a hoof, Apollo stared back at them, impatience evident in every fiber. They both laughed. Prentis picked up the reins, and Apollo trotted up the road again. Prentis slipped his hand into Avery's, and she wrapped both her hands around his.

Eventually, they headed home, Apollo having worn himself out, the picnic lunch having been consumed, and the sun falling toward the horizon. After helping her out of the buggy, Prentis pulled away. Right before he disappeared, he waved his hat, one last farewell.

Even though he could see her no longer, she waved back.

She missed him when he was gone. He was worth any misgivings Mrs. Alfonse Riley or anyone else might have about her decision to marry him.

* * * *

On Tuesday, Prentis woke to a steady rain. Nevertheless, he herded his steers into Wakita and onto the train by seven. In the process, Ulysses injured himself, straining a leg and pulling off a shoe in the mud. Leaving the gelding at the livery, Prentis rode in the cattle car with the steers, since he was wet and covered in mud from head to toe.

The rain poured down, a steady unrelenting torrent. After making the sodden trip to the sales barn, all the mud-caked cattlemen crowded together for the auction, commiserating with one another, taking the edge off by joking about the conditions.

Prentis's steers sold for $1,533.72. Since he'd paid $660 for the lot, he'd made a profit of $7.33 per head after deducting all his costs, an increase of 20 percent from last year. Cattle prices remained high. That gave him $87.96 of pure profit—the equivalent of two free heifers.

He planned to buy those heifers in late May, so they could

produce his own young steers next year. Since it was obvious he'd have to obtain a mortgage, he intended to pay it off with all these farming enterprises. He was determined to leave Avery's savings untouched, but he was full of love and gratitude that she had offered it.

When he returned to Wakita, Ulysses had been reshod. Prentis could have done it himself at home, but he couldn't have his horse travel like that. Unable to ride because of Ulysses's strained leg, he gripped the horse by the halter and walked him home. It took them a while to cover the four miles in the slippery mud and drizzle.

Prentis's boots grew heavier and heavier as mud caked onto them. Water dripped off his hat—*drop, drop, drop*—the entire way. Even with his collar turned up, cold rainwater trickled down his neck, soon soaking all his clothes clean through.

The day had been miserable from dawn to dusk.

Washing off on the back porch before he stepped inside, he discovered there was even mud in his ears. After he had stoked the stove blazing hot, it still took him all evening to warm up. The following day he developed a bad chest cold. The rain continued to fall, day after day. He tried to stay in the house as much as he could, not feeling well at all.

Sitting down to write Avery at week's end, he purposed not to complain. He had to read his Bible and pray before he could write a word.

April 17, 1914

Love of my life,

I hope you and Mrs. Riley can reconcile and that you are at peace. I'm grieved about the situation but appreciate all you said about my faith and your growth. You encourage me, and I can't wait to make you mine.

Everything is already sprouting in the garden, including the flats of our future plantings. Rain is good. I just read Psalm 65 to remind myself of that fact. I'm disappointed that I won't be able to see you this weekend; but God is God, and He's in control of the weather.

I sold the steers on Tuesday and made a nice profit—sale prices were high. Even though I have to obtain a mortgage, we'll pay it off with all our business enterprises. Thank you for offering your savings; but, Avery, that money should be spent on you. Your kind generosity touches me—how I love you!

I'm sitting in front of the fire with my feet up as I write—nice and dry, thinking of kissing you in the buggy, such a precious memory! Soon you'll be mine, and I can kiss you all I want. I'm studying the end of Colossians 3 now, warnings to husbands not to be harsh with their wives. I beg God I may never be so to you. I'm thinking of you and missing you desperately.

With all my heart,

Prentis

The rest of April was soggy; even the mail was delayed. There were no visits, but there were letters sent both ways. They missed one another. Prentis kept Avery apprised of life on the farm: his work, the wheat, the garden, Ulysses's leg, and the lonely bull—now the only head of cattle. Similarly, her letters informed him of her days and her efforts to restore warmth and good fellowship between Mrs. Riley and herself.

Though Prentis had done some earthwork with the plow, hoping to forestall the flooding, still the creek overflowed across the farm's northwestern corner, ruining three to four acres of wheat—all stood underwater. The hilltop with the barn and the house now formed a peninsula at that end of his land. The rest of the farm stood high enough that it wasn't affected. Short of a colossal dam project, he couldn't discern any way to contain the creek during wet springs.

He gave the lost wheat into God's hands. There was nothing he could do about it.

Two-thirds of his land remained in prairie grass for the livestock; one-third was planted in wheat. He broke up some virgin prairie on the back forty, so he'd have more acreage to sow on higher ground in the fall. The work was hard going. It was easier to bust up sod while the ground was soft; but having to stop and scrape mud from the plow, clean the horses' hooves, and check their horseshoes frequently slowed everything and made for mucky work.

It seemed to Prentis that he had spent most of this year caked in mud, traveling in mud, working in mud, planning for mud, and trying to overcome mud. He felt worn down. In the past, mud hadn't bothered him. But now that it was keeping him from Avery, it seemed an obstacle, rather than the blessing of moisture for his crops and water for his well. Even with Sam's company, he was lonely, longing for this wet weather to ease up. Moment by moment, he leaned on Jesus, trying to yield his own desires, so he could submit to God's plan.

By the end of the month, the mares all came into season, one after another. Prentis initiated Apollo into his new position as absolute sovereign of the realm. Though inexperienced, the stallion did his job well, and the mares cooperated. In a human way, this work with the horses was unsettling. He needed to be married, the sooner the better. He couldn't write Avery the particulars—it wouldn't be proper, but he wrote that he hoped all the mares were in foal.

* * * *

May brought the sun, the flowers, and the wheat growing taller; but it took another week to dry out the roads. After this long wait, Ulysses's leg had healed, but Prentis didn't trust it yet. Longing to see Avery, the first day the roads were passable he rode up on his dun gelding.

As he trotted north, adjusting to Hector's gait and habits, Prentis considered his penchant for mythological names. Heroes from both sides of the battle at Troy were represented. Additionally, his young mares were named Persephone, Calypso, and Penelope. These names were more intriguing than Daisy's and Mabel's, who had been named by his mother. When he'd left near the end of his first year of high school, his class in Kingman had just finished *The Iliad* and *The Odyssey*, after studying ancient history that year. Prentis had begun Latin. And then, his father had died. He still longed for the learning he'd missed—he read as much as he could in the evenings.

Preferring Ulysses, he hadn't had Hector out for a while, so they rode hard.

It was Friday afternoon, rather than the usual Sunday visit. Prentis wanted to surprise Avery at the schoolhouse; he felt desperate to see her. He didn't know if the weather would hold, so he made the trip today. There was only one week of school left, so he knew Avery would never expect him. After arriving, he tied Hector to the rail and stepped inside.

Laughter and the sound of young people giving encouragement to one another accompanied the rapid squeak of chalk. With all of that, she probably hadn't heard him come in. Quietly, he slipped into the back, took off his hat, and tried to smooth his hair—a hopeless cause. With his fingertips he felt the indented ridge left by the Stetson's band.

Textbook open before her, Avery faced the chalkboard, sitting in one of the front student desks. Two older students stood at the board, racing to complete a math problem. Bunched on opposite sides of the room, the rest were divided, crowded into desks together creating a clearer demarcation between the two sides than merely the center aisle. The youngest students stood at their desks jumping up and down, Howard bobbing among them. Excited, the students cheered and encouraged their teammates.

Two underlined names were written on the board: *Dorothy* and *Bill*. Under those names, tallies noted the winner of each match, mark after mark chronicling each victory. Dorothy Aves and Billy Cink, apparently now going by "Bill," worked furiously at the board, captains of their teams, which were tied at the moment. These were the oldest students. Whoever won the race to complete this particular math problem would win the contest for their team.

Bill slammed down his chalk and turned, arms held high. His team erupted into cheers. Dorothy finished a second or two later, turning dejectedly. Her team moaned. But wait! Their answers differed. Which was correct? They stepped away from the board so Avery could evaluate their work. Proudly, Prentis watched her calculating in her head. She commanded the room with ease. It was obvious all her students adored and respected her.

"Bill, you've done it!" she said. "Congratulations to you and your team."

Bill's team cheered again. Groaning at their loss, the other side slumped onto their desks.

"Dorothy." Avery circled one part of the computation. "Here's your error."

"Oh, Miss Slaughter, I know how to do that. I let my nerves get the better of me."

"That's what I reckoned. I'm certain you know how to do this. You're usually perfect with your figures. It's difficult to complete computations with a room full of people screaming at you, isn't it?"

Dorothy nodded.

Avery turned to face the room, catching sight of Prentis and smiling widely, her cheeks pinking. His arrival had indeed surprised her. Turning simultaneously, the students stared at him. The boys all grinned, especially Howard, Gene, and Abe. The girls all whispered to one another. He heard someone say, "Teacher's beau."

"No, her fiancé," another said.

"Students," Avery said, her eyes still fixed on Prentis's, "you've done an excellent job with your mathematics this spring.

I'm so proud of you. Everyone tidy up around you and then class is dismissed. I hope you have a wonderful weekend! I'll see you on Monday."

All jumped from their seats and got to work. Then they filed past Prentis, the girls shyly and the boys deferentially, as if they marveled at his achievement—he had courted the teacher, and he had won. The boys thought he'd done a mighty fine job. Inwardly, he chuckled at their clannish male pride in his monumental feat.

Abe stopped and asked if he should take home Avery's horse. Prentis answered in the affirmative; Abe grinned and headed out the door. Prentis tousled Howard's hair as he passed and patted Gene on the shoulder. Both smiled and went on out; they'd see him at the house.

Avery stood at the front, smiling at him. He walked up and embraced her.

"How's the prettiest schoolteacher in Oklahoma?"

"I'm not sure who that would be, but I'm doing fine."

He laughed. "I about burst with pride watching you manage those students, Avery. You're a superb teacher. The boys all looked at me with admiration because I'd won you. I think each woman they meet from here on out will be measured by you to see how she stacks up."

Avery looked at her boots. "Well, thank you, Prentis. Can you come home to eat?"

"I can."

* * * *

Thrilled that he'd come, Avery gathered her books and slung her bag over her shoulder, tidying here and there as they left the building. After locking up, she looked about for Frisky.

"I've lost my horse," she said.

"Abe took her."

"How am I . . ." She stopped short. "We're both riding your horse, aren't we?"

"We are. That is, if you don't mind. If you do, I'll walk, and you can ride."

"I don't mind," she said softly, trying to keep from blushing.

She appraised the dun gelding. They'd never been officially

introduced. Male horses—geldings or stallions—made her nervous; she preferred mares.

"This is Hector."

"Another mythical name." She caressed the horse's soft, silky muzzle.

"So it would seem."

Prentis swung himself into the saddle and extended his hand. Grasping it, she planted her foot in the stirrup, and he hoisted her up to sit sidesaddle in front of him. Wrapping his arms closely about her, reins in hand, he directed Hector away from the schoolhouse.

"I ran this horse hard all the way, just so he'd be patient from here to your house. Hope you don't mind me grabbing the opportunity to hold you in my arms today. I've missed you so badly, and it could rain again tomorrow. I need you close to me today."

After that confession, she didn't trust her powers of speech. Feeling the solidness of his workingman's arms and shoulders, she leaned against him.

"This looks to be a most pleasant, but woefully short trip," he said.

"The neighbors might gossip."

"They might. But we're engaged to be married, we're on a public road, and we're only traveling three-quarters of a mile. We live to please God and to keep from offending our neighbors within reason. As an engaged man, I'd say it's reasonable to long to hold you after a month's absence."

"It is. But remember, the Rileys live nearby and may pass us."

Both twisted in the saddle, surveying the dirt road in all directions.

"No one coming for miles," he said. "Should I walk, just in case?"

"No, I think you can safely stay where you are. The fact remains that we're to be married. That seems to be the main offense, not riding with you on your horse today. She doesn't think I should marry a man who doesn't attend church, whether he's a believer or not."

"Did she say that?"

"Indeed, she did."

"So, no peace has been restored?"

"We're cordial."

"What about Alf?"

"He remains silent on the subject. I'll simply keep trying to mend things."

Prentis sighed, his breath lightly caressing her neck and face. Recalling the taste of his mouth, she was glad the ride was short or this could get out of hand. Her heart pounded as he pulled her closer. Each time she glanced at him, his eyes fixed on hers, filled with longing.

"So," he said loudly, seeming to realize all of this at the same moment, "tell me how school is wrapping up."

Taking a deep breath, she detailed the students' accomplishments. Each had achieved more than she had dreamed or hoped. She would close out her career at this school with satisfaction.

"Next year I won't teach down there," she said. "School boards are reluctant to hire newly-married women because the arrival of a baby might upset the school term. It's frustrating, but I want to devote all my energy to being your wife, so all is well."

"Any school board would be fortunate to have you, married or not. But I have to admit I'll be glad you're there with me."

"I want to help you."

"It will be a gift from God having your cooking to eat and your voice to listen to. When coupled with the joy of having you by my side, night and day, I'll be ecstatic. Having you there with me, rather than miles away, will be like heaven on earth."

"It will be to me as well."

She looked into his eyes. Clearly, there was more he wanted to say. It had been a long absence, and it was obvious his emotions were strong today. His gaze was piercing.

"Avery, you've done an excellent job with all your students, especially that wild young man Billy Cink."

Prentis had aimed toward safer ground once more; she smiled at the direction he'd gone. "You may have noticed that I'm partial to boys, having a tribe of brothers at home. I hope we have six boys of our own."

He laughed soundly. "So do I! More hands to help me out."

Carrying his two-person cargo, Hector walked into the farmyard. Her daddy stepped out to greet them and helped her down before Prentis dismounted.

"Mr. Slaughter," Prentis said. "Do you mind if I consult you about the heifers? I'm going up to Anthony next week, rain or shine. Can we talk in the barn?"

"Glad to. Momma needs your help in the house, Avery. We'll be up shortly."

Quite a while later, Daddy, Prentis, and all the boys came in for supper, the heifers having been thoroughly discussed. All enjoyed a pleasant meal with lots of laughter. But as they stepped out the back door to retrieve Prentis's horse, they sighted thick dark clouds towering on the southwest horizon—more rain. Quickly, Prentis saddled Hector.

"Pray for me, Avery. A farmer has to accept the weather—it's God's handiwork. But it's keeping me from you and eating away my profits when I need the cash. My creek flooded."

"Is it bad?"

"Lost a few acres of wheat. Don't want to grumble. That's like telling the Lord He doesn't know what He's doing. All of this is meant to teach me character and to develop patience. God has a reason that's for my good. I need to study James Chapter 1 this spring."

"All right, I'll join you, now that we're done with Colossians."

"Let's do that. Kiss me so I can get on this horse—I'm racing the rain. How I'll miss you! Don't know when we'll see each other next."

Embracing her, he grabbed her up, lifting her off her feet. Tired of the waiting herself, she drew his face close, kissing him ardently. Though he had to leave, his need for her seemed to overpower his sense of time. One kiss followed another, each more urgent and impassioned. He packed a wet-winter-and-spring's worth of longing into those kisses. It would be a good day when they were wed. Eventually, he put her down and swung up onto his horse.

Wheeling Hector around, he leaned to caress her cheek. "I love you with all my heart."

"As I love you."

Leaning forward in the saddle, he laid his heels to Hector's sides, and the horse took off fast. In the southwest, lightning crackled. She hoped he arrived home without getting too wet.

* * * *

On Monday, a letter arrived with the address scrawled across the envelope. The handwriting on the inside was barely decipherable. He had written with emotion.

May 23, 1914

Beautiful Avery,

I made it home in the pouring rain. If this spring rain were falling next year, I'd be perfectly content to watch the water wash the earth, day after day. You and I would stay in the house and occupy our time with kisses. Then, it could rain all it wanted, and I'd be a perfectly content man. When I'm your husband, a rainy day spent with you in this house will make me the happiest man on God's green earth; and that, my precious girl, is a fact. It's time for me to sit down and read the book of James.

I love you,

Prentis

SEVENTEEN

ON TUESDAY, MR. SLAUGHTER, Floyd, Jerry, and John joined Prentis on the train as it went north through Gibbon. At the weekly livestock sale in Anthony, Prentis would finally purchase his heifers. Both he and Floyd were starting their herds, so they would be looking at fourteen-to fifteen-month-old heifers to breed immediately.

When he sold the steers, Prentis had placed his annual expenses in savings. Now he would spend the remainder on young heifers. His goal was to breed the heifers and then keep them reproducing every year, putting Rex back in with the cows within two to three months after the calves were delivered. During the powwow in the Slaughter's barn the previous week, this had been the group consensus concerning peak productivity.

Surveying the livestock, they all leaned comfortably on the rail. Attempting to ascertain which heifers they should purchase, their group moved as one from pen to pen, voices low to conceal their observations and hats adjusted to shield their eyes. They didn't want any observers to discern which cattle they considered. Subtly, Floyd gestured with his chin, indicating other cattlemen lurking nearby. Prentis panned the room, flicking his eyes over these lurkers, who were obviously trying to determine which stock they had chosen.

Unobtrusively, their group all moseyed to the next pen before he made quiet comments, casually looking over his shoulder first. They sought quality heifers with broad, deep, square bodies and a good coating of flesh. These they would hold onto, guarding their herds from disease. Finally, they found exactly what they wanted and made their choice, ambling among the pens again to conceal their preference—it would become obvious soon enough.

Both Prentis and Floyd would try for heifers from the same lot, but they had second and third choices. They set their absolute limit at $50 a head. This would keep the profit margin right, if any proved to be poor breeders. Any poor breeders would be sold later as beef cattle.

Prentis's one hundred acres in grass could support twenty head of cattle with no additional feed. But he had to start with the financial resources he had, building from there. The mortgage had been secured in Wakita; he'd borrowed $800 of the $2,800 needed to purchase the farm. On his person, he had a check from the Citizens Bank of Wakita made out to his mother for the total. Fred was meeting them today and would deliver the check back to her. Safely in the bank, the year's expenses sat gathering interest, but the remaining cash nestled in his wallet.

If he got his heifers for $50 a head, he could purchase fifteen—the exact number fifteen-month-old Rex could service. Building his herd would require persistence and patience. To raise more cattle, he would need to add more acreage, buy extra feed, or grow and harvest his own.

The sale went as hoped; Floyd and Prentis each got exactly what they wanted for only $45 a head. Keeping their joy in check, they cast one another furtive sidelong glances, maintaining stony faces as they paid up, finally smiling when the transactions were complete. Fred arrived for the closing of the sale, congratulating them on their choice of livestock and then receiving the check for the Oklahoma land. It had been a day of financial transactions.

After eating at the nearby café, they loaded the heifers, always chaotic with panicked cattle, bawling and confused, stumbling up the narrow chutes into the cattle cars through hay dust and fresh manure. To familiarize the livestock with their faces and voices, Prentis and Floyd rode with them. They would serve as the doctors and midwives of their new animals.

At Gibbon, all the Slaughters except Jerry disembarked to help Floyd. Jerry joined Prentis in the cattle car and rode on down to Wakita. Prentis was glad for his help; Jerry would borrow Hector for the trip home. The two men got the skittish heifers home. With Sam's help, they herded them into the corral to put Prentis's brand on them.

The ground was still damp from the weekend's rainfall, so it had been a long, muddy day. There hadn't been time for Prentis to jot a note to Avery, so he asked Jerry to tell her about the sale and to convey his love. Since Jerry was in love with Dorothy, he understood the significance of this message. From inside his jacket, he pulled a thin flat package and handed it to Prentis.

"Avery said to give you this when I left." He patted Prentis on the shoulder and smiled.

After Jerry rode away, Prentis washed on the back porch then carried the small package into the house. Standing by the west-facing bedroom window to catch the fading sunlight, he ripped off the brown paper and slid out a paper-mat folder. When he opened it, there was a photograph of Avery, casting him a sidelong glance, sporting a mysterious and mischievous expression. Some sort of secret joy gleamed in her black eyes. She was so beautiful!

Gently, he ran his thumb over her face, as if to caress her through the photograph. Fastening his eyes on her, he carried her into the living room and set her beside his chair, flopping down to consider her countenance. How he loved her! For quite a while, he sat gazing at her.

Thank you, God! You're so kind to me.

Later he set her on the table and studied her while eating the food left from breakfast. He'd been subsisting on pancakes, bacon, cheese, and anything ripe in the garden. While he washed the dishes, he set her on the window ledge, glancing at her often. Then he carried her back to the table by his chair, lit the lamp, and tried to read. He couldn't focus.

When he went to bed, he set her on the bedside table and gazed at her by moonlight, attempting to fall asleep. He was overwhelmed with gratitude for the photograph, but looking at her made him restless. He couldn't sleep, so he carried her out to his desk, lit the lamp, and wrote a quick letter.

May 27, 1914, the wee morning hours

Beloved Avery,

Thank you, dearest one. I appreciate your thoughtful gesture of having a professional photograph made, wrapping it, and sending it down with Jerry, just for me. You're such a lovely woman!

I carried you about the house all evening, from table to kitchen to chair to bed—you watched me in the moonlight. For staring at your face, I couldn't sleep at all. How I wished it were really you! I had to get out of bed to tell you so. You're now watching me as I write.

I'll be glad when your precious person, and not just your photograph, is here with me. Being able to see your face makes the waiting easier. And yet, it also makes it more wrenching and difficult. There you are, looking at me; I wish with all my heart that it were actually you. I'd be holding you in my arms right now.

How I love you!

Prentis

At last, sometime around the middle of the night, Prentis drifted off to sleep.

* * * *

As May gave way to June, sunny day followed sunny day. The weather returned to a normal pattern for northern Oklahoma. The wheat and the garden flourished after all the winter and spring moisture. Every evening, Prentis stopped by the garden, pulled the weeds, and picked whatever was ripe, eating it raw as he walked into the house.

Rex was put to pasture with the new heifers. In a couple of weeks, Prentis would take him out to rest, and then, back in he'd go. This would be the pattern until July, ensuring that Rex got the job done, producing a calving season from late February through March, as they'd always done at home. While Rex completed his procreative duties, Prentis readied the granary and equipment for the coming harvest and continued his work on the newly broken sod.

Avery wrote that she and Mrs. Slaughter were sewing everything needed for housekeeping, having purchased whole bolts of cloth for sheets, pillowcases, curtains, hand towels, and tablecloths. Avery had set aside her studies, and she thought of him as she embroidered lovely designs on their linens. It filled Prentis with contentment to think of her meditating on him.

While they waited for the wheat to ripen, visits occurred every Sunday. In the buggy, they engaged in long rides and an abundance of kissing. Winter and spring had been filled with the longing of absence, the frustration of muddy roads, and the frenzy of crowding all their talking and affection into the rare Sunday afternoon that the roads were good. But summer provided more time alone together, days extended especially for those in love, it seemed. Warm weather provided a different type of challenge.

Occasionally, Prentis parked the buggy under a tree or on a wooden bridge, and they perfected the newly discovered art of kissing. When he came in the buggy, he drove Apollo. The stallion's impatience guarded against romantic passion getting out of hand. The horse was a Godsend. On one such day, Apollo started down the road without Prentis's cognizance. The taste of Avery's lips and her reciprocating desire absorbed him, until he sensed the buggy's forward motion. Quickly, he released Avery, gave her one last kiss and grabbed the reins. Duly chastened,

Prentis glanced over at Avery, and they both laughed—saved by the horse again.

"I don't think I should come up in the buggy anymore," he said.

Laughing, she straightened her hair, tucking in an errant hairpin here and there. "I think you're right. I could kiss you all day. We'd better stay out of the buggy."

"Didn't know I could love anyone as much as I love you—it's practically overpowering."

"I feel the same."

When they planned to stay safely on solid ground and avoid the buggy, Prentis rode Ulysses or Hector. Sometimes they took Howard along on picnics as a chaperone. He had no idea why he'd been invited; he thought they were awfully nice to take him. For long walks, they held hands and talked non-stop, all alone, just the two of them with God.

They reminded each other often that God was always present, watching all they did. They shouldn't have needed Apollo's impatience to bring that remembrance to mind, but they were glad they had it. They were both on the jagged edge as spring gave way to summer. With time on their hands, waiting for the wheat to ripen intensified their longing for one another.

* * * *

As they awaited harvest, a three-sentence news item on page three of *The Daily Oklahoman* informed them that a Serbian nationalist in Sarajevo had assassinated an Austrian Archduke and his wife on June 28. Prentis gave it a cursory glance; it didn't appear in *The Wakita Herald* at all. But a week later, all of Europe was taking sides.

Austria-Hungary threatened war with Serbia—this made the front page, a one-inch-square tersely worded news feature. Prentis read it, knowing he wouldn't have much time for the paper over the next month. It appeared to be simply another European war, a regional conflict, something to ponder later.

At any rate, it didn't have anything to do with them. It was time to harvest. While he waited on his own wheat, Prentis headed south to help out as harvest began in the Sand Hills.

Watching the grain come in, he hoped for his best yield yet.

EIGHTEEN

FIELD AFTER FIELD AROUND Wakita and Gibbon finally came ripe during that first week of July. None of the pioneer farmers remembered it ever being delayed so long. The heads of wheat drooped, heavy with grain, and the kernels crunched when chewed—dry, but not too dry. Nothing equaled a ripe kernel of wheat, nutty and wholesome, tasting like sunshine itself.

Prentis took his sample to the grain elevator to be tested. It was time! The golden wheat stood abundant. It would be a good return. He expected much more than ten to twelve bushels per acre, the usual result of a dry winter. He hoped and prayed for more, perhaps fifteen. He'd been getting ninety cents a bushel for the last few years.

Maybe he could pay off that mortgage—recompense for the agony of being separated from Avery by all the snow and rain. But on the plains of Oklahoma, anything could happen, therefore everyone hurried to get the wheat cut and safely into storage. They harvested in order of ripening. Providentially, Prentis's wheat came ripe at the same time as Floyd's.

Meeting on Sunday, they divided forces to harvest the two young farmers' fields. After their wheat was in, Floyd and Prentis would help reap the parental crops. Avery and Mrs. Slaughter would feed the southern crew of hungry men at Prentis's farm, Hattie and her mother the northern. Both young women would help Mrs. Slaughter at home. It would take about a month to reap all three farms. They'd finish by the end of July, way behind the usual schedule.

When Prentis heard the Model T chugging toward his farm at sunrise on Monday, he bounded out of the house, brimming with excitement. This was when all his work paid off. He was anxious to get the wheat out of the field and into his granary.

Avery, Mrs. Slaughter, and Howard exited the automobile. Gene, Abe, and John arrived behind them on horseback, having started earlier. Sam ran circles around the entire crowd, barking and wagging his welcome. Exuberant, Prentis grabbed up Avery, squeezing her tightly.

"Good morning, Avery! Hello, Mrs. Slaughter! Thank you for coming."

Smiling, Mrs. Slaughter nodded.

Avery laughed as Prentis set her back on her feet.

"Howdy, Prentisss," Howard lisped.

Noticing a gap in Howard's smile, Prentis grinned. "I see you're missing a tooth, Howard."

"Yep. Sure am. Gene pulled it out with a string tied to the door. Slam! There it went."

They all laughed at his account.

"We're happy to be here, Prentis," Avery said, still chuckling. "I hope we can keep up with you men. Did you receive the supply list I mailed you?"

"I did. Everything's in the house."

"Good. We brought some things we prepared beforehand. Can you help us?"

"Absolutely."

* * * *

Avery leaned into the auto, sorting through the bundles, and then directing Prentis to the heaviest parcels. Each carried a wooden box containing food items or cooking utensils—full crates of supplies. They made several trips. Bringing all his little hands could hold Howard helped. The poultry clucked nervously, peering through the crate's chicken wire; Prentis carried the small coop behind the house, depositing it in the shade.

Stepping into the kitchen, Avery found everything she had specified: a large smoked ham; huge bags of flour, sugar, and potatoes; piles of fresh beets from their garden; butter; eggs; canning supplies; and two empty bushel baskets for Gene and Howard to fill with green beans from the garden. She smiled at Prentis. He'd been thorough.

Sam's welcoming bark sounded as a wagon rolled into the yard. Prentis gave her a quick kiss. Then taking Howard and Gene with him, he headed out to greet the neighbors who had come to help. Out in the yard, she heard one after another return his greeting.

"Pink! Good day for cutting grain."

Or "P.J.! Bet you're glad to get going—it's finally your turn."

Or "Pink, how much yield do you think you'll get?"

Or "Let's hope and pray the weather holds, P.J."

His neighbors thought highly of him; she detected it in their voices and the warmth of their greetings. Peering out the window, she observed each one shake Prentis's hand heartily, some patting him on the back, happy to help him. Avery felt glad to help him, too.

In the cookstove, Prentis already had a fire going nice and low. Momma put in the ham as Avery mixed the dough for the rolls. They would need dozens for each meal. After setting it to rise, she opened the rest of the windows. It was hot in here with the cookstove, and she preferred houseflies to stifling heat.

When she stepped into the bedroom for the first time, she noticed her photograph sitting beside Prentis's neatly made bed. As she raised the windows, she smiled to think of him looking at her face as he fell asleep. His letter about the photograph had touched her heart.

The summertime waiting had been difficult. As she sewed clothing, linens, and household items, she mooned over him, meditating on the kindness of his eyes, the sound of his voice, the ardor of his kisses, and his articulated viewpoints, thoughts, and preferences. During the school year, her mind had been occupied. But now with only sewing to contemplate, she thought of him constantly.

Avery was delighted that she'd see his face each day. Harvest presented a different type of labor than bending over sewing. While Prentis and his hardworking Oklahoma neighbors merged their horsepower and human muscle to cut all the grain southwest of Wakita, she and her mother organized for the assault on their appetites.

* * * *

Out in the barnyard, Prentis introduced the Slaughter boys to his neighbors. They shook hands and chatted, everyone excited, waiting for George Miller to arrive with the binder and the thresher. Prentis had decided to rent the two machines from the Millers, a more economical choice than buying his own equipment.

Here came Mr. Miller, pulling into the barnyard on his tractor hauling the enormous thresher. His son followed, pulling the binder hitched to four horses. Now the fun would begin! Prentis sent Howard and Gene back into the house to help Avery.

After Prentis explained his proposed strategy to the Millers, they all worked together to hitch the sixteen assembled horses to the binder. Everyone had ridden the horses they intended for Prentis to use. One by one, the farm horses stepped into harness, producing moments of disorder and loud neighing complaints. Their combined power would pull the machine through the wheat—more horses, more horsepower. Ulysses and Hector cooperated; but some of the other horses weren't too keen on being hitched with the unfamiliar of their species.

Once all the horses were harnessed together, the younger Miller drove them out into the field Prentis indicated. The cradle that lifted the grain before it was severed close to the ground was positioned off to the right of the binder. This offsetting prevented the wheat from being trampled on by the mass of horseflesh pulling the machine. The binder cut the wheat and bound it into bundles, which came sliding off the conveyor, landing on the ground.

John Slaughter drove two of Prentis's mares, pulling the farm wagon slowly along behind the binder; Abe stood on the wagon bed, ready and waiting. On foot, the rest of the men followed the binder, using pitchforks to toss the bound wheat up onto the wagon, rather than propping them up into shocks—they intended to thresh immediately. Abe repositioned the wheat bundles as they came sailing into the wagon, keeping them orderly for easier transportation. With the binding started, Prentis hurried back to direct Mr. Miller, so the thresher could be positioned.

The thresher was always placed in one central location. Once set up for harvest on a farm, it wasn't moved, and so Prentis had considered carefully what site would be best. He pointed toward the north side of the barn, and George Miller's tractor pulled the heavy piece of machinery that direction. Once Mr. Miller had it in place, he jumped down to connect the thresher's flywheel to his tractor with a thick belt about twenty feet long. They would run the wheat through this machine. Wheat kernels would separate from chaff and stalks, which would fly out behind the machine forming a large pile of straw. Prentis would use it in the barn stalls, making this a prime location. During the winter, the straw pile would also provide insulation from northern winds for the stock kept in the barn.

Turning to head back toward the wheat field, Prentis spotted Avery watching from the porch. With her scientific mind, she had always loved studying the machinery. He knew she found it intriguing. Of course, she would be outside scrutinizing the set-up. He smiled and waved.

She smiled widely and returned his gesture. Prentis spent the morning circulating back and forth, but he didn't glimpse her again. Her hands were full in that hot kitchen. He felt blessed by the assistance of his future wife and her family.

By late morning, the first wagonload of wheat was ready to be threshed. He had hoped the southern wind would blow the chaff free, but as they ran the shocks of wheat through the thresher, the hot prairie wind propelled itchy bits of straw under collars and down shirts. Gradually, the men grew filthier. When they removed their Stetsons to wipe their brows, a ring of clean white skin stood above each man's hatband in sharp contrast to their darkened, dust-covered faces.

The wheat kernels poured out the spout on top, flowing right into the wagon to be hauled to Prentis's granary and shoveled in. The price was going up, so he stored the wheat here on his farm. He would take his grain to the elevator in Wakita when he was ready to sell.

At high noon, Minnie Slaughter stepped out onto his porch and clanged her triangular dinner bell. Prentis heard it over the tractor's engine and signaled George Miller, who cut the motor. All the men from field and barn trudged toward the house, pausing at the barnyard pump to wash up. Thanking each man as he walked toward the house, Prentis shook hands with every one.

As Prentis came through his front door at the end of the line, Avery's wide smile heartened him. She dished up food and poured tea. He kissed her as he stepped up to the counter.

"Your smiling face makes this all worthwhile," he said.

"Why, thank you, Prentis! I'm glad I can help. I hope you like the meal."

"I will." He grinned at her.

Avery loaded his plate with baked ham, buttery mashed potatoes, sliced beets, hot rolls, and cherry pie. He kissed her forehead before heading out the back door to sit in the shade with his obliging neighbors. They chatted comfortably, Howard and Gene among them, eating with gusto and enjoying the camaraderie of the men and their big brothers.

The food strengthened them all for the afternoon.

Behind him in the house, he heard Mrs. Slaughter and Avery washing the dishes. After cleaning up, they would prepare for the second meal. When the late-afternoon meal had been served, they would make pies and cakes for the following day. Somewhere in there, they intended to do his canning; full bushel baskets of green beans now awaited their efforts, picked by Howard and Gene this morning.

When they harvested the far end of the fields, Avery and her mother would load the food onto the wagon and drive it out to them. When the men worked near the house, they would array the food along the countertop ledge as they had done today.

This became the rhythm of the first week of harvest. They all worked hard.

* * * *

Everyone paused for church on Sunday morning except Prentis, who had informed Avery of his intention to sleep late, rest, and read his Bible. Rest was why God had established the Sabbath, he had reminded her. Attempting not to doze off in the pew, Avery envied him his sleep. Maybe flexibility was in order. When they returned home she needed to nap, lest one of her headaches debilitate her.

The following day, the harvest went well, but as twilight approached, dark clouds piled up along the southwest horizon, threatening as they drew nearer. The other men had already headed home, and it was time for Avery and her mother to depart. Avery found Prentis behind the barn, facing the coming storm. Lightening flashed in the distance. As she walked up beside him, he didn't turn but kept his eyes focused on the weather.

"I may lose the rest," he said quietly.

What could she say? God was sovereign over nature. "Let's pray you don't. Good and loving God of the universe, please spare Prentis's wheat. And if You don't, if You know it's somehow best for him to suffer loss, help us to bear it and to accept Your will."

Kissing the top of her head, he pulled her close. "Amen," he said quietly.

It was hard to drive away, but they needed to return home.

Avery tossed and turned most of the night. When she dozed off, dark storms and Prentis's face filled her dreams. No hail swept across her family's farm in the night, but it was twelve miles distant. Maybe Prentis's farm had also been spared. Long before sunrise, she woke her mother, begging to leave early.

When they arrived, all was still, the house dark. As the Model T chugged past the house, Prentis loomed up in the headlights, emerging from the nearest pen. In the sharp shadows cast by the light, Avery couldn't discern his expression. When she parked, he opened the automobile door and pulled her into his arms. Leaving the two of them to deal with this together, her momma turned and walked toward the house to wake the boys and cook breakfast.

"Glad to see you." Prentis held her tightly. "I'm riding out to see what's left."

"Did it hit the wheat?"

"Missed the house and the nearest fields. In the darkness, I couldn't tell—maybe it passed us by. It would comfort me to have you along. Will you come?"

"Of course."

Walking silently through the darkness, they headed for the barn, hand in hand. The first singing of the birds was ending, and it was still pitch black, at least to the human eye. Prentis was deep in thought. Meaningless chatter didn't seem appropriate, so Avery walked along silently. In her head she begged God to hold him up.

After he'd saddled Ulysses and opened the gate, he drew her up into his lap and wrapped his arms tightly about her. As they crossed the newly harvested fields, they didn't speak. There were no words. Sensitive to their mood, Sam trotted quietly alongside.

Avery was glad to see that about two-thirds of the wheat had already been cut. At least their loss wouldn't be total, if the hail had damaged his fields. A faint light glowed on the horizon now, and she detected the uncut wheat ahead, dark in the distance. She squinted. It was impossible to tell. But, as the sky gradually brightened, she realized the sea of wheat was no longer uniform— something was amiss. Prentis pulled back on the reins.

"Let's stop here," he said. "Can you wait with Ulysses?"

"Yes. I'll wait here for you."

He swung down and then lifted her from the horse. Before turning to walk away, he caressed her cheek. The predawn light accentuated the dark circles under his eyes, giving his face a stark and ravaged appearance. She knew then that he hadn't slept either.

Each moment brought more light as he walked toward the wheat. In the distance she saw him pause then drop to his knees, arms heavy at his sides as he sank down upon the earth.

The sun cleared the horizon. The remaining wheat looked like a total loss.

Her heart ached for him. His head dropped, and he was motionless for a great while. Knowing him as she did, she knew he was yielding his wheat to God and attempting to align his will with His. Eventually he rose and walked about surveying the area, stooping to pick up a wheat head here or there, or squatting to poke at something in the damp soil. Then he returned.

"I'm so sorry, Prentis," she said, as soon as he was near.

"The Lord gave, and the Lord hath taken away; blessed be the name of the Lord."

"Amen. We'll get by."

"We will. Our crops are always in God's hands. Still, it was harder for me to praise Him than it should be. My heart was angry, and I needed to be alone with Him to talk it out. Can't judge God for what He's done."

His words challenged Avery. She considered the many times she'd argued with God about His will in a given situation. After they'd mounted Ulysses again, they rode slowly through the entire field. Most of the heads had been shattered and the grain pounded into the earth along with the chaff. The hail had been thick, about marble size by the pockmarks in the mud. Stalks were broken off or bent, with emptied or bruised wheat heads hanging.

"I'll plow it under," he said.

"It will enrich the soil."

"True. A blessing."

Quietly, they rode back, and Avery watched him address the sober-faced neighbors who gathered at his house awaiting the outcome. When he informed the men of his loss, everyone had encouraging words. Most patted him warmly on the back. Milling about together, they commiserated. Farmers all, they understood.

Then all mounted their horses or crawled onto their wagons and headed home.

Prentis's harvest was finished, so he and the boys wasted no time. After gobbling down breakfast, they headed north on horseback to help Floyd. Avery and her momma cleaned up and then followed them to her family's homestead.

After Floyd's wheat was cut, they reaped the home farm, racing the weather lest any additional wheat be lost. The yield was beyond their wildest hopes and dreams. Prentis and Floyd got eighteen bushels an acre—nearly double the yield of dry years, her daddy around fifteen. He told Avery he was going back to planting at the equinox, hang the scientific method. Given the outcome, she agreed.

Optimistic as usual, Prentis said the high yield gave him more than he usually got in a normal year. Never mentioning or bemoaning what could have been, he adjusted. Avery's love for him increased. Her respect for him grew ever higher.

This year's harvest-time discussions had been peppered with international news that affected the outcome for all. While they'd been cutting grain, Europe had gone to war. The Kaiser had sided with the Austrians, who had declared war on Serbia and Russia. The tragedy on European soil would allow them to export their farm products. It wasn't their fight, but the war might result in profit for the American farmer. The price of wheat currently stood at $1.05 a bushel. All of them had stored their wheat in granaries and barns to see if it went higher.

They might all get rich. They didn't want to be avaricious; it was merely a fact.

NINETEEN

DUE TO THE HIGH yield and the rising prices, Prentis would clear enough to proceed with the wedding. Avery felt such gratitude! Together they thanked God for the abundant harvest and the wheat they had gotten in before the hailstorm. God had taken care of them. Once Prentis had his fields plowed and disked for the fall planting, they could marry—he predicted early September.

However, before their wedding day, they still had much to do. August had arrived.

On the weekend, Prentis brought Avery two heaping bushel baskets of ripe vegetables. With Momma's help, she expended several hot days canning tomatoes, green beans, and pickled beets. After the last day of canning, a headache incapacitated her, making her sick to her stomach. Between the effects of the heat and the marriage preparation, there was no time in August for pressing forward with her theological studies. The entire summer had been devoid of study.

Down on his farm, Prentis had been eating the tomatoes right out of the garden like apples, adding variety to his bachelor meals. He told her that he'd left the beets alone because of the amount of time required to cook them. This explained their enormous size! Once the produce had been canned, he took the full quart-jars back home on the following weekend, adding them to the already-filled jars in the root cellar. They awaited Avery's domestic distribution.

That task completed, she attempted to finish the hand sewing on the wedding dress, each stitch bringing her closer to the blessed day. Momma helped as much as possible. Before either of them touched the fabric or lace, they scrubbed their hands and cleaned under their nails, lest any smudge or stain show on the spotless, white garment-in-the-making. They crocheted all the lace with delicate, white thread.

Hattie was a seamstress. She and Avery had designed the dress together—a mixture of Avery's girlhood dreams and designs from the ladies' books. Hattie had taken Avery's measurements before outlining the pattern pieces and pinning them carefully to the various fabrics. Then she had sliced decisively through the material with her sewing shears, ensuring all was perfect. Avery had relied on her.

When they started, Hattie had been large with her first child—the first grandbaby, Avery's first niece or nephew. It had been awkward and uncomfortable for Hattie to bend over the sewing machine. As long as she could maintain a comfortable position while treading the foot pedal and propelling the pieces of fabric under the rapidly bobbing needle, all had been well. Displaying perfect timing, baby Donald was born immediately after Hattie finished the machine sewing.

Everyone took a break to admire the precious baby. As Avery studied Donald's delicate fingers, silken newborn skin, and thick thatch of soft black hair, she couldn't wait to give birth to her own children—hopefully, six boys. Her fear of losing babies seemed to have been conquered. Watching Prentis hold the small bundle endeared him even more to her heart. Having had an infant sister as a young man, his baby-handling skills were expert.

Only the hand sewing remained on her dress. The handmade lace overlaid the white cotton-batiste dress. A ruffled lace collar and elbow-length sleeves completed the fully lined bodice. An eight-inch-wide, hand-tucked cummerbund encompassed Avery's tiny waist, the blouse full above it. Two white, batiste flowers would be set onto this waistband when it was complete.

A deep, lace-edged ruffle skirted the bottom. Underneath, crinoline made the dress full and formal, swishing when Avery walked, making apparent the festive and significant occasion.

Since Prentis wanted this dress for her, she hoped it would be all he anticipated. It remained tucked away in her room on the dress form, covered with a sheet when they weren't working on it. No one had seen it but the three women.

Everything else was complete in Avery's trousseau. Using her last paycheck for her final purchases, she drove to Anthony with Momma to purchase a silk nightgown, a corset of Grecian-Treco, and a sheer chemise and knickers to wear under the dress. She'd never owned anything like this new intimate apparel.

On the way home, Momma gave her "the talk"—explaining the particulars of the marital relationship. Being a farm girl and a teacher, Avery comprehended the mechanics of the matter, but Momma instructed her on a wife's obligations. In short, she was not to withhold herself from Prentis. The marital relationship was to be engaged in as often as her husband needed, regardless of her inclinations. This was Avery's, and every wife's, duty.

When Momma used the word "duty," Avery started laughing, thinking of Prentis's eyes when he kissed her and how she liked his kisses; she loved him completely. How could that ever be a mere duty? Driving down the road, she cast Momma a sidelong glance, and Momma joined in her laughter. Having borne twelve children, Momma clearly practiced what she preached. Loving a man like that had been Avery's dream. Soon it would be a reality.

* * * *

After harvest, Prentis plowed and disked the sixty acres he would plant at the equinox. Completing five to eight acres each day, he worked the land with his horses, the leather strap slung across his shoulder. Ulysses and Hector plodded ahead of him, straining in their harnesses. Wading through the soil's red richness as he wrestled with the plow, Prentis enjoyed watching the earth turn over—fresh and fertile. In September, he would use the spring-tooth harrow right before sowing the grain.

There had been no time for baseball *this* summer. In fact, baseball had seemed pretty insignificant of late. He hadn't thought of it or missed it. He dwelled, instead, mostly on Avery.

Intruding into his mind would come the look in her eyes right before he kissed her—the intensity of reciprocating desire in their depths and what the outcome of that desire would be. Eventually, he'd realize where his mind had wandered . . .

God knew he was trying.

This was the battle in the field and out of it. He strove to keep his thoughts pure, not wanting to taint their coming union by his imagining of it, guarding his actions as well. Coupled with this most difficult and dear temptation was worry about the war in Europe and the gradual realization of a faith lesson that God had been teaching him. His mind was its own war zone.

In Prentis's opinion, the German Kaiser had lost his mind when the Serbian zealot shot the Austrian-Hungarian Archduke and his wife. That act now toppled Europe into war. The Kaiser seemed to have been merely awaiting an opportunity—Germany had declared war on Russia, had invaded Luxembourg, and then had declared war on France.

The Brits had gone to France's aid and were now locked in a land battle with Germany. Canada, with its tie to Great Britain, now entered the war as their ally. Tens of thousands of French soldiers had been killed. Austria-Hungary had invaded Russian Poland. Meanwhile, Russia had invaded East Prussia, and the Japanese had declared war on Germany, attacking a German colony in China, obviously a land grab. All of this had happened in the two months since Prentis had begun harvesting his wheat.

As a peaceful man, this rush to war staggered him. Twice President Wilson had declared that the United States would remain neutral. This war had nothing to do with American citizens. Prentis had read all of this in *The Wakita Herald* and *The Daily Oklahoman*.

Neutral—that was the blessed word. His American citizenship filled him with joy; he thanked God for it. He could marry Avery. This didn't concern them. It wasn't the first time the Europeans couldn't get along, and it certainly wouldn't be the last. But thousands of people were losing their lives as all of Europe went mad. Young men beginning their lives—in love exactly as Prentis was, with young wives and farms that were now being trod upon and destroyed by armies—were being ordered to pick up guns and kill other young men.

Meanwhile, safely on this side of the ocean, he could marry the girl he had loved all his life. God had brought it about. He had used moisture falling from the sky in all its various forms to teach a lesson: God could be trusted to take care of them, even when Prentis didn't understand what He was doing. Prentis felt profoundly grateful.

* * * *

On Sunday, August 30, Prentis drove his wagon north to load up Avery's belongings. Hector and Ulysses did the pulling. Prentis was coddling all the mares—every one of them was in foal, as he had hoped. When he arrived, he pulled the wagon close to the house and ran up the steps, sweeping Avery into his arms when she appeared wiping her hands on a dishtowel.

"It's finally time!" he said.

"Yes!" She returned the kiss he gave her. "Are you hungry?"

"I couldn't eat a bite. I'm too excited. We're loading up all your things to take them down to mingle with mine." He grinned at her.

"You have to promise that you won't unpack anything. It will be fun to do that together after we get home."

"Sounds like the most wonderful thing I can imagine!"

"You may not think so after you see how much I'm bringing." She laughed.

Jerry, John, and Abe appeared from the front room in their stocking feet, their hair at odd angles. All of them had fallen asleep after Sunday dinner, a brief nap being all they'd get today.

"Hello, Pink," Abe said.

"Hello, boys."

Jerry and John both yawned a greeting. All of them laughed together.

* * * *

Upstairs, Avery had pushed the dress form into Momma and Daddy's room, the wedding dress carefully draped so no part could be seen. The boys tramped up the stairs to Avery's room to carry everything else out to the wagon. Several pieces of furniture were being taken. The rest of her possessions included many books, household goods, pictures, and the linens she had prepared. These were boxed and ready to go, crate after crate, all nailed shut. She also had two large trunks of her shoes and clothing.

Hearing all the noise, Gene and Howard appeared, and all five boys helped Prentis load the wagon. Item after item came down the stairs and went out the door with Prentis supervising. Her brothers laughed about the abundance of her possessions, but Prentis never complained. He looked at each of her belongings as if he cherished it, merely because it was hers.

Midway through the loading, Howard asked to sit on Avery's lap. He loved Prentis, but it was now obvious that he was stealing away Avery, exactly as Hattie had stolen Floyd. It was somewhat like losing one's mother. After he had cried a while with Avery comforting him, he pulled himself together and went to help again. Momma came out later with a big cookie for him. She held him in her lap, reminding him that she was staying.

Once everything was loaded, they covered the entire heap with several tarps and tied them down. All of them paused for tea and a piece of pie, and then Prentis hitched Ulysses and Hector back up to the wagon. Jerry, John, and Abe saddled and mounted their horses to ride down to help unload. They would return home in the morning. Gene and Howard clambered up onto the wagon, last-minute additions to the moving party. It was to be a group effort. Avery smiled; this would be a good thing for Howard. Prentis was glad to have them all.

Before he climbed up onto the wagon with the little boys, Prentis stood looking down at Avery, grinning at her with bright eyes. He tipped her face up and gave her a big kiss.

"Now the fun begins," he said.

"It certainly does."

"I'll see you up in Kingman on Friday morning. I'll be the one in the fancy black suit."

"And I'll be the one in the white dress."

"Good! I'll see you in a few days. I can hardly wait!"

She beamed up at him—she couldn't wait either. He kissed her one more time, climbed onto the wagon, and spoke to the horses. The wagon lumbered across the barnyard. Off they went. Grinning, Prentis lifted his hat. The little brothers waved. When

Avery turned to walk back into the house, she practically skipped up the porch stairs.

* * * *

Wednesday a letter arrived, just in time. They would be leaving Thursday morning for Kingman. She carried the letter upstairs to her nearly empty room.

August 31, 1914

My future wife,

In a few short days I'll be the happiest man in the world. All your things are sitting in my house. Just looking at them makes me feel as if I'll burst with joy. I walk from item to item, running my hand across each, thinking, "These are Avery's!" Surely, they're the most beautiful possessions on earth!

All your crates and trunks await your distribution. It will be fun to open them with you—almost like Christmas; but the best gift is arriving with me, dressed all in white—the bride herself. I intend to scoop you up bodily and carry you inside.

I'm so sick of eating cheese, bacon, and cold pancakes for every meal that I can hardly bear these last few days. If I don't see any of those foods at our table for a very long time, it will be just fine with me. My wife will be coming home with me. And, thanks be to God, she knows how to cook! I can hardly wait! You are so precious to me, and not just for your excellent cooking.

Love,

Prentis

She smiled. He sounded hungry. As far as home cooking went, she intended to spoil him. Since she wouldn't be teaching this fall, she would devote her time to making Prentis as happy as possible, in whatever ways he needed to be made content. This would be her wifely mission.

TWENTY

ON SEPTEMBER 4, 1914, AVERY DESCENDED the staircase at Grandma and Grandpa Slaughter's house on her daddy's arm. Standing gathered below, a sea of smiling relatives gasped. But, after a sympathetic glance at Momma, who was crying, Avery fixed her eyes on Prentis. At the bottom of the stairs, he stood mesmerized, looking up at her with adoring eyes. His focus remained riveted entirely on her, as if blinking would deprive him of some significant moment.

Every other detail blurred. She only beheld Prentis's beloved face.

Dressed in his fine black suit and sporting a fresh haircut, he was arresting. That he was enthralled with her was written plain upon his solemn face. Eyes radiant, he hardly seemed to breathe, as if she were a vision, perhaps imaginary or ethereal, or an apparition floating down to him. She couldn't take her eyes off him either. At the bottom, she caressed his cheek, bringing him back to reality. Then a slow, satisfied smile spread wide across his face.

"I can't believe this day is finally here," he whispered. "You're captivating."

And now, she returned his smile. "So are you." That prompted even more happiness.

Shaking Prentis's hand first, Daddy handed her off.

Before turning toward their assembled families, they stared at one another, savoring the fulfillment of their hopes. Then Prentis laced his fingers through hers, and they floated about the room, talking to each family member, feet barely touching the floor, untroubled by the war in Europe or the war of religion apparent in the room.

The Catholic Pinkertons sat opposite the Protestant Dirs, each side scowling at the other—Grandpa Samuel Dir the sternest of all, Uncle Frank and Uncle Albert right beside him. Their arms folded across their chests, Uncle John and Uncle Grant Pinkerton glared right back. The older generations seemed intent on maintaining the hostilities.

Avery and Prentis, along with the Slaughters and the cousins from both sides of Prentis's family—a generation removed from the fight—bounced from one side to the other, chatting with Dirs and Pinkertons alike. Prentis's siblings also remained neutral. With his dashing looks and friendly personality, George Bellew was a powerful peace ambassador, keeping Prentis's mother on her feet, preventing her from settling down on the Dir side— Avery liked him immensely.

Avery catalogued all of this and tucked it away to ponder later. They smiled, talked, and circulated, pausing to eat. She tasted nothing and remembered no conversations. But she would never forget how Prentis looked at her, engrossed in her every word and expression, as if he'd been given the best gift of his life. His eyes hardly ever left her face. When he had to glance away, they bounced right back.

At last, it was time to leave. Floyd drove Grandpa's buggy and Sadie sat beside him—their witnesses for the ceremony. Avery and Prentis climbed in. Without speaking, they sat in the back, gazing at one another with hands clasped. Floyd and Sadie kept up a pleasant conversation, incomprehensible words of daily life, unnoticed and unheeded.

Avery was overcome. Her heart was full. The time had come!

On the way to the courthouse, they took a surprise detour. Prentis had scheduled an appointment at Ritchie Brothers Photography.

"I want to preserve the happiest day of my life for posterity," he said. "I want our children, grandchildren, and great-grandchildren to see how beautiful you are today! This wedding day is the foundation of our family. These photos are for our future."

Avery was deeply touched.

As was the custom, they posed solemnly, staid and proper. Between photographs, they grinned, overcome with laughter as they attempted to contain their joy before sitting or standing sedately once more. All of this required more time than expected, for it took a while to regain appropriately somber expressions for each shot. Finally, the photography was complete. Prentis paid, and off they went again.

Once they reached the courthouse, they filed solemnly into the large brick building, heading straight to the justice of the peace. Before the important and dignified man, clutching one another's hands, Prentis Jordan Pinkerton and Avery Veretta Slaughter repeated their vows.

Each promised to love, honor, and cherish the other, in sickness and in health, for better or for worse, for richer or for poorer, keeping themselves only for the other as long as they both should live. Plighting their troth, looking seriously into one another's eyes, the most binding and solemn words one human being ever speaks to another were spoken reverently, solidly, and passionately with their whole hearts.

Symbols of their love and commitment, each slid a wedding band onto the finger of the other. And then, surprising the justice of the peace, the four of them—Floyd, Prentis, Avery, and Sadie—burst into song after Sadie sounded the pitch. Avery had chosen this old-fashioned, Civil-War-era hymn because Prentis's family loved it. Sadie's soprano, Avery's alto, Floyd's tenor, and Prentis's baritone rang out loud and clear.

After a moment of surprise, the justice joined them, singing bass, rounding out the harmony. Never missing a beat, they all smiled when he jumped in. Wholeheartedly, they jointly raised their praise to God.

For the beauty of the earth
For the glory of the skies,
For the love which from our birth

Over and around us lies.
Lord of all, to Thee we raise,
This, our hymn of grateful praise.

They sang all the verses, Protestant and Catholic, each smiling during their favorite parts. After the concluding chorus, all stood grinning at one another, including the justice. Periodically, heads of the curious had popped around the doorframe throughout the singing, peeking to see who made melody in the county office. Now the ceremony needed to be completed.

"And now, by the power invested in me by the state of Kansas, I pronounce you man and wife, Mr. and Mrs. Prentis Jordan Pinkerton. What God has joined together, let no man put asunder. You may kiss your bride, young man."

And Prentis did. Avery received his most exuberant kiss to date.

Bursting with happiness, they all laughed out loud. Congratulations were offered; hands were shaken; official documents were signed. Hand-in-hand, they stepped out of the office, walked down the hall, and passed out the front doors, where they discovered their entire family assembled on the steps, waiting to send them off.

All burst into applause when Mr. and Mrs. Prentis Jordan Pinkerton and party appeared. Avery and Prentis grinned as they circulated, Prentis keeping a tight grip on Avery, never releasing her hand, hugging and being hugged—a joyous departure. Prentis's mother smiled proudly at him. George Bellew, Daddy, and the boys each pumped his hand enthusiastically. Momma dabbed at her eyes, holding Avery tightly before releasing her and patting her cheek. Howard also had a hard time letting go.

But, at last, Floyd drove them to the station. They had a train to catch.

Prentis carried on their baggage—each had packed a new leather travel bag. Still smiling about finding their family assembled outside, they boarded. When they entered the railway car, everyone on board eyed them knowingly, clearly a bride and groom leaving their ceremony and traveling home. The occasion made everyone happy for them.

Shyly they glanced at one another; then both returned the other passengers' smiles as they searched for their seats. His bashfulness provoked by all the attention, Prentis dipped his head and fixed his eyes on hers a moment before settling their luggage on the rack above. Then they sat, side by side in the passenger car, Prentis on the aisle, heading south. On this Friday afternoon, the car was full, so they remained silent.

Swaying with the train's motion, they held hands on the seat between them. With his thumb, Prentis caressed Avery's hand as he looked past her out the window—plowed fields flying by in rapid succession. Occasionally, his thumb found its way to her ring finger. Then he traced her new wedding band, stroking back and forth wearing a satisfied smile. Glancing at her, he grinned before looking past her again and out the window, his smile lingering. She was mindful of his touch as they rode silently past Gibbon and down to Wakita, where they disembarked.

He alighted first and assisted her. When she had exited, the engine released a loud blast of steam, blowing about her white skirt. In wedding dress and new black suit, their day's activities were obvious once more. Passing people greeted them warmly and offered congratulations. Avery noticed Prentis fighting off an attack of shyness again.

"Will your skirt get dirty if you walk with me to the livery?"

"I'll be fine. I prefer to go with you, rather than stand here without you."

Pleased, he smiled. They made the short walk.

"Wait here," he said softly, "and I'll pull out for you. Livery stables are dusty."

Strolling slowly up and down the wooden sidewalk, she waited. At last, Ulysses came pacing out the door, tossing his head and stepping high, obviously thrilled to be leaving the confines of the livery barn. If a horse could be said to smile, Ulysses smiled. Prentis leapt out to assist her, being especially careful with her delicate, white gown.

After he climbed back in, Prentis flipped the reins lightly, tickling Ulysses. The horse jogged through town, buggy of happy newlyweds in tow, picking up the pace when they coasted into open country. Ulysses didn't need much supervision; he knew the way home.

Prentis leaned in to kiss his bride and then fixed his eyes on her face—he couldn't seem to take his eyes off her.

"You look like an angel. This is the prettiest dress I've ever seen."

"Thank you. Momma, Hattie, and I labored over it for quite a while."

"You made it?"

"Yes. We even made the lace."

"It's perfect." He kissed her, gazed into her eyes, and then kissed her again. "Were you pleased with the ceremony, even though it wasn't in a church and it wasn't your pastor?"

"Oh yes! The justice is a 'minister of God for good,' according to Romans 13. The vows are the same, and the promise is made before God. We're as married as we can be. I took a vow, and I meant it."

"So did I."

Simultaneously, they leaned in and kissed again, lingering and then smiling before Prentis turned to give Ulysses and the road some attention. Avery snuggled even closer—she'd never felt so blissful. It was a cozy ride, fraught with kisses.

Soon they pulled into their curved drive and clattered by the house, heading toward the barn.

He smiled at her. "Can't begin to tell you how wonderful it is to bring you home!"

She returned his smile.

Sam came bounding around from the cattle pen, having been left to guard the place.

"Good dog, Sam!" Prentis then turned toward Avery. "Will you sit in the buggy while I unhitch? I want to carry you in."

"I'll sit."

Avery had never seen a man unhitch a horse so rapidly. Ulysses was unharnessed, groomed, given some oats, led to the water trough, and turned into the pasture. The work was accomplished in nothing flat, her new husband working with focused intensity. Sam attempted to stay out of his master's way, but he didn't always succeed. Prentis asked her to wait while he washed his hands at the pump—he didn't want to soil her dress. Watching Ulysses trot out to pasture, she waited in the buggy, her heart ecstatic with anticipation.

And there he was, face beaming with joy, holding wide his arms. She twined her arms about his neck, and he swung her into his grasp—one swift motion.

And there *she* was, his strong arms cradling her, the motion of his body rocking her gently as he walked toward the house, kissing her cheek or her ear. Twice, he stopped and kissed her quite thoroughly. Enthusiastically, she returned his kisses, which grew more ardent as they made their way across the barnyard.

Pausing at the front door, he had her remove the key from his suit-jacket pocket. As he held her, she turned it in the lock, and the door swung open.

"Welcome home, Mrs. Pinkerton," he whispered.

Countenance beaming, he carried her over the threshold and into the front room's cool shade. Then he kicked the door shut behind them.

* * * *

The next morning, Avery awakened to the gray of predawn. Happiness washed through her before she was even fully conscious. Inhaling slowly, she breathed in the manly scent of her new husband. Lying on his stomach at her side—flesh against flesh, his arm rested heavy across her hips, and his head cradled against her shoulder. They lay entangled in the coolness of the sheets.

The fresh morning fragrance of a late summer's day wafted through the bedroom windows, bringing the chirping of nearby birds and the soft lowing of cattle far in the distance. Prentis slept soundly, so Avery lay perfectly still, recalling the intensity of his amorous affection. More than once, the tenderness in his eyes had given way to desire and then to pleasure. She savored her memories of these new words, actions, and expressions. They were one flesh now.

The beauty of marital intimacy was like Christ and His church. She knew this from Ephesians Chapter Five. *But how?* There was much to comprehend. She would consider this over their lifetime of loving—the ardent focus, the complete intimacy, the utter transparency, the abandonment to love, the ecstasy of consummation. This new marital oneness of body and soul was part of passionate devotion to Christ as well as of marital union.

How difficult the waiting had been! But now the reward of lying safe and tranquil in one another's arms, a storm of exultant, celebratory intensity having transpired in the night.

Avery couldn't help herself. Love-struck, she softly kissed Prentis's head, relishing the sensation of his rough cheek against her arm and shoulder, the warmth of his chest pressed to her side, their legs all intertwined, impossible to tell which were hers and which were his—intimate connection. One of his feet stuck out from under the sheet, hanging slightly off the mattress. She smiled.

Adjusting the position of his countenance, Prentis shifted his head as if he were waking. His eyelash tickled her arm—a blink. His breathing continued slow and relaxed, warm against her skin. Softly, he kissed her arm before turning his head on her shoulder. Lifting her cascading hair away from her face, he gazed at her.

"Good morning, my beloved wife."

"Good morning to you, my dear husband, my very own."

Sleepy-eyed, he smiled softly, the morning fragrance of his body warm and intimate. She traced the shape of his lips before stroking his morning stubble—brown whiskers, not black like the men in her family, thicker than the typical Cherokee scattering of beard. Completely at ease, his blue eyes were clear and peaceful, observing her as she caressed his face.

"Have you been awake long?" he murmured.

"Long enough to meditate on how thoroughly happy I am."

"As am I. Beautiful wedding night—how I love you! Best night's sleep I've had since I began to pursue you. Thank you, precious Savior, for my wife."

"And for my husband."

"Amen. A good morning prayer."

"We have animals to tend, don't we?"

"Not this morning. They're all out to pasture, and I gave the hog extra feed when we arrived last night. All is well."

"So the morning is ours?"

"It is—the entire day is ours and tomorrow as well. We can do whatever you'd like—unpack your boxes, arrange your things, explore the farm, sit by the creek, stay in this bed . . . "

"Let's do all of the above." She kissed his forehead tenderly. And so, they did.

TWENTY-ONE

WHEN PRENTIS WASN'T KISSING her, embracing her, or carrying her back to the bedroom, Avery baked him fresh bread and warm cookies. He sat down to boiled squash, mashed potatoes, tender beet greens, and fried ham. Avery started a shopping list, adding more items each day. The discussion about a cow and chickens was broached. Currently, they had to purchase their eggs and milk. They would travel to town when they ran out of staples, forcing them to return to the world at large.

But for now, they stayed put. There was plenty to do at home.

Several times during their first weeks, Avery's possessions were readjusted as they attempted to discover the perfect arrangement. Clutter and disorder agitated Prentis, though he never uttered a word of complaint. Whenever a mess accumulated, he never even told her that it bothered him. Attempting to be forbearing, he merely surveyed the clutter with knit brows. However, attuned as she was to pleasing him, she noticed.

She tried to maintain order, knowing it was essential. Her fault was that she allowed stacks to grow. If she couldn't see items, she lost them—out of sight, out of mind. So she kept her work in piles—books, papers, and mending. In contrast, he always put each item immediately back where it belonged, neatly in its assigned place. They had to find balance.

He was picky about his socks and his hair. She knew this.

Being a teacher, she was particular about grammar, word usage, and exact representation of facts with sources cited. He knew this as well.

They'd been friends all their lives and had often laughed about these particular quirks, usually his hair, which he had to comb frequently to keep the thick waviness from getting out of hand in amusing ways, especially if he hadn't used pomade. But their disagreements during the first months were about these exact habits.

It surprised Avery that they would argue, for they hardly ever disagreed.

Prentis took a more enlightened view. They were human, he reminded her. Humans sinned. There was also the fact that they were opposites in many ways. This was why they complemented one another so well. But opposites always had disagreements. They prayed together, begging God to help them not to be ridiculous.

But ridiculous, they often were. Emotions ran high.

Prentis hadn't recognized how keenly she could be attached to the exact word—not a synonym of that word, nor a nearby relative of the word, but *that* word, the precise one. Neither had he known how important it was that citations be absolutely correct. The consternation on his face at these particularities tipped her off, but she couldn't seem to let these things go.

And then, they would argue.

"For goodness sake, Avery, I didn't memorize the page number, I merely know which book I read it in." Or, "I know I said 'excited' when 'agitated' would have been the better word, but, Sweetheart, you knew what I meant."

She tried to keep from retorting. But sometimes, she failed.

Until now, Avery hadn't known that socks should be paired, right with left—that there even were a right and a left sock, obvious if one inspected closely, even after the socks had been laundered. A bit of sock wadded up inside his boot irritated Prentis, cramping the movement of his toes or rubbing against his foot. He'd remove the boot, smooth the sock, take it off to investigate if it wouldn't smooth, and then hobble back into the house to find the correct sock.

She tried not to be annoyed when she found him in their bedroom picking apart sock pairs, searching for a left to go with the right, but she couldn't help herself.

"Prentis, I looked at those socks carefully. I'm absolutely certain I put a left with every right. But it's hard to tell. There's barely a particle of difference."

He attempted to bite his tongue, to remember how odd his personal sock preference was. But sometimes, he failed.

Then they felt ridiculous for having been so petty as to argue about socks, verbs, or citations. They apologized. After that, they discovered that making up often involved much more than merely saying they were sorry. This part was surprising, like so much of their early marriage.

A large portion of those first days was spent in the house. Kissing now led to more intimate connection, the marriage vows having been said. But the animals were fed, the garden tended, and the farm looked after. They did all of this side by side, hand in hand, talking non-stop about Prentis's plan for the farm and Avery's desire to have the chicken coop here and the fruit trees there.

Sitting astride Ulysses, they rode out to inspect the livestock, Avery held within the circle of Prentis's arms. Periodically he kissed her on the neck or nuzzled her ear. Sam trotted beside Ulysses, but other than their initial greeting each day, the poor dog was pretty much ignored, only receiving absentminded pats. With linked hands, Prentis did everything with Avery, focusing exclusively on her.

They leaned against one another, always touching in some way. It didn't feel right to walk out of sight now that they were bound together and connected as if they were one person. It was difficult to get out of bed in the morning, wrapped up in one another as they were. Who could sleep at night or crawl out of bed the next day when the one you loved beyond all reason was nearby to talk to, to hold, to kiss, and to draw into intimate embrace?

Marital intimacy was completely absorbing, beautiful, and binding, and it was entirely disruptive, causing amazing tenderness and extreme vulnerability. Somehow it attached

everything they did to this one act, making every single part of
their relationship more significant. Of course, this made perfect
sense to Prentis. This aspect of marriage was exactly as he had
anticipated. What Prentis understood intuitively, she was only
beginning to comprehend.

With all this time and effort being put into it, Avery had
expected to conceive a child immediately, as Hattie had done.
Therefore, she was disappointed when she was still taken to bed
monthly with a migraine as she cared for the cyclical needs of
her womanhood.

With a cold, wet compress over her eyes, she would lie on
the bed, pain and discomfort in her back, sometimes crying
because she was so disappointed. It was ridiculous to cry, she
told herself, ironic even. She had been afraid to have babies, and
now she was afraid she couldn't have them. They were merely
newlyweds; babies would come in God's time.

When Prentis came in from his chores—done all alone on
those days, he would sit on the floor by the bed, studying her face,
holding her hand, and bringing her newly-cooled compresses.
The conversation would generally go something like this:

"Avery, God will bring it about. You have to trust Him and
be patient."

"I know," she would sob, "but I want us to have babies so
badly. What if we're not able?"

"Then God will give us the grace to endure that. He loves
us—He'll do what's best."

"I know," she would sniffle. "I simply have to let God be God.
I'm sorry for crying. And I'm sorry I'm so little help when I'm in
such pain."

He snorted. "You take care of me every single day. I think I
can handle taking care of you for a few days each month."

Then he would stroke her head, easing her temples, her
forehead, and the base of her neck. Once she was eased, he
would prepare scrambled eggs—something that didn't upset her
stomach. These times of the month were difficult, but the care he
lavished on her inspired a loving torrent of wifely emotion. Her
love for him grew deeper still.

Surprisingly, the month of December was now upon them.
How had this happened?

Fall had been completely devoured by the adjustment to new marriage—this had been the absorbing fact, the passionate focus, even as work and duties had been maintained.

* * * *

Prentis's usual fall work had continued unchanged, but now he had the consolation of Avery's presence, her companionship, and her cooking. These facts changed everything. Even arguing with her was a relief. Having her beside him made him happy in every way.

Mentally, he ticked off his work's progression. The fields had been gone over with the spring-tooth, and the wheat had been sown. The cattle had been turned out to pasture after the wheat was thick and green. The hog had been slaughtered, and the meat smoked. They had gone to Attica for Thanksgiving with his family.

And then the wheat had been shoveled out of the granary, transported to town, and sold at the elevator when the price had reached $1.15 a bushel, bringing $920 into his hands. Cognizant of the $460 more that he could have had, but for the hailstorm, Prentis adjusted his expectations. Not wanting Avery to be troubled, he had kept this struggle to himself, walked into the Citizens Bank of Wakita, and banked emergency cash. Then he had traveled to Anthony to purchase only four steers to fatten for the market, far fewer than he had originally hoped.

It had been a blessing to have Avery waiting in the house for him when he returned. If she guessed at his discouragement, she hadn't said a word, but it had been a consolation to have her in bed with him that night. It amazed him that he'd borne living without her for so long.

As war raged on, Europe's motto had become: *Food Will Win the War*. Therefore, he and the other American farmers needed to produce grain and beef. The French, British, Belgians, and Italians relied on the American, Canadian, and Australian commodities markets. He wished he could have purchased more steers. Deliberately, he focused on the blessing, telling the Lord that he was sorry for even comparing what might have been with what actually was.

The hail had been part of a bigger lesson: God would take care of them.

The Europeans would fight, and the American farmer would feed them. Prentis had to lay aside his hope that the upturn in the markets would allow him to pay off the mortgage quickly. Now he focused on making the first yearly payment with the few steers he had purchased and on increasing his farm's productivity. Those, too, were all in God's hands. He was still learning.

* * * *

As he dealt quietly with his financial concerns, Prentis noticed a creeping melancholy coming over Avery. After considering the make of the woman he loved so desperately, he was certain he had discerned the cause. They read their Bibles every day, prayed together, and talked about what they were learning. She had time for theological study and had returned to plugging away at that degree.

But she lacked something vital.

One gray and overcast day, he came in from checking on the new steers to find her wrapped in a quilt, staring at the wall with tracks of tears down her cheeks. Concerned, he sat down on the floor and regarded her face.

"Sweetheart, do you know why you're so sad?"

"No," she sniffed. "I can't put my finger on it."

"I know why."

Expectantly, she lifted her eyes to his, awaiting his solution.

"You need to go to church. You draw life from it, and it encourages your heart. I can see that you long for it."

Staring into his eyes, she untangled one arm from the quilt and cupped his cheek. "But I don't want to go without you. I don't know if I can bear to be there alone. I'm attached to you in every way now."

He had known this conversation would occur at some point. But he felt the same way, comprehending entirely. Biting his lower lip, he studied the bottomless depths of her black eyes. Weekly church attendance had been a lifelong fact for her, something significant and strengthening. Conversely, church for him had been and continued to be a cause of anxiety and upset stomach. Nevertheless, he wanted unity, too.

"I'll try," he said.

"You will?" Her eyebrows raised in surprise.

"Can't promise I'll get in the door, but I'll at least attempt it."

"Where should I, or we, if you're ever able to go—where should we go?"

"There's a small community church about a mile and a half up the road west of here. Has a new young pastor who graduated from your own theology school. I've been investigating. Thought this might be why you were so sad."

"You knew what was wrong and tried to find a church for me?"

"Yes."

"How I love you, Prentis! You're such a good husband."

Overwhelmed by love, he got off the floor and crawled into the quilt cocoon with her, holding her in his arms, spooning.

"Of course I knew what was wrong," he whispered over her shoulder. "I love you more than my own life. That you would even allow me to court you was a miracle—you, a churchgoing woman, and me, a man who doesn't attend. I'm still amazed. I don't want your heart to be broken. I'm going to try. But, if I go, it should be for the right reasons. This is between God and me, not between you and me. I want to go because I know the good Lord wants me to go, not merely to please you—though pleasing you is a mighty powerful incentive."

Softly, he kissed her on the ear.

Avery reached back to stroke his cheek. "You're wise, and you're entirely correct."

"Of course I am." He chuckled softly.

"I'll ride over on one of the mares, if you'll tell me where to go."

"No, I'll drive you in the buggy. I'll get you there safely, and then I'll pick you up when church is over."

"Would you really do that?"

"Absolutely," he said. "You won't mind the churchgoers seeing your heathen husband dropping you off and picking you up, will you?"

"Of course not. My 'heathen' husband is one of the kindest, gentlest Christian men I know. Remember, a long time ago I decided that as far as this subject goes, God's opinion is more important to me than the opinion of any man, or even Mrs. Alfonse Riley for that matter."

"Good." He chuckled as he kissed her cheek. "Then I'll take you, you'll be happy again, and God and I can wrestle this out."

* * * *

When Prentis picked up Avery that first Sunday, he knew he'd been correct. Grinning from ear to ear, she came bounding out the front door, light of step, encouraged. All the way home, she was effusive, talking non-stop.

They needed a Sunday School teacher; she wondered if God would have her volunteer. It would be a blessing to teach again—an encouragement. She liked the pastor very much; he was personable and a good teacher. She told Prentis all about the sermon. Coming up on Christmas, the pastor was teaching on Romans 5, explaining how Christ had redeemed what Adam had done to the human race when he sinned. Avery called this passage one of the most encouraging and explanatory of what Christ had done for them in the entire Bible.

"I didn't know anything could top Colossians in that category," Prentis said.

"Romans 5 is pretty wonderful, too."

"Let's study Romans together, like we did Colossians."

She smiled at him. "Prentis, I loved studying with you during our courtship—the letters, the long talks. It filled my heart with happiness."

"Then let's do it."

"This week, I'd like to look at the first four chapters of Romans, so I can keep Romans 5 within its context next week at church. The pastor's teaching a chapter each month. We'd merely be skimming the surface this week. Is that all right with you?"

"Yep. Looking forward to it. It's what you need."

As she snuggled against his shoulder, Prentis could tell she was thoroughly happy. He loved pleasing her. In studying the Bible with her, however, he knew he was also pleasing the Lord, so he was doubly contented. He leaned in under Avery's hat and kissed her.

Clop, clop, clop. Hector's hooves struck the hard-packed,

frozen road. Prentis paused to contemplate how to phrase his next statement.

"You should also teach the Sunday School class," he said. "Having you prowling around the house attacking my verb choices and lack of adequate citations might end if you have pupils to instruct and an outlet for your gift of teaching."

She stared at him and then burst out laughing. "I hadn't thought of that. Have you felt like a chastened pupil?"

"Have to admit it. Yes, I have."

"Then I'll volunteer for the position. I miss teaching children so much. Thank you."

"Why are you thanking me?"

"It's an hour earlier on Sunday morning, and it's more time away from you. You're my husband—I only want to teach if it's pleasing to you."

"Oh, I'm pleased." He grinned. "I'll be able to speak freely again."

She laughed, but her expression appeared guilt-stricken. "I'm so sorry, Prentis. I was trying not to be a schoolmarm."

"Give you credit for trying. Apology accepted. I've been trying not to care so much about my socks."

"And I give you credit for that."

She leaned against him, both smiling as they reflected on the ridiculous bickering that had often occurred as they adjusted to living together.

* * * *

When they arrived home, the aroma of the food Avery had placed on the cookstove filled the house. After she'd prepared some cornbread, they ate pinto beans that had simmered with a ham hock, slowly bubbling since early morning. Sitting in peaceful camaraderie, they ate silently, savoring their soup, each lost in their own thoughts—Avery considered their conversation in the buggy and the joy it would be to teach again.

"What did you do this morning?" she asked as the meal drew near its close.

"Sat in front of the stove and read my Bible—Psalm 103."

"The brevity of a man's life in contrast to the love of God. I love that psalm. How did it touch your heart today?"

"God was a Father to me. His mercy overwhelms me—His forgiveness first of all and His kindness in my youth and in giving me you. But we're mere dust. Someday we'll be gone, exactly like grass. Our children and our children's children will be left. My decisions and my obedience will affect our future family. I want to be a good father when the time comes."

"I hope it's soon," she whispered.

"He'll give us children, if He wants us to have them." He grasped her hand.

"Yes." Her voice trailed off as she decided not to speak her viewpoint.

His expression invited her to continue.

Pausing in mid-thought, her tone and inflection had given her away. She sat still a moment pondering the passage. When they had children, unity between them in matters of faith would be a vital part of being good parents, but Prentis would have to come to that realization. This was between him and God, as he had said. She wouldn't insert herself, coming between the two of them. She would say nothing. Prentis needed to have God lead him. He didn't need God to lead him through her, provoking him to guilt or resistance.

"Are you ready for dessert?" she asked, changing the subject entirely.

"I'm always ready for dessert."

Avery could tell by the look in his eyes that he knew dessert hadn't been her original topic, but he let it go. She served him pumpkin pie. He devoured two pieces.

TWENTY-TWO

ON CHRISTMAS DAY PRENTIS and Avery traveled to Gibbon, departing on frozen roads in the dark obscurity of predawn. Wrapped in scarves with hats pulled low, they bundled against the wind. In the buggy, they huddled under the leather apron, one of Prentis's hands tucked into Avery's fur muff, grasping both her hands together. This made the ride all the more cozy. His hand and her controversial coat kept her quite warm, even in the biting wind.

Fluttering with anticipation, Avery chattered for the entire trip, for they hadn't been to Gibbon since the wedding. Prentis responded at the appropriate times, but kept shooting her sidelong quizzical expressions and tender smiles. Hard as she tried, she simply couldn't seem to quit talking, but his smiles let her know that he understood her excitement completely.

When they arrived, everyone hugged them tightly, exclaiming and speaking all at once. Momma cried and held onto Avery; Daddy grew teary-eyed, too. Avery laughed at her brothers' comments—Pink looked like he'd been eating, they said. Was she planning on fattening him up? Howard clung to her; Gene said he didn't like the new teacher—Avery was a much better teacher and nicer, too; Abe was doing well at the high school.

With much laughter, they exchanged gifts. Avery had knitted gloves and socks for her daddy and brothers and had crocheted lace collars and cuffs for her momma and Hattie and a blanket for baby Donald. Since she wasn't teaching, she had more time to make presents. Prentis had gotten spinning tops for the boys—Gene and Howard loved them.

Avery received an apron, and Momma had made several pairs of socks for Prentis, prompting a significant look at Avery when he opened the package. Avery gave Prentis a bound, leather journal—blank. He'd been scribbling notes of some kind on loose sheets of paper, and she thought he might like it. He did. Smiling widely, he thanked her warmly and then thumbed through the journal's empty pages, wearing a thoughtful expression.

When Avery opened Prentis's gift, she found a set of bejeweled tortoiseshell combs for her hair. She gasped in surprise—they were so elegant! Immediately, she tucked one behind her ear, turning to model it for him.

"You're the prettiest woman on God's frozen earth," he whispered.

"And I have the best husband."

At the expression of this sentiment, Prentis kissed her tenderly on the forehead.

* * * *

Since getting married, Prentis had been informed by Avery of her supposed frailty. Therefore, he wasn't surprised that the moment the gift exchange was completed Hattie passed little Donald to Avery and headed into the kitchen to help Minnie, excluding Avery from the preparations. Inwardly, he chuckled at her mother's protectiveness.

Round and dimply, Donald was four-and-a-half months old now, cooing as he attempted to communicate. A sweet Cherokee baby, he had dark eyes and a soft black baby-mohawk. Studying Donald, Prentis wondered what their children would look like now that he had brought his blue eyes, brown hair, and pale skin to intermingle with their Cherokee blood. There had been some previous intermarriage in the Slaughter family tree, but he would bring new features to their distinctive appearance. Only time would tell. Avery cradled the baby, rocking and singing.

Prentis knew then that she would cry when they left.

The food was delicious, but now that Prentis wasn't living off his own cooking, it didn't have nearly the impact of those scrumptious meals he'd eaten the previous year. Comparing them with the unvarying diet he'd endured in his bachelor's kitchen, he remembered them as the best meals he'd ever consumed. But now, he was a well-fed husband, though he certainly wasn't getting fat, merely a little less lean and hungry looking.

Beginning his campaign before they had even left home, Prentis had tried to persuade Avery to stay at her parent's house for a long visit. He would come back to retrieve her in just a few days. She refused.

"What if a storm comes and we're separated for a long period of time?" she said.

"We lived through it last year."

"That was different. Now we're one. I couldn't bear being away from you."

Prentis felt the same about her, but he hadn't wanted to be selfish.

After they returned home, Avery was despondent. Prentis wondered again if a longer visit with her mother would have eased Avery's heart. Her female time and a three-day headache occurred within a few days of Christmas—another month with no baby on the way. Having recently tasted the sweet fruit of little Donald—a "delicious" baby, she had called him, Avery grieved. She said she longed for a tribe of little boys.

The sad realization that there would be no baby coincided with inclement weather and, consequently, no church for the next two weekends. There were many tears throughout the end of 1914 and into the beginning of 1915. Avery's crying broke Prentis's heart, but reproduction was in God's hands. As a farmer, he knew this. Prentis dealt with God's sovereignty every day. God was teaching him, and he grew in his ability to comprehend.

However, the fact of church wasn't so easy. It impacted him in surprising ways.

Each week throughout December, as he'd dropped Avery off at church, he had felt disquieted. She'd never said another word, but he knew she longed for him to attend with her, and he yearned to please her. However, he intended to determine if God required or desired church attendance from him. He remained uncertain.

In mid-December, while she was away at church, he had started a research project. Reading Psalm 103 that first Sunday had been the catalyst. Before there were children, this should be resolved. His days were like grass, withering away. It couldn't be put off. His own father had died young. Who knew how many days he himself would be granted? God had been a Father to him, pitying him, redeeming him, and removing his transgressions as far as the east was from the west. Prentis had to hash out with Him the issue of church.

He needed to pray about it, and he needed to read the entire New Testament, gleaning information about the purpose of the church. He hoped and prayed he would then know what to do. This was the note-taking Avery had witnessed, prompting her to buy him a blank journal.

What frightened him so much about hearing a godly man teach from the Scriptures, singing a few songs, trading pleasantries with other gathered believers, and then loading his wife back into the buggy to come home? Nothing, as far as his rational mind could see. But each time he decided to tell Avery that he would attend, he made himself sick with anxiety, memories of his parents' religious disagreements gnawing at his stomach. He even had nightmares about it, waking in a cold sweat, his stomach clenching. It was as if his body had been conditioned by his childhood training to be sickened and anxious about church.

He realized this was because he hadn't yet latched onto God's reason for going. If he had a solid grasp of the whys and knew beyond a shadow of a doubt that God Himself wanted him to attend, then he would go whether it made him sick or not, exactly as he'd shouldered the responsibility for his family after his father had died. It had been the right course of action.

Church, he was still trying to sort out.

Sympathetic and kind, Avery gave him home remedies for his upset stomach—oil of peppermint and warm tea. He suspected she knew why his stomach was in turmoil, but she said nothing about it. Still, Prentis knew his stomach problems were entirely spiritual.

Each time these attacks of anxiety occurred, he prayed. Avery wasn't at all like his mother or his father. The wars of his childhood home wouldn't be repeated, whether he went or not. Fights weren't occurring now. Peace prevailed. There was no pressure to make a decision at this moment. Continually holding this mental conversation, he reassured himself.

* * * *

While the inclement January weather continued, Avery stayed home with Prentis. With hot tea beside them on the reading table and a warm fire in the pot-bellied stove, they each sat in their chairs, feet on their hassocks and Bibles on their laps. Prentis read aloud from Romans 6, intending to read the entire chapter but grinding to a halt after verse seven.

He sat for a moment. Then he looked up at her. "I don't understand any of this. I'm out of my theological depth. There's a lot here."

"There certainly is."

"I haven't been baptized, other than when my father brought in the priest when I was a baby. Does that count?"

"This is an allegory. When you believed and accepted Christ's death as payment for your sins, you were baptized into Him. Metaphorically, you were placed into His death with Him, dying along with Him, since His death was died for you. This frees you from slavery to sin."

"That's a boatload of theology." He paused to reframe his question. "So, it's not saying I have to be baptized in water to belong to Christ?"

"No, it isn't. But you do undergo water baptism to demonstrate your symbolic death with Christ. Going under the water is a symbol of death, coming up a symbol of resurrection. When you're publicly baptized, you're identifying yourself with Christ, a step of obedience that illustrates what happened spiritually."

"Well, that's deep." He appreciated her theological knowledge and her desire to be thorough, but panic rose in his chest.

Avery's eyes remained fixed on his face, awaiting his next thought.

Abruptly, he set down his Bible and stood. He knew anxiety and emotional upheaval were probably written all over his face, because she grew pale and concerned.

"I'll sit here and read," she said, soft and low, "and then I'll make us some dinner."

He wanted to alleviate the worry he saw on her face, but he was in turmoil. Stepping into their bedroom, he retrieved the chamber pot to dump in the outhouse. His stomach was upset again, a regular occurrence on Sundays now. As he walked back through the front room, everything felt bleak. Avery had been sitting with her head bowed, but she lifted her head as he came through, her eyes following him. He couldn't speak.

Out in the barn, Prentis wrestled with God as he checked on his pregnant mares. Persephone and Calypso nibbled oats from his outstretched hands thrust between the slats of the corral. He stared blankly off into space. He felt the unease of a guilty conscience, but he wasn't certain what convicted him. It had something to do with continuing to sin but expecting grace to suddenly free him, the part of the passage that he hadn't even been able to discuss. He was doing that somehow, but he wasn't sure how. He needed to figure this out.

And then, there was the issue of baptism. He longed to be baptized, to make the decision himself, regardless of what his father and the priest had done. He loved Jesus with all his heart. He knew that Christ had died for him, and he had placed his faith in Him. All the early believers had been baptized after they believed. Prentis now wanted to identify himself publicly with Christ, to be known as one who was attached to Him. However, to be baptized, he would need to go to church. The mere thought made him sick. He felt anxious and uncertain about what he should do. His stomach clenched.

Persephone nudged his hand, and he stared into her big, brown eyes. She had finished her oats. He patted her cheek and Calypso's as well, then went to get oats for Daisy and Mabel. When he called their names, they ambled over to the corral fence. Until he felt more settled, he'd stay out here with the mares.

He loved Avery so dearly, but this was between God and him. A cold sweat broke out on his face as queasiness rose in his gut. He leaned his forehead against the top rail.

"God my Father," he whispered, "help me understand what You're trying to tell me. I love You. I want to please You, but I feel sick and guilty for some reason. There are things You've instructed me to do as a believer. These things are attached to the church. I won't be able to obey You unless I join with other believers and go to church, but . . ."

He bent and vomited into the dirt, squatting there until his stomach had emptied and waiting for the nausea to diminish before he stood. The mares stared down at him as he pushed soft stable dirt over the contents of his stomach. As if concerned, each horse took a step closer. Sam made a sympathetic whimpering sound in his throat.

Nickering softly, Penelope crowded close to the stall bars, her head lowered toward Prentis. She hadn't had her oats yet, and now her master was bowed in the dust. Prentis brushed the dirt off his hands, wiped his face with his handkerchief, and then reached through the bars to stroke Penelope's forelock. Distracted, his thoughts weren't on the horse.

"Help me," he whispered. "Be a Father, a Comforter, a Helper, and a Savior to me."

When the wave of nausea subsided, he stood at the barn door breathing deeply of the cold air. Attempting to clear his head, he watched the freezing drizzle, standing close enough that faint droplets landed on his face, cooling it.

God would help him sort this out. He would bring peace, as He always did. Prentis let go. He would go up this path and see where God was leading him, taking each step as God put it before him and not until then.

He felt better. Settling his hat down onto his head and turning up his collar, he headed toward the house to see what Avery had prepared for dinner. He thought he'd be able to eat.

* * * *

Mid-week on January 6, Avery surprised Prentis with a birthday cake, a special meal, and a gift—a copy of *The Aeneid*, yet another story with roots in the sacking of Troy, more history mixed with mythology. He hadn't read this story yet. When he opened the package, he grinned and jumped up from his chair, giving her a big kiss and a tight squeeze before sitting down to thumb through the book, eager to begin.

Now they were both twenty-four. She had turned on August 22, a Saturday, as they made the desperate last gasp to get to their wedding day. He had brought her a silver locket on Sunday, the day afterward—the week before they'd moved her possessions down to his house. But he was privileged to have her face-to-face on his day. Simply having her for his wife was gift enough. The cake and the book made the blessing overflow.

She thrust a candle stub into the cake, lit it, watched him blow it out, kissed him soundly, and then, with great gusto, sang him *Happy Birthday to You*. Enjoying her solo, he sat grinning up at her, tipped back in his chair. Then he pulled her down onto his lap, and they fed each other cake, stabbing their forks right in without even slicing it. Best cake yet!

Frosting got everywhere, resulting in uncontrollable laughter and sticky kisses, and then he picked her up and carried her to bed. Happy Birthday!

Later in January, Avery returned to church. She sang as she worked around the house, so Prentis knew her heart was glad. While she was gone, he returned to his notes about the church, first transferring all of his previous scribblings into the new journal. The snowstorms and freezing rain always occurred mid-week, leaving the roads passable by Sunday. That would have been a blessing had it occurred last year. The previous January had been difficult.

This winter wasn't nearly as wet, meaning his yield of winter wheat wouldn't be as good, but it also meant there weren't as many problems with the horses' feet and the steers seemed to be gaining more rapidly. All the expectant livestock were doing well. Prentis also didn't have to worry about Ulysses hurting himself on muddy roads. Reminded of God's care, he thanked Him. It was surprising how little rain, snow, and mud bothered him this year, now that it didn't keep him from Avery and she was waiting for him inside the house.

Their winter days were spent beside a cozy fire, each working on projects. He repaired leather harnesses, halters, and reins. She crocheted doilies and constructed female workpants to wear around their farm. Pants would make it easier to assist him with the calving, she said, determined to help. Scientist and teacher that she was, he had known she would be. As they worked, they talked quietly, their conversations rambling through many topics. He loved the melody of her gentle, thoughtful voice.

When the weather was bad, he insisted that Avery stay inside the warm house. There was no reason both of them should go out to be frozen and miserable. When he went out in the weather, he was usually welcomed back by the scent of cookies or bread, two foods he loved. As he washed up on the back porch, he felt entirely contented merely inhaling the aroma of the delicious food awaiting him. How he loved his wife!

It was much easier for a man to go out into blowing snow or freezing rain when his wife waited for him inside, probably at that exact moment making him something good to eat. He comforted himself with that thought as he fed the livestock and checked their hooves in bad weather. Unless the weather was particularly bad, they were still in the pasture most of the time. Then he'd bring the horses into the barn and the cattle would huddle on the south side of the windbreak, munching on the alfalfa hay he had put out for them.

Many stockpots of soup were consumed, along with many pots of tea. They read some of their favorite prose and poetry out loud to one another. The cadence of Avery's voice made every story and poem better, Prentis maintained. She said the same was true when he read.

Generally, they went to bed early. It was where newlyweds should be on long cold nights in January—pot-bellied stove stoked, pile of quilts upon the bed, Avery waiting under the covers, head barely peeking out as he finished with the chamber pot, stripped, and jumped onto the bed causing her to giggle. When he crawled under the covers, he felt like the most blessed man on God's frozen earth. On a cold night, it was breathtaking to roll into a warm bed with a beautiful young wife. God was good to have created marriage!

But, at the end of January, she still wasn't pregnant. She didn't weep, but she lay immobile for several days, the slightest sound or glimmer of light causing her excruciating pain. It terrified him. She looked like a corpse.

Opening her eyes a slit, she whispered a few words of instruction now and then. Aspirin didn't make a dent; neither did his gentle massaging of her temples, forehead, or neck. He kept the shades drawn and refreshed the cold compress often. Whenever she had to get out of bed to attend to her personal needs, he assisted her. She could barely lift her head.

Sunday morning came. He knelt by the bed, studying her face—pale and still, dark circles under her eyes, eyelids fragile and delicate. He made a decision and whispered to her:

"I'm riding to your church to let your pastor know you won't be coming."

She nodded almost imperceptibly, not speaking.

He replaced the cold compress, set warm tea on the bedside table, informed her it was there—got no response, bundled up, and headed for the door, begging God to take care of her. Would he arrive back home to find her dead? He now understood why her headaches terrified her mother. He was scared nearly senseless.

Hurriedly, he saddled Ulysses and pounded up the road as quickly as possible so he could return with speed. He was early, so he hoped he didn't have to wait for someone to arrive. As he rode, he begged God not to take her from him. When he trotted into the packed-dirt parking area, another lone rider was also arriving. Yanking his scarf down from his face, Prentis wheeled Ulysses around so he and the other rider faced each other.

"I'm P.J. Pinkerton—Avery's husband."

The other man pulled his scarf down, revealing his face— not much older than he, friendly smile and kind eyes. The man leaned across to shake Prentis's hand. "Tom McKinney. Glad to meet you, P.J. Your wife speaks highly of you."

Providentially, just the man he wanted to see. "Pastor McKinney, glad to meet you."

"Call me Tom."

"All right, I will. Avery's very sick. Need to get back. Wanted you to know so you wouldn't expect her for Sunday School."

That said, Prentis tugged his scarf back up as he turned Ulysses about.

"Is it serious? May I call after church? How can we help you?"

Prentis paused. "Her headaches are debilitating; she's paralyzed with pain. This is the third day. Worst headache yet. Bromide doesn't help, nor aspirin. Frankly, I'm frightened. A visit wouldn't be a good idea. Thank you for asking. But could you have the congregation pray?"

"We certainly will. Don't let me keep you. Give Avery our regards."

Prentis laid his heels into Ulysses. Sensing the urgency of his master, he leapt forward. Tom McKinney watched their departure.

As Prentis raced away, he considered the kind man he had just left. He liked him. From this brief encounter in the cold January weather, he could discern the man's character. Something about Tom McKinney's face and demeanor was humble and approachable, not stuffy, judgmental, or severe, as had been so many ministerial types of Prentis's youth.

Avery had told him about informing Tom McKinney of her conflict with Mrs. Riley. It hadn't bothered the young pastor. In fact, he had been sympathetic. And now, he hadn't chided Prentis or looked at him disapprovingly, even though he didn't come to church. Tom McKinney had treated him as an equal, another man in need, frightened because his wife was in pain. There was empathy on his face, a kinship regarding suffering. Pastor McKinney wanted to be called by his given name, in fact, a shortened version of it: Tom.

All of this gave Prentis much to think about.

TWENTY-THREE

MIDWEEK, AVERY AND PRENTIS were comfortably settled by the hot stove, working side by side, when Sam barked outside. A voice shouted from the barnyard, "Pinkertons! It's Tom McKinney." Both stood and headed toward the door. Prentis was pleased. This would give him a chance for further evaluation of the man.

"Oh, Prentis! Can we invite him for dinner?"

"Gladly."

Her surprised and perplexed expression made Prentis smile. He stepped onto the porch, giving Sam a pat when he ran up to plant himself beside him.

"Tom," Prentis called, "welcome!"

"P.J., hope you don't mind a visit. Figured I'd give Avery a few days to get on her feet. I was concerned and wanted to see if you both were doing all right."

"Don't mind at all. Good to see you. Go 'round to the barn, and I'll help you with your horse. Avery wants you to stay for dinner."

"Wonderful!" Tom McKinney turned his horse toward the barn.

Prentis ducked back into the house and told Avery that her

pastor would stay. Smiling widely, she followed Prentis to the back porch, while he put on his boots and coat.

"This is our first company," she informed him. And so it was.

"I don't mind having only *your* company." He glanced up at her.

"And I don't mind having only yours, but this will be fun. You'll like him."

"Already do."

Puzzled, she stared at him.

"I spoke to him on Sunday."

"But you said you merely delivered the message and then came home."

His hat was on; he was ready to go. "I did."

He wrapped the scarf around his face and stepped outside, leaving her staring after him with an even more puzzled expression. Under his scarf, he chuckled.

Out in the barn, the two men settled Tom's horse into one of the stalls. All the while they discussed the other livestock, farmer-and-rancher talk. When they walked in the back door, the aroma of fried potatoes welcomed them. They smiled at one another. *Food!* As they washed up at the back-porch sink, Tom McKinney commented on how handy the arrangement was, and Prentis gave credit to his father. Then, in they went, both grinning at Avery.

"Welcome, Pastor McKinney," she said, attaching his ministerial label to his surname, as all churchgoers of her denominational ilk seemed to do. Prentis smiled inwardly.

"Hello, Avery—nice to see you on your feet. After P.J. came, I was concerned. The congregation prayed for you. Your husband's face was white as a sheet when he rode in." He glanced apologetically at Prentis. "I've been as worried about him as I was about you."

They all laughed together. Avery seated them at the table, poured coffee, and brought in bowl after bowl of food. The two men smiled at one another as she made each trip. So their little table could seat three, she had dragged over Prentis's desk chair. Tom McKinney ate heartily, complimenting Avery on her cooking. Prentis remembered the hungry hardship of living off his own bachelor cooking. Tom was clearly glad to have home cooking.

The war had to be discussed—the Germans were using dirigibles to attack Great Britain. The zeppelin changed warfare. This newly developed means of air transportation was now being used by the Germans to bomb their enemies from the sky; "Air raids," they were called.

None of them could imagine being attacked like this, as if the clouds themselves had turned adversarial while sailing across the prairie sky. Prentis thought the dropping of a tornado might be an apt comparison. Barely affecting them in America, the scope of the tragedy occurring across the ocean was incomprehensible. Unobserved by any of them, it was inconceivable.

The discussion shifted. Each of them detailed their personal histories—their upbringing, schooling, and early years. In the process, Tom and Prentis discovered they were both passionate about baseball—the American pastime. Both enjoyed playing. Each recounted how they had come to trust in Christ as they grew into adulthood. Their hopes for the future were divulged. Prentis had never had such a companionable conversation with a minister.

Tom McKinney had grown up a farm boy in Kansas and then headed to Moody Bible Institute in Chicago for theological training. Grinning at Prentis, he mentioned that he'd attended the opening of Comiskey Park in 1910. This led to another baseball detour—an animated discussion about the White Sox and Shoeless Joe Jackson before Tom continued his story.

After graduation, he'd married a girl named Mary, and they had worked with the poor and destitute at Pacific Garden Mission. But then, tragedy had struck—Prentis had known that empathy had been written on Tom McKinney's face. His young wife and their newborn had died during childbirth.

As he told how it had affected him, Prentis gripped Avery's hand—it hurt to hear the story; it would be agony to suffer that loss. Battered and heartbroken, Tom had continued his ministry in Chicago for another year, first hurling angry questions at God and then yielding himself, trusting in the Lord's goodness. During that year, he had assessed the situation and had felt that God was calling him back to the plains—small church pastors were needed in Oklahoma as the land had settled in and the next generation came of age.

So he had come and was renting a farm about two miles south of the church. In returning to a rural life, he worked the land while serving as a pastor. Quietness and time for contemplation were benefits he needed right now. He'd been here two years.

After an afternoon of sharing their lives with one another, Prentis realized he'd been given a gift. They were now fast friends, kindred spirits, a trio—a rare thing on this earth, something that must be seized and held onto. During the day, Pastor Thomas McKinney had become simply Tom to Avery, as he already was to Prentis. Tom had Avery's grasp of theology and had been raised in a family much like hers, but he had Prentis's interests and was also a Kansas farm boy.

Tom stood. "Afternoon's gone. Just realized, I need to get home to care for my livestock. P.J., if you need any help with the calving, let me know. I'm only raising steers."

Prentis glanced at Avery. "Avery's determined to help me, but she's never had to pull a calf. We'll see how that goes. May take you up on that offer, if she finds she doesn't have the stomach for it."

Both Tom and Prentis chuckled. Even though Avery had read Dr. Roberts' veterinary book, they were aware of details that she was not. But Avery didn't laugh. Instead her face fell. Prentis squeezed her hand, but she merely looked down and smoothed her skirt.

"Well, on that note," Tom said, a friendly glance at Prentis, "I'd better depart."

Prentis went out to help Tom with his horse, waving as he rode off. He liked the man immensely. Not once had he lectured or preached at him about church. Openly discussing their struggles and their victories, they had shared the details of their lives as equals and had enjoyed the conversation of friends. He was glad he knew him.

Before he headed back inside, he fed and watered all the animals, tossing out more alfalfa hay. As he worked, he talked to Sam. In the house, he knew Avery was upset with him. Nevertheless, eventually, he had to go back in. He dreaded the coming confrontation.

When he entered, he found her sitting at her desk in their bedroom, staring out the window into the nearly dark barnyard.

From this vantage, he realized she had probably observed Tom's departure and his performance of the evening chores as the sun disappeared and dusk descended. Apprehensively, he stood in the doorway, studying her posture. She didn't turn.

"I'm sorry I embarrassed you," he said quietly. "It was wrong of me."

"No, Prentis." She turned to face him. "I'm sorry I embarrassed *you*. I shouldn't have taken up an offense at your teasing."

He didn't answer. He *had* felt uncomfortable, but Tom had looked at him with the understanding expression one husband gives another when it's obvious one of the men has offended his wife, Avery being the only wife who could be offended in this case.

"You were absolutely right," she continued. "I've been sitting in here talking to God about my attitude. I don't know one iota about calving. I've only read about it, and I'm sure it will be more difficult than I imagine. I shouldn't have been offended. You're right: I haven't pulled a calf. Reading about it is clean and tidy, but I'm sure it's messy and complicated. Then there's the fact that the odd hours will probably bring on one of my headaches. It was petty of me not to laugh at your lighthearted way of letting me know that you'll probably need Tom's help."

"Still, I shouldn't have teased. It's important to you. I'd only want his help after you've had a chance to be involved. I want you to experience this, not only because you're a farmer and rancher's wife, but also because you're you. You have to know— you've always had an inquisitive mind. You need to see what you've read applied to the practical situation."

Her eyes had been fixed on his as he made this declaration. Now she stood up and clasped her arms about his waist, looking up at him in the darkened bedroom, her face cast in shadow. "You understand me completely. Thank you. I love you so much."

He caressed her cheek. "I love you, too. You're not only my wife, but my dearest friend; you always have been." Bending down, he kissed her softly.

Her arms went about his neck, and she returned his kisses, responding warmly as she nudged him toward their bed. Then he knew she had forgiven him for his thoughtlessness. He was thankful to be married to a humble and forgiving woman.

It was good to have a wife who both talked *and* listened to God.

* * * *

At the end of the week, the first calf was born. It was too early, and the calf died. Avery cried, and Prentis tried to squelch his disappointment. Against their wills, they now had tender veal to eat. Prentis butchered the calf and stretched out its hide so he could tan it. The soft leather would be useful for delicate items. He had in mind new leather gloves for Avery.

The meat was so tender it melted in their mouths. At this time of year, he could avoid purchasing store-bought ice shipped in from Enid. All winter he'd layered ice into the icehouse during the coldest weather, breaking it off the top of the pond in slabs and then packing it in with clean snow, each layer lined with straw. He stored the meat there, bringing several cuts at a time into the house to keep in the kitchen icebox. They'd have beef every day.

These were the first calves for every one of his cows. It was the trial run. Everything depended on unknown factors. Perhaps they'd end up with more veal. Prentis didn't know if he'd keep the cow that had birthed her calf too soon. Did he trust her for another pregnancy? Unless he could make a profit selling her as beef, his investment on this heifer hadn't paid off.

But for now, he needed to get his four steers to market before the calving began in earnest. Recalling the miserable trip last year in the mud, he felt grateful for cold but dry weather on the Tuesday he headed out. He expended the entire day on the venture and pocketed a good price: $132.69 a head. After deducting feed, transportation, and other costs, that increased his profit to over $12 a head—almost double last year's gain.

Stopping off at the Citizens Bank of Wakita on the way home, he paid the mortgage for the first year and made a large deposit, banking the money until he could discuss strategy with Avery. Then he rode Ulysses home, thanking God for the increase after last year's losses.

He brought Avery a present, purchased in downtown Anthony during the lunch break—a silver toiletry set, engraved in Edwardian script with her new initials.

"Oh, Prentis!" she said, pulling his face down to kiss him. "This is one of the most beautiful gifts I've ever received!"

He grinned; he loved buying her presents, especially adornments and feminine items for her personal use. Having reconciled himself to the fact that his income wasn't going to be as high as he had hoped this year, he had determined to adjust and to put Avery first.

After she had tried out the gifts, they sat by the stove discussing the dramatic price increases for agricultural goods. German submarines now blockaded Great Britain, and beef prices were shooting up. That being the case, after he'd gotten some weight onto the cow that had delivered prematurely, Prentis decided to sell her for beef. Before they made additional monetary decisions, they would wait to ascertain their yield of wheat and the going price. If they made wise choices and the weather held, the war in Europe might result in financial gain. But it was all in God's hands.

* * * *

Near the end of February, calving commenced in earnest— two cows at once. Avery dressed in her workpants, bundled in thick flannel shirts belonging to Prentis, and prepared for a long night outside. Through most of the night, they checked one cow then the other. Strong, that was how she felt as she put her research into practice. Dr. Roberts' tome gave her confidence.

The first birth happened quickly. They missed all the excitement, arriving in time for Prentis to merely apply Umbilicure to the calf's navel, clean it, guide it to the cow's udder, and wash the cow with Antisepto. The calf was large and healthy, too.

"I'm definitely keeping this cow," Prentis told her.

Conversely, after a long labor, Avery now grasped the other cow's head.

After watching the agitated cow and running his hands along her bulging body, Prentis had informed her. "I'm going to check the presentation. Remember your reading."

Avery then discovered that Dr. Roberts had omitted some pertinent information.

Prentis removed his work coat and shirt before rolling up his union-suit sleeves. He slathered on Antisepto, cleansing both cow and man thoroughly, and then in went his arm, disappearing inside the cow. Having read Dr. Roberts, this action didn't shock Avery as much as it might have, but still, sights are far more powerful than mere words on a page. In addition, the odors were earthier and more primitive than she had imagined. She tried not to wrinkle her nose, but rather to fix her mind on the scientific and veterinarian aspects of the birth.

When Prentis was up to his armpit in cow, the water ruptured, drenching him with amniotic fluid as he attempted to adjust the calf's position in its mother's womb. He didn't even flinch. His focus appeared to be entirely on what his hands told him. An even stronger raw and pungent odor now settled upon them, causing her nostrils to flare. All the while, Avery struggled to keep the cow still. It lowed piteously right into her ear, a mournful, distressed sound.

But Prentis wasn't done with the poor thing. With his outside hand, he pushed hard against the cow's pelvic bones—hand flat against her pin bone, all the while pulling on the unborn calf deep inside the cow. Bracing his feet, he leaned back as he grasped the calf's presenting part.

"Traction keeps the calf from slipping back," he stated, without looking up.

"I assumed that was the purpose."

Prentis snorted, but kept his eyes on the cow.

This was all as Dr. Roberts had described, but the good doctor hadn't prepared Avery as well as she had hoped. Now she understood why men didn't discuss this in mixed company.

Though deep in the business end of the cow, Prentis acted as if this were merely another day's work. All along he had worn an absorbed expression as he had first attempted to discern what calf part was in his hand and how best to grip or turn it. With that all sorted out and traction now maintained, he finally glanced up at her. Her face must have betrayed her.

"You all right, Avery?"

"I'm fine. But this is far different than merely reading Dr. Roberts."

He chuckled. "Sure is." He continued to lean back, pulling on the unborn calf.

"The smell of the inner workings of a cow was unexpected."

"Yes, I imagine." He chuckled. "I'm used to it, so I hardly notice."

"It's also difficult to listen to the poor cow." Deep, drawn-out complaints still sounded from the birthing cow. "I empathize too much. I hope to give birth to your children someday."

"Thought it might be like that. I can keep it all business. I'm not a woman."

"I certainly wouldn't want anyone to do to me what you're doing to this poor cow."

"And you wouldn't want her calf to die, killing her too, if I can't get it out."

"Oh! No. Poor thing!"

"This might get even more exciting, if this calf doesn't . . ."

His expression changed. Something had happened. Out came his arm. The cow's knees buckled; down she went. The front feet and head of the calf appeared, the rest following rapidly.

Prentis examined the calf, keeping its head lower than its rear as the mucus and fluid drained out. It appeared lifeless. He cleared its nose. Briskly, he rubbed the tiny calf's chest with an old horse blanket. It uttered little gasps, finally breathing on its own.

Prentis's shoulders relaxed. Avery breathed—she hadn't even realized she'd been holding her breath. After he'd cared for the umbilical cord, he attempted to get the calf onto its feet.

"Get the cow up, Avery." He didn't look at her, but focused on the calf. "Need to get the calf to the udder. Calf's had a hard time of it."

The cow cooperated, to Avery's relief.

Trembling and wobbly, the new calf fell the first two attempts, but soon was up. Prentis positioned it against the cow, butting the side of her udder with its little head then squeezing the teat into the calf's mouth. Finally, it suckled. Cow and calf were fine.

Grinning, Prentis looked up at her. She had tried not to cry, but tears coursed down her cheeks. His eyebrows shot up, bewilderment showing on his face.

"It's a happy ending! Why are you crying?"

"Because it's so beautiful," she sobbed.

Gently, he smiled. "Yes, it is. Birth is absolutely beautiful—a new life, God's handiwork."

Through her tears, she smiled back. The sun was coming up. The birds were singing with joy, as if to welcome the new arrival. All was right with the world.

Watching the calf, they stood together, victorious. Nursing at the udder, it did well; the cow lowed contentedly now. Prentis was seriously in need of a bath from head to toe, but he leaned in and kissed Avery, careful not to touch her garments. How wonderful it would be when the birth they celebrated was their own child, not one of their livestock.

"A job well done!" he said. "Thank you. I think we can pull this off together, as long as a headache doesn't derail you. If it does, it's all right. I'm glad we did these first three together. You were a great help."

"Thank you. I need to get to bed, though. My head hurts, and I don't know if it's lack of sleep, the excitement of the moment, or the approaching monthly event."

"Go on in. I'll be in later. Have some cleaning up to do." He chuckled. "That's an understatement."

* * * *

The bright sunlight awakened Prentis, but something else had penetrated his foggy brain first. What was it? He blinked and stared at the ceiling; looked like noon, about five hours of sleep gained, not bad. Beside him, Avery lay curled into a tight ball. She sniffed—that was the sound that had pulled him from slumber. She was crying. He rolled toward her and peered over her shoulder. Her eyes were wide open.

"Sweetheart, what's wrong?" he asked.

"There's no baby again. I should have known when I got all weepy over a cow."

After hoisting himself up to rest his back against the headboard, Prentis then pulled Avery into his lap, cradling her to his chest so he could gaze down into her eyes.

"If we never have a baby, we still have each other. You make me the happiest man on God's earth. I'm entirely content. I've already been a father of sorts, to Fred and to Millie, and you've already been like a mother to your younger siblings. We'll be fine."

Quietly, she lay in his arms, watching him make this proclamation.

"Do you mean that?" she whispered.

"Absolutely. I'm a satisfied man, perfectly content. If God gives us children, I'll be happy, ecstatic even. But if He doesn't, I'll be fine. You're everything I need and want."

"You're the perfect husband."

"No man is the perfect husband. Not even Adam could pull that one off."

"I love you."

"I absolutely adore you. I'm head-over-heels in love with you. Give me a baby, and I'll be incredibly happy. Don't, and I'll love you just the same."

"Thank you for taking the pressure off me."

"This is God's responsibility, Avery. Remember Psalm 139— our days are numbered before there's even one of them. If a baby of ours is ever to exist, God already has his or her days counted and planned. Let Him have this."

She sighed. He felt her body relax in his arms. "All right, I will. I feel a headache coming. Let's pull the shades and get me some aspirin and the necessities. Maybe we can head off the pain. You'd better get Tom. We have twelve more calves to go, and the mares are right after."

"I'll saddle up and ride down. But first, I want to kiss you for a while. You were my assistant last night, and a better assistant a man never had."

And kiss her, he did.

* * * *

After asking one of the church's elders to look after his livestock, Tom packed a leather travel bag. He inquired about the theological books they had for his sermon preparation. Since they had some of the heavier books, he could leave these at home. Prentis was impressed by the size of Tom's library. It was much larger than theirs, even though Avery had brought an entire bookcase of her own library to add to his.

Tom was available for as long as they needed him. However, if Avery wanted to take over again and play midwife with Prentis, Tom said he'd come home.

Once he was ready, they rode back. As they entered the house, all was silent. The two men stepped back out onto the back porch, talking quietly.

"I'm going in to check on Avery," Prentis said.

"If you'd like, I'll circulate among the cows to check for signs of labor."

"Thank you, I'd appreciate that."

They parted ways. Prentis made a cup of tea and gathered some crackers. In the darkened bedroom, he found Avery lying with a cold compress on her head. Whispering the arrangements to her, he refilled her pitcher, so she had fresh water.

"Thank you," she murmured without opening her eyes. "It's not as bad as last time."

"Good." He bent down to kiss her softly on the lips. "I love you."

For a mere moment, she cracked her eyes a slit and gave him a tiny smile before smoothing her face again and relaxing into the bed.

Out he went. Tom stood waiting in the kitchen. "A couple cows look uneasy."

Prentis nodded. "What say we eat and wash up the laundry from last night?"

"Good idea. Get us all ready for whatever happens."

"That's what I figured."

Prentis stoked the fire in the cookstove, set two large cauldrons of water on to boil, retrieved two steaks from the icebox, and fried them up. They ate the meat with hunks of bread while drinking strong black coffee—hardy fare for tending to birthing cows. After washing up their dishes, they went out to the back porch with the steaming water to tackle the laundry.

Pumping cold water into the washtub on the left, Prentis swiped the bar of lye soap across his blue jeans several times before plunging them into the water, dunking and scrubbing them against the washboard. He repeated the process with his shirts and thermals. Then he ran each through the wringer while turning the hand crank, letting each piece fall into the washtub on the right. Draining the cold water, he repeated the process with warm water and then again, rinsing with cold. Birthing laundry required a bit more work than typical clothing.

As he worked, Tom hung the laundry on the clothesline, whipping the wrinkles out with a flick of his wrists. *Crack!* Meanwhile, Prentis washed the old horse blankets and towels. Within three hours of checking the cows, they headed out, grabbing the Antisepto, the Umbilicure, and a pile of dry towels and old blankets.

They got hardly any sleep that night.

In the wee hours, Prentis crawled into bed with Avery, sleeping until around noon, and then the cycle started again. He tried to look after her as best he could. Providentially, this headache wasn't as bad as the last. After only two days, she rose to become the laundress and cook, maintaining regular hours, so at least one person had a clear head.

Tom and Prentis worked the calving much as he and Fred had done, rotating, sometimes on at the same time, sometimes one sleeping while the other was with the cows. Tom spread his bedroll on the dining room floor. Periodically, Avery assisted them, once holding a cow's head as both men worked to pull a large calf. This became the pattern of their days.

As they worked, they kept up a running conversation about Romans 8—the chapter Tom taught now on Sundays. He did sermon preparation as time allowed. This chapter filled Prentis with joy. The love of Christ overwhelmed him. Nothing could ever separate them from that love.

Prentis recalled the lesson of the previous year. The assurance of God's orchestration of every event, every harvest, and every hailstorm for their good was important to comprehend and to recall with most of the world at war. When added to the fact that no baby was yet on the way, God's providence was an uplifting reality to consider. All of this was undergirded by His love.

Not only did this encourage Prentis, but in their private moments Avery whispered that this passage cheered her as well. God's promises brought peace to her heart. He was glad.

The group conversed about many topics. Of course, the war in Europe had to be dissected. Avery had gone into Wakita for supplies and had purchased a copy of the *Wichita Eagle*, an unexpected surprise south of the Kansas border, somewhat like contraband. Prentis was glad to read the paper he'd grown up on.

The Germans had sunk the British passenger liner *Falaba*,

and the Brits had retaliated by blockading all the German ports. That the Germans would attack a passenger boat filled with civilians was shocking. What did this portend and what appalling news would follow? They were glad they belonged to Christ, a steady source of help in all the chaos.

* * * *

One night the two men sat together by lantern light, watching a laboring cow. In the quiet stillness, Tom related how happy he'd be if Prentis would join them at church. Prentis detailed his current New Testament investigation. Since Tom was now acquainted with the Pinkerton-Dir wars of religion, he understood Prentis's reluctance. Tom reassured him that God would reveal His will to him, since Prentis sought His leading and wanted to obey Him.

"I can feel Him working on my conscience," Prentis said.

Tom chuckled softly. "He's pretty effective, wearing down the hardness of our hearts to get His point across. I know in my life that's how He works."

Prentis nodded. That was exactly how it was. Other than that, nothing else was said about it. Never before had Prentis been treated like this by a member of the clergy.

On Sunday, after the last calf had been born and all had been branded, Prentis drove Avery and Tom to church—the second Sunday of Tom's stay. But now, Tom's horse was tied behind the buggy. He was returning home.

When they arrived, Prentis jumped down to shake Tom's hand.

"Would you like to come in for the service?" Tom asked him.

"Not ready yet, Tom."

Disappointment flitting across his face, Tom nodded and smiled, clapping his hand on Prentis's shoulder. He'd already made clear how much he'd like Prentis to be part of their congregation. Prentis appreciated that he didn't add any words to their earlier conversation.

"We're going to miss your company," Prentis said. Avery nodded.

"I'll come back if you need help. Just come and get me, day or night."

"Thank you. I'm sure Avery and I can handle the foaling. But, if we need you, I'll come. It was a gift to have your help. Good to gain a friend."

"Feel the same. It was a blessing to be with like-minded folks, enjoying quiet talks."

Fast friends now, they shook hands warmly, once more parting ways.

As he drove away, Prentis had to admit that he wanted to stay. He was curious to know what Tom would say about Romans 8, the most encouraging chapter of Scripture he'd ever heard discussed. He wanted to please Tom *and* Avery. They both wanted him there.

However, it was crucial that he understand why church was important before he committed. The day might come when Tom moved away, or either one of them might be called to war, the way things were escalating, and then Prentis would need to know why he should attend. Nevertheless, an impediment had been removed. He had no fear of attending Tom's church.

* * * *

That night the first horse went into labor—Daisy. Prentis had circulated among the mares in the previous weeks, preparing their udders for nursing foals and watching them for signs of impending labor. Foaling was his favorite part of ranching; he loved horses. Growing up caring for the horses in their livery stable had left its lifetime mark.

Now that foaling had begun, after supper every night he checked all the mares. Horses tended to deliver in the nighttime. Carefully watching for the usual signs, he always knew which one would give birth that night. He knew his horses. He'd then wrap that mare's tail, clean her stall, and spread fresh straw, sometimes grabbing a quick nap.

In the privacy of the warm stalls, he loved watching the foals slide out, mother and newborn foal both resting before the final push when the mare rose to her feet, breaking the umbilical cord and finishing the birth. Prentis kept Avery up through most of one night so she could watch. No matter how many times he'd witnessed it, he always felt as if he stood in God's presence when his mares delivered. The event was sacred. It filled him with awe.

It was heartwarming to watch the mare lick the newly delivered foal, nickering softly to it. All the while, the tiny foal stumbled around looking for dinner, knowing it was somewhere under its mother—a God-given instinct. The foal tottered under its dam, wobbling on spindly legs, its tiny rump seeming too high by proportion. Until finally, it nudged its way to the correct spot and latched on, bringing relieved and contented sounds from the mare.

Watching the foal nurse touched their hearts. Avery stood beside him, leaning against the rail with tears running down her cheeks unchecked.

By the end of March, five perfect foals stood beside their mothers—two fillies and three colts. Daisy and Mabel, both experienced mothers, set the good example for the young maiden mares. All the mares nursed their foals well and exhibited excellent maternal instincts.

The Pinkertons never bred their horses in their foal heat. Prentis told Avery he would wait until the cycle a month later, giving the mares about five to six weeks to recover. As their next pregnancies progressed, their milk supplies would taper off. These changes within the mares' bodies would encourage the foals to stop nursing—a gentle way to wean.

Keeping the mares and foals together throughout made for happier, better-adjusted, easier-to-handle horses as the mares taught their foals herd etiquette and survival skills. Once they were weaned, halter and blanket accustomed, well mannered, and trained to respond to basic commands, Prentis would sell them as yearlings.

The foals were superb, and only one calf had been lost. Prentis felt relieved and grateful. He now had seven new heifers and seven new steers. In two to three months, he'd breed the cows again. In the fall, he'd sell the calves or fatten them himself.

In this way, breeding would occur at the same time as last year. Apollo and Rex would soon have work to do. This provided regular seasons of breeding, foaling, and calving on their farm—animal madness brought under control, harnessed for good purpose and financial gain.

A season for everything, Prentis would stick to it.

TWENTY-FOUR

APOLLO WAS ANTSY. THE stallion smelled the mares in their foal heat, but Prentis wouldn't allow the stallion to do anything about it. Supper had been eaten, and Avery was folding the laundry as she took it off the line. The garden had been planted. Nothing required Prentis's attention on the farm this April evening, and the stallion needed a long run. He informed Avery, kissed her at the clothesline, told Sam to stay put, and saddled his skittish horse.

Once they were out on the road, Prentis let Apollo go. On Sunday, he'd hitch him to the buggy for a long ride, if it didn't rain between now and then. Maybe they could visit Avery's family. They'd keep the stallion as worn out as possible until breeding time next month. The scent of the mares was driving him crazy.

The horse trotted to the corner, then headed north, galloping at top speed. Prentis leaned over his neck, giving Apollo the bit. He needed some time for reflection; Apollo needed to work off some frenzied energy—two birds, one stone. The calving and foaling had derailed Prentis's study of the church. Before he could recommence, he had to review. Recapping while he rode would allow his thoughts to percolate. No matter how hard the horse ran there was inner silence for pondering what he had discovered so far.

Spending so much time with Tom and hankering to hear his sermons added an incentive. Prentis had loved the Lord since He had become a Father to him, but was commitment to attend church God's direction and not merely something to please Avery and Tom? What if he only attended for that reason? What would happen when some event tested his resolve? And, people being what they were—sinners, something would definitely test him.

This was why he hesitated.

Reading straight through each gospel, he had taken notes on his observations. Before this, he hadn't ever examined the community of Jesus's disciples, His fledgling church. Therefore, he hadn't realized there were conflicts. But there were, written right into the Scriptures, nothing hidden. In Matthew 18, Jesus had even explained how to resolve discord in the church. Prentis appreciated the honesty and straightforward nature of the Biblical record.

In Prentis's mind, the first-century church, especially when Jesus was with His disciples, would surely have been perfect. He had assumed only the present-day church was flawed, with such judgmental people and constant argument—the part about church that sickened him and made it difficult to attend. He had learned that his preconceived notion was wrong.

Jesus's disciples had possessed varied personalities: zealots, tax collectors, honest men, fishermen, doubters, and a traitor. Whenever He sent them out, they went in groups or by twos, often with conflicting personalities paired. They'd had to cooperate to get the work done. There had been the twelve leaders and at least several hundred other disciples. All had been human. They had done more things wrong than right.

Judas had stolen money from the group; he had been a goat. Jesus had known all along that Judas was a goat, yet there he had been, serving his purpose. The same type of person was in the church today, also serving a purpose. Their very presence tested and refined the sheep.

Apollo slowed to a walk, having exerted himself at full speed for a good distance of the section. Prentis sat back and patted the stallion's neck, pausing in his considerations. They walked past the Miller's farm, Apollo breathing heavily. Prentis waved and called a greeting.

"How you doin', P.J?" George called back.

"Fine. Running this stallion. He's agitated."

George Miller laughed. "You puttin' him to stud yet?"

"Nope, pretty soon."

"I want to see how those first foals turn out."

"Don't we all!" Prentis laughed.

Apollo took off with a leap. Prentis lost his hat. Looking over his shoulder, he spotted the Stetson in the road. One of the Miller children ran out and grabbed it, waving it at him. He'd retrieve it on the second time around the section. Without that hat, the sun would be in his eyes when he headed west, and the farming world would see the true state of his thick wavy hair.

Neighbor greeted and hat lost, Prentis turned his mind back to his considerations. He'd been pondering personalities and conflict in the church. His last thought had been about the purpose of goats. Judas had been one such goat, but what about the others?

Peter had put his foot in his mouth frequently, even denying Jesus. John had a special relationship with Jesus, as had the siblings Mary, Martha, and Lazarus. Doubtless this had caused jealousy. Some of the disciples had been angry when Mary anointed Jesus's feet in the week before His burial. The disciples had reproved parents who brought their children to Jesus. They had misunderstood the repentant women who washed His feet with their tears.

James and John's mother had requested that her sons sit with Jesus in the seats of honor in His kingdom, one on His right and one on His left. They all had seemed to believe Jesus was establishing an earthly kingdom like that of King David. They had even rebuked Jesus when He foretold His death, wondering out loud, "What does He mean?"

Prentis had snorted, as he'd read it. He chuckled again now at their incomprehension.

They had usually been mystified, complaining, tired, or confused. These men had been frustrating, quibbling, petty human beings. The women had seemed to comprehend sooner. It was all written down, nothing hidden to make them look better. He liked that.

In short, they had all been human, like the churchgoers he'd known all his life.

He passed by the Horning's farm now. They worked behind the barn. It looked as though they were branding, or maybe castrating young bull calves. Curious, he peered at their activity, since Apollo walked again and he had time to observe. Castrating it was. All the boys were out there with their dad—no women present.

Prentis recalled when Tom had come to help him complete this procedure and to apply the Horn Killer, stopping the calves' horn growth. Avery had wanted nothing to do with either task. She had even skipped those sections in Dr. Roberts. Recalling her expression, Prentis smiled.

"I don't want to hear even one iota about it," she had said, upper lip curled with distaste, delicate sensibilities offended. "I know my opinion doesn't make one particle of difference concerning what, apparently, *must* occur, but what an insult to the poor calves!"

Amused by his recollection, he laughed out loud. She was absolutely adorable in every way. At the sound of his laughter, the Horning boys looked up and waved.

"Pink!"

"Hello, boys," Prentis hollered, greeting the entire group.

"Baseball game here—Saturday, right after supper. Can you pitch?"

"Count me in."

That sounded fun. He hadn't played ball in over a year, other than tossing a baseball back and forth with Fred or with Tom in spare moments during calving. The Hornings all waved and then concentrated again on the business at hand.

Prentis kept Apollo walking, soon rounding the corner to ride along the east side of the section. Returning to his ruminations Prentis urged Apollo to a steady trot. He reviewed his previous reflections and then continued.

On the night before Jesus's crucifixion, they had been fighting over who would be greatest. That had probably been difficult for Jesus to take. He had stripped off His garments to wash their feet, demonstrating how they should be thinking and acting. Then He had prayed for them at length, begging God for their unity, their comprehension of the truth, and their transformation by it. This prayer had been for the first disciples, and for those who would come to know Christ.

After the prayer, they had left for Gethsemane. All but John and the women had hidden in fear, abandoning Jesus during His most difficult trial. Three days later, the men had doubted the women who had seen Him alive. One had wanted to poke his fingers into Jesus's wounds when He appeared to them, resurrected. They didn't comprehend what He was doing until He rose from the dead and they witnessed the fact—*that* had been when they understood. And then it had changed them entirely.

All had been ordinary people. They had made the same mistakes and had participated in the same arguments. Apparently, there had never been a perfect assembly of people who had loved Jesus, as He deserved to be loved, not even the first group of handpicked disciples. Despite all this, Jesus had loved them. His had devoted His entire self to them, regardless of their hard-heartedness, bickering, and doubt. He had died for them.

It gave Prentis hope. If the disciples in the first century, handpicked by Jesus, had been sinful and uncomprehending and still Jesus had borne with them, then surely Jesus would bear with him as he tried to understand. Prentis was also His own handpicked disciple, though one who lived in Oklahoma in 1915. And maybe, just maybe, Prentis could model Christ's love and follow His example, bearing with judgmental, hypocritical, quibbling people within the church.

He needed to think about this. The idea of the church was growing on him.

Turning west, he now rode along the south side of the section, heading into the blinding light of the setting sun. How he wished he had his hat! Apollo loped now, running fast enough to vent his frustrations.

Prentis now passed the land east of his homestead, a beautiful piece of property. He hoped to buy this quarter section some day. He almost coveted it—he wanted it that badly, ideally situated, lush grassland, flat, perfect for wheat. As they raced past, he kept his eyes fixed on it, forgetting to mind the ridged road. Apollo was sure of foot, so all was well.

All of these meditations had taken him around the section—

four miles. Apollo still had jumpy energy, so Prentis started him around again. As he rode, he prayed about his realizations and discoveries, asking God to help him to understand what actions a man who loved Him should take. After using the concordance to ascertain if he'd missed anything, he would start through the epistles, seeing what they said about it.

In the distance, he noticed a child standing by the road—the youngest Miller boy, waiting to hand off his Stetson. When the boy spotted him, he burst out laughing. Prentis could imagine how his hair must look, probably sticking straight up, wavy and wiry. He thanked the boy, smoothed down the wild shock of hair, and settled the hat back where it belonged. *Ah!*

At the corner, he now turned left, circling counter-clockwise around the western section before clattering across the bridge and arriving at his farm. In the barn, he groomed Apollo, talking to him soothingly. He knew how the horse felt, in a primal and animalistic way. This period in a stallion's life was somewhat like Prentis's final waiting for Avery had been, except the horse had no comprehension of love. It functioned entirely on God-given animal instinct.

The sun dropped toward the horizon, the sky all pink and rosy as Prentis walked into the house. He had a spring to his step and an elated feeling in his chest. Peace was coming. It was pursuing him. The Holy Spirit was guiding and directing him. Allowing himself to be pursued, he felt happy. He went to look for his wife.

It dawned on him that Avery must have found peace in her struggle as well. She hadn't been crying as much, and her headaches hadn't been as severe as in mid-winter, when she had been wrestling with God about their inability to conceive a child.

The winter had been difficult because of these spiritual challenges. Gratitude for her companionship swelled in his chest. Even though his grappling with God had been solitary and private, her nearness had comforted him. He hoped he'd eased her trial as well.

* * * *

On Sunday afternoon, they traveled to Gibbon. Apollo ran hard. The buggy jostled and bumped over the rutted spring roads. Prentis's arms ached by the time they arrived. Everyone spilled out of the house, wearing wide smiles. After Avery had been hugged and he had shaken hands with everyone, they learned that Jerry had asked Dorothy to marry him, and she had agreed. He was over at her house at that moment. There would be a wedding in the fall.

Floyd and Hattie also visited today. Donald was passed to Avery, sampled, and still found delicious. Her face lit up over him, and Prentis expected more crying on the way home. He shot up a quick prayer for his wife's heart.

Donald was now almost eight months old, his face longer and slimmer, his black hair standing straight up. A proficient crawler, he cruised around eating every bit of lint, dirt, or dead bug he could find. Avery sat on the floor with him, digging objects out of his little mouth. Talking non-stop, Howard sprawled beside her, showing her the empty spots left by his newly-vacated teeth, never leaving her side the entire visit, as if he could cram all their missed conversations and experiences into one afternoon.

After staying as long as they could, they finally departed with a wooden crate containing two hens huddled together clucking nervously, and a young rooster, rescued from the tyranny of the older rooster, the mean, combatant chicken king of the barnyard. Avery informed him that these birds would commence her egg-and-chicken enterprise.

Beside them sat a picnic basket, the top fastened down and barely restraining two six-month-old cats, male and female. These were labeled *Adam* and *Eve*, the progenitors of all their future farm cats. The cats would reduce Prentis's loss of grain and feed and would keep the house free of mice. From within the confines of the basket, the two mewed piteously.

When they left, Avery didn't cry over Donald. This surprised Prentis.

"Sweetheart, you're not crying over the baby. What's happened?"

Facing Apollo's racing hindquarters for a moment, she then turned toward him. "You said once that complaining was like telling God that He doesn't know what He's doing. And it is. I would work myself into such agony each month—I made myself sick over it. Then I listened to what you said that day after I helped you pull the calf, I considered God's goodness and sovereignty, and I started praying about it. I gave it to God, trusting Him to do whatever was best and thanking Him for it. Instead of longing for what He hasn't given yet, I turned to what He already *has*—being a good wife to you and working on that Bible degree that has languished through so many interruptions. I got back to work, and I thanked Him for that, too."

He glanced, locking eyes with her briefly before turning back toward Apollo.

"I'm glad," he said. "It was difficult to see you in such pain."

"I'm sorry."

He shot her a quick glance. "No, don't apologize. I understood. I just don't like to see you suffering. I love you."

"You took such good care of me, even during the calving—holding me, encouraging me, admonishing me when I needed it. You're a good husband."

Whenever she said this, Prentis felt entirely content, happy to the core. Keeping his eyes on Apollo until the last moment, he ducked in to deliver a quick peck of a kiss.

"I adore you, Avery." He gave her another brief glance.

"I love you, too."

As he considered her confession, he decided to confide in her. Even though he knew she longed for him to attend church, she had never said another word about it. Therefore, he felt certain he could trust her to leave this between him and God. Briefly, he detailed what he'd been studying. He also told her that he and Tom had discussed it.

"I love the Lord," he said. "I want Him to show me what to do. Don't want to share my conclusions yet. I'm still thinking. But I want you to know what I've been doing. We're one flesh. We need to be united. Keep praying for me."

"I will. Thank you for telling me."

"I appreciate your letting this be between God and me. You're a good woman."

She snorted. "I try."

"You succeed." He flashed her a smile.

She kissed his shoulder then quietly rested her head against it.

* * * *

Spring arrived. Lettuce and beet greens unfolded from the earth, adding delicious variety to their end-of-winter diet. All of the animals grazed in the pasture, pairs of mothers with babies dotted across the newly green grass, including the recently purchased milk cow and her calf—a beautiful sight. Avery loved watching them as she hung the laundry or gathered fresh vegetables.

Prentis followed his annual farming plan, keeping her constantly informed. As spring enveloped and impacted their farming enterprises, tranquility and a sense of happy wellbeing pervaded every particle of their life together. Avery felt settled and content, glad that she had accepted Prentis's pursuit and his love and that they had married.

That he told her everything and she knew all his farming considerations and decisions heightened her sense of being a modern woman, a strong partner. No topic was deemed inappropriate for her scientific and business input. He explained thoroughly any questions she put to him, they discussed the whys, and he took her advice. He treated her as an equal.

Combined, this filled her with a sense of satisfaction.

It was easy to forget that war raged on the other side of the earth.

But, as they occupied themselves with these peaceful springtime farming and domestic concerns, the newspapers arrived in the mail bearing shocking news. Horrified, they read that the Germans had sunk a British passenger liner, the *Lusitania*, on May 7. One hundred twenty-eight Americans had been onboard, and 1,198 civilian lives had been lost—men, women, and children.

That the Germans would so blatantly attack non-combatants appalled them. The Kaiser was ruthless. Hostility and brutality increased. Less than two weeks ago, the Germans had used poison gas on Canadian forces at Ypres. Avery had taught her students about the barbaric medieval tactic of catapulting plague-ridden corpses into besieged castles and towns. This felt the same. Apparently, humanity hadn't made much progress.

However, most days the war didn't even cross their minds. It seemed a faraway event until the papers arrived. But the death of civilians and Americans and the use of chemical warfare brought it to the fore, impressing upon them both the horrific nature of war. President Wilson continued to reassure the nation that America was neutral and would stay out of it.

Nevertheless, word spread via *The Wakita Herald* that young men from the area would gather to sign a document stating their availability for a draft, if one ever came into being. Standing up to the Kaiser in their own way, they would put their names down to go and fight, if they were needed. A celebration of patriotism was planned, complete with the school band and drum corps, singers, and a speaker from Enid.

Prentis and Avery rode in for the event, having no idea who would be so adventurous as to say, "Draft me," assuming single young men. Avery hoped Jerry and John kept their wits about them, even though the document was unofficial, a mere gesture. It was simply a chance to stand in solidarity against the Kaiser, who would have no idea they had even done it.

Therefore, Avery about passed out from shock when Floyd stepped up with the other men—seventy total—and signed the line. If the War College and the president put a draft in place, they were ready to fight. Floyd had baby Donald, another baby on the way now, and Hattie. What was he thinking? Overwhelmed, she gaped at Prentis. Then she found Hattie in the crowd, and the two of them stared at one another, tears running down their cheeks.

But they didn't have much time to fixate on Floyd's action. An approaching tornado ended the festivities, and everyone scrambled for shelter. In the basement of the Methodist Church, Avery stood underground with the crowd, the darkness lit by flickering lanterns, the town's electricity having failed. In disbelief, she stared at Floyd. And he stared back at her—a standoff.

How could he do this? She didn't feel patriotic at all.

* * * *

Throughout the last weeks of May, the weather turned scorching hot, and the wheat more golden every day. By the first days of June the kernels passed the chew test, perfectly dry, but not too dry. The elevator verified and concurred; harvest was upon them.

There were four farms in the family now, since Jerry was renting. The owner had enlisted—he had actually signed up, not the mere token gesture that had occurred in Wakita. The sinking of the *Lusitania* had pushed him over the edge. He wanted to be ready, if America got into it. Along with fourteen other young men, he had left for Fort Oglethorpe in Georgia. Avery thought they were all crazy, especially since the President had urged farmers to increase productivity.

Since everyone's wheat came ripe at the same time, they had a family powwow to decide how to divide forces. Everyone gathered at Momma and Daddy's on Sunday afternoon. Avery and Hattie helped Momma carry out pie and coffee to the men, who all stood with Stetsons donned. Within the circle of wagons and horses, decisions were made. Avery smiled when she noticed Howard scratching his neck and spitting whenever Prentis did.

Daddy kept John, saying he wanted Howard too, because he was the most help. As he said it, he winked at Momma over Howard's head. Oblivious, Howard swelled with importance. Gene was now twelve, old enough to understand the family's efforts to make the baby brother feel significant, so he didn't appear slighted; he and Abe went with Floyd. Jerry had Dorothy's family; Prentis and Avery would rely on Tom, whose wheat wasn't ready.

The following morning, everyone got to work at his or her assigned locations.

The harvest took two weeks. During the work, another disaster struck. As Floyd's crew was threshing, Gene fell off a heavy wagon loaded with wheat. The steel-rimmed wheel ran right over his arm. Cushioned by the soft earth, the bone wasn't crushed, but the weight of the wagon peeled back the skin and muscle, exposing the white bone along his entire lower arm.

Everything halted while Floyd grabbed up Gene, jumped on a horse, and rushed him to the doctor, who neatly stitched the denuded arm back together. There was an abundance of screaming; Abe rode down to inform them. Having been the nursemaid for her little brothers, Avery wished she'd been there to help.

But at least he was alive! Farm work ended one life each year in the Wakita area. Often it was the boys who were lost. They prayed for Gene's recovery.

Fortunately for Avery and Prentis, there were no accidents at their place, and they got all their wheat in—a relief! God's kindness! Together they praised Him.

Avery got through harvest with no headache until it was over, but she never wanted to see another potato, nor did she care if she ever made another pie in her entire life. However, Prentis responded with such gratitude and appreciation that her efforts were worth it. Observing his patient kindness and the pleasant attitude he always displayed, even in hard circumstances, caused her heart to overflow with love for him, as it had done the previous summer.

They got fifteen bushels per acre, abundant considering the dry winter. Wheat was now going for $1.25 a bushel, but Prentis would wait to sell, seeing if the price increased.

A week later, both of them went down to help Tom with his harvest.

One benefit of being an attractive young widower pastor was that every eligible young woman in your church and the surrounding county wanted to help with the cooking when your wheat was cut. Of course, their mommas all came along, each attempting to jostle her girl into position and to draw attention to her daughter's good cooking skills and servant's spirit. As the observant older sister of a flock of brothers, Avery was well aware of these kitchen maneuverings. On the first day, she discovered there was no room in Tom's kitchen. So she bowed out.

For the next two weeks she stayed home to care for the animals and to prepare a pleasant environment for Prentis, feeding him before he left at dawn and waving goodbye as he rode west. When he dragged back in as the sun fell below the horizon each night, hot water was ready for his bath, and she welcomed him with open arms. He always appeared vastly relieved to see her, informing her every morning and every night that she was a tremendous blessing to him.

Loving him filled her with contentment and joy.

TWENTY-FIVE

PRENTIS SPENT JULY TURNING in the wheat stubble on his sixty acres. All the farmers of northern Oklahoma did the same, plowing a month earlier than last year. Near the end of each dusty workday, Avery scanned the horizon. When she spotted Prentis heading in with Ulysses and Hector in harness, she lugged the heavy water pot onto the cookstove. By the time the horses and livestock had been tended and the equipment stored, Prentis's bathwater steamed at the perfect temperature.

Every night he came in filthy and weary, a line of dirt embedded under his collar, his perspiration having caked the dust to his neck. He'd strip off his long-sleeved work shirt and unbutton his union suit, peeling it off his sweaty shoulders so it fell to his waist. Then he'd lean over the back-porch sink, scrubbing his neck and upper body.

Today he seemed particularly weary, so Avery helped him.

Prentis was a handsome man, and strenuous farm labor enhanced the appealing package. Long muscular arms braced on either side of the sink, clothing stripped to his slender bare waist, he leaned, bending over as she scrubbed his hair, neck, and upper body. Pressed close against his skin, Avery's heartbeat quickened and her middle softened, sweet and inviting.

Onto his sunburned neck, she gently massaged the warm water she'd heated, but the sweaty crease of dirt was caked on. Gingerly, she tickled it loose with one finger. When she had thoroughly washed his entire upper body, she worked the hand pump to rinse his hair and to run the soothing cold water slowly over his skin, cleansing and cooling him simultaneously.

"Ah!" he sighed, as she drizzled water across his back and neck with her cupped hands. Rivulets of soapy, muddy water ran down the drain.

"You should get a tractor," she said.

"And miss all this fun?"

She rinsed him one more time and then sniffed, turning to peer into the kitchen. "Can you finish up? It smells as though I need to turn the chicken."

Lifting his wet head—thick brown hair dripping, he laughed. "I'm fairly certain I can wash myself, Avery."

Giving him a teasing shove, she pushed his head back into the sink and headed toward the kitchen. He chuckled. Grinning, she ran up the back-porch steps. His good-natured attitude always made it a pleasure to help him.

It had been a windy day, and he was plastered with dust. As she turned the chicken, she could imagine his dirt-encrusted ankles where his sock tops ended. Opting for comfort and coolness today, he had worn a short-legged union suit under his blue jeans, eliminating one more barrier against the dust.

Catching a glimpse, her conjecture was confirmed. His ankles were filthy.

Altogether wet and bare now, he stood with his back to her, first planting one foot in the sink to scrub his foot and leg, and then repeating the process with the other. The advantage of his long legs allowed him to wash in the sink, the muddy water flowing right down the drain.

As she pounded the mashed potatoes, his glistening skin captured her eyes.

She wanted him. A modern married woman, a Christian, and a suffragette could admit that. God knew it was true. He had created marriage after all. Their love was passionate. Preoccupied by her handsome husband, she turned back to her work.

Thank you, Lord, for that man! Good God Almighty!

Behind her on the back porch, she heard him dump the remaining hot water into the washtub, adding cold water with the pump. Calculating where he was in the bath process, she glanced at the biscuits and peeked at the peas. On the porch, she stocked a supply of towels, clean union suits—long and short, and work clothes, as his mother had done in Kingman. It kept much of the farm dirt out of the house. He would dry and dress before coming in.

Avery fed him chicken regularly now. After setting the two hens on their first clutches of eggs, twenty-two yellow fluff-balls of baby chick had been the result, now grown to eating size. The cockerels went under the knife, runts first, one by one facing the chopping block whenever Prentis craved poultry. The pullets would be laying soon; they'd eaten only a few of them—the slow gainers. In the meantime, they'd been using the eggs from the two matriarchal hens for cooking and breakfast eggs.

The nervous, young rooster had grown arrogant, full of himself now that he had no competition—he even had a swagger. Prentis had named him Napoleon. Smaller than the mean old rooster at her childhood home, Napoleon had gained confidence as the dominant male, strutting about, attempting to conquer the entire barnyard, enjoying free range.

Tonight, Avery would feed Prentis one of Napoleon's sons. The young cockerel smelled delicious. She sprinkled in a bit more salt, anticipating the culinary delight of eating for supper a chicken she had been acquainted with at breakfast.

"The chicken's done," she called to him.

In he stepped, clad in only a fresh short union suit, clean blue jeans draped over his arm, legs and feet bare. "Can a man eat supper in his drawers when it's hot as Hades?"

"It's allowed," she laughed.

Avery had her own blouse unbuttoned to the waist, leaving her chemise showing. She had thrown wide all the house windows, creating more dusting to do. The day had been a scorcher, the flies and the heat oppressive.

"Clouds to the southwest," he said. "Cumulus."

"Do you think we'll get a tornado?"

"Thunderstorm and rain for sure, unless it stays south. Have to wait and see."

They ate in their informal and scandalous attire—she pulled her skirt right up over her knees as soon as she sat down; it was too hot to have yards of fabric upon a person's legs. Today she'd spent much time down in the cool cellar, shucking peas and fanning herself, all the while thinking of Prentis—*poor man*—sweltering in the heat.

Mid-afternoon she had ridden out on Persephone—the colt and Sam trotting alongside—bringing two of the Civil War canteens Prentis used to transport water. His grandpas, good Kansas men, had both fought for the North, passing down their wartime paraphernalia. She had swapped these for the canteen he'd carried out after dinner, so his water was fresh and cool.

Thirstily, he had glugged down the water, emptying one entire canteen then lifting his hat to pour the final drops onto the wet handkerchief he kept on his head. After strapping the second canteen across his chest for later, he had smiled at her.

"Thank you so much," he had said. "I was longing for you just now. Thinking of how a year ago I was pressing toward our wedding day. I drank hot dusty water and dragged myself back in each night to cold pancakes, bacon, cheese, and whatever I could scrounge in the garden. I appreciate your help. I know what it's like not to have it. You're a blessing."

She hadn't cared how filthy he was at that moment. She'd thrown her arms around him. Kissing the top of her head, he had held her close before replacing his hat and getting back to work. When she'd ridden Persephone back to the house, she had smiled all the way.

His love made her happy.

As they sat at the table now, he kept grinning at her. She could tell he was overcome with joy at the thought of this summer, as compared to the last. His white teeth and blue eyes contrasted brilliantly with his sun-darkened face. Below his collar line where his union suit lay unbuttoned to the waist, his abdominal skin was on display—pale and fair.

"You are definitely a white man." She caressed his bare chest.

"And you, my precious girl, are a sweet little Indian. Look."

Grasping her hand, he pressed her palm flat against his stomach. Her light-russet flesh caused his never-touched-by-the-sun alabaster abdomen to appear snowy white. Both examined the dissimilarity and laughed heartily.

"I missed you all day, beautiful Cherokee girl."

"And I thought of you baking in the sun. I could at least go down to the cellar."

"I love you." He leaned in to kiss her.

"And I love you."

"Let's wash these dishes and go sit on the porch. Maybe we'll catch a breeze. Want to enjoy having you beside me."

Once complete, they both headed toward the shady front porch.

"I'd better put on my pants before I step outside." Laughing softly, he slipped on his blue jeans. "A man never knows when his neighbors might show up."

Stepping out onto the porch, Avery surveyed to the east. It was hot as an oven. The light-blue sky shimmered with the heat, even this late in the evening. However, when she looked back at Prentis, she noticed it was much different to the southwest. Now gunmetal gray, the cumulus clouds threatened, towering higher and higher, the sky darkened all the way to the ground and up into the very heavens—a storm was coming. Repeated lightning bolts punctuated the menacing horizon.

With blue jeans on now and union suit still unbuttoned, Prentis stepped outside. Following Avery's gaze, he turned and received a fuller view. Hastily, he buttoned up.

"Most of the animals are already in the pasture. Probably safer for them out there anyway. They tend to cluster down in the creek's canyon—shields them from the wind. I'm letting the rest of the livestock out so they can run if need be. Be right back."

"I'll shut the windows and gather the chickens."

As they worked, a rush of cool air hit, mingling with the hot and humid, carrying sheets of gritty red Oklahoma dirt and debris. It scoured the siding, soft brushings and hard bits driven against the house wall. Flicks and droplets of rain arrived with the dirt, the fragrance carried on each gust. The clouds tinged green now. They'd probably have hail.

The animals clearly sensed the danger. They grew agitated and nervous.

Avery spied Apollo as he charged past Prentis out of the pen and into the pasture, tail high and head lifted, whinnying as he dashed into the wind. The milk cow appeared terrified, eyeballs rolling—showing white. Udder swinging, she and her calf headed toward the creek, Sam herding and barking at their heels.

The chickens were another story; they did not cooperate. Stupidly, they ran about, flapping and squawking, except the more experienced hens. These came right to Avery, who tucked them into their coop. Darting about, she chased the cockerels and pullets, luring them with chicken scratch, grabbing them before they could escape. Prentis helped her with the stragglers. As the first raindrops fell, he shoved the rooster into the coop.

"Here it comes!"

With her, he darted into the back porch. Together they stood at the doorway watching the rain. It soon came down in sheets, pounding the barnyard with walls of water.

The rainfall drowned the sound of their voices. Then, one after another, pea-sized pieces of ice landed, bouncing on the grass, as if leaping back off the earth in surprise at the rapidity of their descent. The barnyard was soon covered with ricocheting hail, now marble-sized. Then the wind picked up, bringing the scent of wet dirt. Prentis pointed to the southwest.

A long rope of white came snaking down from the low wall-cloud that trailed the hail. The finger-like projection could barely be made out. As the hail let up, the descending twister hypnotically captured their complete attention. The serpentine rope grew longer and longer, coiling out to one side like a living thing, searching and groping.

Then the tornado touched down.

Instantly, dark debris winged to the heavens. There went the newly plowed soil of the southwest forty, all of Prentis's work along the creek bed.

"I'm glad the wheat's already in." Prentis kept his eyes on the funnel.

"And I'm glad that twister isn't aimed at the house, barn, or granary."

"Thank you, Jesus."

"Amen."

The longer the tornado remained earthbound, the darker and dirtier it became as it sucked their farm's dirt into the sky. Odd bits of limbs, sticks, old leaves, and straw flew high into the atmosphere as the tornado devoured everything in its path, spewing it out in its wake. Traveling obliquely across their farm, it moved transversely across the grassland south of their house, inhaling a different type of debris there.

Still-green tumbleweeds, dried-out grass, prairie flowers, and dry dung now filled the sky. The tornado's path veered closer, though it looked as if it would pass south of them, traveling on a southwest to northeast diagonal. It should miss their buildings entirely. But still, it drew ever nearer, heavy rain now drenching everything. They could barely see the barn.

Had the twister changed course?

"Let's go down," Prentis said, "just in case."

Grasping Avery's elbow, he secured the door and hurried her into the cellar. In the sheltered corner under the stairs, they sat on the hard-packed dirt floor next to the shelves of canned goods—Avery's summer work of canned garden vegetables laid away for the winter. Today, storm-cellar spiders weren't a consideration, as they usually were when she descended those steps. In the relative calm of the dark root cellar, they still heard the roar of the wind.

Reaching over in the faint light of the dusky-green tornado evening, Prentis gripped Avery's hand, lacing his fingers through hers. Both leaned against the stone foundation, straining to hear sounds of destruction. The cacophony of violent wind still seemed the appropriate distance from their home, rather than bouncing erratically in their direction, as sometimes happened.

"Keep the animals safe, Jesus," Prentis whispered. "You are Lord of the whirlwind."

"Our lives and our possessions are in Your hands. We trust You."

"Amen."

Enduring the roaring volume of destruction, they looked up at the floorboards, as if they could peer through them and out into the farmyard to observe what was happening, trying to see with their ears. Soon they noticed the tenor of the wind quieting and changing in intensity.

Their eyes met.

"Let's go up," he said.

They ran up the stairs, through the kitchen, and out the front door, immediately turning southward to see if they'd been hit.

At first glance all appeared untouched—the trail of damage cut through the open field just east of their property line. Such a relief! Turning back, they watched the twister's progress northeast toward Wakita as the crow flies, bouncing up into the clouds and back down, thicker this time. Avery knew the citizens of Wakita were taking cover.

"Lord," Prentis said, "thank you for sparing our lives. Help our neighbors."

"Amen."

Mesmerized, they surveyed the path of destruction, considering where each neighbor's buildings lay in regard to its path. If it skirted Wakita, it didn't look as though it would hit anyone's homes or barns. But the few trees dotting the Oklahoma plain along its route had been stripped bare of their finery, twisted and broken in its wake, like shattered and gnarled posts stuck into the ground. The destruction left in a tornado's wake always shocked Avery.

Rain fell softly now. Once it eased they would spring into action.

"What should we do first?" she asked.

Like her, Prentis kept his eyes on the tornado's path. "Need to get out there and check the animals. If all's well and no injuries, let's saddle up. Neighbors might need help."

"Where should we start?"

He turned away from the door. "There's a little daylight left. Might get to the closest farms."

He headed into their bedroom, but she remained, watching the twister grow smaller in the distance as if lingering for the grand finale of its dramatic and captivating performance.

"Put on your workpants, Avery," Prentis called, breaking her fixation on the funnel and moving her to action. "Might have some messy work. Tomorrow we need to check on Tom—his farm's directly southwest on the tornado's path."

Considering the possible situations confronting them, Avery dressed quietly, cinching her custom-made pants and braiding her hair. Silently, she laced on her boots as he slid into his, and they headed across the muddy barnyard. An extremely soggy but wagging Sam greeted them.

"Good dog!" Prentis paused to give the faithful dog a good pat.

In the barn Prentis grabbed halters and a length of coiled rope, and they headed toward the creek. Wading through the pasture's damp grass, their pants were soon saturated to the knees. Sparkling through each residual raindrop like a prism, the sun peeked from under the clouds, rays of sunshine brightening the evening in startling relief to the previous atmospheric activity.

"Beautiful!" Avery stopped to gaze about.

Prentis nodded. "God's showing off. First His power. Now His artistry."

She smiled, and he leaned down to kiss her soundly. Cozily, they continued on through the wet grass, hands clasped.

"Got maybe an inch of rain. Should alleviate the dryness. I may have to re-plow that corner though. Looked like the tornado sucked up all my newly plowed soil. Probably as flat and smooth as your kitchen floor now."

"I doubt it," she laughed. He painted an amusing word picture.

They found the animals huddled in the lowest part of the creek canyon and coaxed them out with Sam's help. Prentis had stuffed his pockets with carrot bits from the cellar. The horses loved these. If he could get the horses moving, the cows, calves, and Rex might follow.

Downstream, where the creek came out of the canyon and swept across the lowland of the farm, Apollo charged around, agitated and covered with mud, crossing and re-crossing the widest part of the creek. For now, they dealt with the others.

With his carrots, Prentis soon lured out Ulysses, followed by Hector, and then each mare and her foal. He inspected each horse. All looked fine—timorous, but with no physical damage. Speaking soothingly, he calmed them with his voice and his hands.

Avery followed behind, singing softly as she stroked their cheeks and necks. Soon the mares spread out, grazing, colts and fillies following. Ulysses and Hector stayed close; Apollo still appeared frantic, stampeding about the creek. Sam raced off and ran circles around him, barking all the while. This hardly eased Apollo's nerves.

Rex came barreling up the embankment, bellowing to the cows that now lumbered out of the creek bottom along with their calves. But the milk cow—Artemis—remained stuck in the mud. Her calf stood bawling for her farther up the bank. After putting a rope halter on her and attempting to pull her out—to no avail; she only dug herself in deeper—Prentis put the other halter on Ulysses and slid up onto his back.

"Need to go back and saddle up, so I have the saddle horn for leverage. Have to hurry. Sun's close to setting. Want to ride back with me?"

"I'll walk in with the mares. When you've finished pulling out Artemis, ride up and get me. I'll come with you to fetch Apollo."

"All right. Sounds good." He smiled at her.

Prentis rode hard for the barn. Sam charged away from the creek bottom to join him. Humming, Avery sauntered toward the homestead buildings, attempting to soothe their animals. Stunned, they trudged along, following a straight line toward the barn, as if it offered some type of safety. The animals were all twitchy; the horses' withers kept trembling, as if they expected that *thing*, whatever it was, to rematerialize.

Soon Prentis reappeared on Ulysses, now saddled, Hector and Sam still sticking close. As they all passed her, Prentis smiled and lifted his Stetson wide in greeting as he headed back toward the creek canyon. Laughing softly to herself, she continued on toward the barn.

Avery soon heard the distressed lowing of the Jersey cow, the bawling of her calf, and the constant barking of Sam. Time passed. She could imagine the trial Prentis must be having with that cow. Eventually, a very muddy Jersey and an equally muddy calf trotted by, both herded by a mud-caked, barking dog.

Then over the hill came her husband, slathered with mud from head to toe. One muddy handprint was crusted to his hat from reseating it. His blue eyes peered out of a spattered mud mask. Causing his white teeth to show even more prominently, he laughed.

"Ridiculous cow wouldn't hold still and let me secure her. Gave me fits. Kept digging herself in. She'll probably kick me if I try to milk her tonight. I almost swore at her."

"So much for your bath."

"Looks like I'll need another one. You certain you want to ride with me to get Apollo?" Grinning, he held out his hand to her.

Avery peered up at him. He looked entirely mischievous.

After a hard day of plowing, a tornado, and a cantankerous cow, he still had a playful twinkle in his eye. From the time they were young, this was what she had loved most about him. With his calm and cheerful manner, Prentis was the best boy she'd ever known, the most fun in every way. And now, the boy grinned down at her out of the man's face.

She'd get covered in mud, but she couldn't resist. She gripped his offered hand. He hauled her up and surrounded her with his strong, mud-covered arms. Then he pressed his dirty face against hers, giving her a muddy kiss on the cheek. After a glance at the mark his face had left on hers, he threw his head back and laughed hard.

"You're the best girl in the world," he said, whooping as Ulysses jogged toward Apollo. "God is so good to me!"

She chortled, scooped a large dollop of mud off his knee, and then reached over her shoulder to smear it down the center of his face and onto his chin. That prompted another kiss. He leaned around the other side now, kissing her other cheek, daubing even more mud on her face—so she was even on both sides, he said. She tasted the red dirt of Oklahoma on her lips.

Both of them laughed so hard their sides hurt.

The stallion allowed Prentis to slide on his halter. Then all walked sedately back to the barnyard, where Apollo was secured for the night and Ulysses was let back out to pasture.

As they left the barn in the dusky twilight, Avery took off running, giggling uncontrollably. Prentis laughed when he caught her. Scooping her up into his arms, he covered her face with more muddy kisses as he carried her through the back-porch door.

* * * *

In the morning, Avery sat up, caressing Prentis's chest as she pushed herself up from his body. Gazing at her sleepy face, he threaded his fingers up under her still-damp hair and pulled her head back down to his lips, kissing her lightly on the forehead. Warmly, she responded, pressing her lips to his.

"Let's go help Tom." She stretched as she rose. "I'll fix a quick breakfast."

After slipping on her wrapper, she braided her hair over her shoulder as she shuffled toward the kitchen, yawning widely.

Prentis smiled as he watched her go then began to dress.

They rode up the muddy road on Hector and Ulysses. What they found at Tom's farm sobered them. He had suffered loss.

The roof of his barn had been partially ruined. The landlord would pay for the materials, and Tom would repair it in exchange for lowered rent. But half of his steers had been lost, simply vanishing as the tornado swept through his farm. His horses had run away, their fleetness of foot saving them. He and nearby neighbors had rounded them up and tended to their wounds. Tom thanked God that there had been no further damage.

Prentis and Avery comforted him, as did his parishioners who had come to his aid, many bringing food. But before this he had lost assets far more dear than livestock, so he had experienced God's sustaining grace. He was fine. He ended up comforting all of them. Prentis liked him even more.

Tom introduced Prentis to church members he hadn't met at harvest, most from south of the church. They hadn't been able to assist Tom at harvest-time, because their own wheat had ripened concurrently. All of them shook Prentis's hand warmly. All shared tales of what had transpired as the tornado had bounced across the farmland southwest of Wakita, touching down here, withdrawing into the clouds, and then touching down there.

Several of the men made a trip to town for supplies, and that afternoon the entire group made short work of the barn roof. Avery spent the day picking up debris and piling it to be used for firewood. There was no room in the kitchen again. Mommas and daughters were hard at work in there outdoing one another.

At the end of the day, Tom and Prentis agreed to travel to Anthony. Tom would purchase more steers at the sale barn, and Prentis would help him get them safely home. They would enjoy the time together. His granary having been spared, Tom planned to sell his wheat now and use his profits to pay his yearly rent and to buy the livestock.

On the way home, Prentis and Avery decided to make an anonymous offering earmarked for Tom—money to help with the purchase.

The following day, they began cleaning up their farm. While Prentis groomed the animals, made minor repairs, and replaced a glass pane, Avery began laundering the mound of muddy clothing and scrubbing the back porch, smiling to herself over precious memories of their marital intimacy. It would take a couple of days to clean it all, but she cherished the remembrances.

The remains of the garden having been pounded into the earth by the hail, this year's canning was finished. The chickens were rattled, but laying would recommence soon enough. Avery discovered one cockerel they'd missed when gathering the stragglers. He appeared to have been knocked unconscious by a hailstone. He stumbled in the following night—who knew where he'd been? He was never quite right after that, so she placed him next in line to be eaten.

The following weekend her family came down to check on them. By then, all the mud had been cleaned up and the repairs had been made. They had no other damage worth noting. It surprised them to find that Gene had been wounded again. He'd blown a finger clear off with a firecracker on July 4th. His hand was bandaged minus one digit. Excitedly, he told the story, minimizing the pain. Howard corrected his account, informing them that Gene had "screamed like a girl." Gene retorted that he had not; Howard merely nodded that it was so.

Avery decided that the problem with twelve-year-olds was two-fold: They didn't listen, and they thought they were invincible. They usually recovered from these flaws by the time they reached twenty or twenty-two, if they made it. She hoped Gene survived the summer.

After listening to the horrifying tale and sympathizing with Gene, as there were no additional repairs needed, Avery roasted three of the young roosters—including the hail-damaged straggler—and baked some fresh potatoes dug up from the garden. Momma had brought two pies, and it was a relaxing day catching up on family news.

Prentis informed them of the upcoming trip with Tom to purchase livestock.

Seriously, Howard stood, removed his hat, and fixed his eyes on Prentis. "If you need a man to help out while you're gone, I can look after things."

"Awfully nice of you, Howard. I'm sure Avery would be mighty glad for your help." Prentis turned toward her, his twinkling eyes signaling his amusement only to her.

"I'd love to have you, Howard," she said. "I'll need a man's help around here."

Howard swelled with importance. Hooking his thumbs into his suspenders, he shot an I-told-you-so glance at Gene, who scowled, looking annoyed that he hadn't spoken first. As their parents and the older boys drove away, Howard remained.

On Tuesday, Tom and Prentis departed to purchase the livestock, intending to brand the cattle and leave them overnight at the sale yard under the watchful eye of the proprietor. Then, they would go check on Fred, all alone up in Kingman.

Howard assisted Avery all week. He gathered eggs every morning, milked Artemis, observed the mares and their foals, and played with Artemis's calf—Howard named him Beefsteak. Avery knew the name would stick. She loved having him. So did Sam—he followed Howard everywhere. Prentis enjoyed his company, too, both before he left for Anthony and after he'd returned. While Prentis plowed, Howard and Sam chased the little rabbits and horned toads that hopped about in the dry Oklahoma soil. Sitting with Avery on the front porch, Prentis spoke of Howard fondly as they watched boy and dog herding the chickens around the barnyard.

The following weekend, they drove Howard home in the buggy, arriving to find Gene in bed with a wounded head to match his injured hand and scarred arm. He had been prone to sleepwalking all his life. Now that summer was its hottest, they had thrown wide the windows to catch every Oklahoma breeze that was to be had. On a particularly hot night, Gene had taken a walk right out a bedroom window, falling to the ground and banging his head.

As they drove home that evening, Prentis shot Avery a wry expression. "So. You still positive you want six boys?"

She laughed. "Now that I'm looking at it from a different angle, I'm not entirely certain."

"That's what I thought." He grinned.

Once home, Prentis stepped into their room and returned with a package.

"This is something I bought you in Anthony. Thought it best to wait until Howard was gone to give it to you though. Requires a bit more privacy than we had while he was here. He would have asked some amusing questions."

Curious, Avery untied the ribbon that held the box securely closed. Lifting the lid, she found a sheer, silk negligee.

"You're right about, Howard." They laughed together.

She lifted out the negligee—it was lovely, a chemise, falling to mid-thigh with lace shoulder straps above a bodice the color of Oklahoma mud, a rich reddish-brown.

"I'm paying homage to the night of the tornado," Prentis said.

"A beautiful memory." She gazed up at him from the lingerie.

"I feel differently about the mud this year, as compared to when it kept me from you. It's exactly the opposite now, especially after that tornado—it's worth commemorating. Like to see you slathered in mud again, if I could.

TWENTY-SIX

IN LATE JULY, *THE Daily Oklahoman* arrived with sobering news. In response to the sinking of the *Lusitania*, President Wilson had directed Secretary of War Garrison and Secretary of the Navy Daniels to draft a defense plan. Anger at Germany's policy of torpedoing civilian ships without warning was expressed in print. President Wilson also urged farmers to plant as many crops as they could and to raise as much beef as possible. The American farmer was now a patriot, he said, not only keeping his own country alive, but Europe as well.

Prices would definitely go higher. Wheat now stood at $1.30 a bushel.

For the first time since the war had begun a year ago, Avery doubted that their nation could avoid being dragged into the carnage on the European Continent. In spite of what the president said, she didn't know whether America could remain merely the supplier of food and manufactured goods. Europe was overtaxed. In France and Belgium over a million British men faced off against the Germans in trench warfare. *A million!* British women produced munitions and filled other industrial positions typically held by men.

Additionally, the Ottoman Empire—allied with Germany, Austria-Hungary, and Bulgaria—oversaw an atrocity, a possible genocide. Turkish forces waged war on unarmed civilians within their borders, attempting to eradicate the Armenians—a Christian minority within the mostly Mohammedan[4] country. Horrendous tales leaked out from behind the Ottoman-Turk wall of silence. Though rebuked by their allies, the massacres continued unabated.

With the world gone mad, Avery hoped their country could avoid the insanity, but she was skeptical. She was glad the token "draft me" action Floyd had signed in Wakita was merely symbolic. She didn't want any of the men she knew to go, but neither did she want the madness of the dictators of the Central Powers to prevail. She felt torn in two over it.

As she worried, her head began to throb, the light aura flashing in her visual periphery. The monthly headache had arrived—no baby again. It was almost a relief. The world had lost its way. The thought of bringing a child into such a world terrified her—another thing to trust into God's hands. She longed for babies. Yet now, she was once more afraid to have them.

* * * *

Tom McKinney came to talk strategy. In light of President Wilson's directive, they needed to discern the ideal course for the highest productivity. Quietly, Avery listened as Tom and Prentis bounced around the considerations of alfalfa maintenance and the best use of money and land. Prentis considered taking some of his acreage out of wheat production to plant alfalfa. This was the next step in his farm-improvement plan. Growing his own feed would enable him to buy more livestock. Should he do it? Should he pay off the mortgage or buy more cattle? What should he do with his money and land? Round and round they went.

Avery fed them fried chicken; soon they would have an abundance. Needing chickens to slaughter when the weather turned cold, she'd set many of the young hens on clutches of eggs.

Listening to their discussion, she contemplated something she wanted to discuss with Prentis, evaluating how she should make her appeal. When Tom left, Prentis and Avery stood on the porch waving; their arms draped about one another's waists.

The decision had been made to plant alfalfa now and invest in the farm, keeping to Prentis's master plan for improvement.

Eyes still on Tom as he headed west, Prentis said, "So, what's on your mind, Avery?"

"What do you mean?"

"You weren't your talkative self. You were preoccupied. What do you need to tell me?"

He looked down at her; she smiled a slow smile. "How do you know me so well?"

"From the time we were barely older than babies, you'd sit me down and tell me everything on your mind. Seemed to make you happy. One of my earliest recollections is of sitting on the ground with you, gazing at your face while you explained something in great detail."

"What was it?"

"Don't recall the subject, only your earnest expression—your black eyes staring into mine as you talked your way around the topic. You were absolutely fascinating to me. Still are. After you'd explained everything, you walked off, smiling and contented to have unloaded on me."

"That's so true! I hadn't thought of it. Talking with you makes me happier than anything else I do."

"You've got something to say—I recognize the look. Let's have it."

"Well, there went my introduction."

He chuckled then waited for her to state whatever was on her mind. Reorganizing her thoughts, she looked down at her boot tips a moment, and then she peered up at him.

"I've decided I want to tell you later. It's a surprise."

"Are you certain?"

"Completely."

"Hmm. A surprise. Now that gives me something to be curious about."

"Yes, it does."

* * * *

Prentis's excitement propelled him out of bed before dawn the following morning. As he stepped into his union suit, he detailed the plan. Propped on one elbow, Avery listened, looking so beautiful that he almost pitched his intentions and crawled back into bed with her, but this was the best time and weather to prepare the soil for alfalfa. The tornado had knocked them right out of the dry spell. Rainfall had been regular.

Refocusing, he aimed himself back toward the work.

"I'm going to pace off the creek's lowland. The soil's rich and moist there. It's better suited for alfalfa than wheat. Need to inspect it. Can you call me when breakfast is ready?"

Smiling, she nodded. "Absolutely."

Out he went. As he inspected the land, he felt energized and optimistic.

When she clanged the bell, he headed back in, inhaling the aroma of coffee and bacon as he approached the house. *Delicious!* Animated by what he'd seen during his inspection, he reported how much they'd save by raising their own feed. Out loud, he calculated how many steers he should buy, which of his calves he should keep, and which he should sell. He talked about paying off the mortgage, but he was still uncertain, and it affected his other decisions.

Quietly, she listened to everything, pondering his words and nodding.

After they ate, he helped her wash the dishes so they could go out together. As soon as he'd seen her in her work pants with her hair braided, he'd known she wanted to help.

Both astraddle, they rode Ulysses, Avery held between Prentis's arms with her head leaning back against his shoulder. Sam trotted alongside. Pondering how best to prepare the soil, Prentis silently considered everything he'd discerned earlier, calculating his needs and planning.

Now he needed to think out loud. "It'll take forty to sixty pounds of alfalfa seed." His lips brushed against her cheek. Pausing, her gave her a peck of a kiss.

She nodded.

"Won't disk the plowed wheat stubble here. Need rain right before I plant. End of August or early September—God's timing. After it's in the ground, we'll ask the Lord for more rain."

Again she nodded.

Weighing all of this in his head he paused, strategizing as he stared at the horizon. Decision made, he punctuated his considerations with a smack of a kiss on her cheek again. He loved that she knew he had needed to talk that through uninterrupted.

"Avery, I'm of a mind to shovel out the stalls and the barnyard, haul the manure down here, and spread it on the field. Then I'll plow one more time. It will enrich the soil before I plant."

"That's a good idea. I'll help."

"It will be dirty work."

"I'm a farm girl," she reminded him.

"I'll do the shoveling; you drive the wagon."

* * * *

Near the end of August, Prentis came in for dinner and found Avery crying on the back step, face swollen with tears. The newly arrived newspaper lay strewn across her lap and the back step. Teardrops had left marks upon the page, and the paper had been crushed in her agitation.

"Look at this!" She held up *The Daily Oklahoman,* wadded and crumpled.

Taking a seat beside her on the stoop, he read the article she indicated—in bold at the top, hard to miss. It stated that *The Washington Post* and *The Baltimore Sun* had printed similar news features a week ago, their reports separated by a few days. These papers had written that the military's general staff was preparing to send one million American soldiers overseas and Secretary of War Lindley M. Garrison had requested a statement of military policy.

This sounded ominous.

Prentis folded the paper and pulled Avery onto his lap. "God took care of us when we lost our wheat and when the tornado hit. Can He take care of us if our nation goes to war?"

"Yes," she sobbed, "but what if they take you?"

"My life is in God's hands, Avery. He already has my days ordained. It's always out of our control. Just feels more particularly so right now."

"But what would I do? I don't even have a baby who looks like you to hold and kiss if—" She burst into fresh tears at the thought.

"God would watch over you. But, Sweetheart, they need to keep farmers like me producing food. You know what the president said—they can't take farmers. *Food Will Win the War* is his motto, remember? Why, Floyd must not have been too worried about it, even though he signed that meaningless piece of paper—he just bought the Wakita Dray Line."

She sniffed, lifted her head from his shoulder, and looked into his eyes. "That's true. Do you really think they won't take farmers?"

"I do. The world has to eat."

"Good. But it seems selfish to be relieved, because they'll take someone's husband and brother and son."

"President Wilson will keep us out of this war. He's done a good job so far. These are just rumors. Let's wait and see."

"I'll try not to let my mind run away with me."

"Remember what is says in Philippians Chapter Four—don't be anxious. Take all your concerns to God. Ask His forgiveness for not trusting Him. Thank Him for His sovereign control. Think on the true things, not the possible calamities."

The following week good news arrived. In response to America's demand and to the comments in the national newspapers, Germany agreed to stop sinking ships without warning. The German offensive against Russia also ended. They'd driven the Russians out of Poland.

Prentis tried to keep Avery from fixating on the news. That attempt was futile.

Not only did she have lessons to mail and new units to receive, but she was also inquisitive. Each day, she ran out to grab the rural mail delivery, often crying over the paper.

Several times she had a similar nightmare: The Army came, grabbed him right out of the field, and marched him away, leaving her standing alone and weeping as he disappeared into the distance. In all their lives, he'd never seen her struggle with anxiety as she did now.

To combat these fears and worries, Prentis suggested they begin each day by reviewing Scriptures that encouraged them. Lying in bed together each morning, they quoted these to one another, eyes fastened on the other. Then they discussed how these Scriptures affected them, soothed their hearts, and altered their actions. Starting the day like this fortified them.

Avery feared losing him and having no baby to console her.

At the same time she felt anxious over bringing children into the world at all, in light of its current state. Throughout the day, whenever fear reared its petrifying head, he reminded her of these passages, weaving them into their conversations. In this way, they both remembered the truth and remained strong, although the situation in Europe grew increasingly bleak and Avery's womanly heart was rent.

TWENTY-SEVEN

FOR THEIR ANNIVERSARY, AVERY wanted to attend a movie at The Electric Theater in Wakita: *The Birth of a Nation,* a performance about post-Civil War Reconstruction. This moving picture featured many groundbreaking special techniques. Still, Prentis couldn't comprehend why she wanted to go. The controversial movie promoted the Ku Klux Klan and portrayed people of African ancestry in a patronizing manner. This would be a painful reminder that Avery's ancestors had been treated similarly, attempts to massacre and corral them to extinction having been carried out.

Prentis had grown up hearing her parents recount their family tale to his own folks. He had always listened in, appalled each time he heard them discuss it. He knew *The Birth of a Nation* would remind Avery of the injustices her people had also suffered. Why reopen old wounds?

Additionally, the movie spoke strictly against interracial marriage—*miscegenation,* an offensive term used by misinformed bigots who believed God's law forbade intermarriage. It was obvious from reading the New Testament that race was of no consequence in God's eyes. All social and racial divisions had been removed by Christ's sacrifice. It was stated in practically every epistle. For the Slaughters, intermarriage comprised their entire family tree, including his marriage to Avery. This was another reason not to see it, as far as Prentis was concerned.

"Avery, I don't want to watch this movie and then spend the rest of the evening railing against the inhumanities of the United States government. We've just finished studying Romans 13. We're attempting to remember that God uses governing authorities in His sovereign plan, whether in war or peace. He even uses their mistakes. Why, if Andrew Jackson hadn't carried out his flawed assumptions, your parents would never have met, you wouldn't exist, and I wouldn't have the joy of being your husband. God used even *that* for good."

She smiled at him a moment. "You always disarm me."

"That's my aim."

"Well then, since the outcome worked together for our good, surely we can see this movie without it upsetting us, don't you think?"

"Nope. It's entirely too personal. Negroes[5] and Indians are portrayed in demeaning ways. That will upset you. Then there's miscegenation. That will upset me. How any Christian person can think such a thing is beyond me."

"But we'll miss this important event. Everyone's seen it. Why, when Johnny saw it, he was so hopping mad that he rode his horse out here to tell us about it."

"A good reason to miss it."

"That made me want to see it for myself. As an educator, I should know what the public perception is."

"You know what the public perception is. As a Cherokee and a Christian you know the sinfulness of hard-hearted people. Do you need to be reminded?"

"We're arguing over what to do on our anniversary." She laughed. "We've moved on from verbs and socks."

"So it would seem." He smiled at her.

"Can we please go?"

"Hate to give them my money. However, I'll do whatever you want. You know I love you beyond all reason. I'm simply advising against it. But please, Avery, think about it. You'll cry yourself to sleep. Doesn't sound like a particularly romantic film for a first anniversary."

"Ah, so it's romance you're after?"

"I have romance simply by opening my eyes in the morning and seeing your face."

"Well spoken." She leaned in to kiss him. "You melt my heart."

"Good."

The conversation was tabled for the moment.

Prentis hoped she would decide against the film and choose the opera house instead—they would be playing John Philip Sousa's patriotic marches. However, when he suggested it, she became cynical, saying the Sousa medley had been chosen to soften them up so they could draft their men and send them off to war. He asked what the music selection committee at an opera house in Wakita, Oklahoma, had to do with the United States government's decision to impose a draft. She snorted and walked away, offended by whoever *they* were, muttering that women needed the vote so these travesties wouldn't occur.

She had been particularly opinionated lately, almost cantankerous.

* * * *

The morning of their wedding anniversary, Avery sat bolt upright in bed. The day was still dark and cool, the sun creeping toward the horizon. Overjoyed to see the faintest hint of the sun's return, the birds were making a racket about the coming sunrise.

Preoccupied, Avery counted in her head and then recounted, stunned by her conclusions. Prentis lay on his stomach sprawled across the bed, one foot hanging off the bottom as usual. When she sat up so abruptly, she had displaced his arm across her waist. In his sleep, his hand now plucked at the bedding. When he couldn't locate her, he made a soft and dissatisfied sound, shifting uncomfortably, as if he had lost his mooring—still she sat. Still he slept.

A blissful dream had awakened her: Her own sweet dark-eyed baby smiling at her, burbling. Was she pregnant? When had her last woman's time occurred? Numbering on her fingers, she counted once, twice, three times. Then a slow smile spread across her face. *Ecstasy!* Could it be? That would explain all the recent weeping and crankiness. She'd been afraid she had lost her mind. She hadn't been able to quit crying, worrying, nitpicking, or arguing.

Smiling, heart bursting with love, she scooted back under the covers, carefully lifting Prentis's sleep-heavy arm and sliding in underneath. Quickly, still sound asleep, he pulled her tightly into his embrace. Spooning now, he issued a soft, satisfied exhalation. After one year, they were entirely accustomed to sharing a bed. Now instinctual, he sought her even in slumber.

His skin felt warm against her back. All wakefulness dissipated. Sighing with contentment, she snuggled her head in under his chin.

Much later, she woke again, slowly opening her eyes. The sun shone brightly.

Gazing down at her, Prentis was propped on one elbow studying her face, blue eyes filled with adoration. Regarding her tenderly, he brushed her long hair back from her face, lightly traced the shape of her ear, and lowered his mouth to it. She rolled toward him and smiled. Leaning in, he kissed her forehead.

"Happy anniversary, my beloved wife."

"And to you, too, best husband in the world."

"Been lying here, thanking God. You're the greatest blessing of my life."

"I have to say, that's entirely true for me, too."

"Remember the glorious day? I could barely contain my joy at saying those vows and then bringing you home to make you my own."

"A pinnacle in our lives, like a mountaintop, as if it were a little foretaste of heaven. I love you so dearly."

"As I do you." He softly touched her lips with his. "So, what are we doing today?"

"First, we're looking at the calendar."

* * * *

Puzzled, Prentis watched Avery climb out of bed to retrieve the wall calendar. Carrying it back, she snuggled in beside him. Flipping to July, she touched the *31* with her finger and said, "One." Turning to August, she continued counting, tapping each day, then into September.

"Thirty-six," she said when she reached September 4, this very day.

Then she lay back, regarding him with mysterious eyes.

From this expression, he knew she wanted him to guess.

All right, he'd play the game. Flopping onto his back, he stared at the ceiling, biting his lower lip as he searched his recollections. She had started counting at July 31. Why was it significant? Plowing was in early July, then the tornado and the mud. He smiled as he recalled it.

"What are you smiling about?" she asked.

Turning to meet her eyes, he grinned mischievously. "Mud. I'm working my way through July. Just arrived at the tornado and the muddy aftermath."

She smiled back then pressed her lips together, remaining secretive, giving no clues.

What next? He reviewed July. He'd gone away to Anthony with Tom. Howard had stayed. July had been another bad month for Gene. Frightening news had come in the paper. She'd been crying, afraid to have children, but crushed that once more there would be no baby. He had comforted her—that had been July 31.

"I've got it. July 31 was when the newspaper announced a defense plan was being drafted. You doubted we could stay out of the war."

"And—"

Hmm. Why that day? What came next? He had to think.

They'd prepared the soil for planting alfalfa. He'd sold the wheat. There had been a satisfying quantity of physical intimacy in August. He smiled again.

"What?" she said.

"I recall some particularly good back rubs and the amount of time we spent in this bed."

She grinned at him, but said nothing. Pointedly, her eyes fixed on his, willing him to guess. Tracing back and forth between the events of July and August, he remained mystified.

Then it dawned on him. He was staggered.

Rolling toward Avery, he stared at her. "Are we expecting a baby?"

"I believe we are."

His breath caught. Momentarily stunned, he was speechless.

She stroked the stubble on his cheek. "It's been thirty-six days since my last time of the month. But I'll have to make an appointment with the doctor before we can be certain."

He stared into her eyes. It appeared to have finally happened! He recalled her emotional vulnerability and heightened irritability, and he smiled inwardly—*this* might be the cause. Breaking into wide smiles, they hugged one another tightly.

Prentis found his voice. "Thanks be to God, Avery!"

"Let me see the doctor first, but it may be."

"This is a wonderful anniversary gift. That's all we need to do today—rejoice over this! Don't want to get too excited before you see the doctor, but what else could it be?"

"I can't think of a thing."

They hoped and prayed that it was true. The day was spent rejoicing, planning, eating favorite foods, strolling by the creek, kissing, and thanking God for His kindness.

Avery didn't mention the controversial film, and Prentis didn't remind her.

* * * *

Gifts were exchanged over supper, which was eaten by candlelight late in the evening. Avery reacted to her gift exactly as Prentis had hoped, tea gowns being fashionable just then. Gleefully, she held it up before her and then hurried into their bedroom to try it on.

He followed, lit the lantern, and watched her face.

"Oh, Prentis!" Happiness burst out of her. "It's perfect. So beautiful! I can wear it all this month, while the weather's still hot. And then, my body shape will probably prevent it after that, but I can wear it next summer, too."

At this future possibility, they smiled at one another.

Then she reached into her drawer, drew out a miniscule package, and handed it to him. Simultaneously, they sat down on the bed. Opening the gift, he was puzzled to find a bankbook.

"What's this?" Bewildered, he looked up at her.

"My bankbook."

Awaiting further explanation, he stared at her.

"I'm earnest about this, Prentis. I want to invest in our farm. The world is at war."

"What do you mean?"

"I think, my dear husband, you've forgotten that I have over a thousand dollars banked."

"I had indeed," he said slowly.

He opened the book and thumbed to the balance.

"I'd like you to pay off the mortgage with my savings. Then you can use all the money from the steers and the wheat to expand our operation. With the land paid for outright, we're fine, no matter what happens."

Weighing the implications, he stared into her eyes.

"What's mine is yours," she added. "We're in this together."

"Yes, we are."

"Please, Prentis. Please accept my gift. We're one now. This is the surprise I've been contemplating for so long. I wished I could have given it to you right before we married, when you lost the wheat, but I promised I wouldn't bring it up again. I've thoroughly considered it."

"I'm stunned, Avery. This has been a day of surprises. I'd forgotten all about your savings. Your money may be the key to our success."

"That's exactly what I was thinking."

"I accept your generous gift."

Throwing her arms about him, she beamed and squeezed him tightly.

"I'm glad you planned ahead and were such a frugal woman."

"I can't take credit. Daddy made me make a budget and save half."

"A good man."

Relieved, Prentis threw his head back and laughed. He'd been making choices he didn't have to make. God had given more than double what had been lost in the hailstorm. He could do more than he had dreamed—*all* their spending cash could be spent on expansion and livestock.

God had taken care of them again. As usual, all his worrying had been for naught.

"Thank you, precious wife! I wondered why you were so quiet about these economic decisions."

"This was why. I'm absolutely certain—I don't have one iota of doubt about it."

He pulled her onto his lap, holding her for a great while, unable to speak.

When he felt composed, he prayed, "Thank you, Savior and Provider, for this wonderful wife of mine and for Your provision through her. The day I married her was second only to the day of my salvation, as far as abundance of blessing is concerned. You're a good God, a kind Father to me. I'm grateful. Amen."

Sunday was spent rejoicing. Monday, they went to town.

Avery's savings account was emptied of the amount needed to pay off the mortgage, with a nice reserve remaining. The banker's hand was shaken, and the property title brought home and filed away in a safe place. The mortgage document was burned in the cookstove. He lifted Avery right off her feet, hugging her as the mortgage blazed away before their eyes.

* * * *

What was the world coming to? Joyous celebration was followed by tragic news. In mid-September Avery read the news from Europe. Fighting poison with poison had backfired. The British forces had attempted to use gas on German troops near Loos, but the wind had shifted, and their own gas had killed sixty thousand British troops.

The use of gas in warfare was horrendous, its effects gruesome. The inhumanity of man upon man had continued unabated since Cain and Abel. This was quite clear to her, yet the possibility of a baby overrode every other consideration. She set the news aside, putting these disturbing facts from her mind, as if placing them behind her back. A mother had to learn to turn her mind toward Christ; her child would need her to do so.

She intended to enjoy this blessed time. New changes in her body indicated that she was indeed expecting. She couldn't seem to get enough sleep, she was hungry all the time, and her clothing no longer fit correctly in the bust. But, even without a doctor's confirmation, she had been smitten as soon as she'd counted those days.

The baby was part her and part Prentis, beloved husband and passionate love of her life. Even if they came and marched him away, she now had a part of him to keep. But reading about gas warfare was too much. It brought the type of terror and hopelessness that she wanted to avoid during this happy time of expectancy. She decided to quit reading the newspapers.

In spite of her efforts, she was more vulnerable than ever, she cried often and loved more passionately. Prentis was gentle, patient, and supportive, frequently holding her in his lap.

A week after Prentis sowed the wheat at the equinox, they drove in to see the doctor in town. For the doctor's diagnosis to be certain, enough time had needed to pass. It had now been sixty days; two of her monthly times had been missed.

Prentis waited with Avery in the lobby of the doctor's office, nervously tapping his heel. She knew he was concerned lest this be some calamity within her body, instead of a baby. In recent weeks, she had seen him pacing out in the field, praying she assumed. The nurse came for her. Calm and hopeful, Avery smiled peacefully at Prentis, patting his knee before she left.

The doctor's examination was thorough; she'd never before had this kind of appointment. He confirmed that she was indeed expecting. The baby was due May 7. But, he asserted, it was miraculous that she had conceived at all. Her womb was tipped the wrong way, oddly shaped.

"Will there be a problem carrying the baby until he's due?" she asked.

"Not that I can foresee," he said. "But time will tell."

"Do I need to be careful in any way?"

"Only if you have bleeding or cramps. Otherwise, all is well. The good Lord must have had someone special in mind, someone who had to come into existence."

"I believe that," Avery said.

As she dressed, she considered this. God had made her in a particular way that caused conception to be difficult, so it had taken almost a year to conceive their first baby. No other women in her family had experienced this type of problem, all reproducing quickly and abundantly. Her own mother had borne twelve children. And now, the doctor was calling the conception of her baby a miracle.

Beaming, she fairly floated back out into the waiting room. Quickly, Prentis looked up. He'd been staring at the floor, lost in deep and serious contemplation. Relief washed over his face when he saw her smile. He rose, paid the bill, took her elbow, and walked her out the door.

Outside, she told him everything the doctor had said. His face grew concerned—he asked the same questions. Giving him the same answers the doctor had given her, she assured him that all was well. Then he smiled. He couldn't seem to quit grinning. After helping her into the buggy, they rode through town, Prentis greeting everyone they passed. Still he smiled.

"Since you allowed me to court you," he said, once they were out of town, "I can't even begin to count the number of times I've felt entirely and completely happy. This is one of those times. You and this baby make me so happy I can barely contain it. God is so good to me!"

"I feel the same way. But, apparently, I'm not good breeding stock."

"Don't even think that, Avery." He studied her expression, his face serious. "You're a woman, not a heifer. God governed how you were made. He formed you in your mother's womb—I've read Psalm 139. This is obviously His will. I don't care if this is our only baby. God is in control. We'll trust Him. If He wants to give us more babies, we'll have more, no matter what the doctor says."

She kissed him full on the lips simply for saying that. "That's exactly how I feel."

"Then we're of like mind." He paused, a playful expression growing. "I'll get on my soapbox more frequently, if that's going to be your reaction. Might even become a regular soapbox orator."

Laughing, she kissed him again.

Prentis turned the buggy northward, toward Avery's home farm. "We're telling your parents today. We can't keep this good news to ourselves."

That decision prompted even more kisses.

When they pulled in and announced the coming baby, the news was met with considerable jubilation and congratulations. They ate with her family and left fairly late. Now two grandchildren were due—Floyd and Hattie's in December and theirs in May.

Everyone in Avery's family loved new babies.

TWENTY-EIGHT

AVERY HADN'T EXPECTED PREGNANCY to turn her brain to mush. This surprised her. Her final seminary studies nearly ground to a halt. She felt soft, nurturing, and accommodating. Sharp consideration, serious contemplation, and particularity vanished, lost in the hormonal haze. Avoiding the newspaper seemed a good strategy, since she was indeed bringing a baby into a world at war.

Fatigue dragged her down. It seemed as if she slept all the time. She barely recalled October other than Jerry and Dorothy's wedding, the happy occasion in the middle of the blur: smiling faces, beautiful dress, and fancy cake. All the way home, she had slept against Prentis's shoulder. Then he had carried her into the house and tucked her in.

Every morning Prentis left their bed quietly, so as not to awaken her. Later he returned to find her just awakening, the sun bright. She slept as late as they'd frequently lain abed together during their first year. Time and again, they'd been so wrapped up in one another that they couldn't get out of bed, passionate intimacy stealing morning and night. But now she slept.

After he came back in from the morning chores, they reviewed Scripture and ate a late breakfast together. Whenever she felt bad about it, he laughed.

"Avery, you're working harder than I am, even in your sleep. You're making our baby. The work you're doing is more important than anything I'm doing."

Of course, she objected, stating that his work provided for their family—*beautiful word!* But he always contradicted her. In this case, her work was more significant. She would then reply that she couldn't grow the baby without the food he produced. Nevertheless, he would respond, the baby was of primary importance. That ended the discussion, for that round anyway.

Each time he came in, Prentis told her about everything. He had sold four of their calves and two of their cows, had kept the others, and had bought more steers for fattening—ten in all. He'd done all this and the branding with Tom McKinney's help. They now had thirty-five head of cattle and eleven horses. He reported on the progress of the alfalfa, for its growth would allow him to support all of this livestock. However, he'd also set aside a large portion of their cash for feed and expenses until he could cut the alfalfa in the spring.

Foal training was coming along exactly as it should, Prentis said. All the pregnant cows and mares were doing well. When it got colder, he would butcher Beefsteak; then they would have beef. Providing Avery with plenty of fresh milk to nourish her body, Prentis had increased the amount of milk he took from Artemis.

All the farm news was noted, but she was absorbed with the most basic considerations: sleeping, eating, and bearing their child within her body. That reality seemed to have changed her personality. Food tasted better than ever. She knew some women had the opposite experience in early pregnancy, but she always felt hungry, and sleeping was downright blissful.

After the midday meal while attempting to study, she'd find her head dropping with fatigue. Finally, she'd give up and crawl onto the bed for a nap. Then in the evening she would nod off over her reading or crocheting, head heavy again, hands dropping whatever she held, body slowly sliding down into her chair.

After Prentis had prepared for bed, he would simply pick her up and carry her in. Surprised to be lifted bodily out of the chair, she'd awaken briefly, care for her creature needs, and talk with him, perhaps praying or reviewing Scripture. Then, after enjoying his kisses and intimate affection, held tightly in his arms, she would fall asleep once more, sleeping the sleep of the dead then waking to daylight streaming into the room, his side of the bed empty again.

Sleep was heavy and restorative. In this way, the fall had disappeared.

* * * *

Prentis felt as if Avery had vanished. Her body was present, but her mind and soul were busy elsewhere, occupied with making a baby. She kissed him; he held, loved, and embraced her. They spoke; they prayed; they ate together; they read side-by-side in the evening. But she felt detached somehow, engrossed in the physical work of early pregnancy.

She slept so much! After sliding out of bed each morning, Prentis gazed at her while he dressed, considering how beautiful she was, thanking God for her and the baby. Prentis wanted to be the best father he could possibly be. He would not do to their child what his parents had done to him. There would be no war of religion tearing their child in two. He had to settle this. He now began drawing some serious conclusions.

Taking up where he'd left off during the calving and foaling, he had continued his investigation. During the summer while Avery had been at church, he had taken his time and examined in the concordance each use of the word "church." God had a lot to say about it! He dug in, wanting to discover everything he could.

But now the clock was ticking. A child was coming! Prentis moved on to the epistles.

In the Gospels, Simon Peter had recognized and stated clearly that Jesus was the Christ, the Son of the living God, and Jesus had blessed him. Though he had later denied Jesus as predicted, Jesus had Peter establish the church. This gave hope to Prentis, as did the Apostle Paul's life. Both Paul and Peter wrote that faith along with the teaching and lives of the apostles were like a stone foundation. Upon the rock of Peter's profession and upon Peter himself as one of the apostles, Christ would build His church. It was Jesus's church; *He* would build it.

As a small boy Prentis had helped his father lay the foundation of their house, so he understood the significance of building on stone. It was meant to last. It was secure and held fast.

Jesus Himself was the cornerstone of the church's foundation. He was the Rock, rejected by men, but nevertheless, the precious and chosen cornerstone. Peter called each believer a living stone, used to build the church like a well-constructed building.

As a farmer, Prentis comprehended the building and agricultural analogies. Word pictures helped him see how tightly believers were bound to one another: a physical body with Christ as the Head, a marriage between Christ and His church, a vine and branches, God's family—all of them brothers and sisters. The writers layered one example on top of another, emphasizing unity.

The apostles urged imitation of their lives, not veneration. Scriptural prayers didn't petition Mary, saints, or angels, but God Himself. In fact, "saints" was a title for true believers, yet his Pinkerton relatives talked about these most. His father had called it church tradition, and Prentis definitely understood the importance of tradition to his family. They fought over it.

Having compiled that information, in late July things had taken a serious turn. It had been a tumultuous time in their lives, with frightening war news and Avery battling anxiety. During it all, like a jolt, he had recognized that he needed to act.

Tom had been preaching from Romans Chapter 12 that month. Avery had shared her notes from the sermon each week. This chapter described the church as one body, a familiar analogy. But here was the twist: Something was required of every believer. They were to present their bodies as living sacrifices to God to be used in His church. This was an act of worship and part of their growth. He had gifted each of them to accomplish His purposes.

Prentis had pondered it for months now, since summertime and now into the fall, and he couldn't dodge it. He felt as if a ray of light had fallen from heaven on this one spot—the Holy Spirit putting His finger right here. And there, His finger remained.

As a believer, something was required. This was challenging.

He now understood his sense of guilt: He hadn't been doing what believers were commanded to do. He loved Tom like a brother. Nevertheless, it would be difficult to walk through that church door. Why? Was he stubborn? Was he prideful? Was he still afraid? Was it his natural shyness? He wanted to be baptized; he wanted to serve. What actions should he take?

* * * *

Before Avery knew it, November had blown by. The earth turned brown; the leaves vanished; Thanksgiving came and went; Prentis's mother Addie and George Bellew and Millie were visited—all were excited about the coming baby; and Prentis now talked about butchering. He said that when it froze, he'd buy some ice to get them started.

In early December, the temperature fell below freezing and mostly stayed there. Avery was taken aback. How had this come to pass? It was as if she were emerging from a journey to a faraway place, the first few months of her pregnancy having been slept and eaten away in a foreign land. Her brain grew less foggy, and her energy returned day by day.

When she became nauseated by the smell of wet feathers as they butchered the chickens, it caught her unprepared. Working side by side, Prentis helped her cull the flock down to the best layers and Napoleon; the rest went into the icehouse. While plucking one of the cockerels, after she'd dunked its newly beheaded carcass into the boiling water, she had to drop the bird and vomit.

Gently, Prentis told her to go wash up. He would finish.

"Poor sweet wife of mine," he said softly, as she staggered into the house, turning her face away from chicken plucking, overcome by disgust.

Later he came to her. She had sprayed cologne on a handkerchief and now held it under her nose, inhaling frequently, attempting to rid her nostrils of the horrid odor.

"Feel better?" He sat down on the bed.

"Oh," she shuddered and wrinkled her nose. "Let's not even talk about it."

"All right." Prentis chuckled softly, smoothing her hair back.

Studying his face, she considered him over the wad of handkerchief. He looked different—it felt like seeing him after a long absence. How had he fared? He needed a haircut; he appeared silent and introspective. Contemplating his eyes, she stared into their depths. She'd seen this expression before. He was lonely. She'd been asleep for three months, it seemed.

"I've missed you," she said from behind the hankie.

A smile brightened his face, his eyes registering that she had recognized how he felt. "And I've been pretty desperate for your company."

She nodded. "I'm sorry. I feel as if I disappeared—I don't remember much of the fall other than eating and sleeping."

"You did put away a lot of food," he said affectionately. "Think you slept enough for two people. Your body's been busy getting this pregnancy started."

"Thank you for being such a patient husband."

"You're welcome. Are you here to stay?"

"I think so. I feel more energetic. My brain seems engaged again. I may be here for a while." She grinned at him.

"Welcome back." He returned her grin.

"I felt the baby move for the first time this week. I wasn't sure before; it feels a bit like intestinal rumblings. But I'm certain of it now. He's moving around in there."

"He?"

"Or she." She laughed softly.

"We'll have to start discussing names," Prentis said.

"If we're having a boy, I'd like to name him after you."

"How about we make my outlandish first name into a middle name?"

"I love your name."

"I like my name, too, but I introduce myself as P.J. to keep it simple. Fellows I play ball with call me "Pink"—one syllable, quick to say."

"I'm glad I have the privilege of calling you Prentis."

"I'm happy to grant you that privilege." He smiled at her. "I've always loved the way you say my name. It sounds like a kiss or an endearment. You trail off at the end like a caress. When we were small, you lisped a bit on the end, absolutely adorable: 'Come here, Pwentisss.' I've loved watching your mouth say my name for as long as I can remember."

She pulled his face to hers and kissed him; it was definitely good to see him again.

After all the plucked poultry was tucked into the frigid icehouse, Beefsteak joined them when the snow began in earnest. Avery tallied the foodstuffs, considering their housebound status. They ate beef, chicken, or smoked pork each night, with plenty of milk to drink. The hens were still laying the occasional egg. Canned goods lined the cellar shelves, along with potatoes, squash, and pumpkins on low wooden racks, close to the floor— abundant supply.

They were snowed and iced in, but in want of nothing.

Pausing in her studies, she looked out the window at the new mountain of neatly stacked firewood and the pile of dried cow chips. When had he done that? Surveying the garden spot, she discovered he'd tilled the soil. She'd missed that, too.

The horses were all in the nearest pen, other than Apollo. The foals had grown large, just three months shy of being yearlings—they were beautiful. She'd missed a good portion of their babyhood. Prentis was out in the cold feeding them now, talking to each one, and softly caressing their muzzles, his face close to theirs—greeting them like a fellow horse.

How she loved him! While she'd been sleeping, he'd taken care of everything. She thanked God for him. It was nice to be back.

Reflexively, she stroked her round belly. The precious baby repositioned himself. Her clothing had been altered during those sleepy sewing sessions, waists let out and blouses enlarged with side panels; these could be removed after the baby was born. Momma had written that Floyd and Hattie's new baby girl was named Bernice. Donald was a big brother at only sixteen months.

Would their own baby have siblings? Avery hoped so, but only God knew.

TWENTY-NINE

SNOW FELL, MELTED, MUDDIED everything, and then fell again, making for a frosty weather cycle much like the winter of their courtship. But now Prentis had Avery beside him. Nestled in by the stove, they studied side-by-side, housebound for the entire month of December.

She finished her final Moody Bible Institute study unit and mailed it off right before Christmas, adding extra jubilation to their holiday. He was so proud of her. They would be spending Christmas alone, only the two of them—a first. Prentis was glad to have Avery to himself. Those days would soon end.

He brought in a small cedar to decorate with hand-cut paper snowflakes and popcorn strung onto her red embroidery thread. *A cappella*, they sang Christmas hymns, her alto harmonizing with his baritone. They opened gifts: new boots for him—she'd secretly purchased them when she'd gone into town for supplies one nice day—and a handmade cradle for her, surreptitiously completed out in the barn. She loved it! He tried the boots. They fit perfectly.

Then Avery got busy cooking his favorite Christmas food. She'd made candy and baked two pies the day before, and now she started on the rest. Prentis kept circling through the kitchen to kiss her and sample the cooking. They grinned at one another when they heard Tom McKinney hail them from the barnyard, right in time for Christmas dinner.

"Merry Christmas, Tom!" Prentis called from the front porch.

"Merry Christmas! Hope you don't mind. I was lonely for the two of you. I knew the roads were too bad for a buggy. But one careful man on an experienced horse could make it."

Prentis grinned. "Glad to see you! Need someone to help me eat all this food. Come in!"

Tom and Prentis ate until they could hardly budge.

After dinner, Prentis stretched out flat on the floor before the pot-bellied stove. Tom took one chair, Avery the other; both put their feet up. Recumbent, they began by celebrating the completed degree program. Tom and Prentis both praised Avery for her perseverance. Grinning, she basked in their approval.

Then they talked their way through current events around Wakita, the weather, the war news, Henry Ford's so-called peace ship—the *Oskar II*, and the teaching series Tom would begin in January. He was tackling Ephesians.

Slumped into her chair, Avery grew increasingly relaxed, until she finally dozed off, breathing softly with her chin on her chest. From the floor, Prentis smiled affectionately as he watched her gradual progression toward sleep. Reluctantly turning his eyes away, he looked at Tom. While Avery slept, he needed to talk.

"Just wrapped up my investigation of the church," Prentis said quietly, pointing at Avery.

After glancing her way, Tom whispered, "What are your conclusions?"

"I became a member of the church when I committed my life to Christ. I'm *in* Christ, part of His body."

Sitting forward in his chair, Tom nodded and fixed his eyes on Prentis's.

"Every believer's been given gifts that fulfill a specific purpose within the church, so we can serve Him together."

"Did you study Romans 12?" Tom asked.

Prentis nodded, chuckling softly. "Followed along as best I could here at home. The subject of spiritual gifts was confusing."

Tom returned his smile.

"But this I know," Prentis continued. "I should use the gifts

God has given me. Need to follow His instructions and obey the commands that apply to all believers even today."

"What instructions in particular?"

"I want to be baptized—I'm desperate to publicly identify myself as His. I love Him with all my heart and want to obey Him. My father had me baptized by a priest, but I want to make the decision myself. I've tried to live in what I hope has been a godly way. Now I want to add my public obedience."

"Sounds as if you want this for the right reason."

"That's why I had to investigate on my own."

"Anything else?"

"I need to use the gifts He's given me. And I need to be taught. All the believers then met together to sing praises to God and to encourage one another with teaching and admonition. I need to be there with other believers."

"Yes." Tom nodded. "I wish more of my congregation took this as seriously as you."

"Since you mention it, the hard part will be dealing with church people."

"That's true for all of us. Can you do it?"

"Only with Christ's help." Prentis knew the truth of this.

"It's the same for us all. Christ gives us the ability to work together, to forgive, and to love one another. He modeled putting the interests of others first."

They'd been speaking passionately, their whispers growing in volume. Snuggling down into the chair, Avery sighed and turned in her sleep, readjusting, eyes still closed. Tom and Prentis remained silent. Soon she began to breathe deeply again. They smiled at one another.

"So, how do you want to do this?" Tom whispered.

"That's what I'm sorting out. Think I'd like to start attending now before the baby's born."

Tom nodded.

"Want Avery to know I'm going to obey Christ, so no matter what happens . . ." Prentis's voice cracked. He swallowed hard, trying not to be overcome by the painful possibility that he might lose Avery in childbirth, as Tom had lost his wife.

Tom looked back at him sympathetically.

After a moment, Prentis continued, "I'd like our baby to be

born into a home where unity exists. Realizing I was one with Avery was the first step toward understanding why church is important, but finding out I was going to be a father made this more significant. I want to be a good father. Don't want to put my children through the wars of religion, so I'd like my child there when I'm baptized."

"Of course. It's a serious thing."

"Want you to be more than my friend. I want you to be my pastor and my teacher."

"Thank you. I'm honored. Your faith and pursuit of the Lord encourage me."

"And you encourage me. You've been a kind and patient friend, especially for a pastor." They both laughed softly. "Meant no offense."

"None taken."

"Can you baptize me in my creek? I want to go under the water like Jesus did."

"We have a horse tank we use."

"The creek's somewhat like the Jordan River, though probably more muddy."

Tom smiled. "I'm sure we can arrange that."

Avery blinked open her eyes. Disoriented, she stared at them. Then she slid up into the chair, sitting up straight. "What's being arranged?" she asked.

"I'll tell you later," Prentis said. "Tom's getting ready to go— sun's near setting."

Avery stood. "Let me pack some food for you, Tom. There's no way we can eat all this. I cook like a woman who has six brothers."

Tom went home laden with food and holiday treats. Prentis was left with the task of informing Avery. He prayed for the opportune time. The roads would be too messy to attend church tomorrow, but he hoped he could go with her on January 2, starting 1916 right.

However, before that day arrived, he had to put her back together again when the newspaper was delivered between Christmas and New Year's Day. It contained the end-of-the-year war news. Abandoning her new habit of avoiding the paper, she read it. Casualty estimates were mentioned; entire populations—

men, women, and children—devastated.

"Prentis, I've decided to trust God and the president with your life. I nearly lost my mind over it before I knew I was pregnant. I'm choosing to believe that President Wilson means it when he says he needs farmers—*Food Will Win the War*. But, even if you're safe, I still can't bear this senseless violence. Why on earth did I read the paper today?"

With that, she burst into tears, and he held her close.

They reviewed the passages they'd been meditating on and prayed for the world and for peace, both among mankind and in their own hearts.

* * * *

As Avery dressed for church on the first Sunday morning of 1916, Prentis finished his coffee and left the table. This was the norm. He always drove her. But today, he got out his shaving supplies, stropped his razor, lathered his face, and peered into the mirror, feet spread for stability. Dragging the blade over his skin, he removed his two-day growth of whiskers.

Singing a hymn in full voice, Avery's back was toward him as she buttoned her blouse, now ballooning over her expanded belly—she was now past the halfway mark. She turned to smile at him, and the lyrics fell right out of her mouth.

Speechless now, she froze. Out of the froth of lather, he grinned at her.

"Going to church with you today," he said, lifting his chin to shave his neck, pausing a moment as the blade slid over his Adam's apple, "and ever after, I hope and pray."

"You're done with your investigation?"

"Well," he said, finishing up his shave as he talked, "don't know if a person can ever be finished with their investigation of the church. But I now know I became a member of Christ's body when He saved me, and I should be with the rest of the body. So I'm joining the church. Tom and I talked about it on Christmas Day."

Ignoring the remaining flecks of lather, she wrapped her arms about his waist and squeezed him tightly. Silently, she held onto him for a great while, her head pressed against his chest.

"I'm so very glad," she said at last, softly.

"So am I." He wiped his face and kissed the top of her head.

While he dressed in his black wedding suit, she watched. Prentis didn't think he'd ever seen her look happier.

"I could hardly bear to go without you," she said. "We're one, as if we're one person."

"I know. I wanted to be there just to please you. But I had to know why God Himself wanted me there, so when the difficulties come—and they *will* come, I'll be steadfast."

"I understand."

"Then let's go. Bundle up. It's pretty cold."

As they rode through the wintery weather, both were wrapped up to their eyeballs in woolen scarves, a wool blanket tucked about them. Prentis's rein-free hand was tucked into Avery's muff. That hand felt entirely warm; the other was chilled, even with the woolen mitten. But the ride was short. Within twenty minutes, they had arrived. Hector was stabled in the small barn on the property, and they now walked toward the building.

Provoked by shyness coupled with vestiges of church fear, Prentis's stomach clenched. He told it to be still. This was the right thing to do, no matter what happened. He and his stomach should be right here. He asked God for the ability to expect the best from the gathered church members. Folks he didn't know smiled at him. He greeted neighbors—the Herns and the Millers; and then all of them entered the small building.

Avery stepped into one of the children's classrooms off the entryway, smiling a farewell before turning to her earnest pupils already seated around their table. A fire burned in a small cast-iron stove in the corner, attempting to disperse the cold.

Adults and older young people filed into the sanctuary for their Sunday School class, taught by one of the elders. Prentis had met him during the calving last year. The man smiled and nodded as Prentis came in. Some introduced themselves; some shook his hand, reminding him that they'd met at Tom's house after the tornado. Others were more reserved.

Like Avery's home church, the room was plain, long, and narrow with a pot-bellied stove in the middle. Struggling to make a dent in the cold, it blazed away. Rural Protestant churches seemed to be simple; larger ones in town, like his mother's church, were more ornate. The Catholic churches in Kansas had stained-glass windows and were far more beautiful. Christ hanging there, large and lifelike on the cross, was always arresting.

Either way, the building didn't matter. The people did.

Tom McKinney entered through a side door, spotted Prentis, and smiled widely, making his way through his congregation to greet him. After shaking his hand warmly, Tom sat with him for the class. The elder taught on the *Sermon on the Mount*. Prentis followed along in his Bible. The older man made some points that Prentis had never before considered. He smiled inwardly. This was one reason believers gathered, to teach and admonish one another as they learned together.

Soon the children filed in. The Sunday School hour was over. Avery appeared beside him, sliding her hand into his. Mrs. George Miller took her place at the piano and pounded out an introduction; then Tom stepped up to the pulpit and led them in two hymns: *For the Beauty of the Earth* and *Amazing Grace*. Prentis knew both well. He smiled as he sang, certain that Tom had chosen the hymns today just so he'd feel comfortable.

It was a pleasure to sing with the gathered members. Everyone sang heartily. The harmonies blended seamlessly. Then, in unison, they repeated a statement Tom announced as *The Apostles' Creed*. Prentis had heard it somewhere but didn't know it, so he listened.

"I believe in God, the Father Almighty,

Maker of heaven and earth,

and in Jesus Christ, His only Son, our Lord:

Who was conceived by the Holy Ghost,

born of the virgin Mary,

suffered under Pontius Pilate,

was crucified, dead, and buried;

The third day He arose from the dead;

He ascended into heaven,

and sitteth at the right hand of God the Father Almighty;

from thence He shall come to judge the quick and the dead.

I believe in the Holy Ghost; the holy catholic church;

the communion of saints; the forgiveness of sins;

the resurrection of the body; and the life everlasting. Amen."

The creed contained all the core beliefs Prentis held to be true, but he had one question. As everyone sat down, he whispered to Avery, "The holy Catholic Church?"

"Little *c* catholic," she whispered back. "It means the universal church, true believers all over the world, His church, whether Catholic, Orthodox, or Protestant."

He glanced at her and nodded. All was clear.

"We're a small congregation," Tom said, once they were seated, "so I know you all notice P.J. Pinkerton sitting there with Avery. I'd like to extend a warm welcome to him on behalf of us all. If you haven't spoken to him yet, be sure to greet him afterward. He'll be coming into membership soon." A murmur of whispering followed. Prentis reminded himself that he was here because of Christ, not public sentiment. Tom was still talking. "Now, turn in your Bibles to the book of Acts, and I'll begin by discussing the origins of the church in Ephesus. My overview will take us a couple of weeks before I teach from the letter itself. First, let's pray."

After the service, everyone crowded around to welcome him. Those he hadn't met before introduced themselves warmly. Several others were neighbors and long-time friends. These said they were glad "such a good Christian man" would join their congregation. They looked forward to more fellowship with him.

Embarrassed, Prentis thanked them for their friendship and the help they'd given him over the years. He knew he was a flawed man, but he was glad they'd known he was a Christian. To people who knew him well, at least his actions and his life had conveyed where he stood with Christ, even though he hadn't been attending church.

He caught Avery's eye. She stood against the wall, talking quietly with Tom.

Clearly pleased, she smiled at him.

When they drove home to eat their dinner, she huddled next to him, scarf across her face. Joyful, her eyes shone into his as they discussed the sermon and what they had learned.

It was a good beginning to his coming into the sheepfold with the other sheep.

THIRTY

PRENTIS'S BIRTHDAY WAS CELEBRATED a few days later, making both of them twenty-five now. Avery surprised him with a package containing two handmade flannel work shirts. They were thick and warm, the perfect January gift. She made him a cake and fixed his favorite meal—roast beef. They completed the same festivities as the preceding year, and Prentis thanked God that he had a wife who loved him so much.

Throughout January the weather stayed cold but dry, the mud frozen; they went to church every week. Prentis grew more comfortable attending. His stomach gradually settled down.

On weekdays, neighbors from far and wide stopped by to examine the foals. The five young horses would soon be yearlings, and people wanted to size them up as early as possible. They wondered if Prentis would put Apollo out to stud, since his first offspring were all exceptional. Prentis told them he hadn't made up his mind.

After they left, he confided in Avery what a quandary this produced. Apollo had sired five excellent foals. They would bring top dollar. If he put Apollo out to stud, excellent horses would spring up all over the area, driving down the price he could get for his own yearlings, which were rarities. Stud fees wouldn't defray the difference. All told, he decided to breed Apollo only with his own mares, keeping his herd clean as Dr. Robert recommended.

With Tom's help, Prentis gelded the colts, trying to accomplish the feat before they adopted stallion-like habits. Upset over the grievous insult the young colts were suffering, Avery informed them of her opinion both before and after the deed was done. Practical farmers, they found her objections endearing. Next Prentis took the final steps of halter training each of the young horses, so they'd be ready to go.

When he wasn't with the horses, Prentis was in the house repairing leather goods and working on small tools and equipment, while Avery crocheted and sewed miniscule baby clothing. The baby was due right after the calving and foaling, Avery joining the general birthing parade, their baby conveniently arriving after all the livestock.

They discussed names. Prentis preferred a one-syllable boy's name, easy-to-say, a name that could be yelled out on a baseball field—*Jack!* Avery liked the name when coupled with Prentis as a middle name. He agreed on Jack Prentis Pinkerton—their son's first two initials would reverse his. For a girl, they settled on two of Avery's favorite feminine names. Their daughter's name would be Margaret Ruth Pinkerton.

At the end of January, Prentis came into the house grinning. He handed Avery a parcel. The return address read Moody Bible Institute. Too excited to open it at first, Avery's hands shook; all of her work was condensed down to this one small package. Her heart filled with joy, a moment of supreme satisfaction.

"It's good news, Avery. Rip it open."

Standing by, he still grinned at her. The weight of the achievement paralyzed her; she stared at her name on the front. Finally, she tore into the package and read the letter: She had graduated with highest honors. She could hardly believe it—her progress had been so halting, interrupted, and disjointed. Infant death, courtship, farming disaster, marriage, infertility, war, and pregnancy had been written into her answers as she related her studies to her life.

Of course, Prentis said he had expected these honors for her all along. Given her hard work and diligence, he called these accolades inevitable.

Beaming, she unwrapped the elegantly lettered diploma and held it up for him to see.

"Avery, I'm so proud of you I might burst."

"Thank you, Prentis. I still can't believe it."

"I want you to hang it right here in the living room."

"I thought I'd simply tuck it away in my records."

"Not if I have a say, you won't."

He retrieved his tools from the back porch and got to work measuring and pounding. Then he used his level to hang the wooden frame. Once he had the precious document displayed beside their large oval wedding photo, they both stepped back to examine it.

"Now," he said, "that's exactly as it should be. This is quite an achievement."

Reaching for his hand, she laced her fingers through his, eyes fixed on the diploma. When she tried to speak, her emotions thickened in her throat, garbling her language.

"Thank you, Prentis, for encouraging me to celebrate this."

"You deserve to celebrate."

She wrapped her arms tightly about his waist, squeezing her happiness into him, and then she had a good cry.

* * * *

Minnie Slaughter wrote every week, including special congratulations from the entire family after they received the news of Avery's diploma and final grades. Avery read the letters out loud to Prentis. They wanted her to stay safely at home this winter. They worried about her traveling in her condition and didn't want them to risk it. Prentis thought their advice sound.

He was content to keep Avery at home, tucked in for a quick ride to church each week. It was confining, but warm days occurred periodically in Oklahoma. On those days, she tramped about the farm in her boots, her fancy coat barely covering her large belly. Prentis showed her all his projects and how all the animals fared. Daily, she fed and talked to the hens, anticipating when they would lay eggs again. Most days, she milked Artemis, warmed by the cow's body.

Cozy in front of the pot-bellied stove, they discussed each weekly sermon. Prentis thought Ephesians hit a person hard right from the beginning, such an encouraging letter about God choosing those who would be His. The plan of salvation was God's Plan A, devised before all time and carried out relentlessly, Christ having offered Himself to redeem His own. It was beautiful! Every week Prentis learned something new, even though he had read and studied the letter on his own. This affirmed all he had learned about why believers were to attend church.

Unfortunately, they also had to discuss the war, along with these joyous and encouraging topics. It was an election year, and President Wilson had engaged in a whistle-stop campaign, coming as far west as St. Louis. Prentis read the account aloud as Avery sewed. The president exhorted the American people to be prepared for sacrifices. Preparedness was his reelection theme. He urged support for The Continental Army and the US War College Division.

"That can only mean one thing, Prentis," she said pointedly.

This was confirmed, in Avery's mind at least, when the British conscription law went into effect on February 10. It was only a matter of time, she told him, before American officials did the same. Prentis hoped she was wrong.

At the end of February, ugly news arrived. A vicious battle had begun in northeast France, near the city of Verdun. More than one million men were entrenched; fighting was fierce. Journalists predicted a slaughter, wondering if anything could be gained for either side. If that were the case, the lost lives would be a complete waste of precious humanity—piles of bodies of someone's husbands, sons, brothers, and fathers.

Avery wept all day.

Ominously, at the beginning of March, an army representative arrived at their farm offering to buy their foals. Avery didn't like this one bit. The army had sent him to scour the countryside for the best horses, and he'd heard about Prentis's colts. Though they were just shy of being yearlings, he paid $125 for the gelded colts and $100 for the young mares—top dollar, putting $575 into their pockets. The man promised to return to look at their next yearling herd.

Prentis, Avery, and all the broodmares stood staring after the young horses as they were led away by their new owner—tails and heads held high, jogging away in harness, departing on their unknown adventure. The army would complete their training.

It always saddened Avery to part foals from their mothers, especially this year—she was soon to be a mother herself—and especially to the army, who were amassing troops. What would happen next? Of course, she cried. Everything brought her to tears now. Standing silently beside her, Prentis put his arm about her shoulders.

Finally, he spoke, his voice thick. "We've just done our patriotic duty, Avery. The army needs our horses. You and I can both see where this is heading."

She stared up into his eyes; it was beginning to seem inevitable, and they knew it.

"This," he continued, "is why you never need to worry about the army taking me. Our country needs me right here, producing food and good horses."

Wrapping her arms about his waist, she buried her face in his coat, hating to consider the inescapable conflict and how it would change so many lives. At that moment, the baby kicked against Prentis. A soft and affectionate sigh sounded in his throat as he bent to kiss Avery's head.

"God will take care of us, our baby, and our nation, Sweetheart."

She didn't answer. Clamping her eyes shut, she considered the sovereign care of a good God. Deliberately, she chose to trust Him.

* * * *

Typical for Oklahoma, news arrived of an event that had occurred a week earlier. Acting Secretary of War Hugh L. Scott had asked the War College Division if they had a plan prepared in case of "a complete rupture" with Germany; he wanted such a plan in place, just in case. Alone in the house, Avery read the paper and was shattered. America's entrance into the war seemed a nearer certainty each day.

She sat at her desk, gazing out over the barnyard—Prentis was out there working in the cold to provide for their family and to keep up with the president's demands. Pregnancy had softened her up, but she was a strong woman. She would resist this emotional rollercoaster. Begging God for strength and the courage she lacked, she repented of her anxiety. She would rely on Him, and He would need to help her do even that. Recalling the verses she had memorized and the truth about God that they contained, she felt comforted by His nearness.

When Prentis stepped in later, he seemed unaware of her struggle. The first cow showed signs of labor. He had come to tell her that he was riding down to get Tom. She hugged him, looking up into his face, large pregnant belly between them.

"I'll have something good for you both to eat when you return."

"Thank you, Avery. It's a blessing to have you for my wife. You always take such good care of me." He wrapped up his scarf again, peering over it, his eyes shining. "I love you," his voice was muffled by the thick wool.

"I love you, too."

Then he stepped out to make the cold ride.

Prentis was going to be busy; she needed to be strong.

Once Tom and Prentis arrived, they ate the mound of food Avery had prepared, went out, and got to work. The schedule was much as it had been the previous year; but this year, all three rode to church together, and they lost no calves. By the end of March, they had thirteen new calves, nursing with their mothers, healthy and strong. It had been a successful season.

"I'm happy with these calves," Prentis told Avery as they stood watching Tom ride home. "Rex and the cows I chose are producing exactly the kind of stock I hoped for. Now that our first batch of heifers are grown, in June we'll have twenty cows and young heifers to breed. Lord willing, we'll get a good price for all the steers and provide for the war effort at the same time."

"I hope so." She paused and bit her lower lip. "Now that the calving is safely completed, I want you to know something. My body seems to be warming up to have this baby."

He turned, studying her for a moment; then he laughed. "I don't think I can evaluate that simply by looking at you, like I can for a cow or a mare."

She laughed softly. "Maybe we're going to have our baby early."

"Let's go into town tomorrow and see what the doctor says."

"That's a good idea."

* * * *

The next day the trip was made. The doctor reassured Avery that all was well—the baby wasn't due for another six weeks. The fact that her body prepared for labor was normal. With a binaural stethoscope, he bent low over her abdomen to hear the heartbeat.

"The tubing is too short for you to be able to hear this, Avery. But P.J. could come in here and listen, if you'd like."

"Oh yes! Call him in."

The nurse stepped out of the room and retrieved Prentis. Back he came, obviously excited. The doctor stepped away, allowing Prentis to lean over Avery. He positioned the earpieces as the doctor pressed the oblong cylinder against her rounded abdomen. Holding perfectly still, Prentis got a faraway look in his eyes.

"I can hear the baby's heartbeat," he said softly, his voice tinged with wonder. "It's really fast!" Quickly, he looked up at the doctor, as if verifying that all was right and well.

"That's as it should be. Count the beats, and I'll time them for a minute."

From his front waistcoat pocket, the doctor pulled out his watch and nodded at Prentis, whose face became preoccupied with his tabulations.

After sixty seconds, the doctor said, "Stop."

"One hundred thirty-five."

"Might be a boy."

"Is he all right?"

"Now, we don't necessarily know it's a boy, but it often happens that boys' heartbeats are a bit slower. It's a hypothesis. But everything appears to be fine with the baby."

"Good!" Prentis smiled at Avery.

"I don't expect the baby to be born until May, but when the time comes, you'll need to ride hard to get me as soon as possible."

"I certainly will," Prentis promised.

THIRTY-ONE

ALL OF AVERY'S JOINTS seemed to have slackened, especially those in her hips. Affectionately, Prentis said she waddled like a duck—she knew it was true. Sunday morning, she woke in pain. Off and on, the sensation had been nudging her out of sleep, but she had held onto slumber and ignored it. Alert now, she turned onto her back with her knees bent, attempting to relieve the agony at the base of her spine. The backache felt similar to menstrual cramps.

Hopefully, they'd get to church today, depending on the mares. They were halfway through the foaling. While she waited for the pain to ease, Avery laid her palm flat on Prentis's side of the bed. The bed felt cold, so she knew he'd been gone a while, though last night he hadn't expected any mares to deliver. He was probably checking on the two new foals.

Once the pain let up, she rolled out of bed, utilized the chamber pot, and shuffled into the kitchen to cook breakfast. The small fire he had started warmed the room; the wash water was already heating on the cook stove. She added more wood and set the coffee pot on.

Her hens had surprised her with some early eggs, so today she would make pancakes. Prentis loved them, declaring she could be famous for just these buckwheat flapjacks, let alone all her other admirable qualities. Recalling his words made her smile. Whenever she made them, he ate so many she couldn't comprehend how he could hold them all. His leg was hollow when it came to eating her flapjacks, he said—he simply kept stuffing more in.

Laughing softly, she paused as her lower back cramped again. With her fist she rubbed the sore spot until it eased. It was only April 16, still three weeks before the baby was due, so she determined to ignore this backache. The end of pregnancy was simply uncomfortable. There was no remedy. About thirty minutes later, Prentis came in grinning at her. He had obviously smelled breakfast. The first pile of pancakes awaited him on the back of the stove.

"Thank God, Avery! I was craving your flapjacks."

She smiled. "The water is boiling in the coffeepot."

Turning back to the batter, she paused, motionless as another cramp seized her, pulling at her very vitals—*Hmm, that hurt!* Waiting it out, she then poured more pancake batter, one circle by another onto the sizzling hot griddle. Prentis busied himself with the coffeepot, adding the ground coffee to the boiling water. He liked it nice and strong.

"Are you going to church this morning?" she asked.

"I'm nervous about Persephone, but I can take you over."

"My back hurts today. I don't know if I'll be able to sit."

* * * *

Turning from the coffee, Prentis studied Avery. As she went through the food preparation, he noticed that she paused every five to seven minutes to stand still, her feet farther apart than usual. Sometimes she placed her hands flat on the wooden work ledge, motionless for about a minute. He observed this as she brought him pancake after pancake, which he gobbled down, smothered with maple syrup, his eye on her all the while.

She chatted about the weather, the hens, and the new foals, pausing every five minutes or so to stand, silent and still. The longer she made pancakes, the less she talked. By the time he'd finished as many flapjacks as he could hold, he'd had sufficient time to observe.

"Avery, I'm riding in to get the doctor. We're having a baby today."

"What do you mean? The baby isn't due for three more weeks."

"You're in labor."

"No, I can't be. I simply have a backache today."

"Your backache comes and goes. It's labor pains—I've been timing them."

"Do you think so?"

Motionless, she stood with a distracted look in her eyes. Silently, he watched her, counting in his head. In about sixty seconds, she fixed her eyes on his.

"You just had a labor pain, didn't you?" he said.

"Maybe I did."

"There are times it pays to be a farmer. I have to know when expectant mothers of all types are preparing to give birth. Your body's doing the work, Sweetheart. I'm going for the doctor."

He stepped into their bedroom to change into a clean shirt. Back in the kitchen, he heard something spill with a splat. Startling him, Avery issued a guttural groan of agony. Rushing back in, he found her on her hands and knees, gown and floor wet, face twisted in pain.

"What happened?" He dropped down beside her. "Did you fall? Are you hurt?"

When she could speak, she said, "The water broke—that has to be it. And now—you're not going to believe this—I feel as though the baby's coming."

He scooped her up, dampening the clean shirt and not caring a whit.

"When did this start?" He carried her to the bedroom.

"A while before I got out of bed—so maybe two hours ago. Oh, Prentis!"

A moan came from deep within her, building in intensity. Against his abdomen, he felt her womb rock-hard and straining. This was serious business. Her abdominal muscles tightened, pulling her forward, and her breath caught with the effort. Until it ended, he held her securely.

"Sweetheart, I'm sitting you down. Have to get the bed ready. Hold on. There's no time to get the doctor."

Doubled over with pain, she seemed not to hear a word.

He stripped off their bedding and threw it into the corner. Working frantically, keeping an eye on Avery, he grabbed the pile of newspapers and spread them over their bed, hoping to save the mattress. First one pain and then another doubled her over.

Prentis unfurled his oldest quilt and an old sheet on top of the newspapers, knotted the corners, and tucked them under. After her next labor pain ended, he lifted her to the bed.

Her moaning caused his stomach to clench. There was nothing he could do to ease her pain—he felt helpless. Leaning over her, mere inches from her face, he smoothed her hair back and peered into her eyes. They were unfocused, as if she saw right through him. Gently, he held her face between his hands until she fastened her eyes on his. A glimmer of recognition showed.

"Avery. Have to wash my hands. It's imperative. Be right back."

She nodded and clamped her eyes shut, focusing inwardly again.

Standing over the kitchen sink, he frantically scrubbed, hoping and praying he could deliver his own child as well as he could a foal or a calf. Should he use the Antisepto?

Startling him, she screamed. How was this happening so quickly!

Lord, help me! This is my wife, not a horse or a cow. Please protect her and our baby from my bungling. Please help me!

Grabbing a knife to cut the umbilical cord and her kneading bowl for the afterbirth, he headed back. It felt entirely surreal. He tried to maintain a business-like demeanor, but Avery was his precious wife, not livestock. His heart raced.

He removed her nightclothes as gently as he could, given the circumstances. Totally absorbed in her inner agony, she seemed to be completely oblivious. Once done, he positioned himself between her feet and gripped her chin.

"Avery. Look at me." Her eyes remained clenched, her jaw locked. Soft moans emitted from between her teeth. "Avery!"

Dazed, she opened her eyes. She stared at him, as if from a faraway place—a distant world of pain, far removed from relief. This was how she looked in the throes of her worst headaches, as if she were drowning in agony.

"Sweetheart, try to relax. It will hurt less if you do. You're safe. I'm right here. I'm not moving you again. I'll catch the baby."

* * * *

Sucking in a deep breath, Avery gasped for air. Fixing her eyes on Prentis, she studied his face, attempting to focus. What was he saying? Was he speaking English?

" . . . I'll catch the baby." He looked hard at her, waiting a moment. "Go ahead and push."

Push! Now she understood.

Avery grabbed behind her knees and bore down, screaming with the effort. She experienced sensations she could never have imagined, no matter what Momma and Hattie had told her. She heard her own screams, as if they emanated from someone else—a tribal woman, perhaps an ancient female ancestor—certainly not she, the refined and genteel schoolteacher.

"You're doing well, Avery. Keep it up. I can see the little head."

Well, that information certainly gave her the motivation to push!

She felt as if something primal and uncontrollable had taken hold from the moment the water broke. Now the pain eased, and she regained her sanity. Something felt different now that she could push—she could focus again. Breathing heavily, she lay back.

"Prentis, I'm so sorry . . . I didn't recognize the signs."

"It's all right, Sweetheart. Truly. Just relax and do what your body dictates. I'll do everything I can to make it easier for you."

"I've made a mess in the kitchen."

"Don't worry about it. We're having a baby here." He grinned at her.

She couldn't grin back; this was too overwhelming. "I don't know if I can do this."

"Yes, you can."

"Oh my goodness!"

Here came the pain again. She could tell he had already known it was coming—his eyes told her that he was ready. There was the screaming, erupting from some core of herself that she hadn't known existed until this moment. She *had* to get that baby out. It was the necessary fact of her existence, the absolute imperative!

"The baby has black hair, Avery—lots of it." Prentis glanced up at her, smiling widely. He looked back down. "Ha! What a head of hair!"

A real baby! She wasn't being tortured to no end—such a relief!

Within her, everything strained. She heard herself screaming. But the pain was lessening—time to rest. Easing her gently back against the pillows, Prentis helped her recline.

"Thirsty," she whispered, her voice raspy.

Lifting the glass, he helped her drink. Gulping it down, she stared at him over the rim, grateful once more that he was a gentle, patient, and loving man.

"I love you," she whispered, after she polished off the glass.

"And I absolutely adore you. You can do this. You're nearly done. Listen to me during the next one. Tell yourself that."

"All right."

Closing her eyes, she lay back and dozed off. In that moment she dreamt of a smiling infant and Prentis's face. Here came the pain again—her eyes popped open. He was already prepared.

Grabbing behind her knees, she pushed with all her might. Not even fazed by her yelling, Prentis appeared engrossed in helping the baby ease out gently. She felt him working down there. Into her mind burst the remembrance of the poor cow whose calf he had pulled.

"Stop pushing, Avery. Throw your head back. Fall onto the pillows."

She heard his voice and heeded his words. Feeling as if she were being torn in two from stem to stern, she focused on his voice and stopped pushing. *Oh my!* A sensation of relief followed. *Thank God!*

"The head's out. Ah. Adorable little face . . . Here comes the rest."

Oooohhh! With burning and heat the infant burst forth. Nothing could ever have prepared her for the sensation. It couldn't be described. Wide-awake now, more alert than she'd ever been in her entire life, she reached for the tiny baby—wet, naked, and precious. Beaming, Prentis held him up to her. Through her tears, she smiled back.

"A little boy, Avery." Prentis's voice cracked. "A son."

"Jack," she said softly. "You surprised us and came so soon."

Tears ran down their faces; joy overwhelmed them. *Thank you, Jesus!*

Against her skin, the tiny mouth rooted around, searching instinctively, this most basic of urges placed in him by the Creator. Avery moved him to her breast. Love-smitten, she glanced up at Prentis, and they both chuckled softly at his frantic efforts.

Then Jack latched on and began to nurse. Avery kissed his little head and beamed up at Prentis, joy spilling over. Her heart had been forever changed. She was a mother.

* * * *

The expression on Avery's face drew Prentis to her side. He left his job as midwife and crawled onto the bed, vowing to be the best father a man could ever be. Embracing them both, he admired their son over her shoulder, locking eyes with him. Seriously, Jack stared back with dark infant eyes, all the while continuing his greedy assault on Avery's breast.

They both wept tears of gratitude.

"Father, thank You for this precious gift," Prentis whispered. "Help us raise him to be a good man."

"Amen."

"My heart's full. Thank you, Avery."

She looked up and smiled. "It's my pleasure."

He kissed her on the lips and then gazed back at Jack. "He looks like you. I'm so glad!"

"I was thinking he looked like you—see his nose."

"His eyes and his coloring are yours, though."

Both fell silent, studying their son with affection.

"Loving and being loved changes a man," he whispered.

Avery nodded. "I didn't know I could love with this intensity."

"I feel the same."

"Isn't God good to use love to change us into sacrificial people?"

"He is indeed."

Marveling, they admired Jack's tiny fingers and toes, his little round head, the cuteness of his bowed legs that stayed so tightly tucked up against his body, the exquisite loveliness of his face, and the absolute miracle of his life.

That God loved them even more than this was inconceivable.

* * * *

After dealing with the afterbirth, inspecting, cleaning, bundling, and wrapping—in short, making sure Avery was still all in one piece—Prentis remade the bed with clean linen. Then he tucked her back in with the baby, and both fell asleep.

Before washing the kitchen floor and the laundry, he stood for a while admiring his little family as they slept. Jack's baby chest rose and fell in little gasps, perhaps dreaming of his birth, and Avery wore a blissful expression with their new baby at her breast. The sight moved him.

As he scrubbed the kitchen floor, Prentis heard a horse and rider in the barnyard. Sam barked. Drying his hands, he stepped outside to find Tom hitching his horse at the back rail. They had missed church, and he had come to check on them. It must have shown, because as soon as Tom saw Prentis's face, he smiled his congratulations. Prentis pointed toward the bedroom window and put his finger to his lips. Silently, the two men walked toward one another, grinning widely.

Tom pumped Prentis's hand heartily. "You look as if congratulations are in order!"

"Thank you. They are. We have a healthy son—Jack Prentis Pinkerton."

"Wonderful! How is Avery?"

"Fine. It was quick—three hours from start to finish."

Tom's eyebrows shot up. "I bet that was exciting."

Prentis chuckled. "It was. Especially since it took over two hours for us to even recognize that she was in labor."

Tom laughed softly. "I can imagine what that last hour was like. What can I do to help?"

"I'm tempted to hunker down with my little family, private and isolated, but I think it would ease Avery to have her mother here. She'll know I'm taken care of during the foaling, so she won't worry, and her mother will pamper her. I think a new mother needs that. I'd also like the doctor to come and check both Avery and the baby. Can you take my buggy and ride through Wakita for the doctor and then up to Gibbon to bring back Minnie Slaughter?"

"I certainly can. Just give me the directions to the Slaughter's farm."

* * * *

The doctor arrived about two hours after Tom departed, congratulating them and expressing his surprise at the baby's early arrival. He evaluated mother and child, declaring both healthy. Of course, Jack was small, six pounds even, according to the portable infant-weighing apparatus. But he was early, so it was expected. Everything looked perfect.

The doctor patted Prentis on the back and asked if he'd like to come and work for him. Prentis declined—this was a job he most definitely did not want; the stakes were much higher than with livestock. Then the doctor instructed Avery to come for an appointment in six weeks and departed, smiling as he left.

An hour or so after the doctor left, Tom arrived with Minnie. Keeping it a surprise for Avery, Prentis hadn't told her. She burst into tears at the sight of the beloved face. It had been a long time. Sitting down on the bed, Minnie hugged her tightly.

"Prentis sent your pastor to tell us little Jack had been born. You're a momma now."

Tom leaned around the doorframe. "Congratulations, Avery!"

"Thank you, Tom. Thank you for bringing my momma."

"I've come to help for a while," Minnie said. "At least a week. Daddy's going to come and fetch me. He and the boys will see Jack then."

"Oh! I'm so glad. What a good husband I have! What a kind pastor!"

Prentis and Tom smiled at these comments. Then they excused themselves, leaving Avery and Minnie to dissect the details of Jack's delivery as women always did after a birth. The particulars had to be discussed from beginning to end, and Jack had to be admired from head to toe. Not conversation for mixed company, Prentis and Tom stepped out.

Under the dining-room window, they set up the cot Minnie had brought from home, leaving her carpetbag beside it. Then they stepped outside. Tom offered to help with the foaling, if Prentis needed him.

"Thank you, Tom, not just for offering to help but for sending the doctor and bringing Minnie. I couldn't leave Avery to do that, and I appreciate it. But I think I can handle the three remaining foals, now that Minnie's here. Thank you for the offer, though."

Tom patted Prentis on the back. "Glad to help. I'll head on home now. Congratulations once more. You have a fine son."

"Tom, before you go, I want you to know that I'm mindful of your own wife and son today. How did you bear it?"

Tom paused, gathering his thoughts. "The Lord was my solace and comfort. Only He could help me through it."

Prentis nodded, overwhelmed at the thought. "I can't even imagine."

"I look forward to seeing them with Him in heaven. That will be a very good day. God holds us up through every trial He allows to come our way, even using them for our good, just as He promised."

The two men stood regarding one another, Prentis considering the struggle and the yielding that went into Tom's statements. Tom shook his hand warmly then mounted his horse, tipping his head to Prentis as he left the barnyard. Prentis watched him ride off.

Reflecting on Tom's loss and his response, Prentis sent up a prayer, asking for comfort for him on this day when he had surely been reminded of Mary and his own tiny baby.

Then Prentis pulled his mind back to the pressing issues at hand—back to work.

He checked on the mares and found Persephone readying to labor, but not there yet. All the signs were obvious. Going with the norm, he wrapped her tail, readied the stall, and walked toward the house to take a short nap, if at all possible, since he'd likely be up all night.

He chuckled to himself, a busy day—first his own son, now his horse.

When he came in, he told Avery about Persephone, bending to kiss both her and Jack. While the two of them talked, Minnie went into the kitchen to start supper, and Prentis lay down with his wife and son to grab a little sleep.

And with that, the four of them slipped into the pattern they would follow for the next ten days. Minnie stayed until the last mare had delivered her foal. It was a close family time, all of them admiring, holding, and caring for Jack. Minnie cooked, cleaned, and did up the diapers every other day, hanging them outside on the line—the public announcement of a new baby. As soon as the first diapers appeared on the line, neighbors brought over food, offering their congratulations and peeking in at him.

When Abraham and the boys came down to get Minnie, Jack was introduced to a large portion of the Slaughter family—Grandpa and the tribe of young unmarried uncles. Baby Jack was passed from boy to boy, held, kissed, and exclaimed over.

Gene—who was all healed from his injuries of the preceding summer—said Jack was swell, while Howard declared him "an awfully nice baby." Full of admiration and affection, John and Abe each took a turn holding and kissing him. Both thought he was keen.

Prentis and Avery smiled at one another as each new admirer took their turn. Their proud parental smiles grew wider with each exclamation. They'd ride up to Attica and on to Kingman on the train soon to introduce him to the adoring Pinkertons, Dirs, and Slaughters up there.

Their tiny son would grow up surrounded by a throng of admiring and loving relatives.

THIRTY-TWO

JACK WAS NOW FOUR weeks old, and Avery hadn't asked about the war yet. Quietly, Prentis read the newspapers and didn't mention a word, knowing she would inquire when she was ready. He didn't want to disturb the nest, especially now that her mother had returned home.

Peace and tranquility were essential during the newborn period. This was true for all mothers, animal and human. Eventually, she would discover that some significant events in the wider world had occurred. He'd tell her when she asked, and not before.

A few days after Jack's birth, President Wilson had publicly called for Germany to stop their submarine policy; they'd been sinking all ships in enemy waters without warning. Then, less than two weeks later, about the time Minnie had gone home, Field Marshal Lord Kitchener, the British Secretary of State for War, had asked for American military participation in Europe.

What was occurring in Europe was in startling contrast to the tranquility of his home and their life in America, safe on the other side of the world. Insulating herself in her domain of nursing little Jack and caring for him, Avery seemed to have forgotten the war. She never inquired nor mentioned it. Relieved and glad, Prentis didn't bring it up. That was as it should be during this delicate and precious time.

There was nothing either of them could do to influence the outcome or the course of human history. It was in God's hands. They would pray for peace, and God would orchestrate His intentions in the world, having promised to work it all together for the good of those who loved Him and were called according to His purpose. Prentis held on tight to these promises.

They would trust the Lord, pray, and move forward as He directed.

* * * *

When Jack was six weeks old, they took him to church for the first time, their little family all present. Everyone admired him. Still in Ephesians, Tom explained the instructions for the Christian household. Prentis had gone to church each Sunday since Jack's birth, leaving Avery at home tucked into bed with their son. Each week, he had taken copious notes to share with her. This week they all came, Avery slender again, though more buxom now that she was a nursing mother, Prentis beaming proudly as he held their baby, and Jack adorable in every way.

On this final week of May, Tom focused on Paul's instructions to children, parents, and fathers. Fathers were instructed: "Provoke not your children to wrath: but bring them up in the nurture and admonition of the Lord."[6] Prentis took the command to heart; he never wanted to provoke or discourage young Jack, whom he held cradled in his arms. With bright eyes, the baby looked intently at him.

Jack already smiled when they talked to him. Prentis now focused his eyes on Jack's, momentarily losing Tom's train of thought, his words fading into the background. Prentis smiled down at his son. Burbling a soft baby coo in response, Jack melted Prentis's heart. Glancing up momentarily to catch Avery's eye, Prentis found she was already smiling at him.

Immediately after the service, the entire congregation journeyed to the Pinkerton's farm. Buggies pulled past the barn before all disembarked and walked down to the creek, making their way far enough upstream that Prentis could be properly baptized.

His heart felt as if it would burst with joy at this act of obedience and adoration that he had wanted to complete for so long. He yearned to publicly proclaim himself as one who followed in Christ's footsteps, taking this step of baptism exactly as Christ had done. He wanted to be publicly identified as one of His disciples.

Avery held Jack now, having nursed him in the buggy on the way home. Tom and Prentis waded out into the muddy stream, and all the church members stood on the bank. Tom asked Prentis to share his testimony of salvation.

Standing in the water, Prentis recounted the tale of how God had drawn him to Himself after his father's death. Then he detailed his journey to find God's will concerning the church.

"And now," he said, "here I am, getting baptized. This is where the Lord has brought me. I'd be remiss if I didn't thank God for my wife." He fixed his eyes on hers. "God used her love and patience to change my heart. All my life, she's been a guiding light for me. You draw me to the Lord, Sweetheart. Thank you for your love and for allowing me to be your husband."

* * * *

Avery's eyes welled with tears as she smiled back at Prentis. Her heart overflowed with love for Prentis and gratitude to the Lord for what He'd done. She thanked God for giving her this man as her husband. As she looked into his eyes and held their son in her arms, she was surely the happiest woman on God's green earth, as Prentis liked to phrase it, usually referring to himself as the happiest man. This thought warmed her heart.

Tom smiled at Avery and then at Prentis, and then positioned himself to complete the baptism. "Are you ready, P.J.?"

"I am."

"Based on your profession of faith, I now baptize you in the name of the Father and of the Son and of the Holy Ghost." With one hand on Prentis's chest and the other behind his back, Tom dunked him under. "Buried with Him through baptism into His death." Then he brought Prentis up out of the creek, water streaming off him. "Raised to walk in newness of life."

As Prentis came up out of the water, he was grinning from ear to ear, creek water notwithstanding. The first face he searched for was hers. Communicating their joy without words, they now stared at one another.

* * * *

Once more, Prentis thought his heart couldn't hold all the joy and love God poured into it. Gratitude overflowed as he considered Christ's sacrifice for his sins; the comfort and help of His Spirit; the gentle and loving wife He'd given; the precious son, so tiny and new; the dear friend—his pastor, who now embraced him, patting him heartily on the back; and his surrounding friends and fellow believers.

Prentis was no longer alone. God's love had changed everything!

PRENTIS AND AVERY PINKERTON

EPILOGUE

THIS STORY IS A fictional account of the courtship and early marriage of my great-grandparents. Jack was my maternal grandfather. I portrayed the real people in this story as accurately as possible, including their cadence of speech and pet phrases. I used the language of the time. To flesh out events in the story, I also invented fictional people who wore some of the names common to the Wakita area, since this is a novel, not a memoir or biography.

As this story goes to publication, I am writing the sequel. Here the reader will discover what happened in Oklahoma when America became embroiled in the war on the European continent, who was taken, who died, and how Prentis, Avery, and Jack were impacted.

You can find all my stories here, including the sequel:

http://bit.ly/MelindasBooks

And also here: https://tinyurl.com/melinda-viergever-inman

To receive information when new stories release, subscribe here: http://eepurl.com/cKNoZX

(Endnotes)

1   *Indian* was the term used for Native Americans in 1913-1916. I have used this term throughout the novel.

2   *Bright Star, Would I Were Stedfast* by John Keats, 1819. This poem contains the spelling and word usage from the original.

3   Colossians 2:9, KJV

4   Rather than the term *Muslim, Mohammedan* was the word used in the 1910s to describe the followers of Islam. Webster's Revised Unabridged Dictionary, edited by Noah Porter, published by G & C. Merriam Co., 1913.

5   Though this term is no longer used, it was the proper and accepted term used in the 1910s for African-Americans. "Professor Booker T. Washington, being politely interrogated ... as to whether negroes ought to be called 'negroes' or 'members of the colored race' has replied that it has long been his own practice to write and speak of members of his race as negroes, and when using the term 'negro' as a race designation to employ the capital 'N' [*Harper's Weekly*, June 2, 1906]." Quotation from http://www.etymonline.com. These rules of the time have been applied and adhered to in this novel.

6   Ephesians 6:4, KJV